ALSO BY WOODY CARTER

Theology for a Violent Age
(nonfiction)

NARADA'S CHILDREN

A Visionary Tale of Two Cities

A NOVEL

Woody Carter

Published in 2016

ISBN: 0982730713
ISBN-13: 9780982730713
Library of Congress Control Number: 2015910460
Sleepingman's Books, Richmond, CA.

In memory of Azizah Omenjhud and my dear wife, Jennifer.
And for LaShan and my son, Govinda.

Long ago, the sage Valmiki sat meditating in his hermitage on the banks of the Tamasa. The river murmured along beside the dark, gaunt rishi, whose hair hung down to his shoulders in thick dreadlocks. But otherwise the secluded place was silent; not even birds sang, lest they disturb Valmiki's dhyana.

Suddenly the silence was shattered; the air came alive with the abandoned plucking of a vina. A clear voice sang of the Blue God who lies on his serpent bed, upon eternal waters. Valmiki's eyes flew open. Though he had never seen him before, he had a good idea who his visitor was.

The Ramayana: A Modern Retelling of the
Great Indian Epic
by Ramesh Menon

NARADA'S CHILDREN

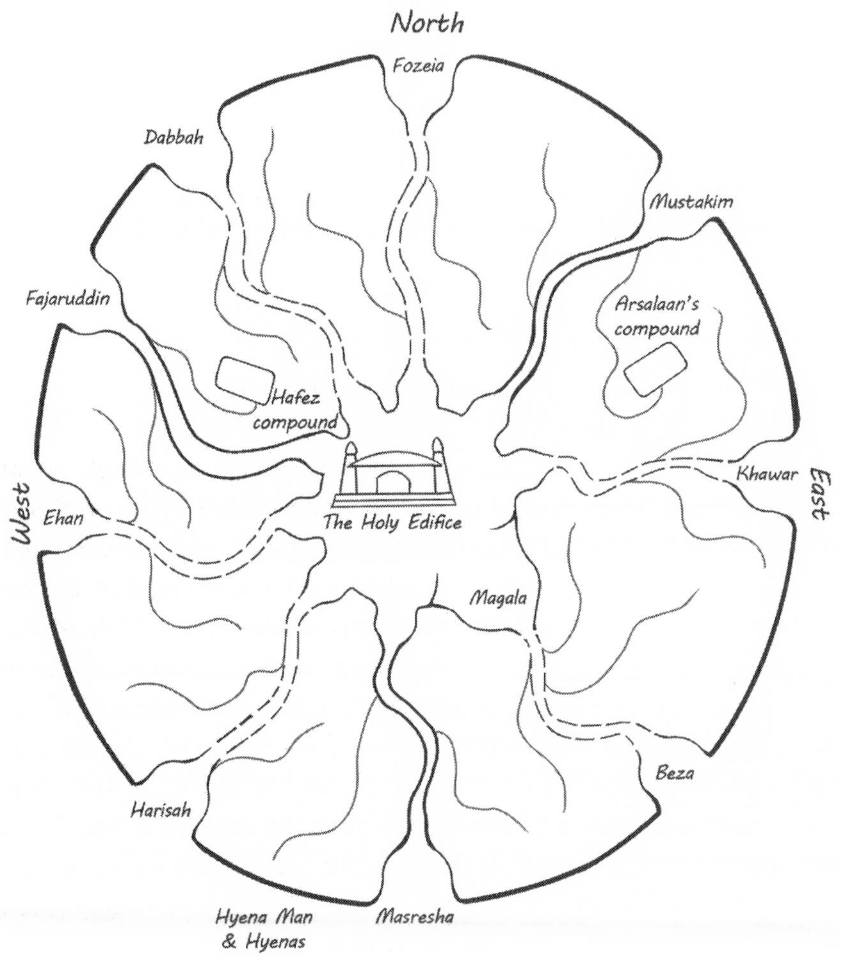
City of Ja'Usa Map
early 19th century
North
Fozeia
Dabbah
Mustakim
Fajaruddin
Arsalaan's compound
Hafez compound
The Holy Edifice
Khawar
East
West
Ehan
Magala
Beza
Harisah
Hyena Man & Hyenas
Masresha
South

CHAPTER 1
THE GREAT MYSTERY

Horn of Africa, Early Nineteenth Century

The luminous star that warmed the earth was high in an azure sky when Narada, the wanderer, placed his hand over his eyes to shield them from the white-hot sun. He peered across a shifting sea of light-brown sand and saw nothing but barren wasteland. A warm breeze brushed across his face and whispered verses from an ancient text well known to him: "Where shall I go from your Spirit, or where shall I flee from your presence? If I ascend up into heaven, you are there; if I make my bed in hell, behold, you are there. If I take the wings of the morning and dwell in the uttermost parts of the sea, even there shall your hand lead me; and your right hand shall hold me." And with this knowing of the inscrutable unknown, the Great Mystery's primal element in human form set off across the desert.

Narada's nut-colored body was lean, strong—not in a muscular way. He had the physique of a man with endurance and the stamina to keep up with the flight of an antelope for days on end. His dark, matted locks, with streaks of light-brown and gold strands bleached by the sun, fell across his shoulders, and his thick brown beard accentuated the reddish-tan of his high cheekbones.

The sun slowly descended over the horizon as a canopy of blood-red, orange, pink, and blue splashes trailed across the western sky. Narada stopped to rest and watch the fleeting day turn gradually into inky blue night. It was the time when daylight embraces the coming darkness and a time for prayer, a time to sense the infinite harmony that mysteriously supports all life from the smallest creature to spirit in human form. It was when land and sea, the heaven's vast necklace of suns and moons and stars, and the frenetic play of birds and insects conjoin, and the noise and confusion in human heads settles down—even just for a moment—to note the passing of the day and the coming of night. And as the blue-black deepens in splendor and white, sparkling jewels beaming from ear to ear adorn the cosmos, the finite world is rocked to sleep by a mystifying hum or soft lullaby only a few hear. While the living slumber through the night, the heartbeat of the universe teaches, nurtures, and replenishes as night's procession gradually recedes into dawn. Searching the heavens to locate the eastern star, Narada sat on the sand, closed his eyes, and merged with the Infinite.

He stirred before sunrise, wrapped himself against the desert's chill in his white shawl, and sat like a tranquil lake to say morning prayers and watch the emergence of a new day. When the sun finally peeked over the horizon, Narada resumed his trek possessing no food or water across the desert. And when the fireball was at its zenith, baking the barren earth with its merciless heat, his sandaled feet were raw and bloody—a testament to the certainty that neither his endurance nor stamina could overcome the dominion of the sun. With his strength ebbing from the grains of sand stinging his face like angry bees and his eyes now tiny slits from the star's white glare, Narada blindly stumbled forward as he tried to recall why he was in the desert; but he couldn't remember. The thought of sitting down and giving up might have been a choice for an ordinary man, but his destiny was a curse to remain homeless and a wanderer, forever. But then there was the fleeting thought that, perhaps, he was on a great and important mission. These conflicting threads—homelessness or glorious quest—held his attention when another consideration surfaced. Was he to endure the desert as a reminder of what it means to be human, for inherent in life is suffering between birth, old age, and, finally, death?

These reflections were a spinning wheel in his consciousness when, in the distance, he thought he saw a faint patch of shimmering greenness playing upon his vision. It hovered in the dazzling heat over the glistening sand. These inklings soon evaporated like drops of water on hot stone as the shimmer of green gradually disappeared and then slowly reappeared, becoming fixed to the land, and the illusion...no, the promise of water filled his mind and swelled his tongue. His footsteps quickened as what may have been a mirage turned into swaying green grass like the graceful fingers of a seductive woman moving to a lyrical melody. Hazy palm trees undulated in the distance and swayed slowly from side to side with a gentle push from a soft desert wind. And as he stumbled forward, kicking up the sand, he sensed, behind the unhurried movement of tall green fronds, the image of a human figure pulling...pulling on something.

The image and movement enlivened his steps as he hurried along on scorched red feet. His arms flapped under a loose tunic like an awkward bird that had forgotten how to fly and was unable to get off the ground. He thought he heard the faint sound of a human voice riding upon the hot air as he fought with the sand to run faster. Reaching the edge of the oasis, Narada realized it was the voice of a woman singing. She didn't seem to notice or hear him approach from the far side of the trees. He tried speaking softly, so as not to alarm her, but his voice like the sudden croak of a frog startled both of them.

The young woman raising water from the well would have dropped the pail back into its source had it not been for the rope tied to the bucket's handle and the other end wrapped tightly around her hand. Once her eyes found and settled on the figure behind the palms, she resumed bringing up the water and securely placed the bucket on the lip of the well. Releasing the rope around her hand while keeping her eyes on the stranger, she cautiously reached for the water bag of dried goatskin lying on the ground. She picked it up and hesitantly offered water.

His cracked lips caked with specks of sand and his hands trembling, Narada stepped out of the palms and took hold of the bag, which he found too heavy to raise to his mouth. Although it was forbidden for an unmarried woman to have physical contact with a man, she placed her hands over his and helped him lift the goatskin to drink. Once she sensed the stranger could hold it on his own, she removed her hands, stood quietly, and stared at him. She then smiled with an unassuming innocence as she searched his dark-brown eyes and placed her light-blue scarf over her head before wrapping it around her shoulders. Only her eyes were visible to the stranger now, and they looked at him without fear, without embarrassment or shame. Cool water rushed down his parched throat while drops trickled along the side of his neck and onto his tunic. Narada lowered the bag and gasped for breath as he looked at the woman standing before him. Captivated by her nut-colored skin and the charcoal dust highlighting her hazel brown eyes, he thought she was beautiful.

"Food you must want," she said to Narada. "To my village, if you come with me, my father, food and rest he will give before your journey you continue. Yes? Unless the Ja'Usu, the Old City, your destiny it is."

Narada tried to speak, but his voice was lost in the desert.

"Come," she said and bent down, placing a circular roll of cloth on the crown of her head before reaching for the bucket. But Narada grabbed the pail's hemp handle to carry the water for her. "My name, Hohete it is."

He bowed to the spirit within her before she walked away and took the footpath her ancestors had walked for ages back to the Old City. Narada followed behind, taking in her sweet fragrance, like ripe almonds soaked in sun-kissed rose water.

Hohete thought about the reception this stranger might receive from the city's Elders. She was certain he wasn't a merchant, and he carried no belongings. How odd for him to show up at the well without a camel or a caravan; yet, he had kind eyes, she thought. And his face, though worn and wrinkled, hinted at both mystery and wisdom.

CHAPTER 2

CITY IN THE DESERT

Approaching Ja'Usu, Narada saw people walking toward an opening in a massive, white stone wall that went as far as his weary eyes could see. The wall was crumbling in places now, breached by tribal warfare, flash floods set off by heavy rains, and centuries of neglect. Fires had destroyed most of the barricade's enormous wooden gates, and those that remained had decayed long ago due to termites and other creatures that crawl in the night.

Once a thriving metropolis, Ja'Usu was now a mere shadow of itself, reduced to asprawling patchwork of family clans related to one another through intermarriage, cultural heritage, and a stilted patriarchal religion. But there was hoarded wealth here, too.

In ancient times, when land surrounding Ja'Usu was green and fertile, the entryway Hohete and Narada drew near--called Fajaruddin, the first or western gate--was guarded by a heavy barrier that took two men to open and close. Fajaruddin was the city's main entrance, wide enough for ten fat oxen to walk through side by side. No one, now, could recall when the archway above the entrance rotted and plunged to the ground or when

Ja'Usu's sentries, standing guard at the gate, had grown old and died. The sentinels were replaced by gatekeepers who couldn't protect or save anyone. They simply watched for strangers and reported at once to Ja'Usu's patriarchs when visitors crossing the desert showed up at the old city's broken-down gate.

Passing underneath the last remnants of the fallen portico, Hohete quickened her step as Narada looked in curiosity at the row upon row of cramped merchant shops that lined both sides of the cobblestone street. Men with skull caps and dyed red beards squatted on straw mats inside shops selling Indian and Persian silks; Egyptian cloth with bright color patterns; sandals, wax candles, frankincense and myrrh, or an assortment of household goods; and sacks of rice and grains. Other shopkeepers hawked teas and small bags filled with raw and roasted coffee beans from sparse fields outside the wall. In other shops along the way, tailors hunched over foot-pedaled sewing machines, making clothes or repairing worn-out garments or anything else an inhabitant was willing to purchase. The men stared at Narada as he passed.

As they turned a corner and walked down a narrower, unpaved lane, Narada noticed craftsmen making earrings, bracelets, and necklaces; others inlayed fine threads of silver and gold into sandalwood frames holding poorly made mirrors. Some merchants stood in narrow doorways and peddled colorful glass beads, semiprecious stones, and pieces of amber strung together on dry cow gut. These workers stopped their labor when they saw Narada.

Along with buying and selling, Narada noted men chewing small green leaves they carefully picked from tiny twigs held in their hands. They packed them inside their jaws as the mass enlarged their checks. Green juice oozed from some of their mouths until they took a piece of soiled cloth or used the backs of their hands to wipe the stain away.

Outside the shops were dark-skinned women, squatting on the ground next to the shopkeepers' doors. These were Ja'Usu's poor who survived on the food they wrestled from the parched, tired soil with rudimentary tools on land that stretched outside the city's wall to the oasis on the edge of the desert. They were the barefoot Oromo, the indigent farmers who saved the best of what they eked out of the land to sell on the streets of Ja'Usu. They covered their lean bodies in shabby white cloth and wore burnt-orange remnants around their heads. In the afternoon heat, the women used their tattered white shawls to cover their faces and their babies from the merciless sun. Black flies followed them everywhere, twitching around the corners of their eyes and mouths and playing upon the babies' faces. In front of them, on laid-out pieces of palm leaf, were small piles of scrawny fruits and vegetables for sale: small mounds of red onion and white garlic and small, wrapped funnels made from fronds filled with turmeric, brown cinnamon, and nutmeg.

The women crouched on cobblestones with infants lying between their thighs as they suckled on their mothers' sagging, rubbery breasts. Some Oromo women carried heavy loads, like beasts of burden, on their bent-over backs. They carried large bundles of dry wood, charcoal, or produce wrapped in earth-stained cloth or chickens in wrapped-up burlap on their heads. They balanced their awkward cargo, walking barefoot over hot stones, often with small children strapped to their backs.

After walking for days alone across the desert, Narada was overwhelmed by this frenzy of activity and smells. The sounds of people hawking wares and bartering for produce melded together in a cacophony of busyness and chatter. The sweet fragrances of spices and the aroma of roasted coffee beans and cooked foods mixed together with the smell of donkey droppings and cow dung left behind as these animals labored down Fajaruddin street. The noise from the main thoroughfare and the chatter of women peddling on the street diminished as they walked farther away from the shops. And although Hohete didn't hear Narada's footsteps behind her, she sensed that he was still there.

A scraggy rooster perched above them crowed and flapped its stubby wings as patches of sunlight made bright splashes of light on tall, whitewashed walls. Narada followed Hohete down a slender passageway and passed large, closed doors on both sides of the corridor. The sun was less intense in these ancient walkways lined by massive stone walls that snaked through Ja'Usu, making a labyrinth of the ancient city.

Hohete stopped in front of a large door of dark cedar wood and knocked. An old man with a short-cropped beard and wearing a white lungi, or cloth wrapped around his waist, opened the door. Before entering, Hohete knelt to touch her father's feet as Ibrahim Hafez looked into the face of Narada.

"Father, from the desert to the well this man came," she said. "Narada his name is, and water him I gave. To Ja'Usu if he came, food and shelter you would gladly give, I said to him."

"Narada...Narada," the old man repeated slowly, getting comfortable with the way the name felt moving in his mouth. "Narada, to our home you we welcome. With us food and shelter yours is; come in."

Ibrahim Hafez led the way into their compound, which had two large buildings made of cow dung, mud brick, and wood. The structures faced each other, and an inner courtyard separated the wide entrance to each house. Ayaat, Ibrahim Hafez's sister, sat in one doorway, shelling snap peas with knurled hands as tiny green pellets fell into her wooden bowl. She looked up from her task, saw the stranger, and smiled, revealing the few teeth left in her mouth.

"Amantahu!" she shouted.

Narada touched his hand to his heart and smiled at her as he followed Hohete's father across the yard and passed under three mature palm trees. A small wooden footstool rested against the base of the tallest tree. Palm leaves started swaying as a gust of wind rustled through the yard, making thin slices of sunlight and shade frolic on the ground. A funnel of brown dust suddenly spiraled up in the air, and the fitful wind left the courtyard as quickly as it came.

Placing his sandals outside the door, Narada followed Ibrahim Hafez into the house and onto a narrow, blood-red floor that ended at a large platform that dominated the room. They stepped on to the dais and sat together on an ornate straw mat that covered the raised area.

Hohete brought water for Narada and her father to drink and then left the room. Ibrahim Hafez noticed his daughter's unusual behavior in the presence of their guest. Ordinarily, she wasn't shy in the company of male strangers and, unlike most Ja'Usu women, would sit uninvited with her father's guests and listen quietly to their conversation. Sitting with men as they talked would be natural for a male child to do, but it was unheard of for a girl or woman, whose traditional place was to stay out of the affairs of men.

When Hohete's mother died in childbirth, Ibrahim Hafez allowed his only child to stay by his side. Perhaps it was his way of comforting his daughter and making up for her mother's absence. After Ayaat informed him that Hohete had come of age, Ibrahim Hafez tried breaking her habit of sitting with men, but she was strong-minded and always found a way to listen in on her father's discussions with others. And besides, he had grown accustomed to her perceptiveness and unconventional ways, like touching his feet when greeting him, and frequently relied on her assessment of people and her plain common sense.

Ibrahim Hafez thought it was extraordinary for his daughter to bring water and then quickly leave. Did she leave in deference to the obvious nobility of Narada's stature, was she just asking her aunt to help her prepare the food, or was Hohete saying with her abrupt departure that she was overwhelmed by his presence and felt compelled to leave the room? Unusually perplexed, Ibrahim Hafez was absorbed in these thoughts.

Hohete soon returned with a pot of sweetened hot tea and two white porcelain cups. After setting the tray on the mat, she poured her father's tea and, without meeting Narada's eyes, served her guest. She then placed a small dish of green olives in front of them and left the room. Sensing her father's apprehension, Narada turned to the old man and appealed to the Great Mystery to put Ibrahim Hafez's mind at ease. They sipped their tea in silence until Ibrahim Hafez asked, "Please, how is it without camel the desert you have crossed? Your belongings, where they are, and where going are you, sir?"

"I am a perpetual wanderer and have no home. I stay in a place for a while, and then I move on."

"Well, why here are you, and how long to stay are you planning?"

"Dear Ibrahim Hafez, at this moment I cannot say why I'm here or how long I will remain in your city, but soon I will tell you."

"Because it is, you don't know?"

"I know but cannot say."

Ibrahim Hafez was baffled by Narada's answer and questioned in his mind whether his guest was mad or a paid assassin and a danger to his family. Narada sensed his host's alarm.

"I understand how it might seem when you invite a stranger into your home and he is unable to tell you why he is here, but I wish your family and the people of Ja'Usu no harm. I give you my word."

"Narada, in my home a guest you are. Here, welcomed you are. Please, with us rest and as long as you like stay. In time, your story revealed it will be."

Hohete returned carrying a small, white basin and a pitcher of lemon water. Her father held his hands over the bowl, and she poured the warm water over them. He washed them as he did for every meal and reached for the hand towel draped over her arm. She then turned to Narada, who washed and dried his hands in turn, and then she left the room. She reappeared this time with a large piece of flatbread in a straw basket shaped like a large, flat dish. And on the spongy pancake was a small mound of chopped tomatoes, onions, and red peppers. After squeezing the juice from a ripe lemon over the mixture, Hohete left, immediately returning with a bowl of hot yellow lentils and a plate with a medley of cooked cabbage, carrots, and small boiled potatoes. Feeling Narada's eyes watching as she placed the food on the bread, she was delighted by his attention.

Ayaat waddled into the room, carrying fresh cooked rice mixed with caraway seeds and a bowl of berbere chicken stew. Hohete took the dishes from her aunt and spooned large portions from each dish onto the flatbread. She then handed her father and Narada newly washed hand towels, and she and Ayaat left the room.

Narada watched Ibrahim Hafez bless the food, giving thanks to Jah. The old man then tore off a piece of bread, using the fingers of only his right hand, and used the bread to gather and pick up food from the basket set in front of them. He turned to his guest and, in keeping with Ja'Usu's custom, fed the first bite of food to his guest. He then fed himself.

They ate from the same plate in silence while absorbed in their own private thoughts. Neither of them noticed Hohete sitting in the doorway leading to the courtyard, watching them. But Ayaat saw and knew what Hohete had done when they were in the cooking room. She had watched her brother's daughter put an extra helping of berbere into the doro wat, or chicken stew, and now Hohete was waiting for Narada's reaction.

When Ibrahim Hafez tasted the wat, he knew what his daughter had done. When he looked at her, she turned away, blushing, and hid her face in her hands. Ayaat, observing from her place, thought Hohete's gesture was silly and foolish. How could a stranger from the desert, not knowing Ja'Usu ways, understand that if a woman prepared food for a man, making it unbearably hot, she was sending him a signal that she cared for him? And if the object of her attention ate the food without complaint, even though it was uncomfortably hot, he was revealing to her without words that, although her food was much too hot and spicy, he would endure whatever he must because he also cared for her.

Overpowered by her own curiosity, Hohete resumed watching their guest as he ate her spicy-hot stew. She waited, intently, to see if he would stop eating when his tongue and mouth caught fire. Would he choke and ask for water as his hair stood on end, or would he continue eating as his insides burned and his head felt like it would explode? Hohete knew he had to be hungry, but if he stopped eating while there was still food left on the bread, she resolved not to pursue to him. But if he ate all of her food without complaint, she would share her feelings of affection with him.

Narada ate with composure, showing no sign of discomfort; and when he finished his meal, he casually wiped his mouth with the cloth Hohete had given him. He then looked at her, not like a man who had been lost in the desert and was grateful for food, but with eyes that radiated a deep tranquility; and she was startled by it. It was neither what she expected nor, perhaps, even what she wanted. She didn't know how to respond.

Ibrahim Hafez followed Narada's eyes and realized his daughter made no attempt to cover her face or lower her eyes while their guest calmly looked at her, and he was irritated by her rudeness. Shocked by her boldness, he wondered when his daughter began caring for this man. *What really happened at the well?* he thought as he turned to look at Narada's face and tried to discern his age.

Lifting her scarf over her head and across her face, Hohete looked into the courtyard as a yellow bird with black wings landed on Ayaat's mud-brick roof. A tiny twig was in the bird's mouth. Unable to comprehend her own thoughts and possible feelings for their guest, she doubled over in laughter and took the tiny bird as a good omen. Ayaat, however, saw something else in Narada's eyes, and knew he was no ordinary man.

CHAPTER 3
MURABBI'S SUMMONS

Sleeping in Ibrahim Hafez's upstairs room, Narada awakened just before dawn. He lit the candle Hohete had left for him beside the cotton mat that was his bed and felt the cool breeze coming from the small, open window on the other side of the room. The light wind made the candle's orange and yellow flame flicker as a wisp of blue-black smoke rose and disappeared in the darkness. He turned to the east, folded his legs, and sat in the stillness with his eyes closed as the world melded into a time of union, when the night made room for the coming of a new day. A rooster crowed in the distance as he listened to the intimate beating of his own heart—the pervasive hum of the universe; and from his innermost silence on the altar of peace, a prayer-song arose of forgotten longing as old as the earth itself.

The nine patriarchs, each ruling one of Ja'Usu's nine family clans, woke early, as they did each morning, to say their prayers at the ancient city's most holy edifice. It was the largest structure in Ja'Usu, built on the backs of the city's poor and the sumptuous holdings the patriarchs had amassed from lucrative trading with merchants that traveled in camel caravans along the Silk Route. They were Persian and Egyptian suppliers who trekked as far west as southern Europe and back again through Egypt and Somalia, crossed the Red Sea into Arabia and Persia, and continued farther east through India and Java until they reached China.

Ja'Usu's patriarchs bartered with frankincense and myrrh and spices and gold, with ebony and ivory and wild animals. They traded short-horned cattle bred to withstand the region's heat. And in return, these lords stocked Ja'Usu's tiny shops with goods and delicacies, even luxuries, from all over the known world.

As a result of their wealth, the patriarchs and their immediate family members wielded considerable influence over all the storekeepers in Ja'Usu. Many of the shops were owned outright by the three largest families, and they employed only members of their particular clan to manage these businesses. But the patriarchs also served as moneylenders and trade brokers. They were the deal makers and breakers for any enterprise of consequence in the city.

Each of the nine main pathways snaking through the ancient city began at one of Ja'Usu's nine gates, and all of them ended in the heart of the city, where the holy edifice stood and the patriarchs or governing council met. It was constructed by Boghdadi Ahmed Ali, a master stonemason from Nubia who lived and died in the city, who, with a Ja'Usu apprentice, built this sacred structure with the only vaulted or dome-shaped roof in Ja'Usu. The holy edifice was not only a public place of worship, where any legitimate city inhabitant could come for morning and afternoon prayer, but also the patriarchs' seat of power; their semblance of government resided there.

This morning was different than all other sunrises because Chief Patriarch Murabbi, the patron and guardian of the people, had summoned Ibrahim Hafez to meet with the council after prayer to hear about his visitor. They had learned about his arrival when Munqad the Obedient, who, while standing sentry at the main gate, saw Hohete and Narada enter the city and immediately ran as fast as his old legs could carry him to Murabbi's house to report the news.

Sitting on the plush maroon carpet, presented as a gift to the council by a visiting spiritual leader from Persia, the patriarchs listened intently as Ibrahim Hafez described the arrival of his guest and what they talked about during their first meal together; however, he left out his daughter's reaction to the stranger's presence.

Patriarch Abdul Muntaqim, slave of him who punishes wrongdoings and seizes retribution, was the first to speak after Ibrahim Hafez finished speaking. He wore an expensive, brown robe that draped around his ankles. It was of fine Egyptian cloth, with gold embroidery around the collar and down the middle of his chest. A gold ring with a sumptuous, wine-red ruby graced his left hand, and he had developed the habit of giving the ring a series of half-twists while he listened to anyone speaking.

"A righteous man you are, Ibrahim Hafez, and our traditions you keep. Your guest from the desert, a more worthy house he could not have picked if on his own he had come, and for advice and protection he had sought you out. But elder, this stranger, Narada, from where does he come from? This to know, we need to. Not every day a man alone crossing the desert to Ja'Usu comes."

"And you say," continued Patriarch Ihtesham, the honorable one, who was dressed in an Egyptian white tunic with matching headdress, "in good health he is? His eyes swollen shut from the sun's glare, they were not? His mouth, dry was it...his lips, cracked were they? Every three months out of the desert, caravans with goods from afar, they arrive. Used to them, we are. But one man alone crossing the desert, how can this be?"

The patriarchs were silent as they pondered the implications of what had been said. "This stranger in Ibrahim Hafez's house, what if a jinn, or spirit, he is?" said old Patriarch Ihtesham, the respectable and honorable one. His white beard was dyed an orange-red.

"Yes...yes," exclaimed Ibrahim Hafez. "Who he was I asked him. A spirit in human form, he simply said."

"A jinn!" repeated Taqiyy, the pious, who usually listened without contributing to the discussion at meetings. "But if a jinn he is...a good jinn or an evil jinn, how to know are we? And why here he is?"

"Narada, evil I don't think so," chided Ibrahim Hafez. "His eyes I saw, and kind they are. In time he..."

"Ibrahim Hafez," interrupted Patriarch Tahawwur, the brash, displaying gold on every finger. "Narada, our customs he may know, you said. How would our traditions he know, if here before he hasn't been? If a jinn, power he may have; and, perhaps, different physical forms he can take. Even a hyena, he could be."

They laughed at this suggestion, except for Patriarch Aschenaki, the distressed, the youngest among them. He remained quiet, with his eyes downcast.

"Even invisible possibly he could be," continued Tahawwur. "Maybe other bodies in Ja'Usu already he has taken, and maybe for a long time watching us he has been. If so, what really does he want?"

Ibrahim Hafez tried to speak again, but Patriarch Tahawwur interjected, "Whether this jinn good or evil is, to find out we must."

The other patriarchs were disturbed by Tahawwur the brash's rudeness in disrupting their guest who was about to speak. They glanced at him with displeasure before turning their attention to Ibrahim Hafez, who was not offended and carefully considered Tahawwur's remark.

"Yes," Ibrahim Hafez finally said, "for sure we must know. But if Narada in Ja'Usu before has been, and a jinn he is, poorly our language he speaks. And if an evil jinn in human form he is, my daughter, Hohete, in danger she may be."

"In danger, all of us we might be," said Tahawwur, confident that Ibrahim Hafez would agree.

"If this Narada fellow good or evil is, how to know are we?" asked Safdar, the one who breaks the enemy's rank.

"Narada with us to meet, let's invite," replied Abdul Muntaqim, slave of him who punishes wrongdoings and seizes retribution, "and then what we must do we will see." And they nodded their heads in agreement.

Aschenaki was very agitated when he left the meeting, and his distress was amplified by the unnatural awkwardness of his body's movement. He bobbed up and down when he walked because his left leg was shorter than the right. His awkward gait forced his right shoulder to pop up in the air when his left foot hit the ground. His peculiar hopping up and down because of his lopsided walk made him especially vulnerable to loose stones and shallow ditches that could cause him to fall and dirty his hands.

Once, as a child, he overheard his mother when she thought she was speaking in private to her sister, Ad'ifaah, about his malady. She confessed that his deformity was caused by a jinn that took out its revenge on him for something that his father had done. Out of respect for his mother and fear of his father, Aschenaki never spoke of the confession or repeated what he had heard to anyone. But after hearing his mother's claim, he blamed his father for his condition. And often, while hopping up and down on Ja'Usu's cobblestone streets, he silently cursed his father's name. He bore in private the weight of his self-loathing.

Aschenaki's lips sometimes trembled when he replayed in his mind this childhood memory, but they quivered this day as he thought about the stranger. He knew it was up to him to uncover the truth, to reveal the evilness in the man or jinn who called himself Narada.

CHAPTER 4

OUR SECRET IT IS

Ibrahim Hafez was sitting on the highest platform in the main room, drinking coffee, when his guest appeared at the top of the stairs. Narada surveyed the room and was intrigued by the intricate color patterns on the baskets that adorned the white-washed walls and the niches where oil lamps, porcelain cups, and saucers from China were kept.

A shaft of light spilled through the entryway, making the red floor below look alive and awash in fresh blood. Three platforms of different heights, like wide stairsteps, took up the entire floor, and a straw rug covered each level with similar-colored patterns as the baskets on the walls. The highest platform was the smallest of the three and reserved for important guests to sit on. The night before, Narada and Ibrahim Hafez had sat and had their meal on the level down from the highest dais, but this morning Hohete's father seated himself on the top platform and gestured to his guest to come and join him. As Narada walked down the stairs and stepped onto the lowest platform, closest to the entryway, he saw apprehension on Ibrahim Hafez's face and understood that his host was startled by his appearance. His loose-fitting pantaloons and long tunic, the color of desert sand, were fresh and unwrinkled, as if they had never been slept in or worn by a man who had just crossed a hostile desert. And the red blisters and welts that had been on his face, hands, and feet when he arrived were completely healed and gone. How could that be? Ibrahim Hafez wondered as Narada drew near and sat in front of him.

"From your journey, the desert crossing, you have recovered, I see," said an astounded Ibrahim Hafez.

"Amantahu," Hohete interjected, entering the room with a tray and smiling at Narada.

"Amantashe," Narada casually replied.

Hohete and her father shared a look of surprise, hearing their guest speak to them in the correct and customary manner. Hohete placed her tray on the rug in front of her guest and served him hot, sweetened coffee with warm goat's milk, pieces of unleavened bread, and the wildflower honey she had purchased from the compound across the way.

Narada knew Ibrahim Hafez had shared their conversation the night before with his daughter and was about to ask him a question when he was distracted by Hohete's attire. She wore a canary-yellow dress that flared out at the waist and rose-colored pantaloons underneath. The silk pants, which fit loosely around her hips and thighs, tightly hugged her legs from her knees down to her ankles, where there was fastened a string of tiny bells. They jingled with the movement of her feet. Her thick black hair was tied into a long braid hanging down her back and was accentuated by the sweet scent of a jasmine flower behind her ear. Hohete felt Narada's eyes watching her as she walked away, and she was pleased.

"Narada," Ibrahim Hafez said, redirecting his attention, "a good rest did you have?"

"Yes, Ibrahim Hafez. I slept well."

"Tomorrow morning, after prayer, Ja'Usu's governing council wishes to meet you. I will accompany you.

"I shall do as you request. Please tell me about your governing council."

"Nine family clans in Ja'Usu there are, and each family by a patriarch is led. In pass times, a gate each clan's responsibility to protect it was, but now most families, poor and weak they are; so no more warriors there are, only gatekeepers. Munqad, the gatekeeper at Fajaruddin gate, when you entered he saw you, and the chief patriarch he told. Here in my house, the council knows you are."

"Why does Ja'Usu have gates?"

Ibrahim Hafez grinned because he delighted in telling Ja'Usu's history. "In ancient times, the Oromo people…the ones selling on the streets you see…a hostile tribe in the region they were. When our women outside the Ja'Usu they went, the Oromo captured, and them they raped and slaves they made them. So to war with the Oromo Ja'Usu warriors went, and the war we won. After the war, the gates we built."

"Why did the Oromo seize Ja'Usu's women? Didn't they have women of their own?"

"Enday!" (This was an expression of surprise.) "Our enemies, their own women they had, but the women of Ja'Usu, the most beautiful they are, so our daughters the Oromo stole…even our wives for their own they took."

Ibrahim Hafez sat quietly, occupied with his own thoughts before he continued. "Our enemies, many problems for Ja'Usu they caused, because even though our weapons superior and our fighters fierce they were, many of our young warriors, their lives they lost. After the war over it was, many women and children a man…a father they did not have. So if in a family two brothers there were, and off to war they went, and only one brother home he came, and the other in battle died, the brother surviving for his dead brother's family responsibility he had. Father to his dead brother's children and husband to his brother's wife he became. Maybe two wives now, and more children to feed and to care for he had. Understand do you?"

"Yes, Ibrahim Hafez, I understand. But your women...your own daughter still goes outside the wall for water."

"Oh yes, now the Oromo too poor, too weak; to Ja'Usu now no threat they are. But after the war, more we did. Ja'Usu women, tight leggings under their dresses to wear they started. Why? Too difficult for a man to take off they are and harder for attackers for them to rape. Today, the tight pantaloons still our women wear. A tradition now it is, but the gates no one anymore guards. Who comes...who goes, only gatekeepers, they watch the gates. Today, like that it is."

"Have any enemies ever breached the wall and entered Ja'Usu?"

"Try they have, but to succeed they have not. Broken glass on the top of the wall we put, and in those days, strong gates at each entrance we had. Who entered or left the city, trained guards they controlled. And the families surrounding each gate, these entrances they guarded and protected. If a gate an enemy attacked, the warriors from the nearest family to the gate, they would defend it. If the enemy too strong was, more warriors from other families to the gate they would go for the invaders to defeat.

"Usu, 'people' the word means, and Ja, 'city' the word means; so Ja'Usu, 'people of the city' it means, and invaded or defeated we have never been," Ibrahim Hafez concluded with pride.

"And you, Narada...in peace I know you've come; but patriarchs, by nature suspicious of strangers they are. Remember, through Ja'Usu's gates, who come and go, the governing council to know they want. And a merchant you are not. So what you say, careful be. Understand do you?"

"Yes, Ibrahim Hafez. I thank you for your words of wisdom and caution. I will answer truthfully the patriarchs' questions."

"What to them you say, to the families around each gate shared it will be. In two hours after the council meets, everyone in Ja'Usu, that here in my home you are, they will know. And about you an opinion they will have. So careful be."

As he walked into the courtyard, Narada felt Ibrahim Hafez's sincerity and the warmth of the morning sun against his face. He saw Hohete sitting with Ayaat on the other side of the palm leaves. Hohete was waiting and was about to cross the yard when a tiny sparrow with a black crescent on its head flew into the compound and landed on the ground in front of Narada's feet. Looking down, he watched as the bird performed an intricate dance on brown spindly legs, its short body flitting from side to side as if it had an urgent message from on high. As swiftly as it landed, the sparrow flew away and perched on the roof of Ayaat's house. He followed its movement as the sparrow turned and bobbed its head several times, before flying away.

"Amantahu," Ayaat shouted with her toothless grin, which made her high cheekbones rise and her eyes squint.

"Hiya Aman, dear Ayaat, hiya Aman!"

"Narada, although our language strangely do you speak, how to know it do you? Before in Ja'Usu have you been?" asked Hohete, standing now in front of him and peering into his eyes to learn the truth she knew was there.

"This is my first time in Ja'Usu, Hohete; and no, I do not know your language."

"But our greetings you speak, and what I say, you understand. How can this be?"

"Hohete, I am simply repeating how people in the streets greeted one another when I entered your city yesterday. That's all. Did I address Ayaat correctly?"

"Yes, our greeting well do you speak; but what I say you understand, and properly you respond. This, why is it so?

Narada smiled, bemused at her bewilderment. "As you speak, I read your thoughts, Hohete, and answer you by sending my thoughts directly to your mind. So you think I'm speaking, but perhaps I am not."

Hohete covered her mouth with the palm of her hand in disbelief while wrestling with the possibility that he was playing with her. "My thoughts and feelings you can read?"

"Yes, I know them."

Her hand still rested on her mouth as if, in this way, she could conceal her thoughts and what she felt.

"You're asking yourself whether I am playing a game with your mind, and I am not."

"Then a jinn you must be," Hohete snapped before abruptly walking into her father's house.

Ayaat had been watching them from across the yard, and after Hohete left, she motioned to Narada to come and sit with her on her doorstep. He crossed the courtyard; and once he was beside her, Ayaat embraced his hand with both of hers. Then, with a large grin, she leaned forward to whisper in his ear. "Who you are, I know…I know," she said emphatically, as if she had seen the depths of his soul—which, if she had, would have frightened her. "To Ja'Usu our Jah has sent you. Is it not so?"

"How do you know such a thing, my sister Ayaat?"

"My Jah, our God, me he has told."

"And who is your God, my sister Ayaat?"

"Many names he has, but only one God there is," she replied with a broad smile.

"For now, let's keep who has sent me our secret."

"Yes, my dear Narada," she said, affectionately patting his hand. "Yes, our secret it is."

Narada stood and walked out of Ibrahim Hafez's compound and onto the cobblestone path, where the allure of roasted coffee couldn't mask the faint stench of raw sewage seeping through the alleyways and underneath the street. An emaciated dog with sagging teats trotted up ahead. The tired bitch sniffed out scraps of food that cackles of hyenas would scrounge when roaming the city's streets at night. Unnerved by Narada's advancing footsteps, the mangy dog scampered away while looking over its shoulder.

Reaching the main street leading to Fajaruddin gate, Narada turned in the opposite direction and walked toward the heart of the old city. This branch of the artery was as crowded as the day before, with Oromo women squatting and selling against whitewashed walls. An older woman, her bare feet knurled with the age of her years, walked in front of Narada, bent over from the weight carried on her back. He thought about lifting her burden and carrying it for her, but he knew she would think he was trying to steal and make a scene. And who would be there at the end of the day when she reclaimed what she couldn't sell, and who would carry her load for her through the gate as she left the city, as all Oromos had to do by public decree, before sunset?

A baby, cradled in a sling across its mother's bare chest, nursed as the mother walked. Her sunbaked arms wrapped around a wooden pole rested on her shoulders. As she made her way down the street with her suckling child, cackling chickens were tied and bound hung in bunches at each end of the pole with their heads dangling upside down. Other Oromo women balanced produce wrapped in tattered cloth or burlap on their heads and held them steady with one hand. And women chewed on small twigs, cleaning their teeth as they walked along in small groups, talking to one another.

A boy with rags draped around his waist and another piece on his head walked quickly passed Narada, leading a small gray donkey. The animal carried a load of dry wood for making charcoal and two water bags tied together over the donkey's shoulder. One sack dripped water while a child ran alongside, trying to catch the drops to drink.

Turning left onto another cobblestone lane, Narada walked past shops where clusters of craftsmen wearing lungis, ankle-length cloths wrapped around their waists, worked. They squatted on storefront floors, inlaying silver and ivory into wooden bowls and small wooden boxes. Other craftsmen labored over gold or silver bracelets or made earrings, and people watched amid the soft medley of the workmen's tap, tap, tap mingled with burning incense of frankincense, sandalwood, and myrrh. Other men carved handles for walking sticks or chiseled hardwood into tables and stools or set about polishing them.

The dirt-poor misery of the many and the privileges of a few disturbed Narada, and he vowed to sow the seeds of discontent and remedy the situation before leaving this ancient city in the desert.

CHAPTER 5

PLANTING A THOUGHT-SEED

Narada and Ibrahim Hafez walked up the cobblestone street leading to Ja'Usu's holy edifice on the hill. Hohete's father had insisted that Narada wear a change in clothing for his meeting with the city's patriarchs and had given him a white lungi and tunic for the occasion. Using one plait to wrap and tie around his other locks, Narada had pulled his hair away from his face and tied it into a bunch on the top of his head. Before entering the edifice, the two of them placed their sandals on the steps and walked through the large entryway into the spacious hall.

Morning prayers were over, and the patriarchs were already assembled and seated in a semicircle on the plush Persian carpet in the rear of the edifice when their guests arrived. Beena, the council's young virgin attendant, was serving the patriarchs their usual morning coffee and biscuits as the two visitors walked barefoot across the immense Persian rug and then patiently stood before them.

Although it was early, dry heat came in waves through the hall's open windows with wooden slats that let in ribbons of light. The sunshine highlighted the rich patterns of beige, blue, and gold threads intricately woven into the carpet the nine council members were sitting on. Now, standing before the council and patiently waiting to be addressed, Narada noticed a black fly that entered the sanctuary; he followed its movement as it meandered its way in a zigzag pattern toward the back of the hall, where the patriarchs leisurely drank their hot coffee and nibbled on their biscuits.

Sitting in the center of the council's semicircular row was Chief Patriarch Murabbi, patron and guardian of the people, who gestured for Narada and Ibrahim Hafez to sit where they stood and offered them a cup of coffee. The young virgin, without waiting for a reply, placed two cups before the visitors and poured them coffee from her Turkish urn; she then quickly left the room.

"Amantahu," Murabbi finally said.

"Hiya Aman," replied Narada and Ibrahim Hafez together.

Starting with Murabbi, each patriarch briefly introduced himself and finished his remarks by placing a hand over his heart and giving an obligatory bow before returning to his coffee and biscuits.

"Your name we understand Narada is? Is that so?" asked the chief patriarch.

"Yes, that is my name."

"Good. Narada you we shall then call. On behalf of Ja'Usu's governing council to our ancient city, you we welcome."

"I thank the council for receiving me, and I am especially grateful to my host, Ibrahim Hafez, and his family for giving me food and shelter." Ibrahim Hafez, sitting next to his guest, lowered his head so as not to bring attention to himself.

"So my name you remember, correct?" asked Murabbi.

"Yes, Chief Patriarch Murabbi, when Ibrahim Hafez delivered your invitation, he shared with me your name and proper title so that I wouldn't make a fool of myself and insult you or anyone. I trust I've said your name and title properly?"

"Yes...yes, perfectly you said it. Thank you."

It was customary for the chief patriarch to open any discussion; and whether meeting with important visitors or merchants or presiding over thorny interfamily disputes, he was always courteous and diplomatic. Patriarchs Tahawwur, one who is rash, and Aschenaki, one who distresses, fidgeted with their hands, unable to conceal their frustration and annoyance with Murabbi's normal politeness and the slow pace of what needed to be the entire council's inquiry. While Patriarch Tahawwur tightly squeezed his hands together, exposing every vein and artery, patriarch Aschenaki twisted his left eyebrow with his fidgety fingers, and his short leg twitched.

"So, my esteemed Narada, tell us, in the desert how did you find yourself?" continued Murabbi.

"I go wherever the Great Mystery takes me."

"The Great Mystery, an unusual phrase that is. Another name for our god, Jah, could that be?"

"Yes, Chief Patriarch."

"Ah...interesting, and traveling alone or separated from your caravan you were?"

"The One-Who-Has-Many-Names is always my companion, so I am never alone."

"And surely, into the desert without water, food, or clothes you couldn't have gone. To them what happened? Where are they now, Narada?"

"I do not live by bread and water alone, but by the grace of the Most High."

Patriarch Tahawwur couldn't keep from speaking any longer and said, "Dear Chief Patriarch, in the discussion, the rest of us—can we now join?"

Then Patriarch Aschenaki, having sat holding his breath far too long, could no longer hold it in and interjected, "Thank you, Chief Patriarch." He was about to continue speaking when all of a sudden the black fly zigzagging around the hall landed on his nose. His hand landed with full force against his own face with a good whack. Everyone else, except Narada and Ibrahim Hafez, broke out in laughter that eased the tension building in the hall. Patriarch Aschenaki's brown skin turned crimson red as he tried to ignore being the butt of ridicule, and he said, "Our brother, Ibrahim Hafez, from him we understand a spirit in human form you said you were. The truth is this?"

"That is true, but aren't we all spirits in human form, or do you think when leaving our bodies behind at death we no longer exist? Is that what your religion teaches you?" Narada sat calmly, alongside Ibrahim Hafez, and looked at each patriarch while waiting for an answer.

"According to our faith," said Patriarch Taqiyy, the pious, the righteous, "when our bodies we leave them, our spirits to a place of peace and pleasure we go. So, yes, since our bodies behind they stay, all of us spirits in human form we are."

"Enough on words with this play!" interrupted Patriarch Aschenaki. "To know we want: a jinn do you admit to be? And good or evil to Ja'Usu do you bring? There, I said it," he concluded, gazing at his fellow patriarchs with a degree of finality and satisfaction.

"I will tell you who I am, Patriarch Aschenaki. My name, Narada, means the wanderer, and I am the son of the Great Mystery, born from his pure thought long before the birth of time. A curse was placed on me by my brother, Daksha, in retribution for a cruel prank I played on his two sons. And our father, the One-Who-Has-Many-Names, whom you refer to as Jah, let my brother's curse stand.

"You see, my brother's sons intended to be creators themselves and wanted to be the first to create a race of men. When they confided their plans to me, I asked them how they could dare to become creators of men before first seeing the ends of the universe. They took my advice, immediately, and started off on an impossible mission because, you see, the Great Mystery's creation has no end.

"So my brother, Daksha, discovering what I had done to his sons, put a curse on me, which I live under to this earth day. I wander the entire universe without rest and will remain homeless until the end of time. So you see, I am not a jinn or spirit, as you would define such a being. I am a force to be reckoned with in our Father's consciousness."

The nine patriarchs and Ibrahim Hafez sat stunned, paralyzed, and had no words to utter. It was as if, after expelling the last drop of air in their lungs, their inhalation took a holiday and refused to come. Time stood still in their holy space as each one tried to wrap his mind around the enormity of Narada's confession. And if they could speak or move, what were they to say to him or do? Should they run and hide in fear or prostrate themselves before this primal force, as he called himself, and bestow upon him devotion and praise?

Narada sensed the internal life of each patriarch frozen in confusion and stilted in thought and decided to plant the seed of disbelief in Aschenaki's mind.

"What a fantastic story that is, Narada," Aschenaki finally said, breaking the spell of bewilderment and fear in the minds of everyone present. "For all of us I think I speak and say, an exceptional storyteller you are. How a living you make, when from place to place you travel, we now understand. A trader of goods or rich merchant selling wares you are not, but a storyteller, and an excellent one at that, you are."

Aschenaki clapped his hands as the rest of the patriarchs and Ibrahim Hafez, who had moved three feet away from his visitor, looked on to see how Narada was going to react. To their amazement he smiled and broke out in laughter. Not wanting to be left out of what they still didn't understand, the other patriarchs and

Hohete's father cautiously joined in applauding while their eyeballs moved wildly in their heads. They looked from Aschenaki to Narada and back again, until they were all clapping in a hysterical and fearful frenzy.

Patriarch Liyaqat, the one deserving of merit, was so moved by their visitor's fantastical story and at the same time relieved that none of it could possibly be true that his body uncontrollably bobbed up and down on the Persian rug as he clapped and clapped and clapped. Finally, exhausted from the group's hysteria, the council settled down and was quiet, though awkwardly, once again.

"My dear Narada," said Chief Patriarch Murabbi, "for a moment please excuse us so among ourselves we may talk. Brother Ibrahim Hafez, with our guest please remain."

Narada and Ibrahim Hafez got up from the carpet and walked away. Hohete's father, his mind still reeling from the story, decided it best to walk a few steps behind his visitor. Recognizing his host was frightened, Narada turned and put his arm around Ibrahim Hafez's shoulders, which had the immediate effect of calming him.

"An idea, I have," Aschenaki said to his companions with enthusiasm, now emboldened by his demonstrated perception and courage to see Narada's incredible farce for what it really was. "From his storytelling, money can be made. And to the people of Ja'Usu, entertainment let us give them."

"This, how can we do, Aschenaki?" said Chief Patriarch Murabbi. Impulsively or out of fear, several patriarchs looked to see where Narada was in their holy space before they decided to join the conversation.

"In our city with one of his fantastical stories in an open place for all to see and hear, our visitor let him the people entertain," said Aschenaki. "Our shopkeepers, tables they can set up; and samosas, sweet breads, and drinks they can sell at Narada's storytelling. His effect on us, did you not see? And if, because of what he says, against him they turn…well, arrest him for a heretic we will, and throw him back to the desert from whence he came. For no one in Ja'Usu on us blame will they lay, if the city's rabble-rouser Narada becomes. Say what do you?"

Patriarch Ihtesham, the respectable and honorable one, was the first to speak. "Well, maybe he is who he says he is; to know I don't. If the story true it be, and an elemental being he really is, what then? His power we don't know, and if a reason to unleash it we give him, what have we done?"

"Enday! Narada on the ground like every other man, he pees and shits. A storyteller he is, that's all," replied Tahawwur, one who is rash, as he stared at Narada, now at the other end of the hall.

"But our language strangely does he speak. In the wrong places his words are said; and, besides, in a public place to hear him, who will be able to?" said Taqiyy, the pious and the righteous.

"If our request to take up he is crazy enough, then our language…the way he speaks and whether loud enough to hear, his problem it becomes, not ours," replied Aschenaki, more confident than ever that his scheme had legs.

"But what if Narada for our proposal does not go? Then what?" asked Patriarch Izzat, the one who possess high rank and honor.

"Then, him closely we will watch," replied Murabbi.

"Our wise patriarch, Aschenaki, right he is I think," said Safdar, the one who breaks the enemy's ranks. "In dealing with this mysterious rascal, it's a good plan."

"I agree," said Abdul Muntaqim, slave of him who punishes wrongdoings and seizes retribution. "As a plan, it is good. From our wandering guest, we make money. His storytelling to Ja'Usu, which nothing it costs us, we give. And if this Narada messes up, none to blame we are, and him we get rid of. That is, unless our people, out of Ja'Usu first they chase him." And the patriarchs laughed softly at their cleverness and blossoming conspiracy.

"But to ourselves, our plot we must keep. No one, not even our brother Ibrahim Hafez, must know," said the chief patriarch.

They chuckled again and turned their heads to see where their visitor and Ibrahim Hafez were standing in their great hall. Only Patriarch Taqiyy, the pious, the righteous, held back his voice and thought about whether they were making the right decision.

Chief Patriarch Murabbi asked Izzat, the one with high rank and honor, to go and fetch their guests. When Ibrahim and Narada returned and seated themselves before the patriarchs, Murabbi said, with sweet sincerity dripping from his mouth, "Narada, by your story very moved we were; incredibly impressive it was. While here in our great city you are, with one of your remarkable stories Ja'Usu would you consider entertaining?"

The patriarchs watched Narada for a sign and silently implored him under a mask of treachery, except for Patriarch Taqiyy, who only stared at the rug.

Narada, knower of all things great and small, peered through their cover of pretense and deceit and saw, very well, the intrigue they were brewing. How would they have known their visitor planted the seed of their trickery in Aschenaki's fertile mind so that he would think this doing was his own?

Narada smiled at them. "I have lived through and told many stories over my years and would like to tell a tale to the people of Ja'Usu…under two conditions."

"Oh!" This caught Murabbi and the others by surprise. "What conditions might those be?" asked the chief patriarch.

"First, this council will agree to supply Ibrahim Hafez's household with food and drink for as long as I am in your city; and second, you allow the Oromo people to also attend and listen to my story."

"That second condition cannot be," said Tahawwur, the rash.

"Dear Narada," said Patriarch Aschenaki, "during the day, the Oromo to walk and sit on Ja'Usu's streets and their wares sell they can, but before nightfall leave the city they must. The council's law it is."

"I accept your rule, Patriarch Aschenaki, and have no wish to violate it. I suggest we schedule my storytelling outside the main gate after sunset so that everyone within the sound of my voice can hear and be entertained."

"Refreshments for our city dwellers...for everyone I mean, our vendors to sell can we ask them...so even our Oromo brethren may buy, if they wish?" politely asked Aschenaki.

"I think that is a good idea."

"Agreed," said Chief Patriarch Murabbi.

Several of the patriarchs, including Ihtesham, the respectable and honorable one; Abdul Muntaqim, slave of him who punishes wrongdoings and seizes retribution; Safdar, the one who breaks the enemy's ranks; Liyaqat, one worthy of merit; and even Ibrahim Hafez were taken aback and put off balance by the rapid volley of the back-and-forth exchange and the speed at which decisions had been made. The governing council's deliberations were always slow and easy, enabling every member to speak his mind. They enjoyed cogitating, like ruminating old cows chewing their cud for the second or third time, over thorny issues or new projects until a decision emerged like sprouting green grass. But this talking back and forth among a few made some patriarchs' eyeballs chase each other from side to side, until Liyaqat buried his head in his hands and silently pled for Jah's mercy.

Patriarch Aschenaki, who had been in on the volley of words, thought he had another superb idea and said, "A platform right outside the Fajaruddin gate let us construct, Chief Patriarch, so Narada everyone can see and something to sit on he will have as his story he tells. Also for mosquitoes to keep away, oil lamps around the whole area we can burn. What to think do you?"

Chief Patriarch Murabbi thought these suggestions were overly generous, as the council had to pay for the extravaganza; but this was Aschenaki's plot, and, knowing his collaborator well, he knew there must be a good reason for such an added expense.

"Narada, how much time your story to tell would you like?" asked Taqiyy, the pious, the righteous.

"Seven nights."

"Seven nights!" the patriarchs gasped.

Stunned silence sat among them.

"A good story is a powerful thing," Narada continued, "and most human spirits can only take in a little at a time. So I would prefer to tell a story in seven installments, every other day for seven nights, ending on the evening of the fourteenth day. Is this acceptable to the council?"

The nine patriarchs didn't know what to think or say or do. They had never heard of a story lasting more than an hour, much less for seven nights.

"Please, Narada," the chief patriarch eventually replied, looking quite exhausted with the whole affair. "You and Ibrahim Hafez, please, again excuse us so your additional request we can consider."

Ibrahim Hafez's head was also swimming; and, at the same time, he was feeling oddly lightheaded from all the ideas floating around and over his crown, like he had smoked too much gunja or chewed too much of that little green leaf, kat. Surely, he would have keeled over from dizziness had Narada not helped him stand and held him around the waist as he seemed to stagger away.

"Narada," Ibrahim Hafez exclaimed in both wonderment and alarm, "for seven nights a story! Even if every other night you tell them, impossible it is. Even after one hour, who will listen? You mean well, I know, and to impress you want, but... and for the food the council has promised, thank you. Very gracious you are. Hohete and Ayaat thank you they will, I know, but a story lasting seven nights! Oh my Jah! Oh my Jah! How crazy that is! Excuse me for so saying, Narada, but crazy it is. To you no offense I mean, but it cannot be done. It cannot be done."

The patriarchs broke ranks and quickly regrouped into a tight bundle to put their incredulous heads together and reexamine their treachery in light of Narada's unexpected request. Aschenaki was the first to speak and rushed to say, "With what he is asking us to go along with, I think we should. No doubt the fellow, as delusional as a desert mouse that mistakes a snake's open mouth for its home he is. Only one night he will last, I bet, before the people, fed up with him they become, and to get rid of him we will be forced. Even to understand what he is saying they will not—that jibba-jabba he be talking."

"But seven nights every other day, that's outrageous. Yes to that, how can we say?" questioned Patriarch Izzat, one with high rank and honor.

"With Aschenaki I agree," Murabbi interjected. "Let Narada himself hang."

Unanimous in their judgment, the council members reclaimed their previous seats on their most coveted Persian rug and unruffled their garments to appear dignified and serious as Murabbi was to render their decision. Aschenaki then snapped his fingers, getting Ibrahim Hafez's attention to escort Narada back over to them.

"Your offer to accept we have decided, Narada," said the chief patriarch, "and anything you request we will give, of course within reason. In all of Ja'Usu, your seven nights of storytelling, every other day, we will publicly announce...and the Oromo we also will tell."

The patriarchs smiled and then applauded as they gazed at one another and Narada, feeling as though they had succeeded in a coup—with the exception of Taqiyy, the pious, the righteous, who clapped with very little enthusiasm.

"But Chief Patriarch Murabbi," said Ibrahim Hafez, who remained deeply distressed, "our guest to Ja'Usu new he is, and the ways of our people to know he does not. Little patience as a people you know we have...of course, about your honorable sirs I'm not speaking...but talk and public speeches we don't abide. Perhaps, our guest just for one night could speak, before another six nights of storytelling he commits to?" Ibrahim Hafez's palms and nose were dripping sweat as he turned to Narada and pleaded with his eyes for him to take back his proposal.

Narada calmly placed a hand on his host's knee and turned to the nine patriarchs. "I'm pleased that you have accepted my request, and I will be prepared to begin my story as soon as Ja'Usu and the Oromo are told and your platform is ready."

"Oh, immediately we will build it, and right away our people will know of you," Aschenaki said, unmasking his scorn.

The sun had passed its zenith when Narada and Ibrahim Hafez left the patriarchs' meeting and headed down the pathway away from the seat of power and toward Khawar gate, the second or eastern entrance to the city. Ja'Usu's main streets, all named after the ancient gate at the end of each pathway, were already thinning of people, with merchants' shops closed and vendors returning home for samosas, tea, and rest to wait out the midday inferno. They would reopen in the late afternoon when the fireball's heat was gentler. Oromo women, however, had nothing to do but remain on Ja'Usu's streets. They'd wait it out in the sweltering heat by covering themselves and their babies with tattered white cloths that sheltered them from the glare of the sun.

Hohete's father was perplexed as he covered his head with his white shawl and walked beside Narada. He marveled how his initial worry and anxiety about his guest's ill-conceived plan abruptly turned into a feeling of peace and well-being once Narada placed his hand on his knee. He also wondered if the bizarre story his visitor told the council was actually true. But how could that be?

"Narada, your story about your origins, true was it?"

"What do you think, Ibrahim Hafez? Do you think it was true?"

"Buried in most stories some truth there is, I think."

"I agree. The truth will be revealed to you and your family before I take my leave."

"Narada, if a jinn or powerful spirit you are, a good one you must be. Please, a blessing grant me before on your wanderings you leave. Ayaat and me, in old age advancing we are, but in peace after death we will not be if Hohete alone remains. In Ja'Usu culture, a women's duty to care for her family it is and the household run, but Hohete no one does she have, no man…no children does she have. So what must we do? Help you must. For my only daughter, Hohete, help I beg you."

"Don't worry, Ibrahim Hafez; we will find a way."

CHAPTER 6

DRY BONES, SADNESS, AND RIGHTEOUS INDIGNATION

Arsalaan crouched on his heels alongside the wall, casually chewing on a twig as he watched Ghazi, the butcher, mumble a sacrificial prayer before stringing the goat up by its hind legs and, in one quick motion, cut the animal's throat. Blood gushed from the open wound in a gurgling red stream as its eyeballs rolled up into its dangling head. The gore splashed into a dirty, wide-mouthed pan set underneath the twitching body until its life drained away; until the animal hung limp on the rope, its carcass quiet and still.

With the skilled hand of one who could peel the skin off a ripe olive, Ghazi removed the goat's brown hide and threw it onto the dirt, where flies waited. His hands were strong and his fingers puffy from soaking in the blood and waste of all the animals he had slaughtered over the years. He gutted them down the middle and reached into their bellies up to his elbow to pull out their entrails. Those, too, he ritually threw to the ground, as it was against Ja'Usu's religion to consume the guts of an animal.

"Those cow bones over there in the dirt, you can have," said Ghazi. "Some meat on them there still is, and the calf guts in the pail over there, yours, too, they are. And if you can wait, this goat's head and hooves and innards for your stinking hyenas also I will give you."

Arsalaan said nothing as he took up the bones and put them in two burlap bags and then searched through the slop in the bucket for the dead calf's intestines. Finding the animal's entrails, he tied a knot at one end of the bowels before scooping up the remaining slop with his free hand and stuffing it into the other end. Ghazi tossed over the goat's innards, which Arsalaan also stuffed into the sack. The makeshift bag swelled up like the bloated belly of a dead dog baking in the sun before Arsalaan closed the other end by tying another knot. He crammed the goat's head and feet into the burlap bag. Then, picking up the intestinal sack filled with coagulated blood and guts, he placed the bag over his head and neck to hang full and plump across his chest. Grabbing the two burlap bags with bones and the goat's head, he slung them onto his back.

Ghazi watched Arsalaan, bent over by the weight of dead animal parts and wasted years, leave his shop. He sadly shook his head as he thought about how far the man had fallen to be called by Ja'Usu's inhabitants the Hyena Man.

Arsalaan, possessing the strength of two men, labored with his burden as he made his way down the cobblestone street in the heat with the flies in pursuit. He staggered down Masresha, which ended at the fourth or southern gate bearing the same name—a title that, in translation, meant "the one who helped us to forget." Arsalaan lived next to the wall right outside the gate, which was fitting for a man obsessed with tortured memories he wished he could forget.

The people of Ja'Usu, even the Oromo, moved out of his way when they saw him coming. Not just on account of the stench or the flies that followed him everywhere but because they thought him mad, roaming the streets stark naked except for the rags around his loins. His dark-brown hair, not brushed or combed in years, was matted and unkempt, with slivers of sun-bleached bone lodged in his tight curls. The inhabitants of the city and, occasionally, traders passing through in caravans ventured outside Masresha gate to watch Arsalaan feed hyenas with his hands and sometimes they grabbed scraps of meat he held between his teeth.

The heavy load he carried, however, was much more than the bowels around his neck or the dry bones on his back. Although he trudged up and down the Masresha to Ghazi's shop every day, it was his memories that weighed on him, gave him nightmares, and had driven him insane. He blamed himself for his father's death; and because of his self-imposed judgment, he made himself suffer, inwardly, as retribution for his crime. Not that the city's patriarchs or anyone in Ja'Usu faulted him for the death of his father or wanted Arsalaan to eke out a living carrying slop and dead bones through the ancient streets. It was his own self-inflicted penance that arrested his life and pursued him down the street each day except for the day when Ghazi, the butcher, was closed.

Ja'Usu's street children, who were orphaned and traveled in packs, sometimes trailed behind Arsalaan and taunted him, hoping he would drop a bag of bones with bits of meat for them to eat. It would be his misfortune and their good luck if he stumbled and fell along his route, giving them an instant to grab a dirty bone and run away.

But on this day, Arsalaan stopped abruptly and jerked his head up, disrupting the swarm of flies surrounding his head.

Narada stood, unmoved, directly in front of him and said, "Who are you, Arsalaan? Who are you?" As suddenly as he appeared, Narada walked away, continuing up the cobblestone street.

Arsalaan glared at the intruder who momentarily interrupted his tortured thoughts as the stranger disappeared behind the crowd of Oromo women advancing toward him. Only then, when he couldn't see the man anymore, did Arsalaan resume his lumbered plod toward the south gate.

Hohete opened the compound door for Narada, latched the door behind him, and quickly walked away. Still, Narada noticed that she had been crying. He knew she was disappointed in him and would have taken her aside to console her if Ibrahim Hafez had not hurried over to speak to him. Ayaat sat, as usual, in the entranceway to her house and watched her brother as he started talking, rapidly.

"Narada, for you I've been waiting. Your platform and the oil lamps, ready they are. The governing council, to know they would like if tonight, your storytelling, you will be ready?"

"Yes, let's begin tonight."

"Actually, Patriarch Taqiyy this morning in confidence he told me, your dais and the lamps, five days ago up they could have been, but among the patriarchs a disagreement there was. To your storytelling who should be invited, and considering a person's status, in what place should they sit? They could not agree."

"I knew there would be disagreement."

Ibrahim Hafez continued speaking hurriedly, eager to return to the council with Narada's response. "The patriarchs, a platform of their own in the front to sit on they decided they also needed. For you above them to be raised it would not be proper, the council, they said. So a platform for themselves to have constructed they agreed. And on their dais, behind the patriarchs, their women and children will sit; except for their first wives beside them will stay.

"The laborers, the platform they built, under Patriarch Liyaqat's direct supervision, but then another problem arose, I was told. If the council's platform in the very front they put it, everyone behind their dais sitting, to see you they would not be able to. So for several days this predicament and the proper way out of this dilemma were discussed."

Narada, finding Ibrahim Hafez's telling of the patriarchs' problem amusing, laughed with abandon. "So what did they decide to do?"

"Well…in the back of the gathering, their platform to build first they decided, so raised up they would be, and everyone in front of them lower they would be and able to see. But then the council realized if in the back they sat, maybe, to hear you they would not be able to."

The council's logic made Narada laugh even more.

"So, finally," continued Ibrahim Hafez, "in the front to stay the patriarch's decided, and whether anyone behind them could see or hear you, to worry about it they will not. So in the end it all worked out, do you see?"

"Yes, I see."

Hohete's father started for the door but remembered something else. "Oh, in Ja'Usu a taleteller you are, and a story you will tell, the patriarchs did not announce. Patriarch Aschenaki, sincere he was not when open to the public he said. Now your storytelling, only for the patriarchs' families and their selected guests it is for." With that said, Ibrahim Hafez hurried out his compound's door.

"Amantahu," said Narada to Ayaat as he approached her sitting in the entrance of her house.

"Hiya Aman…to Hohete, please go and talk. Low she is feeling, and to help her you I beg, please."

Ibrahim Hafez's daughter was sitting on the lower platform in her father's house when Narada walked through the entrance and sat down beside her. She moved over at once to put more space between them and lifted the canary-yellow scarf resting on her shoulders and wrapped it around her head, partially hiding the redness in her eyes.

"Hohete, I am blocking your thoughts so I cannot read your mind; and from now on, your thoughts are your own. So please speak freely, if you wish, and tell me what brings you to tears."

Hohete stood up without speaking and left Narada sitting alone in the room. But moments later she reappeared, carrying a silver tray with tea. She placed the tray between them and poured Narada and then herself a cup. They drank in silence as Hohete gazed out the open door while Narada sat patiently, knowing she was preparing her thoughts to speak.

"My father, how I feel truly he knows," she finally said, "but sad for me he becomes, and he worries; so to Ayaat I only talk, and good that is; because as a Ja'Usu woman, she understands." Hohete paused as she sipped her tea and watched Narada place his cup on the tray.

"Once, married at sixteen years old to a young man named Waheed Nuri, I was. From a good family he came, and my father and his father, for us to marry they consented, so our two families into one family we could become. A good man Waheed was, and with kindness always me he treated. Most of the time, my independence he let me have," Hohete said with a smile as she thought about him.

"As our custom requires, with him and his parents to live I went. A house in their compound for us, they built. But two years after our families joined together, Waheed died, and with child he did not leave me. Waheed's family, a curse they said I was, because their son died and an heir he did not leave. Out of our home me they kicked out, and back to my father they sent me.

And now, no man as their bride—me they will not have; no child will I have, because of the curse upon me that was put."

"You are not cursed. Hohete, you are a victim of your culture's ignorance. It might be difficult to understand or accept, but sometimes misfortune is a blessing because our hardships compel us to grow in ways we would not voluntarily do. Our challenges help us evolve as a human spirit. It does not mean we should look forward to them or welcome our troubles, but when they come, we must accept them and endure.

"I know about curses, and one does not afflict you. I was burdened with a curse a long time ago, and it stays with me. Because of my curse, I do not have a home and must remain a wanderer... homeless, no matter where I roam. But I have learned to make peace with my misfortune, because without this affliction, I would not have understood, perhaps, my purpose: to aid human spirits and other creatures overcome their pain and suffering. Without my burden I could have remained self-absorbed and a trickster."

"My heart, truth it tells me there is in what you say."

Narada was quiet and waited, knowing Hohete had more to say.

"Narada, when at the well you I saw, and your shaking hands so you could drink I held, to rescue me I thought you came. How silly of me. But now, a good and powerful jinn I'm sure you are. At least, Ayaat and my father, they think so. Please, with a man of my own who will care for me and my child have, grant me before you go. To end up old and alone, I do not want to be." Hohete grabbed Narada's hands and held them close to her as warm tears fell over them.

"My dear...dear Hohete, you are a beautiful flower of a woman who will bear a child in your life and experience the embrace of a man who will love and cherish you, but these gifts may not come in the way you imagine."

"What do you mean?"

"If you have faith in me, and your heart is open, I will ask the Great Mystery to find a way to bless you with what you long for."

"I will do anything," she said with desperation.

"No, Hohete, words have power. Do not be desperate and say you will do anything. Let your worries go…open your heart to the One-Who-Has-Many-Names, and Spirit will provide. If you can do these two things, I promise your desire for a righteous man and a child from your loins will be fulfilled."

He wiped the tears streaming down her face with her scarf and kissed her above the bridge of her nose. And with Narada's touch, the worry and pain and sorrow of all the years without Waheed vanished as though they had never been.

Daylight had already faded into twilight when Narada walked through Fajaruddin gate and past a row of hawkers on each side of the road, selling meat samosas, sweet breads, and hot tea. He stepped up onto his platform and faced two hundred people waiting for him. After sitting down on the mat placed there for his seat, Narada respectfully bowed to the nine patriarchs who sat directly in front of him. They were in the very first row with their families and blocked out the vision of anyone unfortunate enough to be sitting behind them.

The council members, their wives, and their mistresses were dressed in their finest silks and robes, the women weighed down by mounds of silver and gold jewelry that they wore in their ears, around their necks and arms, and on their toes. Their oldest children sat alongside their mothers, whose heads were sometimes known to fall to one side from the heavy jewelry they were pleased to wear. When this occurred, a son or daughter, sitting next to them, would be called upon to prop up their mother's head with his or her hand or tilt his or her own head against their mother's crown so she could sit upright. The patriarchs bowed to the storyteller to show their insincere respect, and he politely returned their nod before he got up and walked off the platform specifically built for him.

"What is he doing?" whispered Patriarch Abdul Muntaqim, leaning forward and turning his head to one side and then the other to hear what his colleagues might have to say.

"I don't know," replied Patriarch Aschenaki, who sat closest to Abdul Muntaqim. "Maybe cold feet he has gotten, and this charade no longer appeals to him pulling off?" Several council members, overcome by their feelings of self-importance, were ready to make a public display of their indignation, especially after making such a big to-do in extending their personal invitations to the merchants and shopkeepers sitting behind them. In turn, the shopkeepers lavishly rewarded the patriarchs with boodle and bribes.

The patriarchs watched Narada with suspicion as he walked to the rear of the gathering and turned around to face them. The crowd followed his movements and wondered what he would do next. Narada then parted the gathering with a gesture of his hands and moved down the center of the group as he instructed them to make a wide circle around him. Many onlookers, at first, didn't know what to make of his directive until several people near Narada stood up and told the people around them to move into a circle as they dragged their mats or pieces of cloth behind them. They gestured with their hands and barked orders as people moved, and a circle began to take shape. The patriarchs, with their women and offspring, were annoyed when they realized they had to turn completely around on their dais and were now sitting in back of the people who before were behind them.

Narada slowly walked around the inside of the large ring until he was satisfied that everyone had a place in the circle. Then he motioned for the two men Ibrahim Hafez had employed to bring a stack of dry wood into the middle of the ring, where, once placed, a man vigorously rubbed two pieces of flint together, igniting a spark on dry grass and setting a fire ablaze. Narada watched the flames grow and flicker in the darkness, and the gathering quietly watched him. Pleased with the crackling fire, he walked away from the flames and selected a place in the circle where he separated two people to sit among them.

The people looked on in wonder and anticipation as the flames danced and leaped into the night air as the man from the desert sat peacefully and still. He then intoned in an unknown tongue what the people of Ja'Usu did not recognize or comprehend. And from a mysterious wellspring, deeper than any vibration the people had ever felt or heard, raised a sound that made the ground quake and their bodies tremble until everyone was frightened. But yet, they were unable to move or run away.

And as the ground gradually stopped shaking, and the people's trembling subsided, Narada raised his arms in praise and supplication to the Great Mystery for responding to his prayer. For the Akasha had been opened, permitting Narada to read from the imperishable records of celestial light that contained not only the past but also future human thought and action. And the people were still afraid.

Narada then opened his eyes and said in a voice that all could inconceivably hear, "This story I tell is from the future of a people who have not yet lived, but who will inhabit the earth for an instant almost two hundred years from now; in the year 2003. In the future they will live in another part of the world, in another place and in another time. This story of a future people begins tonight and will resume every other night until coming to a natural end thirteen days from now.

"And in the telling, you will watch and hear words spoken from the mouths of men and women who have not yet lived, in a language that is foreign to you and has not found expression yet, but which has already been recorded in the Akasha Records of Celestial Light. And you will pay attention to their spoken word and understand as their actions give rise to new ways of thinking, bring forth new meaning to old philosophies and your fixed ideas.

"If you try to experience this story by listening with your mind, you will surely be lost. You will become weary and utterly dissatisfied in the telling of it. It will be as if you ate a meal and left the table hungry, with a bad taste in your mouth. So in order to follow my narrative and grasp the story as it unfolds…the images you see, the words you hear and want to understand, the ideas expressed…just look into the fire until your eyes close on their own, and you slip into a collective dream. But it is only a shared dream we will experience, together, as our story begins in another place and at another time."

Most of the people were already staring into the fire now, and many had their eyes closed, except for the patriarchs and a few of their women who heard Narada's voice and whose brains remained scattered. They were lost and completely confused. Their heads craned up and down like strutting peacocks and cautious hens as they tried to uncover what other people were doing. What were the inhabitants of Ja'Usu experiencing that they were not? Why were people watching the flames when all they heard was the unintelligible chatter of a not-to-right storyteller? Several members of the patriarchs' entourage simply closed their eyes and sat like the people they noticed and faked it.

"What about is he jabbering?" asked Chief Patriarch Murabbi, patron and guardian of the people, leaning over and whispering to Adeeba, his elderly wife. She didn't know either and wanted to scream and pull out her hair, but she knew she was not at home and was too cultured and too polite to make a public scene.

CHAPTER 7

A PEOPLE'S DILEMMA

In a distant age and in a faraway land, there is a city nestled on the edge of a great body of water. It is called Oakland in a place named California. It's the year 2003, and Arthur Renfro, at age forty-two, is considered young, because people there live longer. He is in his mechanical wagon, which they call a car or an automobile, and he travels on a wide road they name a freeway or highway. There are many types of cars in many different colors. People in their automobiles are hurrying to work, to merchant houses where people shop, taking children to school, or meeting friends at food houses they identify as restaurants to have their morning meal. Do you see? Wherever they're going or whatever they're doing, the inhabitants of this age, in this part of the world, are always in a hurry, rushing here and there, cramming their lives with responsibilities and obligations and experiences all so very important to them.

The young man we see, Arthur, is on his way to a meeting at an edifice called the Alameda County Public Health Department, where human spirits are paid to look after the health and welfare of the people in their region, called a county. As he rides in his car, Arthur is thinking about the heated argument he had the night before with his woman or wife, Natalie, who left their house in North Oakland and didn't return. He wonders where she spent the night, but he is too preoccupied with other matters to think about contacting her friends to see if she's all right. And he surely doesn't want to admit to himself that he enjoyed the night alone, free from the frequent fights that leave him emotionally exhausted. As Arthur reaches the heart of the city, he sees in his mind Natalie running out the door, crying. She is still in his thoughts as his silver-gray car, named Honda, moves down Fourteenth Street into heavy traffic. He is tired, physically worn out from flare-ups with his wife. These quarrels zap his energy and his spirit, robbing him of his peace of mind. He wonders if his neighbors overhear their arguments but then questions why he should care when the renters—people who pay money to someone else to live in a place—the renters living underneath him have their own bouts of madness. He thanks God that he and Natalie don't have children. The one stable thing in Arthur's life is his work, which is called a job. He manages something like Ja'Usu's governing council, which they name the African American Community Trust. He wonders if Natalie will at least show up for their next session with their marriage healer, a Dr. Brathwaite, who sees them on every seventh day. He knows something has to change.

Arriving anywhere late makes Arthur anxious, as if he'll miss something important being said or someone will question his professionalism…his effectiveness at work. It's this anxiety that causes him to look every few minutes at the watch, or timepiece on his wrist, which makes Arthur rethink his time of arrival. But he fears this repeated action is a symptom of a possible sickness or neurosis or private obsession, so he manages to control this habit when others are around. But today, he's driving alone and free to glare at the slowly moving, thin sliver of metal passing over the numbers on his watch. He stops his car and waits for the red light up ahead to turn green. Do you see?

But when the driver of the car in front of him doesn't move forward when the light changes, Arthur is furious and hits his horn until the poor woman forgets what she's doing and frantically gestures for him to go around her. Arthur jerks his steering wheel to the right and almost slams into an oncoming automobile, and the other driver makes a quick reaction by instantly swerving so as not to hit him. Do you see? Watch...now the angry driver is calling him the hole in someone's ass.

After parking his Honda in the Eleventh and Harrison Street garage (a place where cars are left to sleep), he grabs his brown leather shoulder bag and sprints across the street and down to a place called Eleventh and Broadway. While he rides the empty elevator (see the moving floor going up?) to the fifth level, he hastily tucks his dress shirt in his pants and adjusts his tie before the doors open. And to the entire world, Arthur Renfro's professional persona, or work face, is once again in place, while underneath his personal life is a wreck.

The gathering at the public health department (a big governing council concerned about a people's health) is well attended by people of African descent. They are all tribal or clan leaders and faith healers. They call themselves African Americans, and each one represents like Arthur a different governing council. See Arthur walking into their formal talking place they call a conference room? The people are performing a ritual where, one by one, everyone says his or her name, important title, and the governing council he or she represents. This sharing is almost over when Arthur slides into an empty seat beside a woman calling herself Carol Macklin. She is an attractive manager or handler who heads the cultural diversity, or many-different-people's program, at a council named the American Heart Association.

"Dr. Renfro!" Aaron Campbell, director of the public health department, shouts with a smile as he notices Arthur whispering to Carol. Although Arthur is not a trained healer, which these people refer to as doctors or physicians, it is Aaron's habit to always refer to the community's tribal leaders and heads of organizations or councils with the respectful greeting of "doctor."

"Good to see you, Arthur. You're in time to check in, or speak up and give your name, title, and the name of your organization, sir."

Although most of his colleagues or fellow leaders already know he is the head of the African American Community Trust, Arthur follows the ritual by standing with self-confidence and introducing himself. This council is the only philanthropy, or money-giving organization, that gifts riches and other resources to meet their community's needs and is run by people of African ancestry.

"Like all of you," says Aaron Campbell, "I'm a person of African descent. I've invited you here this morning to share some very disturbing news about the health of black people in our county, including here, in the city of Oakland. I've asked my colleague (working partner), Dr. Harshavardham Tripathi, to attend this meeting. He's our department's lead epidemiologist (one who studies the diseases that many people get) who will present his findings on the alarming pattern of disease among people in our community. After his presentation, we'll have a discussion on how we can come together as African Americans and respond to the issues in his report."

Dr. Tripathi is eloquent in delivering his PowerPoint presentation. See the different colors of moving arrows, dots, and words in that square-shaped white light on the wall? The doctor is comparing the occurrence of major diseases in various tribal lines and among males and females in the region. Based on his staff's, or workers', research, black people in the county...people who look like they could be the descendants of Ja'Usu's inhabitants and the Oromo...are suffering from more diseases at a higher rate than any other tribal population; more than the people of European, Asiatic, or Latin American descent.

By the end of the presentation, everyone in the room understands that African Americans in the county called Alameda and throughout the region are in poor health. These tribal people reflect the general health status of African Americans living on the entire land mass named the United States of America. Out of the nineteen major diseases identified in the county, with names like heart disease, tuberculosis, high blood pressure, cancer, infant mortality, diabetes, sexually transmitted diseases, and hepatitis B, African Americans are suffering and dying from these illnesses far more than any other tribal group. They are dying from fourteen of the nineteen identified major diseases in the area.

"It looks like we got more black people dying in this county than we have being born," concludes Aaron Campbell. "Judging from this report, African Americans in Alameda are in a health crisis. Tomorrow morning this department will host a press conference (a special meeting for scribes and storytellers to get the word out) and issue a press release (a short written story) to publicly announce a health emergency in this county's African American community. We invite all of you to be there. I will also deliver a hard copy of Dr. Tripathi's findings, which are included in this report I am holding up, to the county's board of supervisors (or region's governing council) at their meeting next week.

"Now I'm asking you, as the community's respected black leaders and preachers (or holy edifice talkers), to confront this health emergency now, right now, and tell me what you're going to do about it."

After putting everyone on the defensive, Aaron sits down and gazes around the conference room while attendees look back at him and wait for someone to respond.

The professionals in the room who don't work in health services, including Arthur, are alarmed by Dr. Tripathi's remarks. Although most of them recognize that black-on-black crime and violence and the prison-industrial pipeline (a labyrinth of pathways leading to cages made for people to be locked in for punishment), as well as the diseases Dr. Tripathi presented, are of real concern, they have never thought of sickness setting off a health emergency. A few of the health-care workers present suspected that African Americans were experiencing a health crisis, but Tripathi's presentation and Aaron's report confirmed their suspicions.

The room is quiet, except for a few papers rattling, until the sound of a metal writing instrument suddenly falls to the floor, causing several attendees to turn their heads. Someone coughs, uncomfortably, as the stark reality of what was said and the unbearable silence in the talking room causes that person to clear their throat.

Charles Joyner tentatively raises his hand as he rises to his feet. The audience, and even the walls of the room, feeling unnerved by the prolonged silence, are relieved that someone has an idea and the wherewithal to speak up.

"I'm Charles Joyner from the American Diabetes Association. It would be helpful, Aaron, if you could give us a copy of the report so we can review it thoroughly. I also suggest we form a committee (short-lived council) to speak to your challenge, though it does seem daunting, and see if we can come up with a strategy (plan) to deal with our health inequities." He sits down.

The room erupts in thunderous applause. A young man, dressed in blue jeans (work pants) and a pullover sweater (clothing he places over his head), who is sitting in the front, suddenly stands and proclaims his firm support for Charles's proposal. His enthusiasm is soon contagious as others, now oblivious to decorum and the rules of order, move into impromptu clusters of people to weigh the pros and cons of Charles's suggestion.

Aaron shouts over the den of small group conversations that break out all around him, "Copies of this report will be available on the table at the back of the room right after the meeting, everyone. May I have your attention, please! I would like to take Dr. Joyner's recommendation one step further. If you take my call to action seriously and are able to come together to tackle this health emergency, I will make this conference room available to this group and assign one of my staff to schedule and record minutes (serve as scribe) at any convening you organize. Are you willing to accept my offer?" People voice their approval and clap their hands, and then the gathering adjourns.

Narada suddenly stopped speaking and looked out over the crowd to gauge whether the audience was actually into his story. The gathering was quiet and motionless while everyone's eyes remained closed, as if they sensed the storyteller's tale was far from over and there was much more to come. So they waited in the silence…they patiently waited.

"Since you have grown accustomed to my dream-story of a future world, I will no longer interpret what you see and hear for you," said Narada. "You can now do that for yourselves. As I look around, I know that most of you are receptive to the telling and have begun to comprehend the thoughts and feelings of all the future people you are witnessing. You now understand them on your own terms.

"I confess to you, we do not create new ideas and thoughts ourselves. They are energies that have a life of their own as they move in the ether. We simply become conscious of them when we are relaxed enough and strongly desire to know them; then we become good receivers. So settle into their world with me, and though for you it might be a higher learning, it will no longer be difficult for you to interpret all that you hear and see. And I will help you with your silent intuitive communion. So let us return, once again, and resume our story."

Arthur quickly leaves the gathering and rushes to his office only two blocks away to prepare for his meeting with Alice Tan, a program officer at the foundation. He'll review this morning's presentation and challenge posed by Aaron Campbell, which he's confident she already knows about. And at the close of their conversation, Arthur will affirm the Trust's interest in responding to the health emergency in the region's black community. Arthur reaches his building and rides the elevator to the seventh floor.

"Where you been all mornin'? Keepin' bankers' hours, huh?" Gracie Brown, the Trust's office manager and bookkeeper, shouts as she hears Arthur walking through the door.

"I'm here, ain't I—and good morning to you, Gracie. You always know where I am, so who you kiddin'?"

"No, I don't! No, I don't! I don't know what kinda mess you be into, but if I find out you cheating on your wife, I'm sure gonna tell her, 'cause I got my eye on you." Gracie forms a "V" with her two fingers before pointing them, first at her own eyes and then at him.

"Any messages for me?"

"Now do I look like your secretary? Why you asking me?" She is enjoying the audacity of her own reply. "Arthur, Curtis said he'll e-mail you last month's financial statement tomorrow."

"Good...can you please schedule a board meeting for the first Saturday of next month?"

"Arthur...Ramona's in the conference room waiting for you. And don't forget to wish her a happy birthday. You know how she gets when you forget things like that."

"OK, OK."

After hanging his coat on the hanger behind the door, he heads for the conference room.

"And don't forget," Gracie yells after him, "the white folks are coming for our regular workplace campaign meeting this afternoon at two, so you can't take over the conference room."

"Is that why Ramona is here?"

"Yes...yes!"

"Good morning, Ramona. Happy birthday...so what are you now, turning twenty-five?"

Arthur recalls from looking at her personnel file that Ramona's forty-three, but he knows she welcomes the flattery. Ramona stands up with exaggerated modesty and holds out her high-yella hand like a Southern belle waiting for a gentleman to kiss it.

"Oh, Arthur, you're so sweet," she drawls.

Sitting at the conference table beside her, Arthur is about to initiate a conversation on the progress of the Trust's annual workplace campaign when he's distracted by the sight of something slowly crawling up the wall behind Ramona's chair. Ramona, following Arthur's eyes, slowly turns around to see a big, dark-brown cockroach climbing up the bone-white wall. Ejecting from her chair like a fat woman who suddenly finds her wet toe in an electric socket, Ramona screams as if her hair is on fire. She starts running blindly around the conference table, bumping into chairs as she hysterically scrambles for the door.

Hearing the commotion, Gracie rushes into the room and stands in the doorway as Ramona, now twice around the table, is furiously shaking her dress.

"What's up, what's up?"

Ramona finally finds the door and frantically turns the knob, but the door doesn't open. She is about to collapse right there on the spot, but Arthur opens the door for her. Running out and down the hallway, screaming, Ramona reaches the elevator, forgetting she has left her coat and handbag in the office. A practicing attorney, hearing her screaming, walks out of his office just in time to catch Ramona in his arms, shaking and sobbing from genuine fright.

"Now, isn't she silly?" says Gracie, more to herself, as she takes a piece of scrap paper out of the trash basket and smashes the offending roach, which had apparently stopped on the wall to clean the two moving antennas protruding from its head. "That woman might never come back."

CHAPTER 8

NIGHT VISITORS

When Arthur turns the key and opens the door, the apartment, or living space, is dark, and Natalie is not there. He switches on the lights and looks around a messy apartment, searching for any clue that Natalie has been there. Walking into their bedroom, he opens the door to her closet and examines Natalie's clothes, thinking she may have come home to change what she had on. But after strolling through the rooms, even the bathroom where her lipstick and eye shadow still lie on the sink, there is no indication that Natalie has returned.

It's late, and Arthur wants to sleep, but he's afraid to lie down. So he slouches in his favorite armchair and lets the television (that piece of colored glass in the room that shows moving pictures of people who talk) watch him as he dozes off while waiting for the door to open and Natalie to walk in. A sudden sound from their old refrigerator's (a cold place to store food) noisy motor wakes him with a jolt, and Arthur starts to think he should call the police and report his wife missing. What if something happened to her, he imagines, and her body is lying somewhere in a ditch? If she doesn't show up for their counseling session with Dr. Brathwaite, he resolves to call the cops and file a missing-persons report.

He turns off the television and the living-room lights, ignores the dirty dishes and glasses haphazardly placed in the kitchen sink, and heads for the bedroom to get ready for bed. After undressing and brushing his teeth, taking a hot shower, and putting on his pajamas, he pulls back the covers and lies down on the bed. Arthur hesitates before switching off the light on the wooden stand next to the bed, but he finally does and turns on his side, pulling the cotton sheet and light cream-colored blanket over his shoulders. The apartment is cool and quiet except for the slow, regular drip of water from the faucet on the kitchen sink.

The wind picks up, and Arthur listens to the rustle of leaves on the oak tree outside his bedroom window. A siren shrieks down Telegraph Avenue and then fades into night like a madwoman in heat. A dog barks across the street, and the fragrance of jasmine flowers floats through the slightly open window as Arthur's eyes grow heavy and the promise of sleep clouds his mind.

Then the predictable soft buzzing in his ears returns, along with the sensation felt when moving after sitting on your legs or resting on your arms too long, when the numbness from poor blood circulation is replaced by the feeling of pins and needles percolating through muscles, blood, and skin and the feeling of millions of bubbles rises to the surface from within. This experience of a deep hum overwhelming Arthur's ears and the weird sensation of bubbles rising under Arthur's skin are becoming a regular occurrence just before sleep.

He tried to warn Natalie about this and requested that when she lay beside him at night and discovered him making noises, to please wake him. And when he asked, she looked at him, quizzically, after he explained that sometimes he made noises when having nightmares. But he concealed the truth from her about these so-called nightmares. They aren't bad dreams at all but rather him trying to overcome the buzzing in his ears and the feeling of being a mass of tiny bubbles. And now these episodes are becoming more frequent.

When Arthur was a child and in his bed at night, people he didn't know and other creatures came to visit him. He'd see them sitting somewhere in his room or searching through his clothes. A huge gorilla sometimes came. The large animal would pull out his dresser drawers and look at his clothes before neatly putting them back; or it would play with his toys for a while. Arthur thought the big ape was funny and wanted to laugh, but he was afraid of it. A few times the gorilla even sat at the end of his bed and watched him. It would turn its big head from side to side like a dog does when it's listening to an unfamiliar sound or curious about a thing. Arthur thought the beast wanted to see if he was awake and possibly attack him, but it never did. Arthur would keep very still, not even breathing or making a sound until the gorilla left by disappearing into the night.

When he found the courage to tell his parents and his grandma about these strange occurrences, they would smile and hold him close and say he was just having bad dreams. But little Arthur knew these nightly events were different from dreams, because he would be wide awake.

Sometimes his mama would check in on him during the night and wake him to go to the bathroom. As he grew older, Arthur stopped talking about night visitors. And when asked about his dreams, he'd simply say that he didn't remember dreaming. Eventually they stopped asking about them until, finally, these incidences of nightmarish events receded into amorphous childhood memories as Arthur grew into adolescence.

Seldom as an adult has Arthur been bothered by night visitors—aimless spirits who, for some inexplicable reason, are unable or unwilling to move on. But when they do appear, many are missing limbs or have visible signs of open wounds, maybe because of dying in sudden car crashes or being victims of violent deaths by suicide or by a perpetrator's hand. On the rare occasion when they return and enter his sleeping space, they look at him but never speak unless spoken to; they simply sit or stand around and leave when he telepathically orders them to go. On occasion there are belligerent spirits, who are ill-tempered and wish to do him harm. Arthur's learned to make them go away by addressing them in prayer to the Divine. He's discovered that they don't like references to the Most High.

These current nightly encounters, however, are different—and disconcerting. The buzzing in his ears and the pins-and-needles sensation become so intense that his spirit detaches from his body, and he may find himself walking around his living space or outside his apartment building, flying in the open air. No doubt, there is a certain joy and freedom in these experiences as his essence, his spirit, is no longer bound to or inhibited by his physical form; it remains asleep or lifeless on the bed. Yet, these out-of-body experiences are bewildering because he'll find furniture and other items in his living space that, in his waking state, he knows do not exist, like a beach ball on the living-room floor or an odd-looking table with a set of chairs in the kitchen.

These frequent excursions are causing Arthur to question his sanity. Although, he finds them exciting and pleasurable: the experience of being weightless and invisible; to be able to move through concrete walls, undetected; to fly though the air without a body, feeling neither heat nor cold. Now and again, Arthur looks forward to these out-of-body expeditions. They've made his life so much richer and multifaceted and have given him a new, fresh perspective on the world and the people in it. He experiences an inexplicable dimension of reality that others seem not to know about; and he enjoys concealing this secret.

Tonight he just wants to sleep. So Arthur struggles, suspended betwixt sleep and nonsleep, to make a vocal sound, any willful noise that will break this bizarre chain of sensations. That accomplished, he turns over on his left side and, in a fetal position, falls asleep.

CHAPTER 9

THE MALIGNANT SEED

It's a warm spring day in downtown Oakland. Blue skies and wisps of white clouds are slowly drifting overhead, and Arthur has just finished lunch with Alice Tan and one of her young colleagues, Carl Rupert, at an open-air restaurant in City Center. Their extended conversation about the Trust's possible leadership role in addressing the health crisis facing African Americans went well, ending with Arthur's promise to forward a two- to three-page concept paper to her office for review and feedback within the next two weeks.

Alice and Carl leave Arthur sitting at their outdoor table, where he stays to listen to a Zydeco Cajun band that is the opening act for the Center's free noontime concert series held every spring. Two singers—a middle-aged white man, looking like he came out of the Louisiana bayou; and a heavyset black woman wearing a tight white skirt, and red blouse hiding cantaloupe breasts—stand on a raised stage under a canopy with their four-piece band. They sing into separate microphones, blending their Cajun roots with rhythm and blues as they stomp their feet in cadence with the beat. The music is infectious, and the crowd of office workers on lunch break, sitting in white plastic chairs in front of the bandstand, clap and cheer on the performers while eating takeout salads and fast food from eateries in the Center. People passing through the area stop and gawk at both the performers and audience or slowly meander around the edges of the crowd.

Arthur watches two young children perched on the lip of the large water fountain, listening to the music. The younger male child stays close to his mother and eats from the bag of popcorn she holds in her hand while his older sister claps and dances to the music, oblivious to the people around her.

Arthur walks through the Zydeco crowd, recollecting the African American Health Summit the Trust had convened, and thinks about the mother from West Oakland who came to the expo with her two young sons. She dragged her boys by the hand when she passed him, talking to the director of the YMCA. Arthur remembers her saying to the Y director and him, "Yah know, I had to pull my sons from underneath the bed this mornin' to get here. And I'm sure glad I came, 'cause I learned a lot...I learned a lot! Now, I gotta drag my boys outta here, 'cause they sure don't wanna go. Ain't that somethin'! Thanks for puttin' this on. It's great!" Then she disappeared into the crowd.

Arthur reaches the street and heads south down Broadway to the public health department, acutely aware of the many black and a few Latino men aimlessly wandering around the downtown area. Some stand on corners in front of Walgreens or McDonalds or congregate outside the Goodwill store. Some stand around with rummy-yellow eyes, looking doleful and hopeless at people who try not to notice as they pass them on the street. Holding out their hands, men beg for spare change or food or something they can call their own.

The black, brown, and unemployed nonchalantly enter and leave the Private Industry Council (PIC) office, housed across from City Center. The men check in at the front desk and sit at available computers, typing up or sending out résumés, reading their e-mail, searching for available employment on the Internet, and looking for jobs that, for most of them, are just not there.

Young men saunter up and down the block with no purpose or direction and nowhere to go. They, too, are unemployed or unemployable. They hold their pants up with one hand belted around their thighs, so their trousers don't fall to the pavement. Their black butts hang out, exposing their—hopefully—clean underwear, which, in this defiant act, thumb their noses at convention and shout to the world, "I'm here, motherfucka! I'm not invisible, so you ain't gonna ignore me!" Men drink from open beer cans and smoke weed in public places, 'cause they don't give a damn and have nowhere else to go.

The mentally ill and homeless men and women walk up and down Broadway. Some smell of urine, have unkempt, matted hair, and are dressed in soiled, raggedy clothes and shoes—or may have nothing on their bare, dirty feet at all. Taking refuge in their own private worlds, they engage in conversations with entities no one else sees. On occasion a madman or woman screams his or her rage at the sky or lamppost or anyone who passes and may recklessly punch the air. If they become aggressive with people on the street, police are called to pick them up and transport them to Highland Hospital, where they're placed under a day or two of observation, perhaps given medication to calm them down, and then released once again to the public streets.

After arriving at the public health office, Arthur rides the elevator to the fifth floor to attend the health crisis committee's first meeting. With the images of Broadway's destitute still on his mind, he takes a seat at the conference table with the twelve other African American men and women who have come to participate in the discussion.

Eunice Anderson, the department's community outreach coordinator, soon calls the meeting to order and asks attendees—starting with the person on her immediate left—to state their names, the organizations they represent, and what they hope to accomplish during the session. Arthur looks at his watch and tries to conceal his impatience at these obligatory introductions, when everyone in the room is already acquainted, and interrupts Evelyn Turner from the American Heart Association.

"Ms. Anderson, can we please dispense with these introductions? By the time all of us weigh in, we will have used up at least twenty minutes of our meeting time. We all know each other, so can we get to the business at hand and focus on our community's health emergency?"

"Oh no, Dr. Renfro," she responds with a smile, waving her hand like shooing a fly. "We'll be finished in no time. Evelyn, please continue."

Many of their introductions take seven to ten minutes, and three in attendance can't resist describing the amazing outcomes their health-related programs are achieving in the community. By the time Ms. Anderson reviews in detail the minutes from the previous meeting with the Agency's director and has them approved by the group, over an hour has elapsed. Then, in what comes across as a preplanned or orchestrated moment, Charles Joyner from the American Diabetes Association says, "Let's take the top three diseases from the department's study—coronary heart disease, high blood pressure, and diabetes—and saturate the community with information about these illnesses using flyers and pamphlets, broadcast thirty- to sixty-second spots on local television, place public service announcements on black radio, publish articles in black newspapers, recruit volunteer-presenters who are knowledgeable about these three diseases to speak in black churches...let's flood the community with this information, and then we can move on to tackle another three or four illnesses."

Ms. Anderson is pleased with Charles's remarks and looks around the room to affirm everyone's support. Ms. Turner from the American Heart Association, who's sitting next to Charles, and Fatima Maloud, representing the American Society of Hypertension and seated on Mr. Joyner's other side, nod their two heads in unison, signaling their full support and agreement. The room is silent while everyone, except for Arthur, who taps his fingers on the table, considers their proposal.

"Well, that sounds like a plan," says Andre Swanson, a deacon from Faith United Baptist Church, before the room once again returns to silence.

"I appreciate your prepared remarks, Charles, but before we consider any particular course of action, might we first talk about why we are experiencing a health crisis in our community?" asks Arthur. "Why are our people so sick? If you recall from the report, more than any other racial group in this county, black folk are in deep trouble. We suffer from more diseases and at a higher rate than any other ethnic or racial population. Why is that? Why are African Americans so sick?"

"I think we suffer from constant stress, which leads to poor health and chronic diseases," say Sonia Cespedes, a beautiful, dark-skinned Cuban immigrant married to a Babalawo or Santeria priest named Hector. A singer and dancer, she teaches Afro-Cuban dance to youth, especially, throughout the Bay Area. "I think the racism in this country keeps black people stressed out. That's why people drink and use crack cocaine. They're self-medicating due to trauma and stress in their lives. People are stressed out, man!"

Many of her colleagues laugh, recognizing the truth in Sonia's remarks.

"You got that right!" Ralph Green speaks out. He teaches black history at Ile Omode, an African-centered school in East

Oakland. "And that stress started with slavery. Slavery was like an atom bomb that exploded in the minds of African people. And the radiation from that psychic blast has plagued every generation since and finds expression in a sense of inferiority and self-hatred perpetuated by racial oppression. The destructive energy from that first explosion is a malignant seed that is reinforced, every day, in this white-supremacist country through racial segregation, institutional racism, and the media that constantly portrays us with a negative brush. Damn right we stressed out, shit!"

"Does the truth in Sonia's and Ralph's insightful remarks have any connection to our addressing the health crisis?" Arthur asks the group.

"Ralph is talking about our mental health issues and putting them in an historical context," says Fatima Maloud, "but the ailments we're talking about…at least, in the department's report… are diseases that, for the most part, affect the bodies; so I don't see the relevance of his comments for coming up with a plan for action."

"Your point is well taken, Fatima, but there is a connection between the body and the mind," says Arthur. "Thinking about Charles's proposal and their comments says to me that it's not enough to just saturate the community with information and walk away to prepare for another informational campaign on another set of diseases. I'm afraid that kind of campaign won't do a damn thing to address our health emergency."

"So what do you suggest, Arthur?" says Charles, calling him out.

"I don't know, but whatever we do has to motivate our people to change…to embrace a healthier lifestyle, and in meeting such a challenge, we'll have to question the way we think about ourselves…so we are talking about the mind. The real question is, can we motivate black folk to change?"

"May I have your attention, everyone. This meeting should have been over twenty minutes ago, and we're still here," says Ms. Anderson. "This was a good meeting and a good discussion. Can we agree to reconvene in two weeks at the same time to continue our conversation? It'll give us time to think about what's been said and maybe consider how we might move forward. OK?" Looking around the conference table and hearing no objections, she adjourns the meeting.

CHAPTER 10
INTIMACIES UNWRAPPED

Arthur enters Dr. Maurice Brathwaite's office and sees Natalie already sitting in a corner of the waiting room for their scheduled ten o'clock session with their marriage counselor. She wears a cream-colored spring dress overlaid with an array of tiny pastel blue flowers that nicely set off her dark-brown skin. She's a tall, sultry woman with black hair rolled into a bun on the crown of her head and tied with blue ribbon.

"Hello, Arthur," she casually says while leafing through Jet magazine, as if all was right with the world and the argument they had two nights ago never happened. Arthur's taken aback by her ease and charming smile and irritated by her apparent contentment and acceptance of their current situation while his emotions are running wild.

Arthur sits next to her. "So where have you been for the last two nights?"

Dr. Brathwaite's door opens, and he peeks around the door frame and invites them to come in. "Good morning."

They both take their usual seats at opposite ends of the soft mahogany-colored leather sofa.

"Good morning to you, Dr. Brathwaite," Natalie says cheerfully.

Arthur doesn't say anything as he watches Dr. Brathwaite pick up his pipe resting in the ashtray on the table next to his chair and light it with a match, as he always does at the start of their session. Arthur speculates as to whether Dr. Brathwaite performs his smoking-pipe ritual at the start of all his clients' sessions, and then he imagines what his lungs look like. He wonders what the good doctor would say if one of his patients were to politely ask one day, "Could you please not smoke in my presence? I am allergic to secondhand smoke." Would he comply or refuse to counsel them for taking away his shaman's tool? Maurice Brathwaite certainly had that fatherly look, Arthur thinks as he watches gray smoke from the pipe spiraling in the air.

"So…" Dr. Brathwaite stops a moment to take another draw from his pipe. "How have the two of you been getting along since our last visit?"

Natalie, leisurely lying back on the sofa with her long legs crossed and the top leg gently bouncing up and down, responds, "You know, Dr. Brathwaite, I've realized over the past few days…"

"I haven't seen her since this past Thursday, when she ran out of the apartment," Arthur interjects. Dr. Brathwaite raises his hand, as if stopping traffic, to discourage Arthur from interrupting. Natalie looks over at him and rolls her beautiful brown eyes before turning back to their counselor, who patiently waits for her to continue.

"Dr. Brathwaite, I realized the other day that I still use my maiden name, Marshall, even though we're married, because I'm not comfortable in calling myself…or telling other people that I'm now Mrs. Renfro. I use my maiden name at work and with all my friends. Marshall is still on my credit cards and driver's license, even though Arthur and I will have been married a year next month."

"Why do you prefer to use your maiden name, Natalie?" asks Dr. Brathwaite.

"Because I'm really not comfortable...I'm not settled with him. I don't trust him. I know he sleeps with other women. Has sex with other women. Let's call it for what it is. Arthur doesn't respect our marriage bed and then comes home like nothin's happened and wants to get into bed with me. Well, it ain't gonna happen, baby...it's not gonna happen," she says and snaps her fingers for emphasis as she turns to Arthur with a laugh. "That's why I don't take your name as my own."

"Have you shared your suspicions with Arthur already?

"They're not suspicions. I know what he's doing. I just don't know who with, and frankly, I really don't care. I have asked him about his affairs, and he denies everything, but I know what I know."

Arthur looks uncomfortable hearing Natalie's accusation and senses Dr. Brathwaite's eyes on him.

"And what do you say to Natalie's comments, Arthur?"

"How do you know that I'm sleeping around?"

"'Cause I smell the women on your clothes; I smell them on your body when you lay next to me! What do you think, I'm stupid?"

"Arthur, are you sleeping with other women as Natalie states?"

Arthur feels cornered and resents Natalie and Dr. Brathwaite for calling him out. "Yes, I've slept with other women," he whispers, feebly, in an almost inaudible voice. "Yes, I've slept with other women," he repeats more strongly after clearing his throat, but he avoids their eyes by looking down at the rectangular space rug on the floor. He could be more specific and say he's slept with only one woman since their marriage, although they've met more than once; however, that would bring up more red flags for Natalie that he'd prefer not to discuss under Dr. Brathwaite's bone-cutting scrutiny.

"Well, that's the end of that!" Natalie snaps as she quickly gets up and heads for the door. "Don't expect me to come home tonight, either, because I'm not," she says. Her high heels stab the hardwood floor like a stiletto knife gone mad.

"Is this how you ended your argument with Arthur the other night, by leaving?" asks Dr. Brathwaite.

"Yes," she replies and slams the door behind her.

Dr. Brathwaite lights his shaman's pipe and watches the black ashes in the mahogany bowl turn from orange to gold. Arthur looks at the good doctor with irrational eyes that say, "Now look at what you've done!" However, he knows he's really to blame and sits quietly and waits.

"Do you want to talk about it?"

"About what?" Arthur replies, knowing full well what the doctor is referring to.

"Please don't play games with me, Arthur. Why do you have the need to sleep with other women while married to Natalie?"

"I don't really know, except for the fact that Natalie's not available to me anymore."

"Don't push this off on Natalie. Take responsibility for your own actions, Arthur. Could it be that you're undermining your relationship with her by sleeping with other women, because you don't want to be married in the first place?"

"I don't know."

Dr. Brathwaite sits patiently waiting for Arthur to continue talking, but his client says nothing more. Finally Dr. Brathwaite asks, "When did you come to this realization...before or after you married Natalie?"

"Doc, I've not come to that conclusion, at least not consciously, so I need to give your question more thought."

"Arthur, if we don't pursue this issue of infidelity now, it will remain to haunt you. You know that, don't you?"

Arthur remains silent.

"I would like you to think about this question, carefully, as to whether you want to be married to Natalie or not, so we can return to this issue on your next visit. OK?"

"OK."

They sit in silence together while Dr. Brathwaite resumes smoking his pipe before gazing at his watch.

"You have about twenty minutes left in this session, so what would you like to talk about, Arthur?"

"I learned when I was a child to hide from others what I thought or felt in order to fit in, so intimacy has always been a challenge for me."

"What kind of thoughts, Arthur?"

Arthur adjusts his position on the couch and nervously clears his throat before looking up at Dr. Brathwaite. "I saw ghosts as a child…especially after going to bed. More recently, my spirit leaves my body when I lie down and try to sleep. I find myself walking around our apartment or flying in the air," he says, letting the truth come out.

"What do you mean, you 'leave your body,' and how often does this happen?" the psychologist asks, taken off guard by this particular turn in their conversation.

"If I'm tired and lie on my back, I start to hear this buzzing sound in my ears, and my body starts to feel like a human Pepsi-Cola…you know, when you take the cap off the bottle of soda, and you see all the tiny bubbles begin to rise to the top? Well, I feel something like that. Then I detach from my physical form, which remains lying on the bed, and my spirit—that is, the real me—is free to roam around."

Dr. Brathwaite puts his pipe in the ashtray on the table and leans forward in his chair as if trying to see, for the first time, something he neglectfully missed. "I don't understand you, Arthur. Please describe this experience for me."

Arthur is familiar with Dr. Brathwaite's look of alarm. His parents would stare at him the same way when, as a child, he confided that he saw spirits. But this situation was different. Dr. Brathwaite is a certified family therapist, and Arthur is now an adult. He realizes, while looking at their marriage counselor staring back at him in bewilderment, that he's made a mistake in revealing what he's always managed to keep hidden—at least since childhood—and now it's too late. He has to try and explain.

"Several years ago, before I met Natalie, I was living alone in the apartment I now share with her. At the time, I was seeing another woman named Kathy, who had been living with a jazz musician. I met her after he left her. He played the sax and was a heroin addict, touring Europe and performing with a band. Anyway…Kathy and I started going out, and one night I invited her over for dinner. She spent the night and left the next morning.

"That afternoon, I lay down to take a nap…and I rarely take naps…and thought I was going to sleep, but instead, I found myself out of my body."

"What do you mean, out of your body?"

"I lay there, and this deep humming…buzzing sound started, and then had this pins-and-needles sensation all over my body rising to the surface of my skin. The next thing I knew, I found my spirit sitting up while my physical body was still lying flat on the bed."

"Do you mean you were half out of your body at this point?"

"Yes, that's right…first, I was in a sitting position while still in my body, and then I was completely separated…maybe ejected out of my body. I found myself…I mean my spirit flying through the walls of the apartment and out in the street.

"It felt like I was being pulled somewhere, but I didn't know where. It was daylight, and the sun was directly overhead, but I didn't feel warm or cold. I had no body, so I guess I didn't feel anything. I flew over rooftops and watched people below me walking the streets and entering buildings. Then I found myself flying through the walls of a building and, amazingly, into Kathy's apartment, but she couldn't see me because I was invisible without physical form.

"She was sitting on her bed with the jazz musician she used to live with. His head was cradled in her lap. He was crying, and

Kathy was consoling him. She rubbed her fingers through his hair and told him everything would be all right, that he was the only one she ever loved, and that he should stay with her.

"I wasn't sad or angry. I was more curious than anything else. You could say I was more absorbed in the experience of it all. I mean, how could this be happening to me...being invisible without physical form? It was exciting and very pleasant.

"Then, without really wanting to leave the scene, I returned to my apartment and my spirit reentered my body by hovering directly over it. I opened my eyes and lay on the bed thinking about what I had experienced.

"When I got up, I telephoned Kathy to talk about what had happened, and before I could say anything, she told me that her boyfriend had returned. I asked if they had been sitting on a bed with a yellow bedspread and if his head was resting in her lap. She asked me how I knew. I told her I was there, and, without skipping a beat, she said he'd come home and she couldn't see me anymore. 'I hope you understand,' she said, and she hung up."

Dr. Brathwaite studies Arthur as if he's trying to read something in his client's face. Then he picks up his pipe and gently knocks the mahogany bowl against the ashtray until burnt ashes fall out. "Arthur, you say this incident happened to you several years ago. Have you been experiencing this...this unusual occurrence lately...this leaving your body?"

"Well, the buzzing and the pins-and-needles feeling has returned, and my spirit wants to leave, but I won't let it."

"How do you stop this from happening?"

"It only happens when I'm not fully asleep, so if I can wake myself up by moving an arm or leg, or if I'm successful in making a sound by speaking, then I can stop my spirit from leaving."

"Why do you want to stop when you say you enjoy this unusual, to say the least, out-of-body experience?" asks Dr. Brathwaite.

"I don't know, Doc."

"Does Natalie know about these episodes?"

"No; you're the first person I've spoken to about this."

"Arthur," Dr. Brathwaite picks up his shaman's tool from the ashtray and cradles it with both hands, "I think I need to refer you to someone more experienced than me who can prescribe medication for these hallucinations. I would like to refer you to my colleague, Dr. Joseph Isaacson, and..."

"You mean a psychiatrist?" asks Arthur.

"Yes," says Dr. Brathwaite, getting up from his chair and walking over to his desk. He scribbles the doctor's name and telephone number on the back of his personal business card and hands it to Arthur.

"I'll give him a call this afternoon and let him know to anticipate hearing from you."

"This Dr. Isaacson's a white doctor, isn't he?" asks Arthur.

"He's a good man, Arthur. He knows his craft and cares about his patients."

Dr. Brathwaite starts thumbing through his appointment book to check the time for his next client before noticing Arthur is still standing in front of his desk, looking at the card. "Well, your time is up, so...after you meet with Dr. Isaacson, I'll give you a call, Arthur, and we can go from there," Dr. Brathwaite says. "OK? Good-bye."

Arthur heads for the door, ignoring Dr. Brathwaite's good-bye. He's angry and upset with himself for revealing himself and then getting brushed off with a referral to a white psychiatrist. He tears up the card with Isaacson's name and number and throws the pieces in the air, vowing to never again tell anyone about his out-of-body experiences.

CHAPTER 11

THE AKASHA RECORDS

After concluding the opening thread of his story, introducing Arthur and his future world to the people gathered outside Ja'Usu's walls, Narada closed the Akasha Records of Celestial Light and gave his listeners time and space to reenter their own era and familiar world.

"Have no fear of the Akasha Records' opening," said the storyteller to the gathering. "It is a great blessing that the One-Who-Has-Many Names has allowed us to read from her eternal book. So do not be afraid of the thunderous sounds and mighty roar of which you will have no memory by the time you've reached your homes. But let this narrative remain alive in your thoughts, and speak of it with your family and tribal clans.

"I shall return in two nights to resume our story of this future age. Until then, may you go safely to your dwellings, sleep well the night with pleasant dreams, and awaken in the morning refreshed, and be grateful to Jah for the human spirit that you are, and so it will be...Amantahu."

"Haya Aman," the gathering replied, and the people stretched and lifted their arms. The first night of storytelling ended.

Narada walked alone through the labyrinth of Ja'Usu's streets as the soft light of the full moon followed behind to light his way. He thought about the story the Great Mystery had selected for him to share and wondered what the narrative had in store for the people of Ja'Usu. Suddenly, someone small grabbed his hand and held it tight. Narada looked down at his side onto the innocent face of a young boy gazing up at him.

"Abba...Abba," the child cried, calling the storyteller-sage his father.

Feeling secure walking with his Abba, the young boy and Narada walked hand in hand until the child abruptly stopped, and his body began to shake. It was then Narada sensed what the boy was afraid of: the pack of hyenas coming their way. They roamed Ja'Usu's streets every night and scrounged for garbage thrown over compound walls. They didn't threaten or attack grown men, even though they could easily tear a grown man or woman apart. But abandoned children on the ancient city's streets, alone at night, were a delicacy hyenas would not resist. Perhaps, in their bestial way of thinking, it was a permitted kill, since no one hunted them down at dawn.

Narada picked the boy up, held him close, and stood still as the child's heart raced like a panicked rabbit scampering over dry brush. The child buried his face into Narada's neck as darting shadows larger than dogs swiftly approached and ran past them. Narada then whispered something in the boy's ear and tried to put him down on the ground, but the child held fast.

"Abba...Abba, please...please to hold me it is, Isa."

Then out of the darkness and running toward them was a gang of street youth, who lived by their wits and watched out for one another. They stopped in front of Narada, and an older boy, named Jumah, stepped forward and said, "All right old man, Isa down you can put."

"Abba...Abba," Isa said again, looking into Narada's eyes. When Narada stepped back, the older boy reached out to take Isa from the stranger.

"Jumah, he is still frightened of the hyenas that passed. I will carry him and walk with you back to where you sleep."

"Where we sleep for you to know we do not want, and my name, how you come to know it?"

"I know all your names, as if each of you were my own child."

"Impossible that is," Jumah snapped and turned to the other boys. "Any of you donkey turds to this stranger talked have you, and our names given him?" Some of them said no. Others just shook their heads. "So you lie," said Jumah.

Narada extended his arm and pointed his finger at each boy standing half in darkness and, one by one, called out their names. "There is Basem and Madhi and Yusuf; Rasool and Taanish and Uthman and Gulfam, who prefers to be called Jad; there is Zemuna and Abdi Nor and Ehan and Wasif and, lastly, Masoud, besides Isa in my arms. And then there's you, Jumah."

"How to do that did you?" said Madhi. "You I never met, and my name I never told you."

"Yeah, and me neither," countered Taanish. And they all joined in a chorus of denial. They had never met Narada or told him their names.

Jumah, who was seventeen years old, raised his hand, and their talking stopped. "For those old donkey farts who Ja'Usu they control, working for them you must be. To get rid of us they want, but someone like you to hire for the job to do, laugh don't make me."

"I don't work for them or anyone else to earn a living, if that's what you mean."

Jumah looked Narada up and down in order to gauge his wealth and saw nothing that placed him as a merchant or a trader, but then he had to be sure.

"Rasool, up the path go, and if anyone coming here there is, see."

"Why, Jumah, what to do are you going?"

"Donkey turd, just do it!" Jumah snapped. Rasool ran off.

Jumah turned and looked behind them as the other boys did the same. "Any gold or silver on you, do you have?" he asked Narada, who was smiling at him. Rasool returned and told their leader no one was coming.

"I do not carry gold or silver. I have no need of it."

Jumah, not quite sure how to respond, feared showing any sign of weakness in front of the other boys. "Well, what possessions to have do you?"

"I carry nothing."

"Well, your lodging, where is it? Something there you must have, I know!"

"Where we sleep, for you to know I do not want."

The boys' laughter turned into an uproar, recognizing that the stranger was mimicking Jumah, who had said the exact same thing just a moment ago. Jumah looked at his companions sternly, and their banter abruptly ended.

Narada planted a seed of trust and mutual respect in Jumah's mind and said, "Isa, here, must have strayed from your group and was by himself in the streets when he found me. That was a good thing, because hyenas passed just before you." Narada handed Isa over to Jumah, who reached out to take the boy in his arms. Isa was asleep.

"If you permit me, since I have nothing to give, I will bring food for all of you tomorrow evening just as the sun sets over the western gate. Is that all right with you, Jumah?"

"A fool you must think I am."

"No, on the contrary, I know you are a good leader. You watch out for your friends and protect them from harm. You are no fool. You have a good mind, Jumah. We just need to put it to better use."

Jumah wondered what the man who spoke strangely meant in putting a mind to better use, but he didn't wish to ask standing near his companions, so he ignored the thought. "So food at sunset, tomorrow, you will bring?"

"Yes," said Narada.

"Where to find us, how to know will you?"

"I will know."

"Like our names you knew?"

"Yes, something like that."

"All right," said Jumah. "You can go, but to find you we always can."

The boys opened up a space so Narada could pass, but as soon as Jumah thought the stranger was out of hearing range, he ordered Rasool and Basem to follow him to find out where he lived.

"But what about the hyenas?" asked Basem.

"A knife you got, and Rasool, a spear you have, so if you have to, them fight off." Jumah turned and walked away as the other boys stepped in behind him.

"Tomorrow night, to find us, how will he know?" asked Abdi Nor.

"To know, I do not," replied Jumah.

Narada knocked on the compound door, and Ibrahim Hafez quickly opened it. All of them—Ayaat, Hohete, and her father—were sitting in the open air, talking about the story that was alive in them; its energy kept them wide awake so sleep would not join them.

"In the streets at night with Ja'Usu's hyenas for food they are scavenging, and the street ruffians that rob you walking alone, and you a stranger to our city, we were worried. But nothing but your clothes those ruffians can take," said Ibrahim Hafez with a grin.

"Narada," said Ayaat, "an old woman I am, and my memory, good it is not; but your story, with me it stays. When you said, 'In a distant age and in a faraway land there is a city,' my mind, clear and sharp it became, like when young I was. Now old I am, and well to hear I do not, but your story I remember...everything I saw: people in strange clothes and the strange way they talked; black wheels moving, and on top of them a box with people inside sitting; women and men, together they walked; the women, only in pantaloons they dressed. And that woman, Gracie, to Arthur the way she talked, her did you hear? And the houses, so tall to the sky they reached. It was...it was...to explain I cannot. Great magic it was, Narada, great magic."

"And that Arthur, a handsome man he looks, but a jinn I think he is," said Hohete, glancing at Narada; then, turning back again to her father and Ayaat, she went on, "When as a child, jinns he saw; and now as a grown man, trouble to sleep he has, and in the air his spirit flies. Who really he is, himself he does not know."

"This Pepsi-Pepsi, Narada, what is it? This thing they drink I do not know," said Ibrahim Hafez.

"It is a popular drink in Arthur's world, and when you open the bottle, bubbles like fermented honey rise to the surface, but there is no alcohol."

"I see...but the African people, health problems they have," continued Ibrahim Hafez. "Better care of their animals to take they need, their cows, their goats, their chickens...but I see them not. Places to eat they have, but their food, where grows it? Their soil for planting, where is it? Some plants I saw, but in their world, little earth there is. Mostly gray mudstone on streets and houses there is."

"Abba, in a city they live...a big city," said Hohete. "Much larger than Ja'Usu. That's why their earth for food to grow, you do not see. Our food in Ja'Usu even we do not grow. Outside the city's wall, it the Oromo grow. But to know I want...Arthur with other women sleeps, Natalie, why angry is she? Natural for men with many women to sleep it is, isn't it?"

"And with all their strange and wonderful things," said Ayaat, "the poor people on their streets, did you notice them? To take care of them they do not."

"Our own, to take care of we do not, so the same it is," said Hohete. "And we should."

"Oromo children on our streets, we only have," replied Ibrahim Hafez to his daughter.

"So, of them we should take care of," said Hohete forcefully.

Ayaat, Hohete, and her father turned to Narada seeking guidance on these matters, but he was quiet as he looked back at them.

"So the future this is, Narada? Our future, too, this is?" asked Ibrahim Hafez.

Narada wanted rest and stood without answering his host's questions. Hohete rose after him to serve her storyteller mint tea before he began his silent sitting and said his nightly prayers.

"Well, a fantastical story it is," said Ibrahim Hafez to his sister, Ayaat, rubbing his hands together with noticeable enthusiasm. "And by morning, everyone in Ja'Usu about the storyteller and his story, they will know. At the next gathering, I bet many more people to show up there will be. The patriarchs, to stop them they cannot do."

CHAPTER 12

WAGGING TONGUES

The morning after Narada's story, everyone in Ja'Usu—even the Oromo entering the city and children living on the streets—were talking about the storyteller who walked out of the desert to tell magic tales. Even the patriarchs and their women and children were eagerly telling their friends and neighbors about the fantastical story set in the future. And the people they spoke to, who weren't even there that first night, passed on what little they were told to others until nothing like Narada's original narrative was being talked about. By the time the story spread by word of mouth through the nine family clans and into the streets where Oromo women sat, there were numerous versions of the narrative floating around the ancient city.

One version of the tale had Arthur as a woman married to a man named Natalie; another version had a people in the future dying from a sickness called health crisis; and then there was one account where a community of jinns, looking like Ja'Usu and Oromo people, were flying through the air without bodies and having sex on a distant planet.

Many at the gathering, however, followed Narada's guidance to gaze into the fire until their eyes closed on their own, and they were calm enough to be transported to the future city where the story opened. Without struggling to understand language or concepts that were surely unknown, they were awestruck by the wonder of it all. They followed the narrative closely and the activities of the future people as they went about living their lives. After a while, they settled into the novel experience. It was as if someone was rapidly flipping through a stack of handheld pictures, enhanced by environmental sounds and human speech and where the meaning of strange, unfamiliar words and perceptions were no longer obstacles to their witnessing and understanding what was taking place.

But regardless of each person's experience with the narrative, most everyone in Ja'Usu and the Oromo outside the walls knew that the story was about a city in the future. That alone caused their mouths to drop and their tongues to waggle with questions no one except the storyteller could answer.

By the end of the day, the patriarchs Murabbi, patron and guardian of the people, and Aschenaki, the one who distresses, were both troubled by Narada's narrative and all the talk surrounding it. However, they were troubled for very different reasons. The chief patriarch was upset because everyone around him was positive and excited about Narada's tale when he had no clue what the story was all about. Although he was present when the tale was being told, he didn't hear or understand a word of it. Instead of looking into the fire, he fiddled with his clothes and constantly gazed about as he tried to figure out what others in the gathering were hearing and seeing. Finally, he became so exasperated with the evening's spectacle that his frustration tired him out, and he fell asleep. His elderly wife, Adeeba, nudged him several times when his snoring became so loud and unbearable that she thought he would bring undue attention not only to him but also herself. As a result of his snoring and her poking at his side, she too didn't know what the hell was going on and eventually also took refuge in sleep.

Patriarch Aschenaki's distress was of a different sort. He had heard and watched Narada's story—if "watch" was the right word to describe what he experienced—and, like everyone else, he was captivated by the storyteller's talent to conjure up powerful word pictures that made you believe you saw people moving about and talking. It was a wonderful and potent seduction, but the narrative left him with a strange uneasiness, and he didn't know why. That undefined uneasiness bothered him.

The governing council was supplying the Hafez household with more food than they could eat, so Narada met with Ibrahim Hafez to ask his permission to give food to Ja'Usu's poor. Ibrahim Hafez was pleased with Narada's suggestion, especially because Ja'Usu's age-old religion dictated that those who had plenty must give to those who had little. For surely, Jah's blessings would come to his family in return. So, with his host's tacit approval, Narada sent through the ether a thought-seed and planted it in Jumah's mind.

"Will that stranger keep his promise? Now we will see," said Jumah to his street companions.

"Jumah," said Basem. "Last night when me and Rasool him we followed, him we lost. Down one path he turned we thought, but on us he disappeared, and to find him we could not. Sorry."

"Taanish, Uthman, and Ehan," Jumah commanded, "to the holy edifice in Ja'Usu's center go; and if that stranger with food that way comes, watch and see. Rasool, Madhi and Abdi Nor, to Fozeia the north gate, where last night we slept go; and if he shows up there, come back and tell me. Where we stayed he would know, he said. Go!"

The same two men who stacked the dry wood and ignited the fire on the first night of the story were standing on the steps with two large baskets of food when Taanish, Uthman, and Ehan arrived at the holy edifice.

"Taanish, Uthman, and Ehan are you them?" called one of the men, Imtiyaz, when he saw the three boys. "These baskets, here, the storyteller told us to bring, and for you we waited. Taanish, Uthman, and Ehan is it you?"

The boys were reluctant to step forward or respond to men they didn't know, but the food in the baskets was plentiful, and the man calling out their names said it was for them.

"Our names, how do you know them?" Taanish asked.

"You three by name for the food you would come, the storyteller told us," Imtiyaz replied.

"This storyteller, we do not know."

"Last night, the stranger on the street you met, it was him, the storyteller."

Taanish, Uthman, and Ehan looked at one another, searching for an answer to a mystery they couldn't understand.

"Well, come on! All night we do not have. Your food is this or not?" Imtiyaz demanded to know, annoyed at their reluctance to step forward.

"Yes," Taanish finally replied. "Our names those are, and our food it is. This storyteller, who is he?"

"To know I don't, but six more nights of storytelling outside Fajaruddin gate he will do. While the storyteller in Ja'Usu remains, every day at this time, Tabassum and I two baskets of food right here we will bring. For you to pick up it is. And please, the empty baskets return so your food in them the next day we can bring. Understand?"

"Yes, we understand."

"Good. Amantahu," said Imtiyaz.

"Hiya Aman," Taanish replied as Imtiyaz and Tabassum hastily walked away, leaving the baskets behind. "Wait!" Taanish commanded as Uthman and Ehan rushed to get the food.

They quickly returned to his side as he cautiously looked around to see if anyone was watching or, perhaps, waiting to seize them. Seeing no one, Taanish was the first to cross the road to the holy edifice's steps and grab a basket of food. Uthman and Ethan followed not far behind, together, to pick up the other one. Then they hurried down the pathway toward Mustakim, the fifth or northeast gate.

The Second Evening's Story

Eventide was fast approaching, and the sun was receding toward the horizon, coaxing a pale blue, cloudless sky to clothe itself in pastel colors of red, orange, and pink, and a faint shadow of dark purple. Many of Ja'Usu's inhabitants and Oromo were already gathered outside Fajaruddin gate as the sun now reached the horizon and kissed the face of golden brown sand. Many listeners from the first night were early and already seated on straw mats or pieces of cloth closer to where they thought the storyteller would once again sit. Others, believing the magic was in the fire, claimed a spot in the inner ring or first rung of the gathering not twenty feet from where Imtiyaz and Tabassum placed dry wood in the very center of the circle.

Oromo also gathered but sat to one side, ensuring there was enough required space between them and the people from Ja'Usu. The long, narrow platform, where the patriarchs sat on the first night with their women and children, remained still vacant as it was understood by all that, fitting their exalted station, they would walk in together to make their presence known.

As darkness began to cover the heavens, and a sparse panoply of stars appeared as faint specks of twinkling jewels in the night sky, Narada arrived with Ibrahim Hafez and his family, Ayaat and Hohete. When the listeners saw them, a hush filled the air, and they rose to their feet out of appreciation and respect for the storyteller who brought them a narrative, not out of ancient history or about a mighty battle but from the fantastical and mysterious unknown.

At that moment, when all the people were standing, the patriarchs, with their families in tow, made their grand entrance. Wearing their imported robes and finery, they sashayed past vendors selling sweet breads and, as they approached their exclusive platform, thought the crowd was standing to honor and acknowledge them for arranging the entertainment. Only after reaching their podium with their hands waving in acknowledgment did the patriarchs realize this gathering of people had not risen for them. As seen in their faces that turned ruby red, they were assuredly humiliated and embarrassed. When they regained their composure, recognizing why the people were on their feet, they gritted their teeth and locked their jaws against the storyteller who had dared to draw the crowd's attention away from them.

As on the first night, Narada moved to the far end of the inner ring, away from the platforms built for the patriarchs and him, and the people there made room for the storyteller and Ibrahim Hafez's family to sit among them. But before Narada took his seat, he looked at the gathering, which was now more than five hundred people strong, and noticed the Oromo sitting off to the side and away by themselves. He then left his space in the first ring and walked over to where the Oromo sat. He bid them join the rest of the gathering in the wider circle and face the unlit stack of dry wood in the center of the ring. And under his forceful direction, they moved into the larger circle but nevertheless made sure there was ample space between the last rung of Ja'Usu's people and where they chose to sit.

Even still, the patriarchs were furious with Narada, who was publicly trouncing on Ja'Usu's long-held customs and social norms. Over the past one hundred years, ever since Ja'Usu's warriors defeated the Oromo, the Oromo had grown accustomed to subordinating their lives to the whims of the city and the dictates of the patriarchs who enforced the rules. They were insulted by Narada's infringement on their power and control—so much so that Chief Patriarch Murabbi made a mental note to bring him and his offense immediately before the governing council to air their grievance.

Returning to the space reserved for him in the inner circle, Narada stood and respectfully bowed to the patriarchs and their families before sitting, once again, among the people to begin the second night of his story. He signaled Imtiyaz and Tabassum to light the sacred fire; and, as their torches sent the dry wood ablaze, he intoned in an unknown tongue, asking for the Great Mystery to once again open the Akasha Records of Celestial Light. And from a mysterious wellspring, deeper than any vibration they had ever heard or felt, rose a mighty sound that made the ground quake and their bodies tremble, and the people were afraid but unable to get up and run away.

As the trembling subsided, and the ground gradually became still, Narada raised his hands to the heavens in praise and supplication to the Great Mystery for answering his prayers. Now the Akasha was unsealed, allowing Narada to read, once again, from the imperishable records of celestial light about future human thought and action. He then directed the people to look into the dancing flames until their eyes closed on their own; and once more, after a moment of silence, he resumed his story.

CHAPTER 13
THE MEETING

As twenty-four members of the health summit's leadership arrive for a 10:00 a.m. meeting, Arthur's mind is on Natalie, whom he hasn't seen since she left Dr. Brathwaite's office over a week ago. He knows she's all right, as there are indications she's been in their apartment to pick up clothes and mail. Arthur's actually relieved that they haven't run into each other or spoken on the phone, fearing such an encounter would lead to more conversation about his admitted infidelity. Knowing Natalie, she'd want to question him on who he's slept with, how many times they've been together, and on and on. He's already acknowledged that he's been unfaithful; and as far as Arthur is concerned, giving Natalie additional information would just put salt on an open wound.

Sitting at a conference table at KG Hospital, Arthur calls the meeting to order. "Thank you for coming. It's good to see all of you are able to attend this important meeting. Unless someone objects, I'd like to dispense with introductions and greetings—since we all know each other here—and get to the reason why I've asked you to come."

Dr. Joe Braxton, a primary-care physician and chairman of the Ethnic Health Initiative, interrupts, "Arthur, I think we should at least acknowledge Ellen Granger who's just returned from maternity leave...She and her husband, Charles, recently had a baby girl, and now she's back at the West Oakland Community Clinic."

The leadership claps, nods, and smiles at Ellen, who seems a little embarrassed by the attention. "Thank you, Joe and everyone, especially if you sent an e-mail congratulating Charles and me. I'm sorry about not responding, but I've been inundated with e-mails while trying to adjust to motherhood, so please forgive me if you've tried to reach me and I haven't answered. We named her Abigale Louise Granger...Abbey for short, after Charles's mother. She weighed eight pounds seven ounces when she was born...she's healthy...and she keeps us up most every night. So if I fall asleep during the meeting, please don't think I'm bored or on drugs or anything like that." This last remark draws quite a bit of laughter.

"It's good to have you back, Ellen," says Arthur. "We'll understand if you fall asleep, but if you start to snore, we'll have to wake you up." There's more laughter. "Are there any other comments or announcements we need to address before we begin?" Arthur scans the room for a response.

Dr. Braxton raises his hand and says, "I apologize, but I won't be able to stay for the entire meeting. I have a patient coming at noon and will have to leave at eleven fifteen."

Three other colleagues declared they, too, must leave early because of prior commitments and also apologize to the group. Arthur then tells leadership that as a result of their success in convening the Health Summit, the Trust has been asked to come up with and implement a community action plan to address the health emergency in the community. He shares with them the meeting's agenda and requests that they, once again, come together to collectively envision what such a plan of action might look like; to use the morning to establish guiding principles or value statements that can inform their work as they move forward in developing a plan.

The leadership is silent, and Arthur takes their silence to mean his colleagues are comfortable with his agenda. He highlights the findings presented at the public health department's meeting with the conclusion that African Americans in the county are facing a health crisis.

"At the end of that meeting," says Arthur, "a committee was proposed to come up with strategies to address the crisis. That committee met for the first time last week. Sonia, Eunice, and I attended the session. Sonia...Eunice, please, can you share with the group your thoughts about that discussion?"

"I was struck by the fact that the people who attended talked about our community as if they, themselves, weren't a part of that community," says Sonia. "It was as if the health crisis people of African descent are facing doesn't really affect them, personally, or their families. I found this attitude disturbing. I'm Afro-Cuban, and I know that my family living here have chronic health issues we didn't have in Cuba."

Leadership sits quietly for a moment until Eunice Anderson speaks up. "As director of community outreach for the department, I try to keep up with what's happening in other Bay Area counties and also on national public health issues. African Americans, not just in Alameda County but all over the Bay Area and around the country, are suffering from poor health, and the condition is chronic. The difference between Alameda County and other regions is that our department is willing to call it what it is—a health crisis in the black community."

"I didn't attend that meeting, but I want to add," says Aaron Campbell, "that we are not overstating the impact of this crisis on African Americans...We have to face it and do it now. We can't afford to get stuck in committees and discussions for months and months and come up with half-ass solutions. If we act and do it right, we can be a model for other counties with high populations of African descent. So I do hope that by the end of this session and the next, we can decide how we as community leaders are going to address, in a meaningful way, this very real health emergency. That's all I've got to say."

"Here's the challenge as I see it," continues Arthur. "And this point was brought home by that committee's discussion. We can't just saturate our community with information and public health bulletins using the media about the diseases that plague us and expect our poor health to change and get better. It's not. We can't talk and inform our way out of this crisis. We're challenged to find a way to motivate our people to change, to encourage black folk to alter their lifestyles and make better health choices and decisions, to change the way we live in the world."

"Oh, yeah…Good luck with that! That's very ambitious," shouts Reggie Johnson from United Youth Leadership. "And how are we supposed to do that when we're dealing with parents—at least where I work—who are not even there for their kids? How do we encourage these parents to make better health choices for themselves and for their kids? I just don't see it…I'm sorry, I don't."

Reggie's comment initiates several private conversations as people begin talking to colleagues sitting next to them or across the table.

"Wait a minute…wait a minute," exclaims Carol Anderson from Black Youth Radio. "I don't understand what you're saying, Arthur. Please explain."

Aisha Middleton, a naturopathic health practitioner who owns her own business, interrupts and says, "Look, Carol, let me give you an example. Everyone knows by now that cigarette smoking is unhealthy for you and causes cancer, but that doesn't necessarily mean that you're going to stop smoking. Everybody knows that regular, daily physical exercise is important, but that doesn't mean you're gonna get off your duff and start exercising. And I agree with Reggie—motivating people to change is real hard, especially if they don't want to. Even supporting people who say they want to improve their health and well-being is hard, because they have to break bad habits and replace them with good ones. For most people, that's difficult…it's hard.

"So is everybody clear on this point—about the challenge of motivating people to change?" Arthur asks.

"Yeah, but how we gonna deal with this motivation thing? That's what I wanna know," says Reggie Johnson. "'Cause black people are under a lot of stress, man…and the stress is killing us, and it's from constant racial oppression. And I'm sure it underlies our poor health."

"Before we tackle the how, Reggie," exclaims Arthur, "let's take a few steps back and first figure out a few value-based principles that we all can agree on in developing any motivational plan. If we can't identify what we all stand for now, I guarantee we won't be able to move forward when it comes to taking action. Reggie, we'll address the how at a later session."

Following this exchange, Arthur divides leadership into four workgroups and asks each cluster to choose someone to write down whatever comes out of his or her group's discussion. Two clusters begin their conversations in heated debates about defining the word "principle" and whether "value statement" means the same thing. About forty minutes later, Arthur reconvenes the entire leadership and asks each group to share the results of their discussion.

After four presentations and an animated conversation, leadership settles on four statements to drive the development of any action plan: take personal responsibility for one's own health and well-being; ask for support from others when necessary to make better lifestyle choices and improve health decisions; speak up within family and in faith communities when unhealthy lifestyle choices are being made; and finally, strive to remove inner obstacles to enable the power and voice of Spirit to work within and through us.

Cheers and clapping erupt as Arthur congratulates leadership on finding consensus on four propositions everyone agrees should guide the work ahead. Even two of the three colleagues who had to leave early stayed to contribute to the discussion. Arthur agrees to draft the meeting's summary notes and e-mail them to members for review and comment. A follow-up convening is scheduled in two weeks, and the session is adjourned.

Aaron Campbell walks over to Arthur to say how pleased he is with leadership's outcome. He also suggests that Arthur share what was accomplished with a Dr. Hachi Lightfoot and gives him her contact information. "She's a very creative and socially progressive physician and might have some ideas on how we can convert these four principles into community action. Call her," he says before walking away to talk to two other colleagues still in the room.

Sonia greets Arthur with a smile and congratulates him on facilitating a productive session. She's about to leave when Arthur grabs her arm.

"Sonia, does Hector still do readings?" he asks.

"In Santeria we call readings *consulta.* It's not like reading tea leaves, Arthur, or something like that; it's a sacred ceremony, and, yes, Hector does consulta. Why?"

"I apologize for calling it a reading. I meant no disrespect, Sonia. Do you think Hector would be willing to do a consulta with me?"

"I'm surprised, Arthur, that you would ask for one. Most professionals like yourself know very little about Santeria and would never think about a consulta. Why do you wish one?"

"I have my personal reasons…it would not be appropriate for me to discuss them here."

"I understand. You know Hector's still learning English, so if he agrees, he'll want me there to interpret. Would that be all right with you?"

"I'd be comfortable with that."

"OK, I'll talk to him and give you a call," Sonia replies while lightly touching his arm before walking away.

Arthur and John Sutton, chief executive officer and president of the East Bay Y and associate pastor of a nondenominational church in Berkeley, take the elevator down to the lobby and walk past the information desk out into the open air. A middle-aged African American man with mixed-gray and matted hair approaches them and holds out a shaky hand, begging for change. His disheveled clothes cannot mask the smell of urine that assaults the nose as he stands in front of them.

"My brothers, have any change you can spare?"

John and Arthur reach into their pockets and hand over whatever coins they have.

"God bless you, brothers...bless you." And he slips away into the passing crowd like he was never there.

Immediately, another man of African descent advances toward them and angrily demands money as if it's his birthright to claim. They're taken aback, not just by his aggression but also by the way his request is actually a command.

"Sorry, we already gave all our coins away," says Arthur as they proceed to move on.

The man, now behind them, shouts for everyone to hear, "Yous think you're bad niggas 'cause you wear the white man's suit...witcha cell phones and shoulder bags and shit! You ain't nothin' but chumps...chumps! Go ahead witcha baaad selves."

The sky's overcast, and a mass of steely gray clouds floats aimlessly like puffed-up snails on parade. The dull grayness weighs on Arthur as they head north on Broadway, and he wrestles with his emotions from their encounter with the last man.

"The poor man is disturbed, Arthur. Don't let him get to you," says John as they continue walking.

"I'm fine, John, but the man was unnerving."

"Yes, I feel the same way...unsettled by it all. Arthur, this morning's meeting was a good one. You know, leadership has evolved into an effective working group as a result of the health summit. People speak their minds more than ever, but they also trust and respect one another, which makes all the difference in the world. We've proven that we can work together, and it feels good. And only the Trust can convene this group and guide the work ahead. You know that, don't you?"

"Why do you say that?" asks Arthur.

"Because most of the people in that conference room...not all, but most...are senior executives or heads of organizations that, given their titles and positions, must fulfill the obligations that come with their office. They must represent a diverse array of constituents, not just black folk. They can't show favor to one ethnic population over another. And the internal politics of these institutions...the vast majority of their board of directors...I'm sure are mostly white, 'cause they have the influence and the money. They'd throw these high-on-the-hog negroes out with yesterday's trash, if they thought they were race men or race women. You hear what I'm saying? So we need an organization like the Trust to unapologetically represent black interests, especially since we, as managers in multicultural institutions, cannot."

"I understand. You know, many of them would prefer to meet and talk in my office rather than me coming to visit them, especially if we're gonna talk about black folk. I sympathize with their dilemma. Can we grab lunch, or do you need to get back to your office?"

"Of course...of course...as CEO I make my own schedule."

"Well, I don't know. Don't you have to consult with your multiple constituencies before making that decision?"

"You a funny man, Arthur Renfro."

"How about going to Ensarro? It's not far from here on Grand," says Arthur.

The sun breaks through the clouds momentarily, and as they cross the intersection at Harrison and Grand, shafts of sunlight splash upon the gray pavement while they walk beside Lake Merritt. It's the noon hour, and office workers are on lunch break; young mothers are pushing strollers as joggers and skateboarders pass them on the concrete sidewalk. Huge, gray-chested, black-feathered geese strut about the grass or on the pavement, fertilizing the ground with dark green poop while they nonchalantly waddle along.

"Black folk are no longer the flavor of the month or the year—or the century, for that matter," says John as they pass Fairyland and continue down Grand. "This capitalist country exploits black talent and creativity; and except for these very few, we're in the way or, at best, irrelevant and are definitely being left behind…Hell, not just black people are irrelevant," John continues as if having a conversation with himself. "A whole lot of people are being left behind.

"With the advancement in technology and more and more machines taking over jobs people used to do, fewer folk are finding meaningful, good-paying work. I mean, how many people do you need to push a button to make the machine stop or go, huh? And now computers can even do that? Hell, they don't need our fingers to push buttons anymore. Just hook the damn contraption up to a computer terminal and let it run itself…and it don't need a lunch or dinner break at that! Ain't that something?"

"The US only needs consumer-holics—a populace that does nothing else but buy, buy, buy," Arthur replies. "But damn if I know where consumers are supposed to get the bread to consume, if they don't have jobs.

"America is becoming a third-world country, John, with the relatively few who have and the rest of us who have not. The middle class is shrinking; and along with its demise, our economic and political power is eroding away. And we're so preoccupied with keeping our jobs and homes together we're oblivious to it all. But it's obvious...self-evident."

"And those in power who jump to the corporations' bidding... especially the Republicans—the white people's party...hell, even the Democrats, they don't want people to focus on the real governance structure of this country. Less government, and more and more Wall Street and the media industry. And the Republicans got a good strategy goin' on to divert attention away from examining corporate influence and control. Anytime an election comes around, they start using racial codes like 'welfare cheats' and 'people who think they're entitled' to stir up fear and resentment to galvanize the white vote. So, if you're a white man and don't even have a pot to piss in, you may be bad off, but you ain't black, and for that reason alone, you can stand up tall and be proud. Yes sah! I ain't black! I'm white. Now, ain't that some shit!"

Arthur laughs freely, enjoying John's humor and company. A young Latino boy and his little sister pass them on roller skates, wildly swinging their arms left and right like the long limbs of a grandfather clock gone berserk. A seagull suddenly swoops down close to the children's heads, and the little girl screams her brother's name as she skates faster to catch up. A breeze from the lake suddenly picks up as the sky grows dark with the false promise of rain.

They walk into Ensarro, where two waiters are busy serving the lunch crowd, and find seats at the only vacant table in the small Ethiopian restaurant across from the lake. Solomon, the young owner, walks over and welcomes them as he places two menus on the table with glasses of ice water.

"Would you like something to drink?" he asks.

Arthur orders tea, and John is fine with water. Then, with pen and small pad of paper in hand, Solomon stands over the table and waits to take their order.

"Let us have a moment," says John, and Solomon walks away. "It'll be interesting to see how a plan gets formulated from those principles. They'll certainly keep our feet to the fire when we start talking about programmatic ideas, but I'm curious who suggested that last principle about removing the inner obstacles so Spirit can work through us. Who came up with that?"

"It was my contribution to the group I joined," Arthur replies.

"I knew it...I knew it was you. So how do you define the implied spirituality in your principle, Arthur? Because you're not talking about religion, you're talking about spirituality in a universal sense, aren't you? How are you thinking about spirituality?"

"I didn't give it much thought before I said it."

"Well, that statement has been adopted by the group, so you better explain it."

"I guess what I was thinking about is how everything is always changing...everything. And as human beings, we're always in transition...never arriving at any final destination. We're born, grow into adulthood if we're lucky, and then old age until death comes to claims us."

"All right, gentlemen, may I take your order?" says Solomon, abruptly reappearing at the table.

"We need a few more minutes, Solomon. I haven't even looked at your menu yet," John replies.

"No problem," says the owner and again leaves as John leafs through the menu.

"OK...OK," continues Arthur, slightly leaning across the table. "So we're all in this process of becoming, but what are we becoming—that's the real question. We either move forward in life and become better human beings or backward in life and ultimately turn into terrible people. And do you know the sad thing, John? The opportunities for our youth to better themselves are shrinking. And if this white-supremacist society has its way, people of African descent and our culture will remain nothing more than a resource to exploit."

"That's a very cynical outlook, Arthur. You know that, don't you? And what you describe, how does that relate to your value statement...removing inner obstacles?"

"The question remains, don't you see? Is it possible for us as a people to choose and shape our own destiny, or are we doomed to the rubbish heap delegated to us by white America? That's what this principle is really about. If we're to shape our own destiny, then we need to find a way to remove the obstacles: poor health; growing up in public schools that deliver a substandard education rather than demanding schools prepare our youth to compete with everyone else to get into college or get ahead in the proverbial marketplace; also, mass incarceration and unemployment for our young men and women, and it goes on and on...But in spite of all that stands in our way, can we as a people shape our own positive, life-affirming destiny?"

"Sounds a little grandiose...too ambitious to put into a community action plan," says John. "Don't you think?"

"Yeah, you're right. I get carried away sometimes. Perhaps we should revise that value statement and say, 'If you do dirt, you get dirt thrown back; and if you do right...well, maybe you're more at peace with yourself.' I don't know."

"Are you at peace with yourself, Arthur?"

"No, I'm not, John. I have many inner obstacles and much work to do."

"So do I, Arthur; so do we all."

"Are you gentlemen ready to order?" Solomon asks with a smile.

CHAPTER 14
TAKING FLIGHT

The couple from Saint Croix often argues, and the police were called to break up their knock-down-and-drag-out fight less than a month after they moved into the ground-floor unit, directly under Arthur and Natalie's flat. The walls to the old two-story, three-unit building are thin; and, given the couple's frequent bouts, Arthur has grown used to hearing Arnell's loud voice and the fights that often escalate into her throwing pots and pans at her husband. When thinking about the Crosian couple going at each other and the number of confrontations he's had with Natalie, Arthur begins to wonder whether fighting and arguing in the building is contagious. He resolves that something has to change in his relationship with his estranged wife. Either they find a way to settle their differences or make a clean break of it and file for divorce.

But tonight is different as the fury of their habitual quarrels escalates. The Crosian woman snatches off her short husband's pajamas and chases his naked black ass out the door and into the hallway. She runs after him with all the fury of an unleashed tropical hurricane. Arnell then beats her husband, Neville, with a broomstick as he pleads for his life and runs up the stairs.

"Arta…Arta!" Neville screams. "Open the door! Open the door!"

Arthur rushes to his doorway and opens it in time to pull Arnell's screaming husband in and quickly shut the door on the fury behind him. As red-hot rage slams against the door, he locks the deadbolt and turns to confront the Crosian man's uncircumcised penis that is dangling in front of him.

"Neville…Neville! Come on outta dair!" Arnell screams, banging her fist against the door. "Come on out, you mudder fucka—come on out!"

"Jesus," says Arthur, "couldn't you grab some pants before being chased out?" He hurries pass Neville to find clothes for his nakedness. Trailing behind, his penis dangling between his thighs, Arnell's husband struggles to be heard over the clamor still banging on the door.

"Arta, we nevah fight before moving to dis place—nevah!" shouts Neville, his bloodshot eyes brimming with tears.

"Here, put these on," says Arthur, throwing him a pair of his old khaki pants to wear.

The banging suddenly stops, and Neville and Arthur stand still, listening. Arnell's husband cautiously tiptoes on his bare feet to the door and presses his ear against the wood.

"She's gone," he whispers. "I think she's gone."

Arthur silently makes his way to the door and looks though the peephole. Arnell appears to have left, but then again, she could be sitting on the floor right outside the door, out of sight, waiting to pounce.

"Thank you," Neville says as he pulls Arthur's khakis up over his backside. Arthur walks past him and into the kitchen. "We nevah fight before coming to dis place."

"Would you like some tea?" asks Arthur, filling the kettle with water and placing it on the lit stove.

"Somet'ings not right," Neville declares.

"Can I make you some tea?"

"Oh, no…tank you, Arta. We nevah fought before; now we fight-ting all the time."

"Well, join the club, Neville. I'm sure you've heard Natalie and me at it."

"Yeah, man! It's bizarre, all of us fight-ting up in here. I'm going to tell Arnell, when she calms down, we have to move from dis place. We have to get out now."

Clutching Arthur's pants around his small waist, Neville heads for the door.

"You think it's safe?" asks Arthur.

Neville slowly turns the deadbolt lock while listening for any sound from the other side of the door. Apprehensive, Arnell's husband cautiously cracks the door open and listens for a sound…any sound, but there is none. Arthur watches him, and he can see from the relaxed expression on Neville's face that the dimly lit hall is now empty. Arthur walks to the door and notices his neighbor, Mrs. Valencia, or her heavyset daughter, Julia, closing their apartment door.

Neville crouches down on the landing and looks between the narrow wooden poles in the bannister for any trace of life at the bottom of the stairs. The hardwood floors creak under the Crosian's weight, and the sudden noise causes Neville and Arthur to momentarily freeze in place. Bringing his knees to the floor and bending forward, Neville presses the side of his face to the floor to look down the stairs in search of any sign of Arnell.

Seeing Neville's covered backside, Arthur is reminded of the night the police showed up to wrestle with the big woman beating up her short, skinny husband. Their fight spilled out into the street, with Arnell's nappy hair standing on end as if every strand was at war with itself. Although it took the two policemen—one white, one black—to restrain her, they simply wrote a report and didn't take Arnell to jail. Looking out the window of their second floor apartment, Arthur and Natalie heard the cops laughing at the little man with the big wife before turning off their red, blue, and yellow flashing lights and driving away.

Neville is already walking down the stairs when Arthur closes his door. As he takes the kettle off the burner, the telephone rings. It's Sonia.

"Hector agrees to do a consulta with you and wants to know if you can come to our house on Saturday afternoon at three?"

Arthur agrees and asks if there is anything he needs to bring. Sonia relays his message to Hector, who says in Spanish, "Just tell him not to forget to bring himself and a donation for the Orishas and Egun."

Arthur overhears Hector laughing in the background as Sonia says good-bye and hangs up the phone.

Arthur lies in bed, thinking about the consulta. He wonders if, during the ceremony, his secret of flying without a body will be exposed, and whether he'll be comfortable with Sonia being there. He likes working with her and worries that after the ceremony, she'll think he's mentally unstable—or worse, insane. Arthur realizes he doesn't know what to expect from this Santeria ritual, and the unknowing makes him anxious.

His mind drifts in the stillness when suddenly he remembers he didn't return Natalie's phone call. What must she think of him? Would she reason he's trying to avoid talking with her? As his eyes grow heavy, Arthur promises himself to call her first thing in the morning. He starts to fall asleep. Then the buzzing in his ears abruptly begins, but the pins-and-needles sensation that usually follows doesn't materialize. Without warning, half his spirit, from the waist on up, detaches from his physical body and sits straight up while his lower half remains wedded to his physical form still lying on the bed. It happens so quickly, as if his spirit's inclination is to forcibly release itself to get up and leave. Arthur's spirit looks around the room and then over at the Venetian blinds in the window next to the bed. Streaks of light from a passing car come through the open slits in the blinds and make their way across the bedroom wall before disappearing in the darkness.

As if the light is some type of signal, Arthur's spirit now lifts entirely out of his body and passes through the windowpane into the dark and empty street. It rises in the air past a streetlamp with a golden-yellow glow and flies up into a cloudless, ink-blue sky. The night air is cold and crisp, but his spirit does not feel the chill—only an unconscious sense of relief, free from the burden of existence within a physical form. And it gazes into the heavens, with its broad canopy of twinkling stars, flying higher and higher, intuitively knowing that by the strength of its will it's able to move and flee. But suddenly a feeling of doubt creeps into consciousness as Arthur's spirit wonders whether it might never return to the body left lying on the bed. As soon as the thought arises, a latent fear sets in and slows its ascension pulling his spirit down.

Dismissing these thoughts by focusing on the joy of freedom and flying, his spirit quickly changes course and swoops down to fly over rooftops and trees and glides above the few people still walking the streets before soaring over Lake Merritt and into downtown Oakland. Then, following the bright red taillights of moving cars onto the freeway, Arthur's spirit swiftly heads toward the Bay Bridge and follows the traffic past Treasure Island into downtown San Francisco. He then swoops nearer to the ground like an unseen night bird over the heads of young, white professionals entering and leaving upscale restaurants and bars on Market Street, high on the exuberance of alcohol and unrestrained youth. With the immediate thought of lingering for a moment, Arthur's spirit hovers over a group of Pacific Gas & Electric workers. They wear white hard hats and yellow rubber coveralls as they work under a bright white light in the middle of the street. He observes two men alternately peering into a dark manhole as they talk to one another; a third worker drinks something from a Styrofoam cup as he stands next to a utility truck and watches three stray dogs trot, one behind the other, across Market and head south down Third Street.

There is nothing Arthur can compare with this feeling of weightlessness and total independence from his own physical form—this lightness of being in an altered reality, this mysterious, magical feeling, so exquisitely alive and well with sheer exuberance and energy; and to be invisible and move about at will, faster than the speed of light, high above the world and the creatures in it without inhabiting a material form. He wonders if there are others like him who have the ability to leave their bodies. He ponders what it would be like to visit Europe or countries in Asia or Africa and becomes giddy from the miracle of it all. And in that instant, strapped with a mix of fragmented and unfocused thoughts, he feels once again uncontrollably drawn as his spirit is transported through the darkness back to his apartment and into his bedroom. And without Arthur's conscious intention, his spirit floats, full-length and face up, over the body identified as Arthur, still lying on its back in the bed, and slowly descends into it. Arthur then opens his eyes but intuitively senses he should remain absolutely still while his spirit settles in, again, and fully aligns itself with his physical form.

Dr. Brathwaite's recommendation and referral for him to see a psychiatrist quickly drifts in and out of his consciousness and is replaced by the conviction that what he experienced tonight was not a hallucination. It was as real as him lying in his bed. And if, perchance, he imagined it all...well, it was an enjoyable excursion that he could learn to live with.

Slowly sitting up and getting out of bed, Arthur turns on the light and walks over to the full-length mirror behind the bedroom door. He intently studies his appearance in the looking glass and sees nothing unusual about the way his body looks. Then he moves in closer to examine his face and eyes. They, too, seem normal; and as he raises his hand to let his fingers touch his cheeks, he smiles at his likeness in the mirror and knows that all is right with him.

CHAPTER 15

SOCIAL EXPERIMENT

Arthur's in his office, reviewing the Trust's financial report from the previous month, when the phone rings. He answers it. "Hello, Arthur here."

"Hello, this is Dr. Hachi Lightfoot. I just left Aaron Campbell at the public health department. He speaks highly of you."

"Good. Aaron's comments might balance out the people who don't speak so highly of me, Dr. Lightfoot."

She laughs. "Please call me Hachi; everyone else does. May I call you Arthur?"

"Please do. I'm glad you've taken the initiative to call. Aaron suggested that I reach out to you, but you beat me to it."

"Aaron's told me about your project and the principles your summit leadership has come up with. And I must say I'm impressed the group felt the need to develop these statements. I have some ideas about how they might be applied. So I thought, before leaving the downtown area, I'd call and see if possibly you're open for lunch today. I know it's short notice, and you probably have a full schedule, but I thought I'd give it a try."

"What a pleasant surprise," says Arthur as he hastily thumbs through his calendar. He has a one o'clock meeting with Giorgis, the Trust's new website administrator, which he decides he can reschedule.

"Yes, Dr. Lightfoot—Hachi, let's meet for lunch. How about in forty-five minutes at Miss Ollie's on the corner of Ninth and Washington? Do you know that restaurant?"

"Yes, I know it. I'll see you at Ollie's at noon."

"Good, see you then."

Gracie walks into his office as he hangs up the phone. "Now, don't you forget to sign the checks I'm leaving on the conference table. Don't let me come back from the bank and see those checks haven't been signed. Percy said he'd stop by in the morning to also sign those checks, so they need to be ready. Do ya hear? It's the fifteenth of the month, and they gotta go out."

"Yes, Mother."

"Don't you 'Mother' me, 'cause I'll box your ears if you keep that up," Gracie says, laughing more to herself as she starts for the door. "Oh, you got a phone call from someone named Valerie Hamilton. She says she's coming to San Francisco for a conference and wants you to call her. Here's her number. Is that somebody I should know about?"

"You don't have to know all my business."

"You better stop messin' with me, 'cause I got Natalie's number, so watch out. And Natalie...she also wants you to call her. And her birthday's coming up, so whatcha gonna do about it?"

"I don't know, but thanks for reminding me...and please phone Giorgis and tell him I need to cancel our meeting this afternoon. Ask him if we can reschedule for the same time next week and apologize for me."

"OK," replies Gracie, who's already halfway down the short hall heading to her office.

Arthur arrives at Miss Ollie's early to secure a table where he and Dr. Lightfoot can have a private conversation. Almost immediately, a middle-aged woman with a light-brown complexion and long, silver-gray hair, carrying a brown leather folder, arrives and scans the room. Arthur stands and waves, knowing the woman is Dr. Lightfoot. Seeing him, she walks over to his table, where they formally introduce themselves to one another. After going up to the counter and ordering peas and rice, a house salad, and a Caribbean dish of Achee and Saltfish they return to their table and sit across from one another.

"Dr. Lightfoot, I'm sure that your schedule, like mine, is normally filled with appointments well in advance, so I am surprised that both of us could arrange this impromptu lunch meeting so quickly. It certainly is my pleasure. Tell me, Hachi, does your name hold any special meaning?"

"My mother's ancestry is Black Seminole from North Carolina, and when I was young, she used to call me Hachi, which means river or stream. I don't know why she called me that or why the name stuck with me, but it did."

"And how about Lightfoot, is that Seminole Indian, too?"

"A lot of people ask me that, but it's not. The origin of Lightfoot is actually English. It comes from northern England and means 'one who is light on their feet…a runner who delivers messages.' So what can I say? My ancestry is a mixed bag…Native American, English, and African. And how about you? Tell me about your family."

"It's interesting…although most African Americans have mixed ancestry—and, if you think about it, probably carry DNA from around the world—we tend to only acknowledge our African ancestry."

"As you well know," interjects Hachi, "in the Antebellum South, you were considered black with one drop of African blood, even though many mulattoes could pass for white—and did. But today, many African Americans and consequently their children will most likely identify as African American." Hachi reaches across the table and lightly touches the back of Arthur's hand. "I'm sorry for interrupting, please continue."

"Well...my grandmother—we called her Nanna—she was half Pamunkey Indian. She said she was born in 1901, even though her birth records show something different. Her family lived somewhere along the Chesapeake Bay in Virginia.

"Once Nanna showed me an old photograph of her father she kept in a box. He wore a Native American headdress with a tail of feathers trailing down his back to the ground. He also had on an all-leather shirt and matching pants with tassels hanging under his arms and on the back of his legs. He wore moccasins, just like you'd see in them old Western movies when white men dressed in war paint and played Indian chiefs.

"She said he road in Buffalo Bill's Wild West Show for a living as it traveled up and down the East Coast. The photograph was taken at one of these shows. Nanna's father was a devote, fundamentalist Christian—Baptist, I think—and legally married to her mother, an African woman who was also Christian. I never knew their names. But when Nanna gave birth to my mother out of wedlock, her father, the Indian chef, disowned my grandmother and her child—my mother, his grandchild—and he never spoke to his daughter or saw my mother again."

A young waitress with hemp-colored locks, gathered and tied on the back of her head, brings their food. Arthur unwraps his napkin holding silverware.

"And what about your father's side of the family?" asks Hachi.

"My father never talked about his parents, but my dad's father was a white man who owned the only general store in a small southern town somewhere in North Carolina. His father had an affair—you know how that goes—with his black housekeeper;

and as a result of that union or rape, my dad was born. My mother said he was ashamed of his mother and didn't like to talk about her."

"Why was he ashamed of her?"

"I don't know. But here's the interesting part…apparently, his mother was very sick after he was born, or maybe she just didn't want him. I don't know, but his white father intended to raise him in the same house with his white wife and three white children. Ain't that some stuff!

"Supposedly, the white wife had a nervous breakdown and was institutionalized, and his half-siblings refused to let their father bring my dad into their home. So my father grew up with his mother's people, but his white father paid for everything…even supported him through college."

"Are you going to write that story about your family someday?"

"I've thought about it."

They eat in silence together, remaining in the privacy of their own thoughts, until the hemp-haired waitress returns to bus the table.

"So, Aaron gave you the four principles the leadership team wants to incorporate into any community action plan?" Arthur asks, once the waitress leaves.

"Yes. I read them and was impressed by the way the guiding principles are about getting people to take responsibility for their own health. It's a good start, Arthur, and I've given some thought to what you're attempting to do. Would you like to hear my suggestions?"

"Most definitely."

Dr. Lightfoot then describes how an effective community program could be framed around leadership's four principles, if its members are willing to lead the way by dealing with their own health issues first, thus setting an example. She suggests the group create a social laboratory and then expand the initiative to include others. Start with one issue like the metabolic syndrome, or the biochemical processes involved in the body's normal functioning and its risk factors, whether habits or traits one inherits, that increase the chance of developing a disease.

Upon hearing her plan, Arthur's eyes light up, and a broad smile surfaces on his face. "Dr. Hachi Lightfoot, I think you've just talked yourself into a job. Do you have the time, and are you willing to conduct such a social experiment as you so nicely describe?"

Recognizing it would be impossible to carry out the experiment if leadership decides not to support it, they agree that Hachi's idea must be introduced at the group's next meeting. She also agrees to prepare a short concept paper on the proposal as a hand-out piece for leadership's discussion.

CHAPTER 16
A QUESTIONABLE GIFT

A little before noon on Saturday, Arthur opens his mailbox to find, among newspaper ads, monthly bills, and other correspondence, an unexpected letter from Natalie. Returning to his apartment, he throws the other pieces on the dining room table and sits down to read his wife's letter. It's clear she doesn't want him to know where she's staying as no return address is provided. He studies the envelope closely before placing it under his nose to smell possibly its contents—a curious habit Arthur also performs on food to assess how fresh it is before eating. This particular bent in his personality irritates Natalie when eating at restaurants or sitting at their kitchen table at home. She finally refused to eat with him unless he breaks this habit—or, as she refers to it, his animalistic ritual. Arthur tears open the envelope and reads Natalie's two-page letter.

Dear Arthur,

I apologize for leaving our last session with Dr. Brathwaite so abruptly, but although I knew you were having extramarital affairs, it was hard to hear the truth come out of your mouth. I went back to where I'm staying—and I know you think I'm staying with another man, but I am not. I'm not like that. I'm staying for now with my friend Karen in the Oakland Hills.

I came back to her place and cried about you and our marriage. I was angry at you and still am for hurting and disappointing me. Don't you value our marriage, Arthur? How could you just throw it away? And you want me to make love to you when I've known for some time you're sleeping around. I can't, and I won't.

I guess you've noticed that I come to our apartment during the day when I know you're not there. I really don't want to see you now. I see the way you're living and sometimes have the urge to wash the dirty dishes and straighten up the place, but I don't. I don't even sit on the bed. I quickly change my clothes and pick up a few things. That's all.

It's been awkward, to say the least, since we haven't talked in the last two weeks. And although you might not believe it, I do miss you, and I still love you. I cry at night thinking about you. And it saddens me to know this is where we are in our marriage when our first wedding anniversary is coming up at the end of the month. But this is our reality, isn't it? Maybe we got married too soon.

I want you to know that I need to have a three-month trial separation from you. I feel you need the space to decide whether you really want to be married to me, and if you do, can you really make the commitment to be loyal to our marriage vows? Maybe you can't. I don't know. That's for you to decide. I know it's not all your fault. I, too, have some things to work out about myself and my relationships with men—especially with you. I've made my own arrangements to see Dr. Brathwaite to talk about them. I hope you continue to see him on your own, but of course that's up to you.

Dear Arthur, I sincerely want to say that I love you and think you're a brilliant man and have so much to offer. I hope you will use this time to work on yourself, so if and when we get back together, we'll be a better, healthier couple and can think about having children, which you know I sincerely want. But I have to be with a man I can trust.

Natalie

P.S. I'll stop by in the next day to two to pick up my clothes and other things and leave you with my key so you truly have your own space. You can always reach me on my cell phone. Cheers.

Arthur's heart is pounding by the time he finishes her letter. He questions why she couldn't just sit down with him and have a conversation like two adults instead of sending him this letter. Did she think he'd be angry and lose his temper? He's in emotional turmoil now, feeling empty and truly alone, and wishes they could meet over dinner and work things out together. Arthur rereads her letter, searching for clues about Natalie's state of mind, and assesses whether he should reach out to her in some way. He weighs in his mind whether he could offer her a peace offering like inviting her to dinner, but he knows in his heart that Natalie would not accept any kind of reconciliation, at least not now.

Arthur is confused, driven by feelings of disappointment and remorse mixed with anger and self-pity as he throws her letter on the cluttered dining table and walks to the bedroom to lie down. Reclining on his back, he's reminded of the complete freedom and weightlessness he experienced while unleashed from his body when he glided through the air. He wonders what it would be like if his spirit could leave his physical form, now, and fly in broad daylight.

Arthur focuses on his breath, allowing his body to relax. When he's almost given up trying, the slight buzzing in his ears begins and gradually grows louder. Then suddenly, commanding Arthur's full attention in what feels like a powerful energy source, an apparition materializes on and over him. It looks like a human skull without flesh, and it is waving bony white arms back and force across its chest. It is draped in stark black cloth, and Arthur intuits that the spirit is warning him of danger.

He's startled by the ghost, and then panic sets in as he bolts straight up in the bed, and the spirit instantly disappears. Arthur jumps out of bed and runs to the bedroom mirror to gaze at his reflection in the glass. He thinks he looks quite normal, but he feels something in him is not right and is out of kilter. Returning to the bed, he lies back down, afraid to close his eyes for fear the buzzing will start again. As he lies there, he realizes his spirit, which already started to rise from his body, was forcibly made to return to his physical form when he abruptly sprinted from the bed. As a result, body and spirit were not yet in full alignment with one another. Resting there and thinking about the sudden appearance of the apparition, Arthur has no doubt the spirit saved his life.

Turning over on his side, Arthur falls into a light sleep and drifts into dreaming. He finds himself walking in a dark, musty tunnel when the earthen ceiling opens and lets in a shaft of brilliant sunlight that makes the floor underneath him visible for the first time. Accustom to walking in darkness, Arthur places his hand over his eyes to shield them from the sun's glare. He feels warmth on his face and looks down at his hands and feet. He notices sandals on his feet and that he is clothed in a full-length brown robe that covers his shoulders down to his ankles. He then realizes that he's grown old and gray with the passage of time and, thinking back, cannot recall life outside this dark, dreary passageway. Looking down at the ground beneath him, he notices a cobblestone street, which is a pathway littered with human skulls and human bones packed tightly together. They line the floor for as far as his old eyes can see. Latent thoughts that have been buried for eons now rush into his consciousness; he's alive and alone and has been walking on these human remains, unaware of any other existence, for a long, long time.

Arthur looks up at the sun, which no longer hurts his eyes but soothes his face and warms his limbs. A gentle wind rushes through the opening as he breathes cool, fresh air. At that moment he rejoices in his self-awareness that he exists, that the universe knows he is there, that he is loved by his Creator, whom he had long forgotten—and most of all, that he will no longer have to stay in this dark labyrinth of a tunnel anymore.

When Arthur arrives at Sonia's small, wood-framed house, nestled on an upward slope near Mills College, Hector is in the backyard, planting vegetable seeds. Sonia opens the front door just as the rim of the sun reappears over a bank of white clouds. Arthur turns to face the warmth and golden-yellow brightness, as if he's seeing the sun after a long absence or recalling the distant memory of a dream. Sonia, wearing a full white cotton skirt with ruffles at the bottom, a white blouse, and a white head wrap that contrast her dark-brown skin, greets Arthur with a smile almost as bright as the peek-a-boo sun. She ushers him down a narrow hallway and into a comfortable living room.

"Hector!" she yells. "Arthur is here." She invites Arthur to sit and leaves the room.

Instead of sitting, Arthur casually walks around their living space and notices a small wooden table next to a wall with a statue of an African man placed next to a dark wooden bowl with liquid. Arthur is tempted to bring his nose to the bowl to discern its contents but resists the urge out of respect for Sonia and Hector and their African-rooted religion. Framed photographs of what he assumes are family members are positioned around the statue and bowl, and a garland of small yellow and green glass beads are around the statue and laced among the family pictures. A burning white candle rests in the middle of the table in a clear glass jar.

Above the tabletop, on the wall, is a large print in a plain wooden frame. It's a colorful picture of a mature African man with gray hair and adorned in an elaborate yellow-and-green robe. In one arm he holds a bouquet of yellow flowers. Etched in the background is a large golden ring or circle, and the man's other arm is raised and pointing upward. Hector will tell him later that the figure in the picture is an Orisha, a semidivine being whose name is Orumali, and is a master of divination who knows the past, present, and future of everyone on earth and has the power to influence one's destiny. Hector is a priest or Babalawo of Orumali who gives counsel through intermediaries in a consulta.

After surveying the rest of the living room, Arthur returns to the wooden table with photos and burning candle, recognizing it as Hector and Sonia's family altar. It honors Orumali and Egun, the spirit of their ancestors, who together protect their loved ones. The altar is the cornerstone of their faith in Santeria. The scent of frankincense and myrrh fills this quiet, peaceful house, masking the sound of urban traffic and the hubbub in the streets.

Arthur sits in a reclining wicker chair nestled in a corner and immediately feels a powerful energy force piercing his body. Getting up, he examines the seat and surrounding space, slowly passing his hand over the chair like a priest giving absolution, and again feels a charge of energy emanating through his skin. Hector calls out from another room in Spanish that he needs to take a shower and change his clothes before doing the consulta. At least, that's what Sonia conveys as she offers their guest a glass of iced tea.

"Thank you," says Arthur, pointing to the wicker chair on the other side of the living room. "Who is in that corner over there?"

"Oh you felt that, huh?" Sonia says with astonishment. "That's my father. He's always here. I'm surprised you noticed him. Most people who visit are not aware that he's around. I'm impressed, Arthur Renfro."

Arthur sits down on their brown velvet sofa, and Sonia pulls a red-and-black hassock over to sit near him. Resting her elbow on her knee, she looks with curiosity at Arthur's face and inquisitively asks, "Did my father frighten you?"

"Oh no, I'm used to spirits standing in corners." They laugh as Sonia turns her head to adoringly glance at the space her father sometimes inhabits.

Hector appears, dressed in white with a long strip of yellow and green cloth over one shoulder and wrapped around his waist. An embroidered yellow and green kufi, or brimless cap, rests snuggly on his head. Sonia's husband, as if in the act of bathing and getting dressed, has metamorphosed into the Babalawo or Orumali's priest who is in the room. Several strings of multicolored beads are around his neck, including glass beads matching the yellow and green colors in his hat and shoulder cloth.

Sonia and Arthur stand up, and Hector nods while offering only a slight grin. He arranges items he's carrying on the short-legged tabletop in the center of the room while Sonia quickly slides the hassock she's been sitting on over to the coffee table, and then Hector gestures for Arthur to come and sit down.

Orumali's priest now sits on the other side of the table. He explains in English that it's hard for him to conduct a consulta in English, and asks Arthur in English if he will give his permission for Sonia to interpret. Arthur nods his head in consent before Hector closes his eyes and starts chanting in Lacumi, Santeria's liturgical language. Of course, Arthur has no idea what Hector's saying and wonders if Sonia, who has pulled up a chair next to her husband, understands the Yuroba dialect her Babalawo is intoning.

Orumali's messenger continues his invocation to his Orisha and Egun, asking for their blessings, allowing him to open the doorway to their unseen world where the ancestors' perspective on Arthur's life can be revealed. Orumali's priest is now completely absorbed in his incantation while he places a large white candle on one end of the table and lights it. Arthur watches as he lays a rectangular straw mat on the table and takes two small pieces of animal bone from a small, green, velvet pouch. The Babalawo interrupts his intonation only long enough to ask in English for Arthur to hold out his hands, and then he puts a small piece of bone in each palm and gestures for him to close them.

The Babalawo resumes chanting as he removes his epuele chain, a string of small alternating yellow and green crystal beads, from a place Arthur doesn't see and gently throws it on the mat. He studies the formation of the beads for a moment before asking Arthur again to hold out his hands, palms up. He then drops the bones in his open hands again and commands Arthur to press his palms together, rubbing the bones back and forth. When Orumali's messenger directs him to stop, he asks Arthur to make sure only one bone is in each hand before telling him to open them.

The priest looks at the bones in Arthur's palms and, without commenting, picks up his epuele and throws it on the mat again before resuming his chanting. This ritual is repeated several times. Arthur intently watches the priest's facial expressions as if he might find in his features a sign, an indication of what Orumali's messenger might be seeing, thinking. The last throw ends in silence as the Babalawo abruptly stops his incantation to study the beads that lie before him.

He no longer asks Arthur to rub or show the bones in his hands but rather gives his full attention to the crystals on the table. He groans and mumbles to himself, seemingly unaware of anyone else in the room, before picking up his epuele chain and throwing it again and again. Finally, Orumali's messenger looks up from the table and folds his arms as Sonia fixes her eyes on him. He looks at Arthur with a smile before saying in English, "Man, you got some stuff goin' on. An adventure you're having, huh?"

Arthur remains unmoved, and he keeps silent. Hector looks over at his wife and asks if he's using the word "adventure" properly, but Sonia's not sure as she doesn't know yet what her husband is thinking. Hector turns to speak directly to Sonia in his Puerto Rican Spanish, waiting every now and again for her to translate for him.

"First of all, I want to tell you that your ability to leave your body is not a curse but a gift. Your spirit will want to leave whenever you're under stress or depressed," she says for her husband, who waits patiently to continue.

"Where does this gift you say I have come from? Why do I have it?" asks Arthur.

"You were born in the middle of a snowstorm, so your spirit is not attached to your body too tightly." Hector continues waiting for his wife's translation.

Whatever connection or logic there is between snowstorms and Arthur's ability to vacate his physical form remains elusive to him, but he doesn't share this response with them.

"Do you live in a house or apartment?" Hector asks in English.

"I live in a second floor walk-up in North Oakland. Why do you ask?"

Hector hesitates for a moment and then says something in Spanish to Sonia before looking at Arthur with a serious expression. "There is an evil spirit in your building. You must move as soon as possible."

Sonia then interjects, "You're in great danger staying there."

Hector looks again at his wife and tells her something else in Spanish, and they begin an extended conversation. Finally, Sonia turns to Arthur. "For now, you must return here, soon. Hector wants to prepare a protective necklace for you to wear around your neck at all times. You should wear it under your clothes next to your skin."

"It seems like he said more than that, because the two of you talked for a long time."

"I was explaining to Hector what kind of work you do and saying to him it would be hard for you to wear all-white clothes to work every day. That's when he advised me he will prepare beads for you."

Hector looks at Arthur for almost a minute before leaning across the table and saying, "You're one of us, you know?"

"I'm what one of you?"

"You should be initiated into Santeria."

"Why do you think that?"

"Because," Hector continues in English, "you hear and see spirits. You should study and become a Babalawo—one of

Orumali's priests—because you were born with the ability to connect with the spirit world."

"I will give it some thought," says Arthur.

Hector stands and holds out his hand, letting Arthur know his consulta is over. He wants to ask Hector how much is appropriate in making a donation to the Orishas and his Egun, but decides against it, given the sacredness of the consulta and the gravity of what was said to him. So Arthur writes what he considers to be a generous check and puts it on the coffee table. Sonia, who had momentarily left the room, returns with a glass of water for each of them and commands them both to drink. After finishing his water, Hector makes the sign of the cross several times over Arthur's heart, chanting something in Lacumi.

Arthur thanks Hector, who never once looks at Arthur's check, and says good-bye before Sonia walks with him to the door.

"Arthur, please call me soon so that I can tell Hector when you will return for your beads. Knowing Hector, he'll need two or three days to prepare them for you. Will you?"

"Yes, I will, Sonia, and thank you for setting up this consulta. Your husband's given me a lot to think about, and I am grateful."

"Be careful, Arthur," Sonia says and closes the door behind him.

CHAPTER 17

SHIVA AND PARVATI

Two hours had passed by the time Narada finished the second round of his story, and his listeners remained still with their eyes closed. After sealing the Akasha, the storyteller commanded those gathered to open their eyes and gaze at the fire that was still ablaze in front of them. Narada said to them, "All that you heard and felt, before tonight's story began, will be forgotten by the time you reach your dwelling. But the narrative itself will remain alive in you. Speak freely about it, and bring others with you the night after tomorrow. Tonight, sleep well; and when you wake, give thanks to Jah for your life and your energy restored."

He clapped his hands, and the fire was immediately extinguished. "Amantahu," he shouted to the crowd.

"Hiya Aman," they replied, as many lifted their heads and raised their arms to the night sky, and the second night of storytelling was over.

Then an unusual event occurred. As Ja'Usu's inhabitants passed vendors on the side of the road leading to the Fajaruddin gate, they noticed to their amusement that all the hawkers were fast asleep. They were not shouting about buying sweet breads or something to drink; they were on the ground behind or in front of their makeshift stands, lying flat on their backs or sitting on their rears with their backbones leaning up against their stands, all fast asleep. Even when the people passing by shouted or laughed at them, they did not wake, and some were even snoring.

When the patriarchs saw their hired workers sleeping, they were even more furious than they were with Narada for making the Oromo move closer to Ja'Usu's ring of listeners. As the rulers of the city walked down the path back to the main gate with their families, they cursed and shouted at their vendors, who did not even budge when kicked. Patriarch Safdar, the one who breaks the enemy's rank, and Patriarch Abdul Muntaqim, slave of him who punishes wrongdoings and seizes retribution, were so outdone by the sleeping hawkers snoring that their forceful kicks missed and sent them flying in the air, landing on their backs and dirtying their fine Persian and Egyptian robes. They both had to be rescued by members of their families.

Narada strode through the Fajaruddin gate and walked down the main street as those who had heard his story moved out of his way. They raised a hand to their chests or heads and gracefully nodded in greeting as he passed them. After reaching Ja'Usu's holy edifice, he turned south and walked down Masresha to its gate. Once at the southern entrance, he stopped and looked up at the night sky, which displayed twinkling stars like an expansive array of precious jewels around Great Mother's neck.

A clan of giggling hyenas soon invaded the stillness, followed by their maniacal laughter and whoops as they lowered their hindquarters and raised their heads to sniff the cool, crisp air. They cautiously moved closer to investigate the figure standing in the darkness, slowly surrounding him.

Arsalaan, the one they called the hyena man, sat with his back against Masresha's crumbling white wall and watched with suspicion as the stranger in the shadows walked through the gate.

Narada took a step forward when Arsalaan suddenly got up, shouting and punching the air, trying to distract the hyenas from getting any closer to the man standing and gazing into the darkness. The storyteller calmly turned to look at the hyena man, now hopping from one foot to the other like a man whose feet were being scorched by burning coals. The sight of the hyena man's yelling and frantic movements was hilarious to Narada.

The hyenas, heads held high and ears cocked back, looked poised to attack. Their mouths closed, the manes on their backs erect and their hindquarters high, they moved brazenly closer to the storyteller as they sniffed the air. Several scavengers were distracted by Arsalaan's antics and wavered between watching the one who fed them and the stranger whom they could dine on that night. The more Arsalaan stomped and screamed, the more the storyteller laughed, until the hyena man, completely spent, dropped to the ground in exhaustion.

"When you are able to get up, Arsalaan," said Narada, still laughing, "please light your oil lamp and come and sit by me." He continued ignoring the fifteen or so hyenas that encircled him.

After the storyteller sat on the ground and folded his legs, he extended his arm and slowly lowered his open hand, commanding the animals to lie down on the ground like obedient dogs. Arsalaan saw and was astonished at the scavengers' unusual behavior. They had never done this for him or anyone he could remember. Although he had conquered his own fear by holding scraps of meat between his teeth to let hyenas feed from his mouth, he understood that he never really had power over them. Arsalaan was safe from attack only because he fed them.

Seeing what the stranger had done, Arsalaan did as he was asked. He lit the oil lamp and held the light as he walked through the ring of hyenas lying quietly on the ground. Once inside the docile animals' circle, he sat in front of the stranger, whom he recognized as the one who had stopped him on the street.

"So, you it is!" said Arsalaan with surprise. "The storyteller, are you? The one everyone about is speaking?"

Narada studied the young man's face and saw that Arsalaan's mind was in conflict with his soul. For natural to every spirit was the intrinsic awareness that it came from joy, that for joy it lives, and that for joy it will depart once again. But Arsalaan's mind was consumed with the pain of his father's death and the self-inflected guilt that he had caused it. So while his thoughts filled him with self-loathing, his soul retreated from the internal battle of challenging his mind, deciding, instead, to wait until Arsalaan's death, when his spirit would be set free.

Reading this conflict in the madman's eyes, Narada gently tapped his forehead with his finger, forcing Arsalaan's spirit to leave his physical form. His soul, now free to go, traveled across a vast divide before reaching foreign soil to suddenly materialize in another mature human body. While it was unsettling for Arsalaan's soul to find itself in an unfamiliar human form, it also felt relief and welcomed relinquishing the burden of existence in a troubled young man.

Arsalaan's spirit in its new body was surrounded by a slow-moving mass of people who did not notice his unexpected arrival. They simply continued moving forward, all tightly packed together, advancing into the inner sanctum of an ancient temple built of granite rock. As far as the eye could see, an undulating wave of men and woman streamed forward, forcing Arsalaan's spirit in a new body and everyone in front of and behind him to move forward, pushed by the sheer weight of the human caravan. No one talked or complained about the congestion or being pushed beyond endurance. It was impossible to stumble or fall in this passageway or walk over to the side to allow this sea of humanity to pass on by. As the spirit of Arsalaan's new body was taller than most, the men and women behind him leaned against his back so they could move along faster than the people near them.

This new awareness of forced movement brought him near to panic when those near him started chanting: "Nataraj Nataraja Jay Shiva Shankara Nataraja, Shivaraj Shivaraja Shambho Shankara Shivaraja." They sang in praise of Lord Shiva, the Hindu deity who clears away the old and shattered and makes way for the creation of new life. They intoned this Sanskrit verse over and over again with such passion and joy that Arsalaan's spirit was caught up in the crowd's ecstasy as it, too, started chanting in praise of Lord Shiva. As the people and Arsalaan's new body moved forward, they entered a large room. His spirit was drawn to the raised area in the center of the chamber, where a huge mound of black marble molded into a phallus-shaped stone rested on a pedestal, symbolizing Shiva's energy and potential. Directly above the mound was a large, inverted cup, representing the creative energy of Shiva's divine female counterpart, Parvati. Arsalaan's soul intuitively grasped the union of Shiva and Parvati as the eternal process of creation and regeneration. At that moment when the hyena man's soul in a different body was experiencing the cosmic union of Shiva and Parvati, Narada planted a thought-seed in Arsalaan's mind, still lodged in his original physical form and sitting with the storyteller outside Ja'Usu's ancient wall.

"It is your generation's responsibility, Arsalaan, to prepare and make way for the next wave of souls to be brought into this life. Who will be born from your loins, Arsalaan, and how are you preparing for their coming?"

Arsalaan's mind was receptive to Narada's thought-seed, but he was not prepared for the instant return of his own soul from a distant place, which settled back in him with a jolt. Its homecoming made the young man's eyes open wide and stare straight ahead while causing a silly grin to break out all over his face. Still, the life-negating thoughts that imprisoned his psyche were stubborn and refused to be dislodged as Arsalaan's relaxed, smiling face transformed into a grief-stricken, tortured mask.

"My own father I have killed," he blurted out. "Against Jah and man I have offended, so to suffer I must. For me, the life I used to live, over it is."

"You did not murder your father, Arsalaan."

"Wrong you are," he replied with a hint of anger. "Of what you speak of, you do not know. From a broken heart my father died, after the shame and dishonor on my family I brought. This stain my father could not bear. And for my disgrace with his own life he paid, and for that, pay I must."

"You truly are your father's oldest son. And in Ja'Usu tradition, you were to obey your father's wishes and assume the role of family patriarch when he asked you to do so. And yes, you disobeyed him. Instead of becoming patriarch, you told your father to lift what you considered was a burden. You pleaded with him to give the honor to your younger brother, whom you said was better suited to be patriarch and represent your clan."

"Truth there is in what you say. Houses for Ja'Usu's poor to build, and the art of roofing from a Nubian mason, to learn I wanted. A master builder to be I desired."

"But your rejection of becoming patriarch and your actions did not kill your father. He was a patient man with a strong will and thought that eventually you would accept your rightful position as patriarch of the family. So he was prepared to wait for you to make the right decision when someone decided to poison him."

"This to know, how do you?" asked Arsalaan.

"I know many things great and small."

"Well, to believe you, I do not."

"Yes, you do," said Narada.

"My father—who poisoned him?"

"If I told you, you would take revenge, and that action would set you back another ten thousand years."

"About ten thousand years, what do I care?"

"If you take revenge, Arsalaan, your spirit will be obstructed in its evolution for the next ten thousand years, because it will take that long in Earth time to overcome what your revenge will set in motion. Not just for you, but for others in your clan. And your father, who remains for now in the spirit world, does not want to be the cause of that."

"What my father wants, how could you know?"

"He is talking to me as I am speaking to you."

"Talking to you, how can that be? What is he saying?"

"He begs me not to reveal his killer, because he knows you will want revenge, and that act will devastate your family," said Narada.

"But why? Our right to take revenge, it is. To comprehend, I do not. All that you say for me to believe, it is hard. Too much, it is."

"I understand."

Arsalaan looked at the stranger with alarm and moved back as far as he could without stirring the hyenas. "Sir, who are you?"

"Your people say I am a jinn that has taken on human form, but I am much, much older than any jinn."

"Should afraid I be?"

"I have given you no cause to be alarmed. That was why you chose to come and sit by me."

"Here, why did you come?" asked Arsalaan.

"Your soul cried out to me."

"On Masresha you I saw. In front of me you stopped."

"Listen carefully, Arsalaan. Your mind flutters like the wings of a hummingbird, obsessed with fragmented thoughts that constantly feed your torment. But your soul that is spirit identifies with Spirit. They are one and the same, and all that is and ever will be. But the intensity of your anguish over your father's death blocks your soul's ability to inform your thinking and has imprisoned it. So when your spirit became aware of my presence, it cried out to me. That is why I am here. I have done what I could. The rest is up to you."

"To me the rest is…what to do? Look, mind…soul…spirit, understanding I do not have," said Arsalaan with some frustration, unable to thread the meaning of it all.

"In time you will, Arsalaan; in time you will."

"The hyenas, who you are do they know?"

"No, but they sense a power stronger than they and do as I command."

"The storyteller all of Ja'Usu is talking about, are you?"

"Yes," said Narada.

"So, what is it you want me to do?" Arsalaan finally said, not knowing what else to say or do.

Narada stood and started to walk away before stopping to say, "You are born on Earth to exercise your free will, so the spirit within you may grow through the experience of living. If I told you what to do, Arsalaan, I would be interfering with your learning, which I cannot do."

And he continued on his way into the city, but not before planting another thought-seed that settled through intuition in Arsalaan's now receptive mind: Clean up your old house, live in it, and begin life anew.

"By what name you should I call?" shouted the hyena man as the storyteller reached the Masresha gate.

"You may call me Narada or storyteller. It is up to you," he replied without stopping or turning around.

Arsalaan watched him walk away and disappear into the night, and then he became distracted by the hyenas waking from their sleep. He had just reached for his oil lamp and stood to go sit by the wall when, suddenly, it occurred to him to return to the compound and house he had built so very long ago.

CHAPTER 18

ENCOUNTERING THE MADMAN

Morning prayers had ended, and Ja'Usu's men were putting on their sandals and leaving the holy edifice when an old, blind Oromo man with a young boy was seen standing on the temple stairs. Jabir and Wakeel, who had finished their prayers, approached the old man and asked why he was in Ja'Usu so early and what he wanted.

"To the governing council to speak, I want."

They looked at the old Oromo from head to toe and asked if he was carrying a weapon, which he was not, and then Wakeel informed the patriarchs that the Oromo man wanted to speak to them. After having their morning meal served at the edifice, they had stayed behind to discuss the state of the city's wealth—which they saw as their very own—and conduct the business of the city. On hearing the Oromo's request, Chief Patriarch Murabbi, patron and guardian of the people, asked their Ja'Usu brother to politely tell the old man to come back another day, as the governing council was too busy to entertain his affairs. In truth, they were not preoccupied with anything except waiting for their servant-girl, Beena, to refresh their coffee and bring some more biscuits. And while they lingered, they wrapped themselves in cotton shawls to guard against the morning cold. Chief Patriarch Murabbi was especially sensitive to the chill seeping through the open windows and, to the chagrin of the other patriarchs, called for Beena to close the open wooden slats in all the windows before serving them their coffee.

They sat idly on the Persian carpet, avoiding each other's eyes and not having any conversation. Some yawned listlessly while others became grumpy because they had to wait longer than usual for more of their morning meal. After a while, Chief Patriarch Murabbi intruded on their silence and said, "When our storyteller come closer in the circle the Oromo were told, very disturbing it was. His actions he must explain. To bring him before us, we must."

The patriarchs looked at each other to see who and how many of them supported old Murabbi's demand, when Patriarch Taqiyy, the pious and righteous one, spoke up. "You may I remind, his storytelling outside the Fajaruddin gate so the Oromo could attend, we agreed."

"Yes," replied Murabbi, "but anywhere to sit they wanted, it did not mean."

"As you may recall," said Patriarch Izzat, one who is held in high rank and honor, "with Ja'Usu people in the circle, the Oromo in the back, Narada directed them to sit. Before, off to the side they were sitting." Several of the patriarchs nodded their heads in agreement.

"Well, I still do not like it," concluded Murabbi.

When Beena arrived with more coffee and biscuits, the issue of where the Oromo sat was forgotten as quickly as raising their warm biscuits to their mouths. But Patriarch Aschenaki, the distressed, was troubled not about where or how near or far the Oromo sat but whether the story the Oromo were hearing would cause them to think about their own status in Ja'Usu. He thought about Arthur's comment to his friend, something about black people being nothing more than a resource to exploit, with no collective power to do nothing more than be passive…something or the other. And then this Arthur fellow questioned whether it is possible for a people to choose and shape their own destiny. Such thinking, he thought, could be dangerous.

Would the Oromo begin to think Narada's story was really about them? And did not the storyteller say to the council that words had power? A shiver went up Aschenaki's spine, but then he thought he might be making a big deal out of nothing. He had to remind himself that the Oromo, with their silly nomadic superstitions, were not bright enough to draw such heady conclusions. And besides, this whole storytelling idea was his own, so how could he tell the council the story they were listening to could be dangerous? He took comfort in knowing the narrative would end in five more nights and vowed to keep these random thoughts to himself and out of any future conversation.

Therefore, instead of sharing these disturbing notions with his fellow patriachs, Aschenaki dismissed his musings and said to the council, "This Arthur fellow, weak I think he is, because his women he cannot control. His woman, away from him she runs, and another woman…this doctor person, what he should do she tells him. And a jinn he must be, but he does not know it. Crazy I think he is."

"Yes, right you are, Aschenaki," replied Patriarch Liyaqat, one worthy and deserving of merit, eager to talk about Narada's story. "Jinns in the future surprised to hear I was, and with all their thingamajigs and contraptions, very little about spirits they seem to know. And that big woman on that little man beating up, did you see? Now, a Ja'Usu woman…huh, something like that could never happen."

"To understand I do not," said Patriarch Abdul Muntaqim, slave of him who punishes wrongdoings and seizes retribution, "how these people money to make. Anything to trade, I do not see; no gold, no silver exchanges hands, so how themselves to support do they?"

"The woman on the speaking machine that called Arthur… Alice Tan, herself she calls," replied Patriarch Ihtesham, the respectable and honorable one, "something of value him she will give. Maybe like our silver and gold, it is."

"What for," interrupted Patriarch Tahawwur, the rash, "healthy people to make? For wrong do not get me. For those black people of the future I feel shame, because descendants of Africans they are, but money for better to make them feel, no sense does it make; a waste it is. If no businesses they have, well, how better can they feel…huh? Like our vendors they are. For someone else, not themselves they work. Tan's money take, yes… but businesses they should make. That's what I say."

"What mean do you?" interrupted Aschenaki. "The children of slaves, they are. Like slaves, still they think. A kind of syndrome they have, and sick it makes them. So for them sympathy to feel, useless it is. Their own way let them find. Money for them, I would not give."

"Maybe the Oromo of the future, they are? Maybe the future children of the Oromo, they are? What to think do you?" Inquired Patriarch Izzat, one with high rank and honor, scanning their semicircle for a response. The origins of the future black people in Narada's story was such a new and odd idea that no one knew quite what to think or say. It was a notion just beyond their collective contemplation, except for Aschenaki, who dared not share what he thought about the subject.

"The Oromo, our slaves they are not," said Chief Patriarch Murabbi finally. The council members laughed, finding their chief's comment amusing.

"Then, what are they?" asked Aschenaki.

"If slaves they were, as they please they would not come and go. Oromo a conquered people they are, that's all."

"When the sun sets in the west, out of Ja'Usu they must be," Patriarch Taqiyy, the pious and the righteous, replied.

Several patriarchs, including Aschenaki, were visibly uncomfortable with the turn in the conversation and were relieved when Taqiyy, the pious and the righteous, continued, "Well, a fascinating story I think it is. No one in all my sixty years to Ja'Usu ever has come and a story in the future has told. Our stories from the holy books about our prophets and our god, Jah, only we tell. Needed and good to study they are, but Narada's story, magical it is. Moving pictures with words of a future people in a future world he paints. About their problems, and how with them they wish to deal, he tells us. In the future you feel as he is speaking; everything to watch is there. Narada's story for five more nights continues it will. Happy, me it makes."

"Your comments, euphoric and almost blasphemous they sound, Patriarch Taqiyy," said Aschenaki with a sardonic smile.

The patriarchs were surprised at Taqiyy's enthusiasm for Narada's narrative, and a few of them wondered if he had stayed up the night before, chewing kat before morning prayer. But the thought about kat was immediately dismissed as he was a patriarch and governing council member, and it was much too early in the day to think about such a deviant pastime.

"Well, for you so very pleased I am, Patriarch Taqiyy, the storyteller you are enjoying," said Chief Patriarch Murabbi. "But what to know I want, why last night all our vendors to sleep they went? And why to wake them we could not? That's what to know I want."

He glanced at their faces, searching for an answer that did not come. His expression was transfixed, like sitting on the toilet with anticipation when one is absolutely constipated.

Hohete caught Narada as he was leaving Ibrahim Hafez's compound. "Today, with you may I walk?"

She wore tight, burnt-orange leggings that rose up to her knees and then ballooned out underneath her loose-fitting light-blue dress. A bright green scarf was draped over her head and on to her shoulders, covering her face so that one could only see her eyes lined with charcoal dust.

Narada looked at Hohete and was reminded how beautiful she was, especially her eyes. He replied, "I thought it was discouraged for unmarried women to walk alone with men in Ja'Usu's streets, Hohete."

"Narada, it is, but already married I was, and a child and man I lost, so bad luck I am. No man or family my father for me they will ask, so with you to walk, what does it matter?"

"Come then, Hohete, let us walk together."

"But customary it is a little behind you for me to walk, it must be."

"Well, what does it matter, Hohete, if today you walk beside me?" And they both laughed as Narada echoed her own sentiment exactly.

It was a clear morning with no clouds in a pastel blue sky, and the sun was warm and pleasant. Spirals of white smoke rose from chimneys as women prepared their meals or heated water to give their children a skimpy washdown. The swish of stick brooms, made of dried olive-tree stems and bramble bush blown in from the desert, could be heard as women swept courtyards or scrubbed the entrances to their homes, making them shine the color of blood.

Hohete walked behind Narada down the narrow cobblestone lane from her father's compound to Fajaruddin where the street widened, with its open shops and Oromo women squatting next to whitewashed walls. But once they entered Fajaruddin and walked east toward Ja'Usu's center, Hohete caught up with him and walked by his side. She wanted to take hold of his arm, but such a display of public affection flew in the face of culture and tradition and, therefore, was frowned upon. So Hohete dismissed her desire and was content with walking beside her storyteller, despite the stares of disapproving or, perhaps, jealous eyes of women who concealed their emotions behind colorful scarves and black mascara.

The Oromo women they passed, while seemingly indifferent to Hohete, smiled at Narada and greeted him, nodding their heads as the two of them walked by. Reaching the holy edifice in the center of the city, Narada and Hohete turned northeast and walked up Mustakim, leading to the fifth gate that, as was Ja'Usu's custom, bore the same name as the road that led to it. Before reaching the entrance, they turned off Mustakim and onto a narrow lane, and Hohete asked, "Narada, where going are we, do you know?"

"Yes, Hohete, we are going to visit an old friend."

"You have friends in Ja'Usu, you never said."

The well-worn path was narrow and led into an isolated section of Ja'Usu between the Mustakim and the Khawar gates, where fewer inhabitants lived. The meager passageway conspired to make Hohete walk behind Narada as they continued down the lane. A blackbird glided overhead on invisible air currents and watched them as they moved along a shaded patch of broken cobblestone. Narada observed the bird that drifted on ahead of them before it began circling above a compound that was awash in sunlight.

When they arrived at the compound, which did not have a door, Narada walked through the opening; Hohete was uncertain whether she should follow him. Reminding herself she had nothing to fear with the storyteller around, she stepped through the entrance into a large, shabby courtyard, where, as she guessed, no one seemed to live. Pieces of broken mud brick and a shabby assortment of trash littered the ground. Even the large doors to the three empty buildings in the compound were gone. Hohete was about to peer into one of the houses when she was startled by a noise and looked up to see. Standing on the dome-shaped roof of the largest building was a figure of a man silhouetted by the harsh glare of the sun. She raised her hand to her scarf to make sure her head and face were covered and called out for Narada in alarm.

"Storyteller, is that you?" shouted Arsalaan from the rooftop. "To find me, how did you?"

He then saw Hohete and carefully moved to another spot on the roof so he could see her better. Now Hohete clearly saw him. He looked wild and unkempt. His chest was bare, and he wore dirty rags for clothes around his loins. His thick, nappy hair stood on end, and Hohete imagined that mice could nest in it without him ever knowing. Narada returned to her side, and she held his arm while she was looking up to see the man's face.

"Most everyone in Ja'Usu seems to believe the holy edifice is the only building in the city that has a dome-shaped roof. Who constructed these buildings, Arsalaan?" asked Narada, solely for Hohete's benefit.

"The Nubian's apprentice I was. With mud brick to build and a roof to vault, he taught me. After the holy edifice we finsihed, this compound I found, and these houses I built."

Hohete felt at ease with Narada standing near as she placed a hand over her eyes to block the sun's glare and gaze at the mad-man on the roof. She noticed the filthy rag around his head, the sweat that soaked his bare chest and back, and the flies that delighted in landing on his face. He did not seem to care.

"Why are you here, Arsalaan?" asked Narada, again for Hohete's benefit.

"Last night, humans you said on Earth for their free will to exercise they were put, correct? And since what actually happened to my father you revealed, here to return I decided and do what I set out to do; houses in Ja'Usu I will build. So this woman next to you, who is she?"

Before Narada responded, Hohete exclaimed almost in defiance, "Ibrahim Hafez's daughter, Hohete Ibrahim I am."

Arsalaan was quiet while he removed the rag from his head, and the memory of her father came back to him. "Your man, Waheed Nuri, how is he?"

Hohete was taken aback by Arsalaan's question. How could he know her late husband, and was he insulting her by inferring he was still alive? She was puzzled by his question and did not answer him.

Narada understood the muddled thoughts in both their minds and broke the awkwardness of the silence between them. "I am pleased you decided to return to this house and will start building homes for the poor, but you will need laborers to make mud brick and to work the construction."

Arsalaan laughed and almost lost his balance while standing on the dome-shaped roof. "Yes, storyteller, laborers I will need, but hard that will be once the hyena man they find out I am."

"There are many poor in Ja'Usu, Arsalaan. People will trade their labor for a piece of gold or silver or something to eat. You will have no trouble finding them. They will find you."

Arsalaan finally grunted to acknowledge that he heard what was said and abruptly resumed work on his roof. He ignored his visitors as if they had already left. Hohete decided she did not like Arsalaan for the impolite way he treated them. As she followed Narada out the compound and onto the narrow lane, she realized who was standing on the roof. Over the years since Waheed's death, she had seen him on Ja'Usu's streets, carrying bones and the bowels of dead animals with a host of flies trailing behind him. The people called him the "hyena man" and stayed clear of him when he passed. No one called this madman by his name, even when they knew it. But Hohete never once imagined that this man could possibly have family in Ja'Usu, let alone know Waheed. How could Narada, a stranger in Ja'Usu, call that madman an old friend? Hohete was also eager to know whether Narada found Arsalaan rude and insulting and if the hyena man was mocking her when he asked about Waheed. So instead of staying behind him, she quickly caught up with the storyteller to ask about this madman and Narada's relationship to him. Narada anticipated Hohete's interest and was prepared to answers all her questions—except for who killed Arsalaan's father.

CHAPTER 19
ALL THAT CRAWLS IN THE NIGHT

Narada knew who was following him and was amused that Jumah thought he could find out where Ibrahim Hafez's compound was near Fajaruddin gate. Narada also understood that, even though he had now been supplying Jumah's street family with food for almost two weeks, the boy was still wrestling with whether or not to rob him. He was sympathetic to the boy's constant need to find food and shelter for his little band of street youth. He also protected them from the clutches of Ja'Usu's governing council, which was ever ready to arrest the boys. Because Jumah was older and committed to the group, they looked upon him as the parent they did not have; they relied on his leadership and judgment.

When Jumah caught up with Narada on the Dabbah road leading to the seventh or northwest gate with the same name, the storyteller planted a thought-seed in his mind: I wonder what will happen to us once the storyteller leaves and the food stops?

"Hey, storyteller, in this part of Ja'Usu, here what are you doing? Only poor people and shunned families here they live."

"Every day, I walk and see a different part of Ja'Usu. Is this where you and your boys live?"

"In Dabbah area to stay we are forced by Ja'Usu's council. If here we stay, us they will not bother. But if in other areas of the city us they find, the council, us they will try and catch—especially if some important donkey turd gets robbed. Then, even in Dabbah, us they will hunt."

"And what will they do if they catch you?"

"If someone gets robbed, even if nothing to do with it we have, we get picked up. And if the council, one of us they suspect, a hand or a foot as punishment they will cut off."

"So let me guess, your street family only steals from those who have no importance to the council…such as visitors to the city, like me. Am I right, Jumah?"

"Thanks for the food, storyteller. Your promise you kept; glad I am."

"Where are your friends today?" asked Narada.

"Somewhere safe stay until I get back, I told them."

"So, Jumah, will you return to robbing and stealing after I leave and the food runs out?"

"Survive we will," said Jumah. "What else do can we?"

"What would you think about working for food and shelter?"

"Who in their right mind us is going to hire? Living on the streets we are, and from the streets everybody in Ja'Usu knows we are. Like the people on the street in your future story, like them we are. Nobody about us a donkey turd gives."

"Oh, you have been listening to my story."

"Yeah, behind the hyena man way in the back we sit. But Isa afraid of snakes and scorpions he is, so sometimes whimpering he starts, and the story to follow I cannot."

"Well, from now on, Jumah, I will command all that crawls in the night to stay away from the area so Isa will not have to be afraid, and you can follow the narrative. Please tell him that."

"Storyteller, as crazy as the hyena man you are, but in a good way. The crawlies to command, you can do? "

"If you wish."

Narada's reply made Jumah laugh, and for a moment he forgot who and what he was as he kicked his feet in the air like a carefree soul with no pressing responsibilities. But when the piece of sharp metal he carried as a knife fell from his waist to the cobblestone, he caught himself feeling and playing like a child. His impulsiveness felt awkward, and he wanted to run, feeling open and vulnerable in sharing a fleeting joy with someone he did not know.

"Suppose, Jumah, you could feel as happy as you do right now every day, knowing you do not have to rob or steal to survive, anymore…knowing no one was out to capture you or your friends anymore. If you and they are willing to work and learn a skill, perhaps I can find you steady work."

"So what crazy donkey turd to work for pieces of silver or gold is going to give us?"

"Why would they be crazy, because if you were them you would not hire you?"

What the storyteller said was true, but Jumah kept his thoughts to himself and said nothing as they continued down Dabbah road. Once they reached the gate, Narada said, "If you meet me at Mustakim gate tomorrow at noon, I will show you a way."

And Narada walked away, up a narrow lane that led to Fozeia, or the north gate. Jumah watched Narada recede into the brilliant sunlight that flooded the lane as Arsalaan had once done before on Masresha when he was still the hyena man.

The Third Evening's Story

The purple-pink and bright-orange splash trailing the sun's procession over the western horizon lingered as luminous stillness on the lip of the desert. Ja'Usu's inhabitants were already gathering for story night and staking out a place on the ground as close as possible to the circle's center. The Oromo were also assembling, but they were standing off to one side waiting for Ja'Usu's people to be seated first before they found space on the outer edges of the ring. More than 750 people were already settled and waiting for the storyteller as more of Ja'Usu's populace arrived, eager to hear Narada's story.

As twilight descended into night, and the first blush of twinkling stars and planets became visible in the celestial heavens, the patriarchs with their women and children in hand passed through the Fajaruddin gate. Seeing the enormous crowd, they were shocked by how large the storyteller's audience had become. This time the vendors were outside the gate hawking their wares, as Chief Patriarch Murabbi had admonished them for falling asleep. They were shouting to the multitude, peddling sweet hot tea, an assortment of sweet breads, and meat and vegetable samosas. Murabbi and his elderly wife, Adeeba, nodded approvingly as they made their way past the peddlers and stepped onto their dais to take seats on their platform.

A moment later, as soon as those in the gathering closest to the center spotted Narada and the Hafez family passing though the main gate, they stood to welcome them. When the people in the innermost circle rose, those behind them also stood, although they could not spot the one they were patiently waiting to see. Of course, the patriarchs and their entourage remained seated, as it was unfitting for them to rise for someone they considered beneath their station—except for Patriarch Taqiyy the pious, the righteous, who stood with the rest of the gathering to welcome Narada for his third night of the story.

Imtiyaz and Tabassum had just finished stacking dry wood and desert brush for the evening's fire and remained in the center of the ring, waiting for instructions to light the kindling as Narada, Ibrahim Hafez, Hohete, and Ayaat made their way toward the inner circle. Once there, the Hafez family stayed next to him as Narada first raised and then slowly lowered his hands for the people to sit as he remained standing. Then, first turning to the north, and then to the east, and then south, and finally to the west, Narada bowed in each direction in reverence to Mother Earth.

He then sat on the mat reserved for him and noticed the masses of people who had come to hear his third night of the story. Peering into the darkness accentuated by scattered tiny flames from oil lamps, he looked for the Oromo, who had found places to sit, again, at the far edges of Ja'Usu's circle; and behind them were Jumah's boys and Arsalaan, who sat apart from everyone.

Narada motioned to Imtiyaz and Tabassum to light the fire the people now considered sacred. He then closed his eyes and prayed to the Great Mystery for all to hear. And even though no one but Narada knew the purpose or function of the blaze, the people intuitively related their ability to hear and watch the story unfold with the life of the fire.

Narada listened to the sparks ignite and looked at the nascent flames flicker in the darkness as everyone silently kept their eyes on him. Those who had been present during the first two nights of storytelling closed their eyes as soon as the fire was lit and, on their own, entered their quiet space within. They waited patiently for the story to begin as they discerned in the stillness the perceivable sound of what was unknown—the Aum, the Amin, the Amen, the Holy Ghost. Some of the people were absorbed by the hum, the omniscient heartbeat of the universe.

Now the fire was ablaze as its crackling flames lit up and warmed the night. The people looked on in wonder and anticipation as the flames danced and leaped into an ink-black sky, and Narada sat in silence, with his body very still. He then intoned in an unknown tongue that the people of Ja'Usu and the

Oromo did not recognize or understand. The earth shook until the people were afraid.

And as the trembling subsided in throbbing tremors, Narada raised his arms in praise and supplication to thank the Great Mystery for responding to his prayer. For the Akasha now opened again, letting Narada read from the imperishable records of celestial light the future of human thought and action. The people's fears gradually diminished as the ground stopped shaking, and they settled into a communal trance.

Narada opened his eyes and said in a thundering voice, "Now, all the crawling creatures moving among those here, go underground and sleep until I choose to wake you." And the multitude of snakes and lizards and toads and scorpions and sand crabs and fleas and anything that crawled did as they were commanded.

Then, directing his words to the gathering, Narada said, "If you try to experience my narrative with your mind, you will surely be lost and confused and will quickly tire of listening. But if you let yourself relax and stay very still, allowing your inner vision to witness the story as it is revealed, the narrative will be easy for you to follow."

Ending with these tidings, the storyteller once again read from the Akasha: "Once upon a future time, in a distant world, in a different age…"

CHAPTER 20

AN OVERGROUND RAILROAD

Arthur calls the leadership meeting to order and states that because he has not received comments about the summary notes from the previous meeting, he'll move on with today's agenda.

Roy Thomas, director of minority affairs at Unified Way, raises his hand and says, "I'm sorry I couldn't attend that meeting. I was at a two-day conference, in Chicago. I just want to say the four principals agreed upon are a great achievement; however, I think we should revisit these principles and consider the impact on this leadership group if we continue to support them the way they're written."

"Please explain," says Arthur.

"Well...I mean they raise a lot of questions," continues Roy. "How are we going to implement these principles...I mean really, Arthur? And are we talking about involving other minority groups, like Latinos and Asians, who also suffer from chronic diseases and may also have a health crisis on their hands? There are only black people sitting up in here. And it seems to me politically unwise for us to focus our sole attention on the health issues of African Americans when the Bay Area's demographics are definitely multicultural."

"Mr. Thomas, it's unfortunate that you were unable to attend Aaron Campbell's meeting at the public health department or the last two sessions of this group," says Arthur. "If you had been present, I'm confident you'd have a better appreciation for the issues we're challenged to address. The last meeting was a working session where those present developed the principles or value statements you have mentioned, and they've already been unanimously endorsed and approved."

Arthur, seeing that Roy wants to continue, explains the rules and voting system. Then, after summarizing the conversation he had with Dr. Lightfoot at Miss Ollie's, Arthur asks Aaron Campbell to introduce her to the leadership. Arthur is relieved he doesn't have to facilitate this segment of the meeting and allows his thoughts to drift back to his consulta. He recalls telephoning his mother in New York after leaving Hector and Sonia's house to ask about the weather on the night he was born.

"Arthur, you were almost born in the backseat of a taxicab," his mother recalled. "It snowed so hard, I almost didn't make it to the hospital. In Freedman's lobby they put me in a wheelchair and immediately rolled me into the maternity ward. Lord, I had to hold my legs together to stop from spitting you out on that cold marble floor, Arthur! That was a night I'll always remember."

His mother's words made Hector's consulta all the more plausible...that this leaving his body is a gift...that he should be one of them...that he's in grave danger remaining in his apartment. Arthur's mind drifts into wondering about the menace Hector claims is in his building. How would he go about finding a new place to live, let alone find the time to return to Hector's for protection beads, given his workload and efforts to secure more funding for the new project? Then the image of the skull and crossbones that appeared out of nowhere jars his thoughts, and applause interrupts his daydreams.

"Many of us as health professionals and community leaders tend to think, act, and talk about the African American community as something outside of ourselves," Hachi begins, "as if we're not part of the community we're here to talk about or serve. And as a result, we're susceptible to that disease I like to call I-know-best-what's-good-for-our-community-disorder. I, too, suffer from this disorder at times when I see patients and advise them on their treatment options or on how to manage their illnesses. And that's part of our job, right? But the reality is that your advice or treatment will only be effective if the patient or client is willing to follow your plan. So the real question is, how receptive or motivated are they to follow your advice or your directions...the prescriptions you write out for them?"

"I agree with your perspective, Dr. Lightfoot, and know exactly what you're talking about," says Dr. Joe Braxton. "I have a family practice up on Pill Hill, and there's a physician in our office who is at least 100 pounds overweight. At one of our weekly staff meetings, he was asked how he treats his patients who are overweight and diagnosed with type two diabetes. He said he puts them on insulin. Someone asked him, 'Do you recommend that they try to lose weight and change their eating habits as a way to manage their diabetes?' He said sure. So another doctor said to him, 'How you gonna tell somebody that they're overweight and they should change their eating habits when you're terribly overweight yourself?'"

The room fills with laughter. Dr. Lightfoot suggests they serve as role models and begin as an experiment with the whole group serving as support to each participant's efforts to make better health choices. Then questions arise about how changing their behavior as professionals will help an entire community.

"This strategy reminds me of the conductors on the Underground Railroad," Reggie Johnson, youth program director from United Youth Leadership, interjects. "You dig what I'm sayin'? One conductor on the underground…well, they could help a few runaway slaves only get so far, but when you had a whole network of conductors each doing their little part, that's when the Railroad, carrying an enslaved people to freedom, took off. What you talkin' about is a modern-day overground railroad. Maybe we could call our role as community models 'health conductors'…health conductors on the overground railroad."

There is much laughter, but uncertainty lingers.

"Well, exactly how would that work?" asks Fatima Maloud from the American Society of Hypertension. "Do you mean this large group of twenty, possibly thirty-five people would get involved in my personal business? I don't know if I'm up for that, Dr. Lightfoot."

"Don't you see," replies Dr. Lightfoot, "in asking that very question, Fatimah, you're having to deal with principle number two: we will ask for support from others. How you handle both your need for privacy and, at the same time, find support from the group will inform the overall experiment—and, in the long term, the development of a community action plan. Perhaps leadership needs to be divided into smaller support groups with no more than three or four people in each cluster. Members in each group could then share with one another what health challenge or challenges they choose to work on during the course of this pilot study. You could exchange phone numbers so those in the same support group could contact one another to find out how a member is progressing in addressing his or her personal health concerns. Maybe group members can get together once or twice a month to participate in a health-related activity, together. You could mutually agree, for example, to walk Lake Merritt together or meet at a restaurant after work for conversation and a good healthy meal…take an aerobics class together…be creative.

"And the reason group support is important, even necessary, is that we need to be held accountable to each other. If we share with one another in our small clusters what we specifically plan to work on, healthwise, knowing that we're going to be asked about our progress during a telephone call or in a group meeting, we have a better chance of actually following through on our commitment to ourselves. Does that make sense?"

"But I think, Dr. Lightfoot, we still need good health-related information," says Samuel Spivey, representing a parent education program in West Oakland. He hadn't attended the last leadership meeting. Several members nod their heads or voice their agreement following his comment.

"I fully agree. That's why I suggest that the entire leadership… I mean those participating in such a social laboratory meet, perhaps, once a month for the duration of the experiment for a workshop on some aspect of the metabolic syndrome." Hachi stops and waits for the response she knows will come. She didn't anticipate Dr. Braxton to be the first to speak up.

"Brilliant idea, Doc…for those of you who don't know, the metabolic syndrome is a constellation of conditions or traits that you may have that make you prone or susceptible to any number of chronic illnesses…coronary heart disease, diabetes, stroke, and other diseases…conditions like a large waistline—especially excess fat around the stomach; a high triglyceride level—a type of fat found in the blood; low HDL—sometimes called good cholesterol, because it removes the bad cholesterol from your arteries; a high blood sugar level, which leads to diabetes; and high blood pressure, which, over time, can damage your heart and lead to plaque buildup in your blood vessels. If you have three or more of these risk factors, you're more likely to ultimately suffer from one of the diseases I've already named and more. So you see why the good doctor suggests we take a look at the metabolic syndrome.

"But I want to add another piece," continues Dr. Braxton, "that we should focus on in any social experiment, as you say, and that is: we need to deal with stress. Man...chronic stress is killing us. We'd have to learn stress reduction, stress management, because stress is the root cause of so many diseases."

Several more questions and answers ensue before Arthur calls for a vote on Hachi's proposal. Then John Sutton from the YMCA slowly raises his hand and patiently waits to be called upon. Arthur knows whatever John has to say will affect the outcome of a vote.

"I have two comments," says John. "First, Dr. Lightfoot, are you prepared to facilitate such a project if we approve it?"

"Yes."

"And second," directing this comment to Arthur and the leadership, "I would like to suggest, if we do vote to accept Dr. Lightfoot's proposal, that the program committee come back to this group with a very clear goal for the project."

"Point of clarification, John," says Arthur. "Are you also saying that you would like leadership to vote the project up or down once the committee returns with its findings?"

"That's correct."

Arthur quickly asks who seconds the motion, and then the group takes a vote. After completing the count, the vote to move Hachi's proposed project forward carries eighteen to four; the motion passes, and the meeting is adjourned."

It's a little after three in the afternoon when Arthur returns to his office and receives a message from Gracie that Alice Tan from the Foundation has called. Immediately, he picks up the phone to call her back and is surprised to learn from Alice that she has already talked with Aaron Campbell at public health about leadership's meeting with Dr. Lightfoot and is keen about her self-help model. She likes the culturally rooted approach to alleviating the health crisis; and even though the health emergency itself would take years to turn around, she believes the Trust and its leadership can make a difference. Alice surprises Arthur by telling him she's already met with her staff and the Foundation's vice president for programming, and he's agreed to give the Trust a general support grant for one year out of his discretionary fund to support Hachi's experiment.

"This is wonderful news, Alice. I know we wouldn't have gotten this immediate support if you didn't believe in the Trust or the work of the leadership group."

"Don't thank me, Arthur. Thank Ralph Needleman, our vice president, when you see him and Aaron for his wholehearted endorsement of your project. Ciao," she says and hangs up the phone.

CHAPTER 21
EL SEÑOR IS BACK

Arthur knocks on his neighbor's door across the hall to see how El Señor is doing. Knowing Natalie liked cats, he had brought her a male Siamese kitten as a birthday gift. It didn't work out, though, because neither of them was ever home, and the kitten commenced urinating on the carpet instead of in its litter box. They were going to give it to the American Society for the Prevention of Cruelty to Animals, but their two neighbors down the hall—Mrs. Valencia and her daughter, Julia—volunteered to care for him. Mrs. Valencia wanted the kitten because it was male, and she desired male energy in her apartment to replace her late husband, Señor Valencia, who died a year earlier while in the house. She renamed the cat El Señor and, like with her husband, only speaks to him in Spanish.

After peering at Arthur through the peephole, his neighbor opens the door, grabs Arthur's arm, and pulls him in, quickly closing the door behind him. It's just an odd habit of hers.

"Do you know what El Señor is doing?" she asks.

"Oh, Mima!" Julia exclaims as he goes to sit on the sofa.

"Oh no…Arthur, do you know what he's doin'?" Mrs. Valencia says before switching into Spanish.

"Mima, speak English; Arthur doesn't speak Spanish."

Without taking another breath, Mrs. Valencia shifts back to English. "This cat, he goes around and around in a circle...faster and faster until he gets the speed and—voom! Straight up the wall. Meda! Meda!"

Extending her outstretched finger along the invisible path the cat takes on the floor and around the room, Mrs. Valencia repeats, "El Señor, he gets the speed. Meda! Meda! El gato runs in a circle around the room and straight up this wall, here...here to the ceiling...then drops to the floor. Can you believe that?" she says, not quite believing it herself.

Arthur looks over at El Señor, who's curled up in the woman's dead husband's chair, resting on a large brown pillow. "Do you have any trouble with the cat peeing on your carpet?" he asks.

"Oh, no," Mrs. Valencia replies with a hint of reproach. "He has his own bathroom."

Sunlight streams through the living-room windows onto El Señor's sleek, wheat-colored fur. His tail lazily waves to and fro, until he seems to forget he has a tail and drifts off to sleep.

Mrs. Valencia rushes over to her precious El Señor and says, "Vente! Vente! Show Arthur what you can do!"

"You know he's not gonna do anything 'cause you ask him to, Mima," says Julia as she washes the dirty dishes in the sink. El Señor opens his beautiful blue eyes to look at the pleading woman in front of him before yawning out of boredom, stretching his legs, and resuming his siesta in her late husband's chair.

"Ayee, por Dios!" exclaims Mrs. Valencia, raising her flabby, light-brown arms over her head in exasperation. Arthur laughs easily, thinking that El Señor knows he commands the household and the two women in it.

"Why is it that tenants who rent apartment one, downstairs, never seem to stay?" Arthur finally asks the two women.

"Neville and his wife, Arnell, left yesterday in the middle of the night."

"Did they take their furniture with them?" asks Julia.

"I don't know."

"Si, everybody leaves," Julia continues. "And the tenants before them stayed less than a year."

"Remember the fight they had when Neville ran up the stairs and into my apartment?" Arthur asks. "Neville told me he thought it strange that he and his wife fought all the time after moving into this building."

Mrs. Valencia places her index finger to her lips and motions for Arthur to cease talking. Julia stops washing her dishes and seems a little uneasy. Quickly rushing to the front door, Mrs. Valencia opens the peephole and looks into it before making the sign of the cross three times across her substantial bosom. After closing the tiny metal flap, she turns and says, "Arthur, we shouldn't talk about these things."

Julia hastily wipes her hands on a kitchen towel and pulls up a chair next to Arthur, who is still sitting on the couch.

"What things are you talking about?" Arthur inquires.

Julia now presses her finger against Arthur's lips. Mrs. Valencia joins him on the sofa but faces the front door as if suspecting that an intruder who hears anyone talking will break in.

"Let me tell you something, mi amigo..." confides Mrs. Valencia.

"Mima!" shouts Julia.

"Shush, Niña —he's got a right to know," her mother says, moving closer to Arthur on the couch. His eyes glance at each of them like neurotic glass marbles going from one face to the other, dumbfounded by the expression of foreboding on Julia's face.

"Know what...what is it I need to know?

"My uncle, Enrique, used to own this building," Julia reveals. "That's why Mima and me were able to move into this building."

"Enrique was my middle brother," says Mrs. Valencia as a point of clarification. "There's Hector, Paolo died...and then Enrique he died too, and then my—"

"Mima, we're not talking about your brothers right now, OK?"

"Oh, sorry..."

"OK," continues Julia, "my uncle Enrique owned this building. He rented that apartment downstairs to this man from the south or maybe from Guyana. I'm not sure. His name was..."

"Julia, don't!" Mrs. Valencia says in alarm.

"Don't what?" Arthur asks, looking at both women.

"Mima doesn't like saying his name. She's afraid he might hear us talking about him and enter our apartment." Julia and her mother lean in closer, and Arthur moves closer, too, until their three faces are almost touching.

"Well...go on," whispers Arthur. "You don't need to say his name, but please continue your story."

"He was an evil man and always drinking. He rarely left that apartment and usually had the liquor store deliver what he drank," Julia discloses. "Sometimes, you'd see him walking down the street with a bottle of liquor and cursing as he walked. And when he drank, he sometimes kept the front door to his apartment open. And when he couldn't make it to his bathroom, he'd relieve himself on the wall in the hallway.

"My uncle wanted to get rid of him, but the man went to a tenant's rights organization, and they took Enrique to court. The judge told my uncle that since the man had a long-term lease and paid his rent on time, he couldn't legally be evicted. So we were stuck with him."

"But what does this evil tenant have to do with Neville and Arnell moving out?"

"Ayeee, por Dios!" exclaims Mrs. Valencia. "One night Julia was coming home, and that man had his door open drinking and cursing. I was waiting for her at the top of the stairs, because I knew he was trouble. When he saw Julia pass his door, he stumbled into the hallway..."

Julia suddenly places her hands over her eyes as if her mother's words bring back a flood of painful memories. "That nasty man pulled his...you know, out of his underwear and was shaking it at her. Julia ran up the stairs, and..."

"When I got to the top of the stairs and turned around," Julia continues, "I was more angry than scared. He was still playing with his...his, you know, and saying something I didn't understand. Drunk—he was drunk! And I got so angry that I said to him, 'Why don't you drop dead? Just drop dead!'"

Mother and daughter fall silent, sit back on their seats, and gaze at one another as if to see who will speak first while Arthur waits patiently, looking from one woman to the other. Mrs. Valencia is the first to lean forward, and she whispers, "That same night...that evil man, el murió. He dropped dead! Dead!" she says and quickly slaps her two hands together and then away, like they were two appendages passing in the night.

"How did he die?" Arthur asks, his mouth wide open.

"We never did find out," answers Julia. "But since then, no one has been able to live in his apartment for too long."

"We think he's never left the building," Mrs. Valencia confides. "He's angry, and his spirit is not at peace. He's still here; and if you let him, Arthur, he can make trouble."

Arthur now sits back on the sofa and remembers Hector's admonition—there's an evil spirit in your building, and he can do you harm. He realizes he hasn't returned to the Babalawo for his protective beads. He now sees he's been reckless in not taking Hector's warning seriously and take steps to move out of the building. Julia and her mother look at him and wonder what he's thinking.

"Well," says Arthur, "if you believe his spirit remains in that apartment and menaces the building, why do you stay here?"

"Do you see our altar over there with Mother Mary on the wall, the holy water, and that burning white candle?" asks Mrs. Valencia, pointing to a corner of the room. "We own this building now, and she protects us from him."

"Is it because of his spirit that you pull everyone who visits into your apartment and then quickly slam the door? Do you think he might try to enter with them?"

"He might try, but he can't stay in here with Mother Mary watching over us," says Julia.

"And all the hair on El Señor's back would stand up on end, if evil enters here," asserts Mrs. Valencia.

"Thank you for telling me. If I'm going to continue living here, I better learn to protect myself as well."

"Si, we want you to stay, Arthur," says Mrs. Valencia. "He cannot hurt you if you protect yourself."

Arthur returns to his flat, and as he sits alone at his own kitchen table, he surveys his apartment and the mess surrounding him. Arthur wonders if Julia's evil spirit has anything to do with his own constant fights with Natalie. And again, he recollects his encounter with the skull and crossbones that appeared in his bedroom. It certainly was a warning sign. He questions whether that spirit was also present then. It all makes sense now, as unearthly as it feels and sounds.

CHAPTER 22
BALL AND JACKS

Arthur arranges for the ad-hoc committee to meet at Silvestre Collins's small bed-and-breakfast on Pill Hill, well situated between downtown Oakland and Summit Hospital, where primary-care physicians and medical specialists have their offices. A former IBM executive who took his retirement money purchased this old vacant mansion and converted it into an urban bed-and-breakfast.

Early, Arthur sits in Silvestre's ground-floor living room, sipping coffee and reviewing the day's agenda as he waits for committee members to arrive. If Hachi's project is going to win the approval of leadership, they must agree on the ultimate goal of the project, identify the objective measurements to monitor progress, and work out the remaining details he can incorporate into a proposal for Alice Tan.

The room is comfortable and meticulously designed, with cream-colored wallpaper imprinted with thin, red-and-gold vertical lines. A cushy red-and-gold sofa regally sits as the centerpiece of the room on a plush, caramel-colored carpet, adorned with an array of handwoven Turkish floor pillows. Two matching armchairs with tan seat cushions complement a long, dark wood table, nestled under a large bay window with lace curtains. A large fireplace framed in exposed red brick dominates the room.

Morning light streams through the bay window and sheer white curtains, accenting the metallic sheen of a pot of fresh coffee and carefully arranged white porcelain cups on the table. A large canister of hot water and a variety of caffeinated and herbal teas are equally displayed alongside an assortment of fresh muffins and bagels with cream cheese on a sterling silver tray. Next to the platter, a crystal glass bowl filled with cut-up pieces of fresh cantaloupe and ripe watermelon sits alongside a silver serving spoon set at an appropriate angle on a small white dish near the bowl.

Dr. Hachi Lightfoot, Aaron Campbell, and the retreat's two facilitators, Ron Upchurch and Aisha Middleton, arrive together; and, after reading the sign posted on the wall, they take off their shoes at the front door. Silvestre stands patiently at the entrance to his living room and proudly smiles as he ushers his guests into the space where Arthur's waiting for them.

"Welcome to Silvestre's Bed and Breakfast, my humble abode," he says with a practiced humility that underscores the utter splendor of the room.

The doorbell rings, and the proprietor quickly returns to the front door to greet the rest of Arthur's guests: John Sutton from the Y, Sonia Cespedes, and Doris Whitehead, who at the last minute is substituting for Ellen Granger from West Oakland Community Clinic.

Before the retreat gets underway, Arthur formally introduces Silvestre to the committee and invites him to speak to the group. The proprietor welcomes his guests, offers a brief history of the home, and describes the facilities and services while passing out a brochure and his business card. With a grin, revealing the large gold tooth in the front of his mouth and holding his two hands together like an opera singer getting ready to perform an aria, he says to the group, "Your lunch this afternoon will be served in the adjoining dining room at twelve thirty. Please be so kind to be seated at this time, because your two chefs…Charles and I… have no wish to serve you a warmed-over meal. For your dining pleasure, today, you'll have black rice pilaf, your choice of grilled chicken or salmon, a tossed green salad with a homemade balsamic dressing, fresh-baked biscuits, and a surprise dessert."

After committee members serve themselves and find a place to sit, Ron Upchurch, a tall, lanky, middle-aged brother wearing a West African dashiki, stands in front of the fireplace, where he has already placed a potted leafy green plant and a glass of water on the floor. Holding his African drum between his knees, he raps a forceful and intricate rhythm, ending in a rapid pulsating cadence before calling out: "To God who is called by many different names, we give thanks and all praise as we mourn for the lives of our ancestors who were maimed and killed in the slave trade, who died in dungeons or in holes of slave ships during the middle passage, we say Ashe."

"Ashe," the group repeats, and he pours drops of water on the plant as a libation to the Creator and to the ancestors.

"We also honor our ancestors who were enslaved and survived in spite of their suffering to bring forth future generations, and we call upon them to share in our deliberations, especially Frederick Douglass, James Forten, Sojourner Truth, Harriet Tubman, and so many…many others, let us say Ashe."

"Ashe." And the water flows.

"And for those who led slave rebellions and gave their lives for us—Denmark Vesey, Nat Turner, John Brown, Gabriel Prosser, and so many, many more, say Ashe."

"Ashe." More water is poured.

"And we remember those of our immediate relatives who have passed over, and we invite them to join us here today. Speak their names, and we'll all say, Ashe.

"Daphne and Robert Whitehead," someone exclaims.
"Ashe."
"Roland Clark," another says.
"Ashe."
"Azizah Omenjhud."
"Ashe."
"Robert Campbell."
"Ashe."
"Sandra Middleton."
"Ashe."
"Rosa and Antonio Cespedes," says Sonia as her eyes fill with tears.

"In the name of all the generations that have come before us and for those still to come, we say, Ashe...Ashe...Ashe."

There follows a warp in time as each of them taps into the collective memory of a people and cultural feelings of sorrow and loss, of remembrance and hope. Arthur, sitting in a straight-backed chair, starts to daydream as he gazes out the bay window, when he notices on the ceiling a dazzling blue radiance moving across the room before slowly descending into the far corner of the living room. The luminous light settles in an area near the floor, and Arthur stands to see this strange occurrence more clearly, detecting something stirring in the light.

"Arthur...Arthur!" Aisha Middleton calls, but her voice is distant to him as his eyes are fixed on the luminescence in the corner.

He leaves his chair and walks slowly toward the light, as if its radiance might evaporate or disappear if he makes a noise or disturbs it in any way. He stops after a few feet and is stunned by what he sees in the glow: a small human figure sitting on the floor in the center of the brilliance.

Arthur's colleagues look at him and are puzzled by his bizarre behavior. They don't see the light in the corner or what he's watching on the living-room floor. He is transfixed by the brilliant blue light as he resumes walking toward the glow and is in awe as he peers into the brightness. In luminous light is a young, dark-skinned girl, playing with jacks on the floor. She tosses something small and round in the air in front of her and quickly snatches, with the same hand, tiny metal pieces off the floor before the little sphere hits the flooring. But the orb makes no thumping sound when hitting the surface.

The young child is absorbed in her play. Each time she throws the ball up in the air, she increases the number of jacks she tries to pick up, and each successful attempt completely delights her. Arthur looks on in disbelief and moves nearer to the light when he notices her hair's braided in two pigtails set high on each side of her head. She's barefoot but wears a spotless white dress that highlights her dark-brown skin. The little girl is utterly resplendent in her innocence and beauty.

Arthur leans over and is about to reach his hand into the light when, without warning, the young child looks up at him with large, luminous eyes and smiles, "I freed a thousand slaves. I coulda freed a thousand more if only they knew they were slaves. I shall help you." And with that declaration, the girl in the brilliant light vanishes. The corner that a moment ago was radiant suddenly seems dull and ordinary as Arthur stands, dazed from the vanished flash of light and departure of the vision.

He turns and faces his colleagues, who are standing and staring at him.

"What's the matter, Arthur?" says Aisha. "Why did you leave us to go and stand in the corner?"

"Did you see her?" he replies. "There was a little girl here... right here." He points to the spot. "And now she's gone."

His colleagues look at one another, obviously perplexed and confused and not really knowing what to say. "Arthur...is this some kind of a game you're playing? Because there's no one there," says Ron.

There is an awkward hush as they look on and as Arthur comes to grips with the confusion on their faces. "I'm sorry…I'm not quite sure what just happened, but I thought I saw a ghost or something right here, after that last "Ashe."

"What did she look like, Arthur?" says Sonia, taking his comment seriously.

Arthur looks down at the corner again before turning to look at them and scratching his head. "I'm sorry…I apologize…let me get some water. Please continue the session." But instead of going to the table under the window to pour a glass of water, he turns and walks through the dining room and opens the two-way door to the kitchen.

Arthur startles Charles—a short, stocky man with a white apron tied around his large waist—and Silvestre by his entrance. They are preoccupied with preparing their guests' noontime meal. Charles is standing over the stove, sautéing diced onions and garlic in a frying pan, while Silvestre is chopping celery on a wooden board.

"Can I help you?" asks Silvestre, drying his hands on a towel as he walks over to Arthur standing in the doorway.

"I know this will sound strange, but I was wondering," says Arthur, "has anyone died in this house since you've lived here?"

Charles lowers the burner under his frying pan to sauté the onions and garlic a little more slowly so he can hear without appearing to butt into their conversation.

"Well…no," replies Silvestre, "not since I've been here. Now, I can't vouch for the people who may have died in the house before I bought it. This old mansion was built in the early 1920s, so there's a good chance someone died here. But that had to be a while back. Why do you ask?"

If Charles had been a dog, one would have seen his ears perk up and stand at attention. He doesn't even breathe for fear he'll not hear Arthur's answer.

"Well, Silvestre," says Arthur, "do you think there're ghosts in the house? 'Cause I just saw one."

Silvestre seems to take Arthur's comment as an affront to his proprietorship, like something was found unclean, while Charles's eyes pop out of his head. Silvestre picks up his hand towel resting on the sink and hastily wipes his hands, as if doing so will make both Arthur and his question go away. Charles cautiously glances around the small kitchen and then over his shoulder for fear that something might try to sneak up on him. He then hastily grabs the saltshaker from a kitchen cupboard, pours some into his hands, and throws it three times over his right shoulder.

"Listen, y'all," Charles quickly drawls, "if y'all gonna talk like that, I wish the two of you get the hell out of my kitchen. I'm tryin' to cook this here food, and I don't need to hear no ghost stories. Ya hear me?"

"I apologize for disturbing your cooking," says Arthur. "Perhaps I dozed off and was just dreaming. Sorry to disturb you," and he leaves them to their cooking.

"Strange fellow," says Charles as he turns up the burner on the stove and returns to his pots.

Arthur returns to the living room as Aisha is saying to the group, "When Harriet was twelve years old, she was severely hit on the head with a heavy metal object by a plantation overseer. He was angry with her because she wouldn't tie up a runaway slave who had been captured. She remained unconscious for days.

"Another enslaved woman cleaned Harriet's wound and bandaged her head. They thought she would die, but after many days, Harriet stirred and gradually recovered from her injury.

But for the rest of her life, she suffered from a kind of sleeping sickness. She'd drop asleep without warning at anytime and anywhere, having no control over falling unconscious or when she would wake up. Now, can you imagine having to lead slaves north and manage all of them…walking through the woods and swamps in the cold winter months, which they say is when she liked to travel, suffering from that kind of illness?

"So you're right, Hachi, Harriet had to learn to live with this condition and, as a slave, assume responsibility for her own health and well-being with a sleeping disorder she couldn't control. Maybe this is why she became good at using herbs and spices and poultices. So her story does support the first principle—taking full responsibility for one's own health. And we need to share her story with health conductors-in-training in some way, especially those who feel challenged in making positive changes to their lifestyle and living up to their decisions."

"When did we adopt the name 'Health Conductors'?" inquires John.

"At the last leadership meeting," says Sonia. "You were there when Reggie talked about the project being an overground railroad and calling those who accept the challenge of dealing with their own health issues and serving as role models for others to follow. I think he called them health conductors."

"But we didn't vote on the name," John retorts.

"Leadership hasn't voted on anything yet," quips Ron. "And they won't until this committee comes back with a proposed plan of action."

"Let's not get stuck, 'cause we're making good progress," says Aisha. "We were talking about Harriet Tubman's life as a good example of leadership's first principle."

"Our challenges seem light compared to what she had to go through," says Sonia. "Maybe we can produce one of those rubber bracelets. You know, the kind people wear around their wrists? Lots of people wear them nowadays with a saying written on them. And they come in all colors, too. We could have one made that says, 'What would Harriet do?' And hand them out at training. So anytime any one is in doubt or feels like giving up on themselves and needs support, they have their bracelet to remind them, saying, 'What would Harriet do?' What do you think?"

The group is momentarily distracted when Arthur takes his seat, and his colleagues turn to him.

"Is there something wrong, Arthur?" says Ron.

"No, everything's fine. I just wanted to check on our lunch," Arthur replies. "So I hear we're using the term 'health conductors.'"

"Yes," Aisha replies. "It just sort of caught on after Reggie used it."

"After you left," Ron continues, "we reviewed the agenda for the day and made a little adjustment. John suggested that we tackle the hard stuff first, which is program goal and progress measures, and then go back to program details. Is that all right with you?"

"Yeah, that works."

"Good."

I've done a little research on John's concerns," says Arthur. "So would it be appropriate for me to speak to the issue of goals and measurements now?"

"Yes," says Ron, relieved and pleased that Arthur has rejoined the group and is ready to engage in their continued discussions. "This would be a good time."

"Well, I started thinking about the critical mass bike riders in San Francisco who return to the downtown area once every month to take over the streets and highlight the need for a more bike-friendly city. I got curious about the origin of the term 'critical mass' and why they use it. It turns out this concept was evident in China long before cars were on their roads, when most people were still riding bikes.

"They didn't have traffic signals then or traffic cops, either, so when bicyclists got to a crossroad, they had to stop and wait until it was safe enough to cross the intersection because a lot of bikes were passing from right and left directly in front of them. When enough riders showed up who also wanted to cross the road, the traffic in front of them had to stop. Why? Because the growing number of riders at the intersection who wanted to cross the road would put so much pressure on the bikers in front that the bikers at the head of the line would be forced to move forward. So the cyclists coming from their right and left would be forced to stop. Do you understand?" asks Arthur.

"So far..." someone tentatively says. "So what does that have to do with our project?"

He explains that there's a natural law for this concept called critical mass, or reaching the tipping point. If you can change 10 percent of any field, you change that field forever. So the Chinese bikers could be considered a field, just like the African American population in the Bay Area can be considered a field. Thirteen percent of the population in the region is people of African descent, which translates into 465,000 people. Ten percent of these inhabitants amount to 4,650 people.

"So if we set as our goal reaching ten percent of our population in the Bay Area and support them in making better health decisions...Don't you see?" Arthur continues sensing their hesitation and is now quite animated by his vision of it all. "OK...take our young black men, for instance, who wear their pants around their thighs instead of their waists. As ridiculous as they look, waddling down the street with one hand holding their pants up to keep them from falling—where did that start? How did that fashion statement begin, huh?"

"It started in the jails and prisons," John replies. "The men weren't allowed to wear belts for fear inmates would use them as weapons or, perhaps, to hang themselves. Now how many black folk you know gonna hang themselves? So jailers took their belts away when convicts entered the system, and they gave them prison clothes to wear with no belts, and most often the pants didn't fit. The pants would be too big. So prisoners had no choice but to walk around with one hand holding up their oversized pants."

"Yes," Arthur exclaims. "Black and Latino men coming out of jails and prisons got so used to wearing their pants like that, they just continued the practice even after being released. And it became a weird badge of honor signifying they'd done prison time. Now, if you wear your pants like that, you're a bona fide gangbanger. You paid your dues.

"So when enough men came out of prison and continued wearing their pants down while walking around city streets, it eventually caught on, and men who hadn't even gone to jail started copying that fashion statement until it became a fad among many black men and even other youth; it reached a tipping point; it reached critical mass. Now do you see?"

"Hell, I've even seen some old dudes walkin' round with dare pants like dat," says John, arousing much laughter.

"Arthur, are you suggesting that the purpose of our action plan be training health conductors in our community until being a health conductor becomes a fad and we reach critical mass?" asks Aaron.

"Yes and no…not exactly, but suppose we train enough health conductors having influence over the health behavior of their family members and close friends that, together…conductors and those they influence, allow us to reach the tipping point, so that living a healthier lifestyle in our community becomes fashionable—chic—a self-perpetuating fashion statement, like our young men wearing their pants under their asses."

"OK, Arthur," says John. "If our programmatic goal is to reach that critical mass number of, what did you say...4,650 people of African descent...ten percent of the African Americans in the Bay Area, how many health conductors would we need to do that?"

"For argument's sake, let's say that each conductor influences at least four or five people they know—'cause they will impact others." exclaims Hachi. "How many conductors would we need then?"

"Well, if we take Hachi's estimate," says Aaron, "and we have a thousand health conductors, they'll probably influence four to five thousand people."

"Plus the conductors, themselves—bingo!" shouts John.

"Yah, that's it—that's it!" Aaron declares. "The purpose of our project, then, is to reach the tipping point—to achieve critical mass. And we measure progress and our ultimate success by monitoring the number of conductors trained and, somehow, figuring out how many people conductors actually influence over time in changing health behavior."

"So if I may," continues John, "the inference here is, if we reach the tipping point, the program will become self-perpetuating—like the brothas with their butts hanging out—and at that point we should begin to see a reduction in the health crisis now facing our community."

"We'll have reached critical mass," says Aisha. "I like it...I like it."

Everyone's energetic and overjoyed by this surprising revelation except for Doris Whitehead, who remains unmoved and whose facial expression looks troubled and frustrated. The two facilitators notice and encourage her to speak up and share whatever's on her mind. Doris's face quickly turns to anger as she chides the group for not including representatives from low-income families and poor people in their discussion. She tells them she's been sitting there all morning, and all she hears is middle-class black people talking about action plans and social change without any input from people who suffer from more health problems than they do. She is offended by their arrogance. Tears fall from her eyes as she lowers her head and wipes them away with the back of her hand.

The group is taken aback by Doris's abrasive reaction as Arthur looks to the retreat's facilitators for assistance on how to handle the situation. Aisha finally tells Doris that she, personally, had no idea their conversation was affecting her that way and that she raises a very interesting point. But Doris immediately takes offense to Aisha's comment.

"Interesting—you find it interesting!" she interrupts with a sneer, now clearly emotionally distraught.

Hachi suggests the group take a short break and approaches Doris to help her on her feet. Looking at his watch, Ron realizes it's lunchtime and proposes they take up Doris's concern after lunch, at the beginning of their afternoon session. The committee's enlivened interaction and delight in the morning's accomplishments dissipates like an intermittent spring shower that comes and quickly passes. It's replaced by tension and the heaviness of a possibly brewing tropical storm.

Hachi and Doris are the last to enter the dining room as Arthur stands and invites the troubled woman to sit next to him at the table. While waiting for their meal, he leans over and says to her, "I personally apologize for perhaps not being sensitive to your concerns. I understand our discussion upset you. I don't think any of us had any intensions of doing so. I'm glad you raised your point…not having anyone here to represent low-income families."

"Well, I'm also sorry," replies Doris softly, "for putting a pin in everybody's balloon. Y'all seem to know each other well and are having such a good time. I was thinking…maybe I shouldn't stay for the afternoon part, but I haven't yet made up my mind."

Arthur asks if her boss briefed her about the project and the purpose of their retreat. Doris confides to him that she was asked to attend at the last minute, as Ellen had an emergency that commanded her immediate attention. He then reviews with her how the program started and the results of the previous leadership meetings. He tells her that to address the community's health inequities, they first have to begin with themselves and learn what it will take for them to address their own health problems to discover what works and then refine and adapt the program to appeal to a wider audience, including low-income people and their families.

He says, "I have no doubt that, before we engage them, we'll have many conversations with people from low-income groups and work with them in determining how best to alter the program to fit their specific needs."

Silvestre sets two plates of food in front of Doris and Arthur and steps away. Arthur picks up his fork and begins to eat when Doris leans over and says, "Low-income families are much sicker than you all. How long do you think they're gonna have to wait before this program gets around to them?"

"I don't know. What I do know is that we've been in poor health in body, mind, and spirit for more than four hundred years…ever since slavery, so it's gonna take some time to make us whole."

"OK," Doris says with reluctance. "It seems like you've already given a lot of thought to this initiative."

"We all have, Doris…we all have," Arthur retorts. The two of them eat the rest of their meal without any more conversation.

At the start of the afternoon session, Doris surprises everyone when she apologizes to the group for what she refers to as speaking out of turn. She mentions her exchange with Arthur at lunch and says she now has a better understanding of the project and what the committee is attempting to accomplish. She tells the group she's thought about what Harriet would do in this situation. And she came to the conclusion that Harriet...being the good Christian woman that she was...she would stand up and apologize.

"I have five siblings, and I'm the first in my family to graduate from college," she continues. My mother raised us, and we was dirt poor. Sometimes all we had was white bread and some thin soup to eat for breakfast, lunch, and dinner. On good days, we had peanut butter and jelly sandwiches. So my ears perk up when I hear people talkin' 'bout poor black people and low-income families, 'cause I grew up in one. And it annoys me when I hear people talk about what they need or what they should do when they've never ever asked them, directly, for their opinion on what concerns them. That's what I thought was happening, here. But after talking with Arthur over lunch, I realize I was mistaken, and I apologize for my disruption."

Hachi reminds the group that their third guiding principle relates to speaking out about unhealthy practices, even when one is in the minority, and thanks Doris for her courage in speaking up. Everyone agrees.

After Doris's apology, the afternoon proceeds without incident as the committee settles on a three-month time frame for the pilot project and agrees that the members willing to participate in the experiment meet once each month on a Saturday morning for preventative health training. The group also asks Arthur to follow up with Joe Braxton from Ethnic Health Initiative about finding a physician, preferably of African descent, to talk about the impact of chronic stress on people, and also ways to reduce and manage stress.

A little before four in the afternoon, the facilitators are about to invite everyone to give their closing remarks when Sonia asks, "In addition to the bracelets, why don't we make Harriet Tubman the patron of our project? We can find a photo of her—I'm sure there are some—have it enlarged, and display it at training sessions."

"What do the rest of you think?" asks Aisha.

"If Harriet is the patron of this initiative," replies Doris, "we should also ask participants to read at least one book about her life so we can share her stories throughout the training."

Aisha and Arthur glance at one another, knowing they're having the same thought. Doris used the word "we" instead of "you," indicating she's now vested in seeing the committee's work move forward and, no doubt, will want to join their social experiment as well. But then another thought occurs to Arthur as he recalls the little girl playing with the ball and jacks. He wonders whether, in some odd way, the little girl surrounded by light was the spirit of Harriet Tubman. He should have asked the child her name.

CHAPTER 23
TELL ME...SAY IT NOW

Arthur leaves the foundation after dropping off the Trust's three-year proposal to Alice Tan when his mobile phone rings. It's Valerie, who is in San Francisco for a weekend conference, staying at the downtown Hilton. She wants to see him, and they arrange to meet at the hotel that evening for dinner at six o'clock. It's rush hour as Arthur drives across the Bay Bridge toward San Francisco along with the hundreds of other cars and trucks. Traffic moves slowly, and he reminisces about the last time he saw Valerie and their lovemaking. Natalie is right; he has had an extramarital affair, but with only one woman, Valerie. He wonders if telling the truth would help his relationship with Natalie. But if he told her, he reasons, he'd have to stop seeing Valerie. He realizes he's not prepared to do that, at least not yet.

The traffic halts to a momentary standstill as he reflects on the fact that he's known Valerie since college when they were just good friends. While never finding themselves in each other's arms—fearing a romance, perhaps, would ruin their friendship or encourage a commitment neither one was prepared to keep—they embraced unbridled conversation sharing their uncharted dreams and aspirations and, on occasion, their fears and uncertainties to one another.

The stalled traffic gradually begins to move again as Arthur tries to remember when after graduation their friendship turned into an occasional love affair. It was so long ago. And besides, he ponders, why does Natalie think he's sleeping around when he only sees Valerie two or three times a year? The thought dissipates as he exits the bridge and drives into San Francisco's Financial District. After parking his car in a public lot and walking over to the Hilton, Arthur takes the elevator up to the third floor and knocks on Valerie's door.

"Arthur, is that you?"

"Yes, it's me. Were you expecting someone else to also knock on your door?"

"Oh, you funny man!" She opens the door wearing one of the hotel's white terry-cloth bathrobes, loose in the front.

"Hello, Arthur, it's about time you got here, or was I supposed to wait all night?

"It's just fifteen minutes after six, and I said I'd be here around six o'clock, so why are you complaining?"

"I wanted to take a bath before dinner but didn't want to be in the tub when you knocked on the door." She smiles, very much aware of the impression she's making and kisses him on his cheek. Her slender, brown body is visible under her open robe that doesn't hide the lilt of her firm, beautiful breasts that she knows he admires so well.

Arthur grins, knowing what she's up to as he walks into the room and she closes the door. He's enchanted by the fragrance of frangipani that fills the space but sees no incense burning.

"I'm sorry I'm a little late."

"The bath is already prepared, and I won't be long," Valerie asserts as she walks to the bathroom door, stopping only long enough to look back and say, "I hope you don't mind, Arthur.

Do you? You can also join me," she adds, artfully laughing as she disappears through the open door.

He takes off his shoes and haphazardly throws his clothing on a chair and carpeted floor, before walking to the bathroom door and looking at her soaking in the hot, sudsy water. There's something magic between them, this dance they play, needing neither soft music nor romantic words for the air to turn electric. Arthur looks at her hazel-green eyes that change color with the nuance of her moods. And when she fixes her eyes on him, he knows he's never able to turn away. Valerie delights in the effect she has on him, when in that moment when time ceases, her presence enchants…beguiles him.

The bathroom is dimly lit by the two white candles resting at each end of the bathtub, creating silhouettes of dancing shadows on the white marble wall next to the tub. Valerie lies back, her head resting on a folded towel, as she leisurely closes her eyes and sinks up to her chin in the hot water.

"Arthur, are you comin' in or just gonna stand there staring at me?" she asks before opening her eyes to look at him again. Arthur steps into the frothy suds as she slides back, opening a space for him to sit down. But he finds the water uncomfortably hot, stinging his calves and thighs, bringing him to a sudden halt when the heat reaches the tender skin between his legs.

"So…what have you been up to since I last saw you?" asks Valerie with her arms wrapped around her knees, showing genuine interest.

He slowly stretches his legs in the water and rests his feet next to her body. "Usually, I have to make upfront cash commitments to people and organizations to launch new initiatives; and after promises are made, I look for resources to carry the project out. It's scary sometimes, because I'm making pledges on the allocation of funds with money I don't really have. But this time around…with this new community health initiative, I'm receiving a grant before we even get started, and it feels good."

"Arthur, I'm truly interested in your work, but more importantly, I'm interested in you…your personal life. So how are you and Natalie doing?"

"We're going through a trial separation."

"Oh…trial separation…what's that about?"

"She says she needs space away from me for the next few months."

"Why?"

"She says she can't trust me, knowing I sleep with other women."

"Does Natalie know about us?"

"No, not really."

"You've hurt her Arthur, and she may not forgive you. I'm so sorry I've brought you grief. And how do you feel about this separation?"

"I have mixed feelings about it all. I love Natalie and don't want to see her unhappy, but we have a lot of arguments that upset both of us. So, most of the time, we're on an emotional rollercoaster. Now that we live apart, I feel relieved and more relaxed, and that's the honest truth."

"Maybe we should stop seeing each other, Arthur." Valerie looks at his face to gauge his reaction, but there's none for her to see. "Do you remember, Arthur, my saying you weren't ready to get married?"

"Yes, I remember. And how is your husband, Ralph?" Arthur quickly asks, wanting to change the subject.

"He's the same…still working all the time."

"And how do you handle that, as much as you like sex?"

"Arthur, I don't like sex, as you put it. I love to be made love to. There's a difference, you know?"

"What do you mean?"

"I'm surprised you don't know, Arthur. I wouldn't make love to you if I didn't love you, darling, and know that you also love me."

"How do you know I love you?"

"I know...trust me Arthur, I know you," Valerie says, lightly laughing at her own conviction.

Sitting in the hot water, they're both absorbed in their own private thoughts for a moment until Valerie breaks the silence when she abruptly stands.

"Take me to bed, Arthur." She steps out of the bath and wraps her wet body in a towel.

"Don't you want to go out for dinner?" he asks.

Valerie takes another towel from the rack and wraps it around her hair as she looks at herself in the bathroom mirror, considering Arthur's question. "We can order room service later, if you like. I really don't feel like getting dressed now and leaving the room. Are you disappointed?"

He smiles at her. "I'd much rather stay here and make love to you."

Valerie looks at him and rolls her eyes. "Arthur, why do you think you and I never got together and made a go of it?"

"Valerie...we're like two people walking together down the street, but never in step with one another. I mean, we try, but one of us is always playing catch-up. When you were seriously dating someone, I was free and available; and when I was with someone, you were free and available. And then you decided Ralph was the one, and you got married. Besides, you always liked West Indian men, and I just didn't fit that bill."

Valerie doubles over laughing and falls across the bed, causing the towel around her body to become undone. "Arthur, you're funny! Why do you think I only like West Indian men?"

"You married one, didn't you? Besides, that's what you told me. Don't you remember saying that when we were at Howard U?

"I told you that because getting into my pants seemed to be the only thing on your mind most of the time. And I wanted more than that from you. I needed you to be my friend."

Valerie lies on her stomach with the soles of her feet raised toward the ceiling, looking at Arthur with her chin resting in the palms of her hands. Her eyes have changed color from hazel brown to green.

"Arthur, can you do me a favor?" she quizzically asks him.

"How could I deny you anything?"

"Can you please come over here and kiss my black butt?"

He's captivated by the expression on her face, as if she's just asked him to fetch a glass of water. And the innocent audacity of her charm moves him from his chair to her bed, where he leans over and softly kisses her where she has commanded.

"You're a freak, you know, Arthur," she says to him, "and I love that about you. Maybe I'm just in love with you, Arthur Renfro."

She feels the wet warmth of his tongue on the roundness of her firm, round cheeks as Arthur kisses her with long, unhurried strokes until her behind starts to rise and fall with anticipation.

Valerie slowly turns over on her back and says to him in a breathy whisper, "Arthur...Arthur...make love to me...make love to me."

Arthur moves up to her mouth and kisses her on her full lips. Valerie's fingers dig into his back as she desperately pulls him close. She grabs him around the small of his back and holds him tight, kissing him all the while as she wraps her legs around the back of his thighs and the warm perspiration from his body now mingles with the wetness of her soft brown skin. They hold fast to one another as if the world and its people no longer exist, and their physical and psychic boundaries, defining where one begins and the other leaves off, no longer exist or have any meaning.

"Tell me, Arthur...tell me...say it now," she softly whispers in his ear.

"I love you, Valerie. I love you, muchly."

⁂

The midmorning sky is overcast as Arthur drives back across the Bay Bridge to Oakland. A light mist falls on his windshield, heralding the coming of spring, but precipitously stops as if the clouds can't decide whether to shower the Bay or head further south where rain is most needed. Cool air rushes through Arthur's half-open window on the passenger side as he keeps up with the sparse traffic crossing the wide expanse and recalls the note Valerie left.

Dear Arthur,

After all our beautiful lovemaking, I thought I'd let you sleep and regain your energy. You're gonna need it if you come back tonight. I left early for the conference's breakfast session and will be gone the rest of the day. Hope to see you around seven? Here's my room key in case you return before me.

V

He smiles, thinking of her, and believes Valerie might be right; she does know him well and perhaps understands him better than he knows himself. The thought certainly contradicts what he knows to be true, as he's told her nothing of his out-of-body experiences and his seeing ghosts. He then questions: how much does he really know about her? She speaks very little about her life with Ralph, and he imagines that her relationship with her husband is very different from the one she shares with him. Yes, she says he works hard and is seldom home, but how are they together, when they're alone and in bed? He tries to imagine what it might be like for Valerie to make love to Ralph. And when she's loving Ralph, does she ever think of him? He contemplates asking her as he rubs his thumb against her hotel key in his hand.

Arthur turns the key in the lock and walks into his apartment, closing the door behind him. The living-room blinds are shut, sealing in the darkness. Groping for the wall switch, he turns on the light and sees his clothes on the floor and the pile of dirty dishes he left in the sink. The sight of the mess depresses him. Taking off his windbreaker and throwing it on the back of a chair, he wades into the kitchen to tackle the soiled pots, pans, plates, bowls, cups, and glasses in front of him.

After putting on rubber gloves Natalie keeps under the sink, he picks through the pile and removes the dishes and glasses from the basin and sets them aside on the counter. Then he takes out the two greasy pots and a frying pan and places them on the other side of the sink. Moving the grimy silverware to one side, he scoops up rotting food left in the basin and pops the rubber stopper in the drain. Turning on the hot water, Arthur reaches for the dish soap and squirts the green liquid into the water as he watches the sink fill up, making the white foam bubbles rise. Turning off the water, he picks up a dirty pot and reaches for the worn-out scouring pad before coming to the conclusion that he has little energy or willpower to stand over a sink right then.

Peeling off the gloves, Arthur heads for the bedroom to lie down. As soon as he's on the bed, he falls into a light sleep and starts to dream that Natalie is in the apartment, screaming and crying as she furiously stabs her white wedding dress with a butcher knife. The fabric begins to bleed as she drags her tattered dress into the bathroom and tries stuffing it in the toilet while blood drips down the side of the bowl and onto the white tile floor. The toilet water turns blood red and, after filling the basin, spills out onto the floor. It spreads like molten lava over the bathroom tile and into the bedroom, where Natalie is now sitting on the bed, slashing the white sheets with her knife.

Arthur suddenly awakes in a cold sweat and sits up on the side of the bed. Hastily tucking his disheveled shirt into his khaki pants and putting on his shoes, he grabs his jacket and keys and rushes out of the apartment. The air is cool, and rain drizzles on his head and down his face as he walks to the BART station on Ashby Avenue. He feels strange and somewhat at odds with himself and wonders if he should go back to the house and drive his car.

After buying a BART ticket and climbing the stairs, he paces up and down the platform as he waits for the train to San Francisco. Fifteen minutes pass before the BART arrives, and Arthur boards the second to the last car. Finding an empty seat, he zips his jacket and pulls the collar up around his neck. The car is half full of people reading Kindle and magazines, fiddling with smartphones, or listening to music or something with earbuds crammed in their ears. Arthur notices a young Latina mother trying to comfort her toddler, who is making a scene and fighting to get off her lap. Giving up in frustration, she surrenders to the child's wishes and lets him stand on the floor between her legs as he turns his attention to pulling out items his mother has in a plastic bag.

BART stops at several stations before descending into the tunnel, racing past gray steel and concrete shafts underneath the bay. Arthur looks through the window into the darkness as the train picks up speed and descends deeper into the tube. Light bulbs whiz by like solitary fireflies, their pulsating glimmer swallowed up in blackness. It's raining lightly in San Francisco when Arthur climbs the stairs at the Embarcadero and starts down

Market toward the Hilton Hotel. The street is crowded with tourists and shoppers while street merchants spread pieces of plastic over their tables to protect their merchandise for sale. A troupe of teenagers wearing T-shirts and tight jeans and oblivious to the weather sprint by on skateboards while a group of young women pushing strollers and chatting to one another pass Arthur without noticing him.

He takes the elevator to the third floor and uses Valerie's card key to let himself in the room. The bed is still unmade, and towels remain scattered across the floor. Soon there's a knock on the door.

"Housekeeping," a female voice says, accompanied by a light tapping on the door.

"Can you come back later?" Arthur replies and waits for a response, but the housekeeper has already walked away, pushing her cart in front of her.

Taking off his jacket and dropping it on the floor, he finds a fresh hand towel in the bathroom to wipe the rainwater from his head and face. Returning to the room, he notices his windbreaker on the carpet, which reminds him of the dirty clothes in his apartment and the untidy mess he left in the kitchen sink. Feeling disgusted now about his habit of throwing things on the floor and his general uncleanliness, Arthur feels an overwhelming urge to return to his own unit and finish cleaning up as he first intended to do. Giving in to this impulse, Arthur grabs his jacket off the floor, checks for the card key in his pocket, and hastily leaves Valerie's room.

After getting off the hotel elevator, he walks past a party of white teenage girls standing in the lobby with suitcases and duffel bags, waiting to check in. They're all wearing yellow T-shirts with red basketball insignias on their backs; they're animated and chatting together like wild geese impatiently waiting to fly. Arthur passes through the hotel's revolving door and out onto the busy street, where people are irritated because he's blocked what they consider their right-of-way.

Reaching the BART station at Powell and Market, Arthur descends the stairs two at a time, buys another train pass, and rushes down the long, narrow flight of stairs to the platform below. The train is entering the station as he runs to where he guesses the last car will stop, hoping to bypass the lines of people already queuing for the BART. Quickly boarding the car, he takes a seat and crouches in the corner, watching the rest of the passengers as they disembark or hop on the train. He's amused by the number of people who play it safe and avoid each other's eyes and wonders how many of them are really faking their sober preoccupation with the electronic devices in their hands. And although most of the riders seem rather young and ethnically diverse, they dress alike in drab wash-and-wear colors, making them all look the same.

Three hard-looking, overweight women, two white and one black women swagger onto the train at the Embarcadero stop, and Arthur swears the car tilted in their direction when they boarded the train. They enter the car and scowl at the male passengers around them, as if they climbed into a boxing ring and dare any man to take them on in a fight. One of the fighters in the trio sports a close-cropped haircut and wears blue jeans, a red plaid shirt, and work boots, and her biceps are so muscular she looks as if she could chop down a redwood tree with one single blow of an ax.

Arthur muses over the realization that although he and the three women he's watching live on the same Earth and breathe the same air, the world they live in is out of his grasp. He begins to question whether the world he inhabits and the planet they live on are both contrived realities; different, yet manufactured narratives out of which he and they live out their lives and interpret the world around them. And if this is true, doesn't that mean that everyone's reality is what they believe it to be? Then what is real? Arthur shudders with the thought that everyone's fixed reality is both pervasive and all delusional.

Arriving at the Ashby station, Arthur scrambles from the train and down the stairs into the open air. The sun plays hide and seek with steel gray clouds silently moving overhead in a shadow play most pedestrians are too preoccupied to notice. He picks up his pace with determination and resolves to finish cleaning his apartment in time to shower, change clothes, and meet Valerie at her hotel at seven.

After entering his building and mounting the stairs, Arthur opens his front door and switches on the light. The apartment is dark and colorless, and the stuffiness from stale air and closed windows accentuates the odor of garbage piled high in a trash bin next to the sink. Arthur's nauseated by the smell and wonders how long he's been living this way.

Pulling off his windbreaker and throwing it over a kitchen chair, he again puts on the rubber gloves he left on the counter. The dishwater in the sink is cold, and the soap suds are now a white film on the surface of the water. Arthur's eyes catch the silent movement of a black fly landing on the pile of smelly garbage. Overcome by nausea, he runs to the bathroom and holds his head over the toilet. His stomach heaves up and down, but nothing comes out.

Returning to the kitchen, he desperately searches the cabinets for a trash bag to pick up the garbage on the floor. Finding none, he hastily decides to hire someone to clean up the apartment for him. Peeling off his rubber gloves and throwing them on the counter, he searches his apartment for a phone book he can't seem to find. Giving up, he grabs his jacket and is out the door before realizing that he's left his house keys on the kitchen table. Luckily, in trying the doorknob, he finds it unlocked and opens the door as he suddenly realizes he needs a change of clothing to take to Valerie's place. Holding his breath while passing through the kitchen, he rushes into the bedroom and grabs a clean shirt and pair of pants from his closet and then opens his chest of drawers for underwear, an undershirt, and a clean pair of socks.

In the bathroom he snatches his toothbrush and hair brush before returning to the bedroom, where he throws all the items on the unmade bed. Arthur's not sure what to do next as he stands in the doorway between the bathroom and bedroom. Seeing all the articles on the bed, he recognizes he needs something to put his things in and scrounges around the closet for his overnight bag. Not finding it, Arthur becomes agitated, thinking that Natalie must have taken it. In frustration, he stuffs his clothes and other items into a brown paper shopping bag and heads for the door before remembering his keys on the kitchen table.

He's relieved, once again, to be in the open air and not having to put up with the stench of garbage, even if it's his own. He walks to the BART, his shopping bag in hand, and buys another transit pass before climbing the stairs to wait once more for the train to San Francisco. He is on the platform for less than ten minutes before the BART pulls into the station, and he boards the car, finding a seat next to a window. It's not until he's underground and crossing the bay that Arthur realizes, while looking at his reflection in the glass, that he's clutching the shopping bag like someone who appears to be not all there. He laughs out loud, making some passengers in the car stop what they're doing momentarily and look his way.

At the Embarcadero station, Arthur climbs the stairs and walks the few blocks to the Hilton hotel. Arriving a little past three in the afternoon, he strides through the lobby and passes two men and two women standing together with backpacks and climbing gear near the front desk. Getting off the elevator at the third floor, he walks down the hallway with his shopping bag in his arms and, noting the sign on the door knob, realizes that the housekeeper has straightened up the place and gone.

The telephone rings as he opens the door and goes to pick it up, thinking it could be Valerie calling to check in on him. But what if it's someone else? He's perplexed about what to do when the phone stops ringing. He then puts down his brown paper bag, hurriedly takes off his clothes, grabs the clean towel and washcloth that were placed on the bed, and walks into the bathroom, only to be startled by his own nakedness in the mirror. He doesn't recognize himself or the face staring back at him in the looking glass. His body appears large and puffy, and he tries to think back to the previous night when he and Valerie were in the tub. He questions whether he now looks the same as he did then. He can't remember, but he is repulsed by what he sees and feels a sudden compulsion to immediately get dressed and leave.

Throwing the towel and washcloth back on the bed, Arthur once again puts his dirty clothes on, grabs his card key, and walks out the door. He rushes down the hallway, fearing he might run into her and have to explain. When he gets to the elevator, he worries about the door opening and Valerie catching him standing there. Seeing the exit sign, he bolts through the exit door and down the stairs. Once in the lobby, Arthurs makes a dash across the hotel's polished marble floors and into the streets. Although there is now no need to quicken his pace, he fights off the impulse to run as he heads back to BART for the train across the bay.

He's exhausted by the time he boards the train and slumps down in an empty seat. Looking at his watch, he notices it's ten minutes to four and realizes he hasn't accomplished a damn thing but ride BART through the Transbay tunnel back and forth all day. And now he's on the train, again, returning to the

East Bay. He begins to question what has possessed him to ride BART back and forth, like he's spinning around and around in a revolving door. Underneath his thoughts, a fear grows as he promises himself that this time, he will stay put when he reaches his apartment.

Arthur's legs ache after climbing the stairs and opening his apartment's door. He collapses into his living-room chair, and it dawns on him that he's left the shopping bag of clothes in Valerie's room. It weighs on him that she will find his clothes in a paper bag until the thought is an obsession. Wondering how he could have possibly left them, he chastises himself for his forgetfulness and worries about her thinking it strange and so unlike him to carry clothes around in a paper bag. Or would she think, perhaps, that someone from housekeeping left them by mistake and telephones the front desk to inquire? And what if someone saw him with the bag and tells her he was there? Though physically exhausted, his promise to stay put and cease the back-and-forth rides is undermined by a compelling desire to retrieve his clothes from Valerie's room. Every fiber of his being screams from within for him to get up and get his clothes. Arthur wrestles with his judgment and fatigue and the toll it has taken on his body and mind in constantly crisscrossing the Bay. His brain is on fire, and his emotions are raw, making it difficult for him to focus and bring clarity to his thoughts. No sooner than he sinks into an erratic sleep, he's suddenly jolted awake, driven by the obsession to retrieve his clothes. Weary, feeling half mad, Arthur staggers from the chair, finds his jacket and keys, and leaves the apartment.

This time, the train ride is a blur crossing the Bay. He passes through the hotel's revolving door and by the front desk like a body coerced into putting one foot in front of the other. Taking the elevator alone to the third floor, Arthur plods down the hallway like a defeated man and pulls the key card out his pocket.

His hand trembles, and the room key falls on the carpet in front of her door.

Tears well up in his eyes as he opens the door and he stumbles over to the bed. The bag of clothes is right where he left them on a chair in the middle of the room. He feels utterly helpless as his mind demands he get up, take his clothes, and exit the room.

Getting up, he grabs the paper bag and, in desperation, throws the clothes on the floor. Arthur sits defeated on the chair and uncontrollably weeps, knowing he can no longer physically move or obey whatever's compelling him to get up and make another trip back across the bay. Closing his eyes with tears running down his cheeks, he silently prays to a god he doesn't know or has never truly acknowledged. And as he pleads for help, a gray film or hazy fog rises up out of Arthur's body, and with the filth's departure, the compulsive feeling to flee dissipates until it's gone, like it was never there.

Arthur is sitting like a human lump on a seat, feeling drained and weary, finding what has just occurred incomprehensible, when without warning, a frightening thought surfaces in his consciousness. He intuitively realizes he's been possessed this day; this riding back and forth on BART was not of his doing. It was the spirit Rosa and Julia fear and do not dare to mention by name, the one that haunts the unit downstairs and roams the apartment building. Hector had warned him and had offered him protective beads to guard against this evil.

Arthur's eyes are heavy, and he wants to sleep, but he is afraid the entity might return or is still in the room. If spirit possession can happen to him, he reasons, it could happen to anyone—or can it? What made him susceptible to its influence? How could this entity enter his body, without him knowing, and overpower him? And if possession happened, could this thing return and reenter him again?

A sudden tremor passes through his spine, and he shudders as it runs its course straight up his back. He realizes he remains as vulnerable as that little girl in the fairytale walking alone in the forest, unaware that a big, bad wolf is stalking her. He's at a loss on how to protect himself from an entity he cannot hear, smell, or see; from a thing that has the power to possess him at will.

Arthur closes his eyes and sits brooding, attentive to any sound or noise, yet oddly at peace as he listens to the silence that embraces him. He suddenly hears voices in the hallway as two people pass the door and recede down the corridor. He recollects Hector's consulta and his explanation of why he leaves his body; that his spirit is not securely attached to his physical form; that his spirit wants to escape when he's under stress or depressed. He must find a way to ground himself, to bind his spirit more tightly to his physical form, to prevent unembodied entities from entering and forcing him to act against his own will. He thinks about Hector's protective beads and decides to return for them as soon as possible. "But will beads be enough?" he asks himself.

A revelation surfaces in his consciousness: he must learn to sit quietly with concentration and focus as a way of nourishing his spirit and keeping unclean spirits out. Then, without warning, Arthur hears a voice that, unbeknown to him, ascends from the intuition of his own soul. "Establish a personal relationship with the Divine," it says; and once again, the room settles into silence.

He's startled by the utterance and quickly opens his eyes, only to see Valerie standing in the open doorway looking at him. "What did you say?" he asks.

"Nothing…I didn't say a thing. I just opened the door and saw you sitting there."

CHAPTER 24

OLD BLIND MAN

Two hours elapsed before the Akasha Records of Celestial Light were closed with a prayer, and Narada directed his listeners to open their eyes to gaze, once again, into the fire blazing in front of them. And he said to the gathering, "Everything you have heard and felt before we resumed our story will be forgotten by the time you reach your dwelling, but the narrative will remain alive in you. You will be eager to talk about the story, and I encourage you to invite others to attend when you return the night after tomorrow for the next leaf of the tale. I promise you will sleep well tonight and wake in the morning, feeling grateful that you are alive and your energy has been restored."

Those who heard him were silent and feeling the residual effects of the story as he spoke, until Narada clapped his hands and the fire extinguished itself.

"Amantahu," he cried out.

"Hiya Aman," the people replied, and they lifted their heads and arms to the night sky as if giving thanks to the Most High; and the third night of story ended.

But this evening, as the gathering dispersed and the inhabitants of Ja'Usu returned to their mud-brick homes, and the

Oromos left for their makeshift shacks outside the wall, Narada stayed behind. He confided in Ibrahim Hafez that he was to have a visitor; a man who could not enter the city at night was coming now to see him.

Hohete overheard and was puzzled, while Ayaat, still absorbed in Narada's story, just said, "And so it must be," before reaching for Hohete's arm; and together, they walked away.

Not long after the Hafez family departed, a tiny orange-yellow glow appeared in the darkness and advanced toward Narada who sat, waiting. An old Oromo man, led by a young boy carrying an oil lamp, emerged from the blackness and stood before the storyteller. The old man, whose name was Daanish Nour, rested one hand on the boy's shoulder while the other held a long wooden staff with a shepherd's crook. His blind eyes stared into the darkness as he waited for either his grandson or the storyteller he knew was there to instruct him where to stand or sit. Narada rose and took Daanish Nour's arm and directed him to sit on the straw mat he had been sitting on. Ma'Mun took his grandfather's staff and, after placing the oil lamp on the ground, sat next to his elder resting the shepherd's crook between them. The young boy waited patiently for someone to speak and watched flying insects drawn closer to the lamps' flame as one by one they fell to the ground with scorched wings. But as soon as Narada sat on the bare ground facing the blind man and the boy, the insects stopped coming, and the flame in the lamp grew merciful and still.

"Who you are I do not know, but a rare being you must be," said the blind man with a smile. "Me, on the ground I should be, while on your mat you should remain. Much older than me, you are I know. My little life to the longevity of your existence when compared, one blink of an eye the length of my life to yours is. In your presence deeply honored I am, here with you to be sitting."

And the old man bowed his head in reverence to Narada as his grandson beside him did the same.

"I know you well, Daanish Nour, and I am well pleased with you," said Narada. "I honor your age in Earth years, old man, and the wisdom you have gained not only in this life but from the trials and tribulations you have experienced in the many lives you have lived over the past three thousand years. I met you long before the birth of Christ, when your soul was still young and self-centered. Do you remember when we met?"

Before the old man could respond, Narada gently tapped his forehead with a finger, and Daanish Nour was taken back to an earlier life when they first met. The blind man's inner vision saw a young boy with fair skin beating a mangy little dog with a stick. The dog was whimpering and trying to escape, but the boy had it pinned down with a forked tree branch. A stranger interrupted him and asked, "Why are you beating the dog?"

"Because I can," answered the boy curtly and resumed whipping the animal.

"And what does your father say to you when he beats you?"

The boy abruptly stopped and turned to the stranger, who was also a youth, perhaps five years older than him. "How do you know my father beats me?"

"I can see the welts and bruises on your arms and legs."

"He beats me when he is mad."

"Because of something you have done?"

"No…any time he gets mad, he takes it out on my mother and me. And I hate him for it."

"And then you take it out on this little dog?"

"Yes."

"You are just like your father, then."

"I am nothing like my father."

"Oh, I see," and the older youth walked away.

"I am not like my father!" the young boy shouted after him and let the little dog go. It quickly scampered away.

"Understand I do not," said Daanish Nour, "who am I supposed to be?"

"You are the little boy beating the dog. Do you see the birthmark on the boy's right ankle? You still carry this same mark on your ankle."

"Yes…yes, the white mark on my grandfather's ankle, I see," says Ma'Mun, looking down at his grandfather's leg. "A small leaf, it looks like."

"And in this scene with the boy, storyteller, where are you?" asks Daanish Nour.

"I am the youth who walks away."

"Well, this earlier life for me to see, a blessing it is. But since my birth blind I have been, so whether the same mark as the boy in the vision I have now, for myself I will never see."

Ma'Mun reached for the oil lamp and brought it close to his grandfather's right foot. "There…there, grandfather, a small patch of white in the shape of a leaf it is. To feel it would you like?" The young boy looked at his grandfather and then the storyteller with a mixture of fear and wonder, so Narada planted a thought-seed of peace and serenity in the child's fertile mind. It immediately took root.

"Many things in dreams I see. Where these pictures come from I do not know. From past lives these images are they, storyteller?"

Narada did not answer and waited patiently for the blind man to once again speak. The old man intuitively understood the storyteller's silence and decided to reveal the reason for his visit.

"Each night to your story we Oromo listen, and in the day about it we talk. Oromo and the African Americans in your story, much in common we have. Maybe harder they have it. To know, I do not. Even though Mother Africa in their blood

African Americans have, by an alien culture controlled they are. And that alien culture, African blood to subdue it wants. Inside them this alien also lives. Maybe why in poor health this people of African descent, spiritually sick they are. At war with himself, this African American, he truly is.

"From your story about these future people, we Oromo, much to learn have we. Although Ja'Usu people, African skin like the Oromo they have, to Ja'Usu we Oromo, inferior we are. And to their will submissive we must be. The power to rule and wealth they have for Oromo to hold back, they use it.

"Storyteller, to the Oromo your narrative says inferior we will stay if we do not break loose like the African American of the future is trying. This inferiority, to our children to pass it we will, and to their children pass it they will, and to their children's children on and on it will go...and like today it is, Oromo will stay."

"You are wise, Daanish Nour," said Narada. "The Oromo mind was receptive to the thought-seed of being less than your brethren when your people were defeated in battle by Ja'Usu over one hundred years ago. Inferiority took root then and has been passed on through each succeeding Oromo generation to this day. And that thought-seed is reinforced today in the way you live your lives as Oromo in your dealings with Ja'Usu and each other. Your people have adapted well and survived, but, Daanish Nour, what will it take for Oromo to thrive?"

Young Ma'Mun sat quietly listening to this adult conversation and looked at his grandfather, who was in deep reflection; but he, too, considered the storyteller's question and suddenly blurted out, "We must confront Ja'Usu to address our grievances."

"Yes, that too, my little one," said Narada. "Was that why you and your grandfather went to the holy edifice to speak to the council?"

"Yes," said Daanish Nour, "but they would not see us."

Narada waited for a moment before asking, "Daanish Nour, what speaks to you when you saw that glimpse of an earlier life?"

"To have lived before, I never knew. But many lives I have lived you say then true it must be. This being so, from one life to the next, change is constant I see."

"And so it is for all of creation, this yearning to evolve and grow, this relentless change and transformation through cycles of birth and death and rebirth, the Great Mystery, our Creator, compels us to undergo. She entices us…teaches us by the supremacy of her love emanating throughout her creation encouraging our devotion in self-surrender. The Great Mother calls us home. So you see, my friend, the Oromo, too, must change and grow. The Great Mystery wills it so."

"And how to change must we?" asked Daanish Nour.

"It may no longer serve the Oromo to live as nomads in the desert; instead, strive to build community together and take care of one another; let every man and woman become a hollow reed the One-Who-Has-Many-Names will play like a bamboo flute to channel her love into the love of family. Consider all Oromo one family where the needs of every child are the charge of everyone. And above all else, bring your lives in harmony with Divine Will through devotion nurtured by daily quiet sitting. In this way, you will grow in communion with the Most High, and she will teach you. It never fails; she will respond."

"Of this sitting quietly I know nothing, so to learn this thing how to do?"

"Before I leave Ja'Usu, I will teach Ma'Mun if he is willing, and I through him will instruct anyone who is willing."

"Abbabba, I am ready," said Ma'Mun.

"For this quiet sitting, to worship Jah will Oromo have to give up?"

"No, sitting quietly will bring you closer to Jah. But instead of only speaking to Jah in prayer, you will learn to listen…to hear the Great Mystery intimately speak to you through the intuition of your soul."

"And in the Oromo, this subordinate feeling, will it be extinguished? Will quiet sitting root it out?" asked Daanish Nour.

"Communing with the Divine will change the Oromo's way of seeing the world, which, in turn, will alter how he will be in the world. And when quiet sitting becomes part of daily family life, the divine healing that comes from deep devotion will protect the Oromo from feeling inferior to Ja'Usu or anyone else no matter what they may say or do."

"What else must we do?"

"The Great Mystery has placed men and women on Earth to learn and exercise free will, so I can say no more."

For some time, the old man and his grandson sat in silence with Narada, who welcomed their company. Although the night air had grown cold coming in from the desert, the blind man and the young boy were both content and at peace, even feeling invigorated by being in the storyteller's presence as if the energy radiating from his body was warm, soothing, and healing.

As the three of them sat in silence, Daanish Nour casually raised his head to peer into his accustomed darkness, only to notice a canopy of luminous, twinkling specks of light that he had never seen before. The sensation was different from the sudden pain or momentary flashes of white light he experienced when, on occasion, he stumbled and fell and hit his head. These pinpoints of light did not flash or pull away.

When he raised his hands to touch his eyes, he never expected to see his gnarled fingers on his raised hands move across his face. Ma'Mun noticed immediately and shouted, "Abbabba, you can see! You can see!"

Too astonished to speak, the old man slowly looked down at the ground and saw, for the first time, the wooden staff lying between him and his grandson. Hesitantly, he reached for the smooth wooden stick he never thought to see and then examined his right ankle for the birthmark the storyteller pointed out. Then he began crying so loudly that his grandson was startled and fell over backward.

Ma'Mun quickly got up, shouting and dancing in a wide circle around the storyteller and his grandfather, who by now had forgotten his old age and was up on his spindly legs, laughing and waving his hands, following his grandson around in the circle. He then abruptly stopped and looked at the storyteller as the first human being he had ever seen and fell to the ground, lying prostrate in front of him, and reached with his fingertips to touch Narada's feet.

"Lord...lord, such a blessing I do not deserve," he cried. "For allowing me to see, you how can I ever repay?"

"I apologize for asking you to confirm a birthmark from a previous life you could not see."

"My lord, you how can I ever repay?"

"Daanish Nour, I am like an imperfect flute made from an old reed the Great Mystery chooses when to play; and on this clear night, she has graced us with her music of healing and rebirth. Do you hear it, old man? Do you hear it, Ma'Mun?"

And in that instant, into the ether, the faint, buttery sound of a flute was heard emanating from Narada himself. And the raga was the mood of the night, proclaiming the mystery of rebirth and renewal as the three of them, beguiled by a melody as ancient as the Earth, itself, danced and sang and hopped about for joy.

Before they departed near dawn, Narada made Daanish Nour and Ma'Mun promise that the old man's miracle of sight would be attributed to Jah, and not to Narada, for nothing that was said or done could have any other source but Him. And even though they vowed to keep his secret, the storyteller planted a thought-seed in their minds to help reinforce their promise.

It was deathly cold when Narada returned to Fajaruddin gate and turned around to survey the arid land and desert in the distance. He watched the silent sliver of the sun peek over the eastern horizon as he clapped his hands once, so the little crawly creatures in their burrows or sleeping on the land could once again wake up and live their life's purpose.

CHAPTER 25

THREE WILTED FLOWERS

Ibrahim Hafez heard a knock on his compound door, went to open it, and was stunned to see the hyena man standing in the doorway with three wilting yellow flowers in his hand. He noticed right away that the man had taken a bath or dipped his ragged clothes in water, because he did not smell as foul as he usually did, and the flies were not as numerous swarming around his nappy head. He might have laughed at the site of such an absurd visitor with flowers if it were not for the serious look on Arsalaan's face. Unruffled and determined to be polite, Ibrahim Hafez gave the customary, informal male greeting, "Amantahe."

"Hiya Aman," said Arsalaan.

"You may I help?"

"To your daughter to apologize I have come."

"My daughter...Hohete, you mean?"

"Yes."

"What to you is she?"

"Abba," Hohete interrupted as she and Ayaat approached the door.

"This man to apologize to you he says he wants," her father replied, stepping back a little but still blocking the door.

"Oh my Jah!" said Hohete. "What do you want?" she asked while the entire Hafez family now stood at the compound's entrance.

Arsalaan did not know what to say as he had not thought that far ahead and did not expect to be talking to all three members of the family, so he held out the three dying flowers and waited for someone to take them. Hohete stepped forward, undaunted by the fact that she wore no scarf around her head and face, and said, "So, what do you want?"

"To apologize to you I came. So sorry, I am. That your man and my friend, Waheed Nuri, died I did not know. Good friends we were when another kind of life I lived. Amends to make I wanted, and these flowers to you I bring. When my compound I left, still well they were, but the sun has been harsh I see, and dying they are. Perhaps, in water or something them you could put?"

Hohete's face softened as she took the flowers from him. "For the flowers I thank you, and your apology I accept. Waheed, him how did you know?"

"The holy edifice's master builder, from him I learned, and with him I worked. Sometimes, on the edifice how the work was progressing, Waheed to see he came. The son of a patriarch he knew I was, and why a laborer I chose to be, to know he wanted. To become a master builder like the Nubian, him I told, and houses with dome roofs for Ja'Usu's poor to build I wanted. By my idea he was intrigued. Then my father, he died, and...and a little mad I sort of went."

Ibrahim Hafez and Ayaat were quiet and watched the hyena man, who now stared at the ground until he raised his head and said, "For a favor may I ask you, Hohete...please?"

The Hafez family looked at one another, not knowing how to respond. Then Hohete replied, "Arsalaan, what is it?"

Ayaat and Ibrahim Hafez were stunned to realize that Hohete actually knew the hyena man's name. "This man do you know?" asked her father.

"No, but one morning when with Narada I went walking, I met him. To me he spoke."

"And..."

"And...that is it. To me he spoke," she replied before returning her attention to Arsalaan. "How may I help you?"

"My family's compound I want to visit. To see them, I have not since...well...for many years, them I have not seen. The way I look and am dressed, them to see I am not fit." Arsalaan reached into his raggedy loincloth, pulled out a tiny piece of fabric, and started to hand it to Hohete but, instead, thought it best to give it to her father. "In this pouch, silver there is. Some decent clothes for me to wear for my family to visit, if for me you bought, most grateful I would be. Like this to see me, I do not want them."

"Like this you let us see you," Ibrahim Hafez replied with a bit of ridicule.

"But sir, in my family you are not."

"And my daughter, these clothes for you to purchase, why asking her are you? She to you, what is she?"

Arsalaan did not know what to say, and Ibrahim Hafez turned first to Ayaat and then to his daughter for an answer.

"Even though in Ja'Usu family I have, when hyenas to feed I chose, upon my family disgrace I brought, and me they disowned," said Arsalaan. "In this city now, me no one will claim. So since a friend of the storyteller you are, perhaps, to help me you would, I thought."

"Well..." said Ibrahim Hafez, clearing his throat, but then Ayaat interrupted him.

"Dear brother, let Hohete for herself speak."

"Arsalaan, the clothes for you I will buy, so your family you can visit. But if this I do, you something for me you must also do."

"For you, what can I do?"

"Yeah," said her father, "for you what possibly can he do?"

"Hush," said Ayaat to her brother.

"A bath you must take, and your hair you must brush. Your family, even with new clothes, like that smelling and looking as you do, to see you they must not."

Arsalaan did not seem embarrassed or shamed by her request. "Even though a house I have, a way to bathe I do not. But a hand basin I can buy. All right would that be?"

"No, your whole body, a bath it needs. In two days come back, and my father, with your bath he will help you."

"I will?" said Ibrahim Hafez.

"Yes, brother, you will," Ayaat replied, "and Hohete and I, the hot water with salts, we will prepare."

Arsalaan and Ibrahim Hafez were surprised by Hohete's demand and stared, bewildered, at one another as they both struggled to get comfortable with her arrangement, already knowing they would comply.

"Hiya Aman," said Arsalaan and walked away before Ibrahim Hafez could close the compound door.

The people who recognized Arsalaan as the hyena man still moved out of his way when passing him on the street as he walked back to his unfinished compound. But while he looked the same, there was something unusual or unfamiliar about his gait that enabled a few of Ja'Usu's inhabitants to see him differently. The hyena man usually walked with his head and shoulders extended forward, so if he stopped suddenly he could lose his balance and fall on his face. This familiar stride was probably exaggerated by the fact that he usually carried a bag of bones on his back and a sack of animal guts around his shoulders that made him stretch his neck and hold his head up high. But today his steps were different. Arsalaan was erect and more relaxed as he strolled first down Fajaruddin, past the holy edifice where his brother might still be in session, and then crossed over onto Mustakim as he headed home.

Or perhaps, his movements were less frantic and more at ease, because he was preoccupied with a new and strange awareness.

Rather than struggling with unfounded guilt about killing his father, he thought about Hohete and why she made him feel so uncomfortable. Was it because she was married to his friend, Waheed, who had passed away, or because she, unlike most Ja'Usu women, looked him in the eyes when she talked and said what she pleased? Arsalaan's private deliberations abruptly came to an end upon entering his compound when he heard voices coming from one of his three houses. A middle-aged Oromo woman then quickly walked past him, carrying a copper teapot and a set of small glasses. She slipped off her well-worn sandals at the door and entered the mud-brick house where the voices were coming from.

Walking to the entrance and looking inside, Arsalaan was surprised to see Narada seated, cross-legged, on an ornate straw mat, talking to a young boy whom Arsalaan at first did not recognize. Then it struck him who this youth was, and he stormed into the room, ready to grab the boy and physically throw him out.

"Oh no, kidding me you are!" shouted Jumah to Narada, jumping up as soon as he saw Arsalaan. "This man…the hyena man, to work for him you want me? Kidding, you must be."

Arsalaan and Jumah were about to exchange blows when Narada forcefully demanded they both sit down. Arsalaan was the first to reluctantly sit, while Jumah stood over him, glaring, with his fists in a knot.

"Jumah, please sit down," Narada requested again, gently.

The Oromo woman had stepped to the side when the disturbance began and now returned to the mat to serve them hot, sweet tea and dry biscuits. Given the Oromo custom to serve the eldest first, she first poured Narada's tea, and then Arsalaan's, and finally Jumah's. After she set the copper pot on the mat, Narada gave her a silver coin, and she quietly and quickly left the room.

Narada watched small black flies aimlessly circling each other. They rode the warm air currents in the open doorway as the late-morning sun illuminated the room. He calmly drank his tea while Arsalaan and Jumah sat looking daggers at each other. Out of respect and deference to the storyteller, Arsalaan was the first to relinquish his stare and raise his glass to drink his tea.

Narada broke the silence with a laugh, catching Arsalaan and Jumah by surprise as they turned to look at him. "The two of you remind me of the flies at the entrance," he said, pointing toward the doorway. "They are flying nowhere in reaction to light and the movement of the air, while their lives slip away with little purpose or meaning. But the life of a human spirit is a blessing, because each being is unique and has a singular place and purpose in the Great Mystery's cosmic scheme. You are born of human spirit, capable of uncovering the purpose of your life and not moving about aimlessly like the flies circling around and around in the air."

"So our meaning…our purpose, what is it?" asked Arsalaan, picking up a biscuit.

"I cannot aide caterpillars in changing into butterflies by helping them shed their cocoons. If a butterfly struggles to break free from its covering, and I assisted it by peeling away its protective sheath, it would surely die. The struggle to break free is the journey each butterfly must accomplish alone—and so, too, with you. What it means to be a human spirit you must realize and take action on your own; that is the sole purpose of your life. And when your desire for self-knowledge grows strong…so overwhelms you that nothing else matters, then the purpose of your existence and how to fulfill that purpose with an unwavering mind will be revealed to you.

"But at this moment, Arsalaan and Jumah, you are preoccupied with basic survival matters like food, shelter, and clothing. Are you not? This is why I have brought the two of you together.

"Arsalaan, you have walked away from being the hyena man, but you are confronted with a new challenge if you are to fulfill your dream. And Jumah, you are coming upon two crossroads:

one is most immediate, and the other...well, you will be faced with it soon. And the choices you make will affect not only you but also the boys who see you as their leader."

"Explain, storyteller, because a challenge that involves him I do not see," said Arsalaan.

"And no donkey turd crossroad with him in it, for me there is not," Jumah said as he resumed glaring at Arsalaan across from him.

"Arsalaan, you said you want to build houses for the poor. That worthy task will require many workers...trained laborers willing to contribute to this great work of yours. You will find many among the Oromo who are also in need of the housing you envision.

"Jumah, you and your boys live from day to day by robbing and hurting people, especially the poor. I would like the two of you to consider working together, so Arsalaan, you have the workers you need, and Jumah, you and your young men can pay back what you have mercilessly taken from those who do not have. Working with Arsalaan, all of you can acquire a trade that will support not only you but also your families to come. This is the proposal I would like the two of you to consider."

Jumah was the first to speak and burst out laughing. "Me and my boys, for this crazy hyena man us to work with him you want? Kidding you got to be."

"Storyteller," said Arsalaan, "these ruffians, from me they steal. When animal bones I carried, they tripped me up for my bones to take."

"When hungry we steal, and on those old dead bones to hyenas you give, meat there still is," replied Jumah. "This donkey turd, he smells, and with the hyenas he lives. Work with him I cannot. Out of here I am."

But when he tried to stand, Jumah found his backside stuck to the straw mat. And as much as he twisted and turned, he could not move from his place. Arsalaan laughed at the street youth's predicament until he, too, tried to stand and found that he also was stuck to the mat. And now Jumah started laughing. The two of them squirmed and jerked around until finally they looked at Narada, who sat calmly watching both of them struggle.

"With the actions of human beings to interfere you do not, I thought you said, because free will we must have," said Arsalaan.

"That is correct."

"What the donkey turd is this! Let me go!" Jumah shouted.

"Both of you have the right to make your own decisions," continued Narada. "I cannot take away your free will. It is against the Great Mystery's law. But I can make it convenient for you to sit and talk to one another until whatever you freely decide comes from your heart, with calm thoughts, and is not conveyed out of anger."

"But agreed already we have. To work together, we cannot," said Arsalaan. "Jumah, with me to work he will not; and with him and his hooligans to work, with them I cannot."

"Hooligans!" Jumah cried. "Well, at least out of our minds like you we are not. And a donkey turd house to build, a crazy man like you, carrying guts and bones, how would you know?"

"Oh, I almost forgot. I need to ask both of you for a kindness," said Narada.

Arsalaan and Jumah were both confused and annoyed that Narada could so casually put aside their mutual dilemma of being stuck to the floor to ask them for a good turn. They looked at the storyteller in astonishment and then at each other as they waited for whatever came next.

"Imtiyaz and Tabassum, my fire builders, will be unable to prepare the fire for tomorrow night's story. I was wondering if the two of you would be willing to come to stack the wood and start the fire. It really takes two people to handle with all that needs to be done. The people of Ja'Usu, the Oromo, and I would be most grateful."

You could tell by Jumah's face that it took a moment for him to comprehend what was being asked of him, but Arsalaan was the first to speak. "And if we do it, let us go will you?"

"Yes, if us you release, I will do it," Jumah chimed in.

"Oh, the two of you wish to reach a deal? Well then…I will release you from where you sit in two hours if the two of you stop calling each other names and seriously consider the opportunity to work together…in exchange for your promise to build tomorrow's fire together. Agreed?"

"For two hours!" cried Jumah, "And if your terms we do not agree, what then?"

"Yes, what then?" Arsalaan echoed.

"Well…you will probably have to sit for a much longer time."

"Oh, not fair is that," said Jumah.

"And who told you a fair life it was supposed to be?" asked Arsalaan, obviously amused.

"OK, for your story tomorrow the fire I will build," said Arsalaan.

"Together," said Narada, looking at Jumah.

Jumah sulked for an instant and begrudgingly said, "OK, I will do it."

"What will you do, Jumah?" asked Narada to affirm his commitment.

"With this crazy man the fire for your story I will build, but with him houses to build, I will not do."

"And both of you must stay by the fire, until I come and ask for you to light it. Do you both promise?"

"Yes…yes, we do…we do," they both said.

Narada then turned and walked away, and the two of them immediately started shouting and begging for him to return and let them go. In an instant he was back, and they smiled, thinking he had taken pity on their condition and was ready to let them go.

"Oh, when the woman returns for her teapot and glasses, please give her this silver coin I will leave, here, on the mat." After putting down the coin, Narada quickly left before they resumed yelling after him.

CHAPTER 26

THE FLYING BISCUIT

Morning prayer was over, and the last worshipers were leaving the holy edifice when Daanish Nour, his grandson Ma'Mun, and another Oromo named Kazi took off their sandals and washed their hands, faces, and feet in the fountain's running water. Together, they walked barefoot up the three steps and into the holy edifice to meet the governing council.

The nine patriarchs were just getting settled in the rear of the hall and waiting for Beena to serve their morning coffee and biscuits when Daanish Nour, his grandson, and Kazi approached them. The patriarchs were taken aback by the Oromos' presence and the presumption that they could just walk into their space without being announced.

"Into this holy edifice before being invited, how dare you come?" barked Chief Patriarch Murabbi, patron and guardian of the people.

"Sir," replied Daanish Nour, "yesterday we came and outside waited. Someone from here our message to you delivered that with the governing council to meet we wanted, and to come back today we were told. So invited we were, you see."

"Well," replied Chief Patriarch Murabbi, "today does not necessarily mean today. In the future it just means we will see you. Now go!" He dismissed them out of hand and looked away as if something more important had already attracted his attention.

Beena, the young virgin, who had not yet served the governing council their morning meal, rushed into the hall with tiny white cups in hand and their Turkish pot of sweet coffee. Seeing the council's three guests, she was already turning around to get more cups when old Patriarch Ihtesham, the respectable and honorable one, said, "Beena, more cups we do not need. Our visitors leaving they are, so please our coffee and biscuits serve."

Daanish Nour and his party held their ground and did not leave, to the consternation of the council. The chief patriarch was about to demand again that they leave when Patriarch Taqiyy, the pious and righteous, spoke up in a polite tone. "How may we help you?" The other council members looked his way but said nothing as Chief Patriarch Murabbi grumbled to himself.

"As governors of Ja'Usu, out of respect we want you to know, our women, to enter the city and on the streets sit selling vegetables and other wares, they will no longer do."

"Where will they go?" asked Liyaqat, the one who is deserving, worthy of merit.

"We Oromo, the land near to this holy edifice from Ja'Usu's governing council we want to rent, so a magala, a market, we can have. More convenient for everyone in Ja'Usu from one place to buy Oromo food it will be, rather than from street to street you have to walk. This way, in one place everything Oromo sells, there it will be."

"Why?" asked Patriarch Abdul Muntaqim, slave of him who punishes wrongdoings and seizes retribution. "Your women, suddenly unhappy on the streets are they?"

"We Oromo, this arrangement we have never liked, because our women in the hot sun all day and feeding our babies they must sit, even when your shops in the afternoon close, and no one on the streets there is. Our women, until late in the afternoon for shops to open they wait for Ja'Usu people to come back to buy, they stay. This arrangement we accepted because the war we lost, and to survive we wanted. But more than one hundred years ago that was; the war, over it is, and time now for change."

"This hoax, whose idea was this?" asked Aschenaki, the distressed. "Did the storyteller with this proposal here to come he tell you?"

"To the storyteller or to anyone about our request we have not talked to. For the Oromo outside the wall, to this council to speak I have come."

"The storyteller, in your heads these ideas he has put I think," continued Aschenaki.

"To Narada we have not spoken, but Oromo to his story we have listened; and our eyes about our own poor condition has opened, and changes must be made we want. From the future African Americans we have learned if our lives to improve we want, with the Oromo change must start. So, here, for your permission, land for an Oromo magala we ask."

"Your magala!" said Patriarch Tahawwur, the rash. "Everything in Ja'Usu—everything owned by us it is. The Oromo, nothing you have, and land inside our ancient city, if the council agreed to give—which it will not—any market inside Ja'Usu, by Ja'Usu it would be owned, not Oromo."

Kazi, who was only asked to accompany Daanish Nour and his grandson into Ja'Usu, took a step forward and was drawing his knife when the old man who once was blind grabbed his hand to prevent him from baring his blade. "This patriarch, the will of the governing council does he speak?" asked Daanish Nour.

The nine patriarchs looked at one another, assuring themselves they were all in agreement with Tahawwur's pronouncement, and Chief Patriarch Murabbi exclaimed, "The council, spoken it has. No land will be given." And he bit into his biscuit with such vehemence that a large piece of it flew into the air and wedged between the hairs in Patriarch Izzat's dyed carrot-red beard.

"Get out! Leave us!" cried the chief patriarch, embarrassed by his flying biscuit.

"Well then," said Daanish Nour calmly, "Oromo women no longer the city will they enter for their vegetables and crafts to sell. However, well outside the Fajaruddin gate they will remain, and an Oromo magala they will set up. An hour after sunrise it will open, and when the sun overhead directly it is, the magala will close—or when no more food there is to buy. So in the afternoon, Oromo mothers with their babies in the shade they can feed, and better health they can have...like our future African American brothers in the city, Oakland they call it. All Ja'Usu to the Oromo market outside the gate welcomed to come you are, tomorrow starting. Hiya Aman," said Daanish Nour and, along with Ma'Mun and Kazi, left the patriarchs where they sat and headed for the door.

Patriarch Abdul Muntaqim, slave of him who punishes wrongdoings and seizes retribution, was so angry that he wanted to get up and kill the intruders, then and there. Although Abdul's anger boiled, intensified by the simmering rage of his fellow patriarchs, they were all too old—except for Aschenaki, who walked with a severe limp—to mount a stab-in-the-back attack, much less in their own holy place. So they watched the three Oromo as they strode out of the hall, which left them seething—all except Patriarch Taqiyy, the pious, the righteous, whose family actually owned the land the once-blind Oromo man was seeking.

Patriarch Aschenaki, the distressed, was less upset by the Oromo entering their holy space than he was by the notion that they now felt entitled to live a better life. What he feared in private had come to pass—that as a result of Narada's narrative, the Oromo were now motivated to change a Ja'Usu tried-and-true tradition and policy that put Oromo people in their rightful place under the boot of Ja'Usu governance. Now the Oromo wanted control over their own destiny and were demanding changes. Patriarch Aschenaki understood better than most that if an Oromo magala was allowed to operate, no matter where in the city, and it succeeded, there would be no turning back. The Oromo would then demand more independence and autonomy from Ja'Usu rule. Such unlawful actions, if supported, were dangerous and posed a real threat to Ja'Usu's domination over the Oromo—and, more importantly, threatened the patriarchs' control over the city.

"A problem we have," said Chief Patriarch Murabbi, patron and guardian of the people, as he signaled to Beena to bring them more coffee.

"A big problem we got, and now it to fix, how are we going to do it?" asked Patriarch Tahawwur, the rash.

"This storytelling idea was yours, Aschenaki, so with solutions you better come up with," demanded Patriarch Liyaqat, one who is worthy and deserving.

"I better? My honorable Liyaqat, you as well as everyone on this council on the matter voted. You forget? So this little setback together we must solve," replied Aschenaki with as much composure as he could muster.

"Now...now," said Chief Patriarch Murabbi, "among ourselves quarrelling let us not start. Better and smarter than that we are, so our little problem to solve, our heads together, let us put them. First the Oromo, before out of hand they get, with them how should we deal?"

"As they like, let them do," said Patriarch Safdar, the one who breaks the enemy's ranks. "When Ja'Usu women in our streets the Oromo women they do not find, their dignity lower they will not, and outside the wall to an Oromo so-called magala they will not go."

"And if they do, what then?" asked Patriarch Taqiyy, the pious, the righteous.

"Notices around the city we can put up for anyone outside our walls from the Oromo to buy, a crime let us make it," Patriarch Safdar, the one who breaks the enemy's rank, replied with satisfaction. "And if that does not work…well, our soldiers we can send, and any so-called magala the Oromo establish they can destroy,"

"Safdar is right, I think," said Patriarch Ihtesham, the respectable and honorable one. "Very few of our women outside the gate feel safe, they do not; and with the signs up about an Oromo market, no Ja'Usu from them will they dare buy."

"Most of our vegetables from the Oromo comes; them where are we to buy?" asked Patriarch Taqiyy the pious, the righteous.

"When the Oromo enough sales they have lost, to Ja'Usu's streets their women will return," said Patriarch Liyaqat.

"But until the Oromo give in, our vegetables, where will we buy them?" Patriarch Taqiyy asked, again.

"Hell sir, more meat just eat!" shouted Patriarch Safdar, and most everyone, except for Patriarchs Taqiyy and Aschenaki, laughed with relish and relief.

"So about Narada, who resumes his story tonight, what shall we do?" interjected Aschenaki.

"About the storyteller what to do, I do not know," Patriarch Taqiyy replied. "More and more Ja'Usu and Oromo to hear his story they have been coming. Even people who missed the first two nights, to the third narration to hear they came, and probably more people tonight they will come."

"Right Taqiyy is. My grandson, Omair," said Patriarch Ihtesham, the respectable and honorable one, "the tale every night so far he has heard. Members of my family...the next day after Narada's story, with Omair they meet. The storyteller's narrative he retells, and the meaning of new words to explain he delights."

"And in every one of our families, the same thing happening it is," Patriarch Liyaqat exclaimed. "All over Ja'Usu his story is being talked about. Narada and this Arthur Renfro fellow is all I hear...everywhere they are. Even in my own house, so how now can we stop him?"

Patriarch Aschenaki stared at the ornate Persian rug he sat on with his bum leg outstretched, longing for any idea, when, suddenly, he had an epiphany. "Every night, before Narada his story he begins, a fire he has prepared and ready to light it always is. Noticed have you? That fire he needs for the story to tell. What to think do you?"

"OK," said Murabbi reluctantly, "solving our Narada problem, this information how is it going to help us?"

"Well, suppose a fire Narada does not have tonight. If a fire blazing he does not have, his story to tell he may not be able to."

The council members glanced at each other to gauge whether Patriarch Aschenaki's idea had any merit, until Chief Patriarch Murabbi exclaimed, "Yes, Patriarch Aschenaki, that I have noticed, too. A point there, you have."

"Some truth in what you say there might be, because that fire damn sure the bugs to keep away it does not or anybody warm it does not keep," said Patriarch Abdul Muntaqim, slave of him who punishes wrongdoings and seizes retribution.

"Narada's two fire bugs, whose family are they in?" asked the chief patriarch.

"Imtiyaz and Tabassum in mine they are, along with Ibrahim Hafez and his family," Patriarch Liyaqat replied. "Do not worry,

I will take care of it. A fire for his story tonight, Narada will not have."

"Good. Hopefully, if the storyteller unable to continue he is," Chief Patriarch Murabbi said, "Ja'Usu against him they will turn, and over the city and the Oromo his spell will be broken. Then out of town—and not too soon—we can run him."

The council's two resolutions, to boycott the Oromo market and stop Narada's fire, did not sit well with Patriarch Taqiyy, the pious, the righteous, who was beginning to believe the storyteller's presence in the city and his serial narrative were good things. Narada and his story stirred the people's imaginations and encouraged new ideas and change—those that were long overdue. He privately chided himself for not speaking up at meetings and sharing his views with fellow patriarchs, but he was a lone voice on the governing council and knew his opinions would receive little support. In fact, his views would be looked upon as heretical and possibly treasonous. At best, he would be dismissed from the council and shunned. And at worst, he could be locked up and made to stand trial for subversion and treachery and punished. So, he advised himself, it was best to keep his thoughts private and bide his time while Narada and his story progressed along its mysterious course. But then he wondered, should he warn the storyteller?

The Storyteller's Fourth Night

The nine patriarchs, with their family members in tow, walked through the Fajaruddin gate and were pleased to see their vendors selling sweet breads, samosas, and honey wine to Ja'Usu's inhabitants who came to hear Narada's story. Aschenaki moved in his awkward way toward the patriarchs' private platform with a sneer and glared at the people rushing past him to find a place in the inner circle near the storyteller. As if sitting closer to the charlatan would improve their hearing his subversive story! Little did they know that tonight there would be no story, because Narada needed a blazing fire to seduce his audience into a trance. And this night there would be no inferno.

Aschenaki smiled graciously, instead of showing his unbridled teeth to everyone, as he dragged his deformed foot along the ground and gloated over the fact that he alone on the council found ingenious, creative ways to solve Ja'Usu's problems. Tonight, he thought to himself, sabotaging Narada's storytelling would vindicate him and make Narada look like a fool. Then they would run him out of the city.

When the patriarchs passed their vendors and looked out over the flat land and into the gathering crowd, they noticed two figures in the center of the ring stacking wood for the fire that was not supposed to be. They were horrorstruck that their orders were somehow circumvented or ignored and turned to Patriarch Liyaqat, the one who is worthy and deserving, who also mirrored everyone's shock and growing rage. Pushing Liyaqat's family members out of the way, the patriarchs rushed toward him in a fury, demanding to know why he did not carry out what they mutually agreed—to do away with Narada's fire.

"My dear brothers, wait…wait, nothing wrong did I do," Liyaqat quickly shouted. "As I promised, I did. Imtiyaz and Tabassum, his fire builders, to stay home I ordered them and the fire tonight not to make. To not show, even them I paid."

The council members surrounded Liyaqat with wrath in their eyes and grumbled in both his ears, except for Taqiyy, the pious, the righteous, who looked at the two men arranging the dry wood in the field and wondered who they could possibly be.

"To my house I even invited them, and all afternoon I drank with them," Patriarch Liyaqat continued. "And since our religion forbids to drink, you know I do not. But my honey wine, they loved it. Really good it is. When them I left, they were drinking and to their heart's content singing as well. Maybe even home they did not make it, drunk as they were. So what I was asked,

I did. If someone else readies the storyteller's fire, me do not blame."

The chief patriarch twisted his head to look at Arsalaan and Jumah stacking the wood, only stopping occasionally to watch the people and children coming into the field.

"Well, who are they?" cried Murabbi, patron and guardian of the people, pointing to the two figures in the middle of the circle. The patriarchs twisted their heads in unison, like owls on a tree limb, and looked to the center of the ring, wondering how their plans were thwarted.

"The men with the wood to know I do not, but one of them… the way he walks, familiar he looks," said Patriarch Aschenaki, gazing into the field. "Well…as soon as they leave, arrest them."

"To arrest them, how can you?" asked Patriarch Taqiyy. "No ruling did we put out that a fire at Narada's story to build prohibited it was."

"Edicts or rulings or decrees or commands or public prohibitions or whatever else you come up with, care I do not!" shouted Murabbi. "Those two men, as soon as this spectacle over is, arrested they must be. Do you hear? Arrested I want them!" And he marched off toward the patriarchs' platform, pulling his old wife, Adeeba, behind him. The other patriarchs, each with his own entourage, followed them.

Narada was already seated in the inner circle with the Hafez family sitting next to him. He intently watched Arsalaan and Jumah arrange the wood for the fire while Ja'Usu's inhabitants continued streaming into the field, searching for a place to sit. The Oromo no longer stood off to the side, waiting to see where Ja'Usu families placed themselves. They sat in small groups wherever they chose, even if they sat next to the people from the city. Narada thought about Daanish Nour and inwardly smiled, knowing the Oromos' initiative to sit where they liked was the Great Mystery's doing.

The fullness of the yellow moon rose in the twilight, illuminating the plains and the edges of the dark purple and gray desert in the distance. The latent warmth of the day's heat rose from the earth like an invisible kiss and mingled with the cool breeze coming in from the desert. Over a thousand people were now gathered, and more were still coming. Some gatherers carried tiny clay bowls with drops of camphor oil and thin wicks torn from burlap to light and keep the mosquitoes away.

Narada stood facing the north and bowed to the Earth when many newcomers thought he was bowing to them. So they, too, got up to return his bow, while listeners from the previous night of storytelling understood his bowing was to honor Mother Earth. So they also rose and turned north to mimic Narada's every action. When he turned to the east to bow, the seasoned listeners turned east and bowed; when he turned to the south and bowed, they, too, turned south and bowed; and finally, when he turned west, they also turned west, which completely confused the newcomers, who now did not know who was bowing for what or what they were supposed to do. Some stood still and watched the rotations of the people next to them, while other new gatherers tried to keep up with the crowd by turning around and around.

The swirling bodies only stopped and stood with the rest when they noticed the people near Narada were no longer standing. Then they, too, sat until row after row of gatherers from the inner circle to the outer edges were seated and waiting patiently for the next leg of the story to begin.

Narada motioned to Arsalaan and Jumah, and both of them started lighting the dry wood from opposite sides of the pile. Almost immediately, the wood ignited as yellow, red, and orange flames licked the air, bursting tiny specks of red-hot embers in all directions. The two of them jumped back from the fire, seeing something out of the ordinary in the way the fire danced and played. And in that instant, they shared the same thought at the same time as the wood burned. And they saw each other through the flames, as if it were for the first time, and understood they had actually worked together in stacking wood and cow dung and igniting the blaze. Why could they not work together in building homes for the poor? They both dismissed the thought, knowing it was absurd.

As the fire grew into knowing itself and its potential, Narada closed his eyes and offered a silent prayer to the Great Mystery. Hohete, sitting next to him, felt the closeness of his body and turned to look at him and then at Arsalaan, who was staring at the flames. And now the entire gathering watched the fire intently. Although they did not know the connection, they subconsciously understood their capacity to listen, watch, and appreciate Narada's story had something to do with the dancing flames, as if the fire, as living energy, possessed the power to catapult each listener through time and space to behold the narrative as it continued to unfold.

While many Ja'Usu and Oromo closed their eyes and waited patiently for the story to begin again, some in the gathering watched the crackling fire as it gave birth to a multitude of glowing, red-hot embers. These flashing specks of light, like miniature meteorites, rose into the night sky before disappearing into blackness. Few among the many who looked upon the fire understood that the embers spoke to them of their own mortality. They, too, were born like the embers from the womb of Spirit, only to exhaust their lives in a moment of time before passing away into the unknown. Rather than becoming fearful, they felt an infinite peace, as if they had tasted water from a living spring of wisdom born from the experience of settling into themselves. In this stillness and deep silence from within, they willingly surrendered to an expanded awareness that they, too, were in transition, engaged in a perpetual cycle of constant change. That knowing was intrinsic to the subtlety of the cosmic hum they faintly felt and heard, but still they could not name. Later in time or, perhaps, in another life, they would recognize that cosmic hum as Aum, Amin, Amen, or the sole witness, the Holy Ghost; the constant rumbling drone emanating existence, the intimacy of a heartbeat undergirding the universe. The blaze from the fire warmed their hearts.

Narada, the storyteller, intoned in an unfamiliar tongue that the inhabitants of Ja'Usu and the Oromo present did not know or understand. From a mysterious wellspring, deeper than any vibration or sound they had ever felt or heard, surfaced a roaring that made their bodies tremble and the ground quake; and the people were much afraid, yet unable to get up or run away.

As the trembling gradually subsided, and the ground stopped shaking, the storyteller raised his arms in praise and supplication to thank the Great Mystery for responding to his prayer. For the Akasha had reopened, allowing Narada to once again read from the imperishable records of celestial light, retaining the history of man and woman and illuminating the present and future of human thought and action. And the people were afraid.

Narada opened his eyes and, unbeknownst to others, commanded all crawling creatures among them go underground and the tiny life forms flying in the air to move away until the night turned to day. And the multitude of snakes and lizards and toads and scorpions; sand crabs and fleas and mosquitoes; and everything that crawled or flew did as it was told. Once these directives were complete, Narada picked up where he left off in his once-upon-a-time-in-the-future story.

CHAPTER 27
GOD IS DEAD

It is a little after six on Wednesday evening when eighteen members of the leadership team meet at the Holy Redeemer Retreat Center in East Oakland. Arthur stands at the podium, summarizing the progress made to date in fleshing out Dr. Lightfoot's proposed social experiment and engaging leadership in the development of a community action plan to confront the health crisis facing African Americans.

A large portrait of Harriet Tubman rests on an ornate easel to the left of the lectern. Three latecomers enter the hall as Arthur informs those present that, based on the ad-hoc committee's work and the responses he received, the majority of leadership approved Dr. Lightfoot's proposal. He says, "We're ready to move forward with what shall be called the Critical Mass Health Conductors initiative." The leaders applaud, and Arthur introduces the project's new staff, and there's another round of applause.

After being introduced, Dr. Lightfoot comes to the podium and happily tells everyone to call her Hachi from now on and adds, "Although I will be your program director, I, along with the rest of the staff, will also be an active participant in this social experiment." There's another round of applause.

Hachi thanks everyone for already forming into small groups of three or four per cluster. She explains that before the night is over, each cluster will have a chance to meet so members can share with one another the personal health challenge they're each prepared to work on over the next three months. Groups will also decide on a shared activity everyone is willing to do, together, at least once each month.

After her introduction, Aisha steps up to the podium and, while pointing to the large photograph, explains how Harriet Tubman has been chosen as the initiative's patron and tells the story of Harriet leading slaves to freedom. She describes Harriet as a courageous woman who was countercultural and a revolutionary for the times in which she lived; that she was considered so dangerous by white slaveholders that they put a bounty on her head; that she was wanted dead or alive. "So we honor Harriet as our first health conductor for her unselfish service to others and her bravery," Aisha concludes. "And we look to her for strength and spiritual guidance as we launch our Overground Railroad, to not only free ourselves but also our brothas and sistahs from the health crisis we all face. Please feel free to invite your family members and friends to our two remaining training sessions. They are welcome to attend."

The next speakers are Dr. Joe Braxton and Regina Bradley, who discuss the metabolic syndrome for the benefit of their audience. As their conversation begins, Arthur's thoughts are somewhere else—on his extraordinary encounter with a man he recalls meeting at Ensarro that afternoon.

He had stopped at the Ethiopian restaurant on Grand for lunch, sitting alone with a book on Buddhist meditation while waiting for Solomon, the proprietor, to take his order. Looking up, he casually noticed an older black man sitting by himself two tables away. The man smiled at him, and although Arthur thought the old fellow looked familiar, he couldn't place him or recall any recent event where he might have seen or met him.

Arthur ordered doro wat, a chicken stew cooked in berbere, a red hot-pepper sauce unique to Ethiopia, and injera, a large, spongy pancake made from a grain called teff, and went back to reading his book. He then looked up, discovering the older gentleman standing on the other side of the table.

"May I sit down?" the man had said.

He was a short, stocky man with smooth dark skin and a beguiling smile. If it were not for his overall demeanor and appearance, Arthur would have thought the man was getting ready to sell him something or, perhaps, lonely and didn't want to eat alone. The gentleman was impressive in his clothes and could have been a seasoned tailor in his light gray suit with a blue dress shirt and matching gray and dark blue striped tie. Arthur looked down to the side and noticed his black, soft leather shoes that were immaculately clean and polished. As an accent to his attire, he wore a steel gray fedora with a short brim, that sat squarely on his head.

Had he been walking down Wall Street, he may have been considered a private investment banker meeting rich clients for lunch. He looked oddly out of place here in Oakland, or the Bay Area in general, where casual clothing is fashionable and formal dress relegated to those working in a corporate culture that prides itself on employee uniformity.

Arthur stood up on impulse and said to the older man, "Please, sit down."

"I see you're getting ready to have your lunch," the older man said in a rich voice with a slight southern drawl, "but I couldn't help but notice the book you're reading," pointing to the cover of Arthur's book. "Let me introduce myself; my name is Luther McKinnie. And yours?

"Arthur...Arthur Renfro."

"Mr. Renfro, may I call you Arthur?"

"Arthur would be fine."

"Arthur," the man said slowly, with a respectful familiarity, as if he had known him all his life, "the Buddha's teachings and Buddhist meditation are very fitting for this age, because the Buddha's path is not predicated on a belief in God. In fact, many people in the modern world believe that God is truly dead."

"What do you mean, dead?"

"I admit the term is misleading, because it doesn't explain what's really behind the statement. Some people literally mean God is dead or irrelevant, because the supremacy of God has been replaced by science with its disciplined system of logic and reason. But others have a different take on this God-is-dead business. Many modern theologians, for example, recognize the difficulty in thinking and talking about God as an anthropomorphic being, as some external deity sitting on a throne on high or in a heaven somewhere making commandments and doling out justice. This conceptualization of God is slowly dying and giving way in the Western mind to a more personal, and intimate relationship with the Most High."

"Mr. McKinnie, I know you're not a pastor or preacher, but are you a religious scholar or an academic of some sort?

"You could say that I am, but you would be wrong. But I apologize for veering off the subject."

"What subject?"

"Buddhism, of course...do you know why Buddhism is so popular here in the West, Arthur?" Luther sat back in his chair and waited patiently for him to answer.

"No, I don't."

"Because the question of whether there is a God or not is irrelevant since Buddha's teachings say that a definitive answer to this question is unknowable."

"Excuse me?" said Arthur. Ever since Luther sat down and began to speak, Arthur had this peculiar feeling that things were not quite what they seemed.

Luther picked up on Arthur's confusion and repeated his comments, word for word, and concluded by saying, "Now, do you understand?"

"Yes...yes, I think I do."

"You will see that the Buddha's teachings are elegant in their simplicity and offer an exceptional human development system, tried and tested throughout the ages by millions of followers around the world. The practice of Buddhism is suited to today when so many youth are rejecting organized religion and doing away with God."

Arthur looked at Luther McKinnie and was starting to wonder if his initial take on the man was actually true, that he was an older gentleman who was lonely and simply needed someone to talk to.

"But Arthur, as you consider following in Buddha's footsteps, I suggest you also explore the path of Raja yoga and learn how to commune with the Most High." Luther leaned back in his chair and waited for Arthur to respond.

Tears suddenly welled-up in Arthur's eyes as he heard himself saying in a barely audible voice that no one else but Luther heard, "My professional life keeps me grounded and sane, but my personal life is a train wreck. My wife left me and may want a divorce. When I'm home and alone, I feel a deep sense of emptiness and loss, and I don't know why. A psychologist wants me on drugs because, when I lie down to sleep, I leave my body. And recently, I experienced being possessed by an evil spirit that roams my building; and now I must find a way to protect myself. And you're telling me Buddhism and mindfulness practice may not be right for me, and to read about some kind of yoga?"

Solomon returned and placed a plate with his order on the table. Feeling embarrassed that he had unintentionally exposed so much of his private life to a man he didn't know was unnerving. Overwhelmed, Arthur abruptly left the table, claiming he had to wash his hands. He wished the man would go away, but while walking back to his table, he saw that Luther was still there.

Sitting down without looking at his unwanted guest, Arthur picked up a piece of injera in his hand and held it over the tray as if considering what to taste first. But in reality, he was trying to regain control over his inner turmoil as he looked at the hard-boiled egg in the doro wat; the cooked yellow lentils, mustard greens, and salad fixings on his plate. He well expected Luther to resume talking and thought he would explode, but to his surprise, the man said nothing.

Arthur felt himself becoming angry, because Luther hadn't said a word since he returned to his table. He prayed to God no one he knew would come into the restaurant and walk over to greet him. This experience and his reaction to Luther was crazy, and he laughed uncontrollably.

"Arthur, have you ever been in a situation where you were fearful because you were not in control of what was happening and felt your life was in danger? And at that very moment, what did you say to yourself?" Arthur looked at Luther, whose face was calm but serious. The older man's eyes were riveted on his young companion. "What did you say, Arthur?"

"I asked for God's help," Arthur said in a soft monotone, sensing that the man already knew about his possession experience and how it ended. But how could that be?

"After that encounter, you sat in silence and prayed to the Most High to show you how to protect yourself. Didn't you?"

Arthur found it difficult to speak or swallow; he put down his fork and glanced at Luther, who looked back at him with deep sympathy and compassion. Silence was between them now; Arthur felt a sense of relief and oddly at peace, like a young boy basking in the love and approval of his father.

Luther reached into the inside pocket of his jacket and pulled out what looked like a business card. "I can help you in nurturing your relationship with the Divine, and in doing so you can free the intuition of your soul to guide and protect you from all harm. If and when you're ready, come see me." Luther pushed the card across the table, stood and nodded with the slight tilt of his fedora, and walked away.

Arthur takes the card out of his shirt pocket for the fifth time since receiving it and, once again, studies Luther's handwriting as the panel concludes its discussion and the audience starts to applause. Hachi thanks Dr. Braxton and Regina for their conversation on the metabolic syndrome and what one can do to reduce the risk factors associated with the disorder.

While Hachi and Aisha remain up front to talk to members of the leadership, Dr. Braxton walks over to Arthur and asks what he thought of the panel's first training session. Too embarrassed to admit he heard little of the discussion, Arthur deflects the question by asking Joe if he knows a black physician who can talk to the group about chronic stress and how to manage it.

Dr. Braxton takes out his smartphone and says, "Call Dr. Phil Morgan at the Berkeley City Clinic. He runs an innovative program for treating addicts using acupuncture and meditation for stress management. I think Phil would enjoy talking to this group. I've just texted you his phone number, but I'll get in touch with him in the morning and let him know to expect your call."

CHAPTER 28
THE MIGHTY BILLY

Julia accompanies Mrs. Alvarez on her first visit to Arthur's apartment as the middle-aged Mexican woman speaks little to no English and needs Mrs. Valencia's daughter to make introductions and help negotiate the terms of her employment. Julia knocks on the door, and, anticipating the women's arrival, Arthur answers immediately. As soon as they enter the apartment, Mrs. Alvarez is distracted by the uncleanliness of the place. Julia introduces Arthur to his potential cleaning lady, and Mrs. Alvarez starts rattling off in Spanish that the unit looks like a garbage can. When Arthur asks Julia what the woman is saying, she is reluctant to speak until he prods her into answering. Julia says that Mrs. Alvarez thinks the apartment is messy, but purposely leaves out the part about him living like a pig. Suddenly, the conversation between the two women becomes heated, and all Arthur can do is wait for their discussion to end.

"Arthur," Julia finally turns to him and says, "I know you don't understand what we're talking about, but I'm working it out. Do you mind if she sees the rest of your apartment?"

"No, I don't mind." Arthur remains in the kitchen while Julia and Mrs. Alvarez walk through the rest of the unit.

Julia steps away from Mrs. Alvarez to speak to Arthur in private. Almost in a whisper, she tells him the woman says she can clean it, but wants to charge twice as much as she normally does for a flat this size because she'll have to stay all day. After more exchanges in English and Spanish, Arthur agrees to hire Mrs. Alvarez to clean twice a month; she wants to start that very day. His new housekeeper then looks up at Arthur with a smile and, at the same time, shakes her head. He wonders if the little woman has just put one over on him. Mrs. Alvarez turns to Julia and says in Spanish, "Poor man…poor man."

Arthur meets with Dr. Phil Morgan, who teaches stress management at the Berkeley City Clinic. Phil greets Arthur with a firm handshake and suggests they walk over to the clinic's cafeteria to have their conversation. As Joe Braxton told him Phil Morgan was a surgeon during the Vietnam War, but Arthur is surprised to see how young the doctor looks. As they walk down the hallway, they exchange pleasantries and share how they both know Joe Braxton. It turns out that Phil attended the Saturday Expo at the Health Summit and took Billy Blank's exercise class.

"Man…that was a great session," says Phil. "I take karate twice a week, and let me tell you, my muscles were still sore the day after that session. I can see why Billy's videos are so popular. He's a good instructor. How he's able to present workout instructions and give encouragement while at the same time doing the exercises himself is remarkable. The guy's strong."

The doc orders herbal tea and Arthur coffee, and then they sit at a table near the window. Phil explains that he was an army surgeon in a trauma unit outside of Saigon during the Vietnam War when Billy used to come and work out with the troops. Phil marvels that, judging from the Expo, Billy's routine hasn't slowed him down over the years. He then abruptly shifts the conversation.

"So what can I do for you, Mr. Renfro? Joe said you wanted to see me about stress management."

"Please call me Arthur. Joe referred me to you thinking that, perhaps, you might be willing to talk to our leadership about chronic stress and how to manage it."

"He did, huh...Joe did mention he was involved in something called Critical Mass Health Conductors. What's that about?"

Arthur shares with Phil the origin of Health Conductors and emphasizes it's a pilot project led by a physician named Dr. Hachi Lightfoot. Phil is intrigued with the triad concept and wants to know what type of health activities are groups involved in.

Arthur describes his own triad with Aaron Campbell, John Sutton, and a black South African pastor who decided to join their group. "We chose to increase our exercise regimen and meet at six o'clock every Thursday morning to walk around Lake Merritt. There's another triad of three women who say they're sleep deprived, and they chose to support one another in getting more rest. So, around nine in the evening, someone in their group makes phone calls, reminding their partners it's time to prepare for bed so everyone's tucked in by nine thirty. So you see, these groups are very creative in what they choose to do to improve their health and well-being."

"Is it working for them?" asks Dr. Morgan, laughing.

"I don't know. We'll find out at the next training session when triads share with everyone their group's progress."

Dr. Morgan smiles and says, "I wish I had the time to show you around the clinic, but I have a staff meeting in fifteen minutes. So let me tell you how I would approach conducting a stress management workshop for your leadership. First, I'd talk about what chronic stress is and what it does to the human body over time. I'd then cover the importance of deep relaxation as a way to counter stress and what deep relaxation is and is not. It's not taking up a leisure activity like golf or tennis or reading. It's not even getting more sleep. We'd also discuss what positive effect deep relaxation has on the body and then take your leadership through several simple meditation exercises anyone could practice at home to relieve stress."

"So, you use meditation to manage stress?" asks Arthur.

"Yes, I use it with my clients here and also when I'm invited to other substance-abuse centers. Of course, here at the clinic, we also complement meditation with acupuncture, but simple, quiet sitting techniques alone can be effective if applied fifteen to twenty minutes a day. When is your meeting with your group?"

"We meet the first Wednesday in the month at the Holy Redeemer Retreat Center in East Oakland, between six and nine in the evening. Would this time slot work for you?"

"Yes."

"How long would your seminar be, and what's your fee?" asks Arthur.

"My presentation is about thirty to forty minutes, leaving time for questions and answers. I'll do the workshop for free under one condition: that you don't publicize my work with Health Conductors, ever."

"Why? I would think you'd want to be acknowledged for the service you'll provide."

"While the content material on stress reduction is mine, the information I present on meditation comes from another large organization, which I'm not going to name. They charge a hefty fee for their training, and if it was found out that I gave it to you for free...well, I'd be dismissed from working as a trainer with them. So, let my workshop for health conductors remain anonymous. Do you agree?"

"I agree. And I'll get back to you shortly with a specific date and time for your consideration."

⁂

As soon as Arthur returns to his car and turns the key in the ignition, his phone rings. So he lets it go to voice mail and listens to it. "Hi, Arthur, it's been a while since I've heard your voice, even if it's just your outgoing voice mail message. We need to talk, so please call me when you have a chance...Ciao!"

Her voice sounds cheerful enough, but Arthur listens to her words with foreboding. He fights the urge to call her back right then and there. Instead, he makes a U-turn on Sixth Street and heads south toward Ashby. He glances at his watch, which reads twenty minutes after twelve, and guesses Natalie called from her office. He wonders if she's made up her mind about filing for divorce or getting back together and prefers to talk on the phone rather than meeting him for lunch or dinner.

It's a sunny, warm day, and Arthur decides he's not going to spoil it by returning Natalie's call right away. He opts for waiting until he's home that evening, so he'll have no distractions to contend with and can respond to whatever she has to say.

CHAPTER 29
WAITING FOR A SIGN

Arthur is torn. He wants to talk to Natalie and therefore returns her call. But as he listens to the phone ring, part of him hopes that his call will roll over to her voice mail so he can leave a message and hang up.

"Hello," he hears her innocent voice inquire.

"Hi Natalie, it's me. I'm sorry I couldn't respond sooner, but I had just left a meeting when I got your message and thought I'd wait until I got home to return your call."

"That's fine, Arthur. I knew you'd surface when you had the chance. So, how are you?"

"Work is going well. Perhaps it's that part of my life that keeps me sane."

"What do you mean?" she asks.

"Well...I think about you a lot, and the fact that we're not together. I mean, although the Trust keeps me busy, I miss you in my life and want this separation to end."

"Do you, Arthur? Do you really miss me, or are you just lonely or tired of being alone at night in that messy apartment?"

"It's no longer messy. I hired a housekeeper, and I'm determined to keep the place clean. She started today, and it sure makes me feel better."

"Good…that's a very worthy goal. You know, when I first left, I thought about you, too, every day, and the feelings that came up made me cry. But now, after all this time that has passed, I don't think of you as much…and I've stopped crying. But when I think of you, the question I ask myself is this: 'Do you love me, Arthur?'"

"Now, which question would you prefer I answer first?"

Natalie laughs as if someone has given her a compliment she needs to get comfortable with. "So you've avoided answering any of my questions with asking a question of your own."

"You've asked several questions, and I can't recall all of them."

"You know, Arthur, I know you don't love me. I know you think you do, but you really don't. Maybe you're in love with the idea of loving me, or maybe you're in love with the idea of someone to come home to, but you don't love me, Arthur."

"Now wait a minute, Natalie. Please don't speak for me."

"Well, do you, Arthur? Do you love me?" She could have been talking into empty space for the deafening sound of silence on the other end of the line. He doesn't respond. "Arthur, are you still there?"

"Yes, Natalie, I'm here. It's painful and very disturbing for me to realize that you don't feel that I love you. I don't know what to say. I feel like I've crashed into a brick wall."

"Arthur, you've always had a flair for the dramatic. Just be honest, and tell me, how do you feel about me?"

"Sometimes, I can't distinguish the difference between a thought and a feeling, I admit, but for as long as we've been together, Natalie, I've tried to express my love for you."

"Does that also include when you were sleeping around, Arthur? I'm sorry…I didn't really want to go there. That's not why I called."

"And why did you call? Just to say 'hello' and to see how I was doing?"

"Arthur, most of the time, you do live in your head, so I can understand your confusion about thoughts and feelings. Let me make it easy for you, because I know what I feel. I don't feel loved by you, and that's OK. I felt sorry for myself at first, but I'm over it now. I'm over it. You know, even though I'm thirty-five and you're forty-two, we both have a lot of growing up to do. I own up to it. I wonder if either one of us knows what love is. We just got married too soon."

"What are you saying, Natalie?" asks Arthur.

"I went to see a lawyer yesterday and am filing for divorce."

"Natalie, like you decided without even talking to me first that you wanted a three-month separation, now you're telling me you want a divorce, and we've not discussed it."

"We're discussing it now, Arthur," she says. "And besides, I don't have to ask first for your permission. I can think for myself and am taking care of me."

"Why don't we meet for dinner somewhere and talk about this? Are you open to meeting me?" There is a long pause while Arthur waits, not saying a word.

"No, Arthur, I've already made a decision."

"So, that's it? There's nothing else to say to one another?"

"Luckily we don't have children. I want nothing from you, so I don't see what else we have to talk about."

"Oh I see...you're just springing this on me...deciding to get a divorce, and I'm supposed to come to terms with your decision without any further discussion. Is meeting me and talking about it asking too much of you?"

"No, Arthur. I understand. Just call me back when you want, and we can talk. OK? Bye." And suddenly there's only dead air on the other end of the line.

"Natalie...Natalie?

Although it takes a moment for him to recognize it, she's abruptly left the conversation, like other times when he's sensed she couldn't emotionally handle his tone of voice or the direction of their conversation. Each time she does this, it makes him furious because what he needs is the opportunity to just talk things through. Even though he knows from past experience that if he calls her back, she will refuse to pick up the phone, he dials anyway and listens to it ring. After four loops it transfers to her voice mail, and he listens to her childlike innocence seep into her outgoing message like maple sap dribbling down tree bark.

Instead of shouting into the phone like he wants to, Arthur composes himself long enough to calmly say, "I know this is hard for you, Natalie, and you're doing your best not to get caught up in the emotion of it all. I'm struggling, too, and would like the opportunity to sit down like two grown adults and have a conversation. And if it would be helpful to you, I'm sure we could arrange to meet at Dr. Brathwaite's office. So please call me back… or leave a message to let me know if you're open to my suggestion. I would appreciate it…good night."

Arthur sits and waits, hoping the phone will ring. After ten minutes, with his mind on fire and racing, he gets up and pours himself a full glass of red wine and returns to his living-room chair, mulling over his brief conversation with Natalie.

He questions whether to telephone Valerie to talk about what happened before looking at his watch and realizing that with the three-hour time difference, it's much too late to call the East Coast. His instincts also warn him it might not be a good idea. So, instead, he stands up and searches in his pockets for a phone number and, finding it, calls Luther and tells him he's ready to be introduced to Raja yoga. They arrange to meet, and he realizes to his surprise that Luther lives not far from Hector's and Sonia's place near Mills College.

How could Arthur know the malevolent spirit staying downstairs and haunting the building was now in his kitchen watching him? Like it had done that afternoon when Arthur laid on his bed and, intentionally, tried to leave his body. It would have succeeded and taken over his physical form that day had it not been for the bright light that showed up at the last minute to warn him of danger. But its persistent spirit paid off when it found an opening into Arthur's human form, the morning he returned from San Francisco after spending the night with Valerie. It took pleasure in riding Arthur like a horse on the BART back and forth that day.

It was its good fortune to find someone in the building whose spirit and physical vessel was loosely wrapped. It was determined to wait as long as it took to grab this body, and make this human its very own. Even if it only stayed for minutes at a time, it would learn to enter Arthur's physical frame like a revolving door and wear down his will power so it could come and go as it pleased.

Then it would have the physical pleasure of drinking, again, and getting drunk; of using this human's prick to fuck any woman it could seduce. It would then be free, like any human to do whatever it chose to do. But first, it must be patient and learn how to enter this human vessel like putting on and taking off a leather glove. These thoughts were enough to stir up the tangled web of passions and desires that defined its reality, and it watched the human called Arthur and waited for a sign...any sign.

CHAPTER 30
TALKING POINTS

"Dr. Renfro, how are you this mornin'…have you seen *The Post*?" says Aaron Campbell on the other end of the line.

"No, I haven't, Aaron."

"Well, you should take a look at the article on the front page. It's about Critical Mass Health Conductors and the Trust, and it ain't good. Oh, and it was written by Roy Thomas."

"Who?" asks Arthur.

"Roy Thomas, the brotha from Unified Way who came to the leadership meeting once, when Hachi was presenting her proposal. He lit into the plan because we were only targeting black folk and not, as he wanted, a multicultural demographic to participate in the project. You remember him?"

"Oh, yes…yes, the one I had to cut off because decisions had already been made at the previous meeting."

"That's the one. Check out the article, and be prepared for reporters calling you for your response. I gotta go…talk to yah."

Arthur takes the elevator down to the lobby and picks up a copy of The Post—one of several local black newspapers—from the front desk. While riding back to the seventh floor, he notices Roy has managed to get his photo on the front page, smiling broadly, as if he were a cat that caught a mouse. Next to his picture is the title to his op ed piece, "The Trust's Inappropriate Response to the Health Crisis." Arthur's halfway through the article when the elevator stops, and he almost trips getting off the lift while reading about the leadership team being "a bunch of elitist Black Nationalists." According to Mr. Thomas, this "exclusive group holds the misguided belief that the best way to respond to the health crisis facing the Black community is to address their own personal health issues as an approach to developing a community action plan."

Arthur's incensed not by Roy's critique, which as a Unified Way executive was predictable, but by feeling compelled to defend the initiative before it even gets off the ground. While walking back to his office, he realizes that he'll have to strike a delicate balance in his response between defending Critical Mass Health Conductors and not coming across as diminishing the significance of health inequities in other communities of color. Of course, he'll have to champion the initiative's train-one, teach-one strategy with community activists and faith leaders, some of whom will support Roy's point of view, but that's an easy argument to confront, and Arthur actually welcomes the opportunity to talk about Health Conductors communitywide. In fact, he concludes, Roy's article may have unwittingly set in motion a larger conversation about the nature of community social change and transformation, about community empowerment through self-help as opposed to relying heavily on rousing community support for a change in public policy.

What irks Arthur the most about the editorial, and it surfaces over and over again in dealing with racial politics in white America, is having to defend the right of a people to address their own needs and issues in a culturally rooted way, without having to justify or defend a community's interests or actions to public institutions and agencies or to other cultural and ethnic groups. Why are black people and their organizations labeled as exclusionary or nationalistic for focusing merely on the needs of people of African descent when other cultural and racial populations do it all the time? Arthur instantly realizes when he walks into the Trust that he has slammed the office door.

"What's up with you?" asks Gracie. "Arthur, there's a reporter from The Post on the line wanting to talk to you. Do you want me to transfer him to your desk?"

"Yes, put him through."

"Someone else from *The Sun Reporter* also called, asking for you. What's goin' on, Arthur?"

"Here, read this article, and after you finish, please put it on the conference table." The phone on his desk rings. Arthur picks it up and covers the mouthpiece. "Gracie, if other reporters call, just take their phone numbers and what papers they're from, and I'll call them back." Then into the phone, "Arthur Renfro here."

"Dr. Renfro, this is Scott Bailey from The Post. Thanks for taking my call. Did you read the article in our paper this morning by Roy Thomas from Unified Way?"

"Yes, I did."

"Would you care to comment? How about on his accusation that you head a Black Nationalist organization that's addressing the health needs of W. E. B. DuBois's talented tenth?"

"Let's take one thing at a time, Mr. Bailey. The African American Community Trust Fund is, by its name, an identity-based philanthropy, like the Asian American Fund or the Hispanic Community Fund that serve their respective communities. The Trust is unabashedly a black organization serving a black population. And if my memory serves me well, a nationalist is someone who is devoted to the interest or culture of a particular nation. The Trust is a locally based nonprofit, serving Bay Area African American communities. So the Trust and its programs are not nationalistic. Isn't that right, Mr. Bailey?"

"Well, don't you think it odd that the Trust would address the health concerns of…as Mr. Thomas puts it, a small elitist group of African Americans all sitting in positions of power?"

"His accusation is simply not true. If this was the case, Mr. Bailey, then the Trust wouldn't have utilized its limited resources to convene and host the first Bay Area–wide African American Health Summit last year. Over twenty-nine hundred people—coming from diverse economic backgrounds—attended that two-day event. So I think Mr. Thomas's criticism is grossly misrepresented and unfounded."

"What about his assertion that the Trust's effort to develop a community action plan to reduce health inequities in the black community will only benefit the middle and upper classes and not low-income families and their children? How do you respond to that?"

"That's not our intent, and it's not true. But it does speak to a much larger question, and that's how does social change actually occur within communities? This is where we actually differ with Roy Thomas's underlying perspective on the matter. You see, Scott…may I call you Scott?

"Yes, that's fine."

"Well, Scott, the Trust believes on a fundamental level that social change takes place one person at a time, not primarily through bombarding people with a barrage of health information or using our communities limited resources to complain to government for public policy change. Any community has the right to create its own culturally rooted solutions to the issues it faces; and in this instance, the Trust is piloting a social experiment to learn how to address the health crisis among people of African descent."

"What kind of experiment?" asks Bailey.

"Our leadership team is challenged to discover how best to recruit and train a cadre of community health volunteers. But first, we have to learn from this self-help approach and, in doing so, figure out how to best motivate individuals to make better behavioral and lifestyle changes. So it's an organic process we're undertaking, and as this Initiative develops, we expect our demographics will change to also include poor and low-income volunteers and their families. And we'll adapt the model as we go along to meet the needs of those changing demographics, but we're not there yet."

"But why aren't Hispanics and Asians represented in your social experiment? I mean, we live in a multicultural part of the world. Shouldn't they, too, be included?"

"Scott…at the root of the health problems African Americans face, no doubt, is chronic stress and a deep sense of victimization at the hands of a white-supremacist America dating back to the inception of slavery. And I think people of African descent remain under siege in a country that continues to find it difficult to confront its own racist history, to own up to centuries of its systemic and structural racism and racial discrimination against not only black folk but other people of color. Black folk are unhealthy because they live in an unhealthy environment.

"And while other communities of color may have to confront similar issues in terms of racial oppression, none has to grapple with the history and specific impact of slavery and its aftermath as do black people. So our response to the health crisis has to take into account this peculiar history. And there's collective agreement among Summit leadership that a multicultural approach to our health crisis is neither viable nor appropriate. Now, if other organizations serving a multicultural population wish to tackle health inequities, the Trust is here to advise and help, but our priority is to serve people of African descent."

"Do you mind if I quote you on what you've just said?"

"I trust that you will and not distort my words, Scott."

"One last question, because you've mentioned so much. Given what you've said, how does the Trust plan to tackle what you see as an intergenerational crisis?"

"We're trying to discover the answer to your question now in the launching of Critical Mass Health Conductors. But one thing I'd like to emphasis is that the Trust and its leadership are focused on community empowerment. We recognize, as a community and as individuals, that we must take responsibility for our own health…our family's health and well-being. No organization, no matter if they are a public agency or private institution, can do this for us. We must take responsibility for ourselves."

"And what do you see as the Trust's biggest obstacle in making all this happen?"

"Engaging our youth…our young people, so that ultimately they lead the way."

"Thank you, Dr. Renfro. I'd like to draft an article and run it by you before it goes to publication. Is that all right with you?

"Yes, that would be fine."

"It needs to be a quick turnaround."

"I promise to respond the same day I receive the draft."

"Thanks for your time. I appreciate it."

"Remember, you got that health conductors' management meeting at two," says Gracie, hearing Arthur's conversation with The Post reporter's ended. "And Ramona, she's still afraid to go near the conference room, 'cause of that roach she saw climbing the wall. Ain't that something, a grown woman afraid of a damn roach! She's comin' in at four to see you about this year's campaign results…and don't forget to sign these here checks. I'll leave them on the conference table so you have no excuse. And don't be tryin' to sneak outta here, telling me you gonna get some coffee or tea, 'cause I ain't goin' for it."

"OK, Mama. I'm not going anywhere."

"Don't mama me, 'cause you know I got your number."

"Good afternoon, everybody," says Percy Groves strolling into the office; a robust high-yella man who once was president and CEO of Oakland's National Urban Assistance League until it went belly-up and forced him into retirement. Always in a shirt and tie and dark suit, he's chairman of the board of directors and one of the founders of the Trust. "Hey, Gracie, how's tricks?"

"Percy, you better stop that ole-time mess you be talkin'. You know ain't nobody these days even know what kinda tricks you talkin' bout. They think you mean somebody standing on the corner, and you know what I mean. And since you're here, can you please sign the checks on the conference table before leaving so I don't have to track you down tomorrow?"

Yeah…I can do that," he replies as he walks past her desk and into Arthur's office.

"Hey, Percy, what's up?" says Arthur.

"Have you seen the article in today's Post?"

"Yes…I read it, and just got off the phone with a reporter from the paper."

"How'd that go?"

"We'll see. He's writing an article based on our telephone conversation and said he'll run it by me before it goes to print, but I don't think I'll have much influence on his final piece. Roy's article unnerved me at first, but on second thought, his article and my public response may open a needed conversation on community self-help and social change. What do you think?"

"I'm glad you see it that way, Arthur, but I hope his untimely article doesn't detract from the work in front of us."

"It's just all part of the job, Percy."

"OK, but I know what you have on your plate."

"Well, Roy Thomas kicked the cat out the bag, so what can I do but respond? Percy, I'd like to review and sign those checks before you receive them, so let us get them to you tomorrow."

"You better explain that to Gracie so you don't get me into trouble."

"I'll handle it."

"Dr. Lightfoot and the gang are in the conference room waiting for you," Gracie says, standing in his doorway. "And I heard what you said about those checks. Now what am I supposed to do, 'cause I wanna pay our bills on time?"

"I'll take them to Percy in the morning and bring them back to you in the early afternoon. Is that all right with you?"

"OK now, I want my checks and I want 'em by twelve noon."

"OK, Sergeant."

"Don't sergeant me, 'cause you know I got your number."

Critical Mass Health Conductors' kitchen cabinet—Dr. Hachi Lightfoot, Mary Roebuck, Herbert Curry, and Aisha Middleton—are already in discussion when Arthur enters the conference room.

"We all read this here article in the Post," says Mary, holding up the paper. "So how are we supposed to respond?"

"I'd prefer that you have no response," Arthur replies, "and if you're contacted by a reporter or someone from the media, please refer them to me. I speak on behalf of the Trust since Critical Mass Health Conductors is supported by a grant to the Trust. I need to be the voice of the initiative as well."

Arthur then shares with the group his phone interview with the Post reporter and suggests that, based on his comments, they formulate talking points for health-conductor leadership. Once finalized, Mary agrees to e-mail the information to leadership that afternoon along with Roy's article. They then discuss progress made to date in implementing Hachi's social experiment.

"What most concerns me, now," Herb says, "is that even though we drafted a quick response to the article in the talking points…it remains to be seen whether this community outreach model, as it is now designed, is really going to work for low-income families and their children. I raise this point, now, because what might be considered effective for the professional class...the middle class, might not work for poor people at all."

"That was Doris Whitehead's issue as well," says Aisha.

"I understand your concern," says Arthur. "You're right, it's come up before, but you know what...right now, health conductors-in-training are from the middle class, and mostly employed; they're mid- and upper-level managers in public agencies and large nonprofit institutions. And so far, they seem to value the current design of the project, which, remember, is a pilot study. I suspect the demographics of the next group of trainees will be this gathering's subordinates; maybe mid-level managers and their subordinates who've learned about this project from someone now in Health Conductors. And we should encourage those currently in training to share with their staff their personal experience in the project, because if this initiative is to succeed and grow, it will be through word of mouth...through our talking drum."

"But eventually, it needs to trickle down," says Aisha, "to low-income families; and if and when this happens, we must be ready. Let's talk to Doris now, and see if she'd be willing to organize a focus group of low-income clients at their clinic to give us feedback on our current model, and see what suggestions they have to ensure Health Conductors will work for them."

"Good idea," replies Hachi, "but let's finish this round of health conductors-in-training, first, before trying to adapt the model while we're still learning how it actually performs."

"Also, we should remember," Mary Roebuck interjects, "that we're trying to recruit and train as volunteers people who are already motivated to live healthier lifestyles, and those consciously trying to make better health choices, regardless of what socioeconomic level they're in."

CHAPTER 31
BUSHY AS A BIRD'S NEST

Narada returned to Ibrahim Hafez's compound after his fourth night of storytelling and sat down on the straw mat in his upstairs room while Hohete served him mint tea. But rather than pour the tea and leave as she normally did, this night Ibrahim Hafez's daughter sat at the entrance to the room at the top of the stairs and commenced to unbraid her raven-black hair as she gazed at the storyteller and said nothing. She just quietly watched him as she enjoyed being in his presence.

"My mind, Narada, still you are not reading it?" Hohete asked with a devious smile.

"I still block your thoughts, Hohete. So I do not know what you are thinking until you tell me."

"Narada," she continued. "The women in your story, I do not understand. As powerful as the men, they are...like Hachi, the doctor. The health solution her idea was, and the people, including the men, now them she leads. And other women in the story there are. At meetings with men, the women sit and speak up; some of them even like men they look.

"And Natalie there is...Arthur's wife, childlike she is, and what she wants she does not know. And love they talk about, but

Arthur does not love her, she says. And Valerie…his mistress, to another man married she is, but Arthur she loves, I think. So confusing it all is. In your story to follow these women for me difficult it is, because them I do not understand."

Narada crossed his legs and sat comfortably with his back against the wall sipping his tea and looked at Hohete, who waited patiently for him to respond.

"The people in the story live in an age when girls can receive the same education as boys. They can go to school for knowledge and learn a skill and apply for work and get paid like men. This means women can live on their own, because they do not need a man to take care of them. They can work outside their compound…their house. In this future time, women also control if and when they have a child. And if they do not want to become a mother, they can stop having children."

"Ja'Usu women an herb to drink that, too, they can do, but sometimes the herb to work it does not."

"If the women in the story chose to have a man," continues Narada, "to have a marriage ceremony and bring children into the world, it is because a woman falls in love and wants the man to be the father of her children. Or maybe she does not want children and just lives with the man."

"So many choices she has," Hohete said as she continued taking down her hair.

"Many choices and many problems…In this future age and in their culture, men and women joining together no longer make an agreement between two families to become one family through marriage. Here in Ja'Usu, the patriarch of each family clan, along with both the fathers of the man and woman, meet to decide if their children will marry. In Oakland, the decision is solely up to the man and woman; their families do not decide. Many African American mothers remain unmarried and bring their children up alone. They may not want to be a single parent, but their family structures are weak. Some fathers support their children while others do not."

"Narada, these things about the future how do you know, when in your story they have not yet happened?" she asked as a smile brightened her face, knowing she had caught him by surprise.

Narada was delighted and amused by Hohete's cunning and laughed as he placed his empty cup down on the mat. "You are the only one in Ja'Usu who believes I am a jinn. So I tell you this: I live in the past, present, and future all at the same time. I am experiencing this future that I speak of even while I am sitting here with you." And he looked at Hohete with great compassion and love.

"Oh my Jah! Oh my Jah!"

Silence sat between them while Narada gave Hohete space to think about what he had said. "So when your story about Arthur you tell, in the future, are you there?"

"Yes."

"When the story you tell, with us also in Ja'Usu, are you here? And with someone else right now in the future, are you there?"

"Yes to both your questions."

"Who now are you with?"

"If I say, it would only make it more difficult for you to understand."

"And such power, by it how do you come?"

"It was a gift...a great blessing given to me by the Great Mystery when I was born, long before the birth of time. But with this gift also comes great responsibility." Narada paused for a moment before continuing. "Spirits in human form also have the potential to be present everywhere at once, but first, they must overcome their fear of going within...surrendering completely to the Great Mystery. And that is very difficult for humans to do."

"This knowledge, for me too wonderful it is. High it is, and to grasp it I cannot."

"In time, Hohete, you will have this experience when nothing but the Great Mystery only matters to you."

"Narada, what you say I believe, but for me something troubles. This gift you have...and powerful jinn you are...then why weak and thirsty coming out of the desert you were, when at the well you we met?"

"What would you have thought, Hohete...your father and Ayaat...everyone in Ja'Usu, if I walked out of the desert looking rested and very much alive?"

"Impossible for any man to do that would be, even if by caravan you traveled. So all a disguise it was?"

"No, Hohete, I needed your help, and I was grateful to find you at the well. I had to endure what any human would have suffered crossing that hot and barren land."

"And at the well our meeting an accident it was, Narada?"

"Oh no, everything that is and will be is for a reason."

"And that reason, what is it?"

"The Great Mystery has dreamed this creation into being for her own pleasure, Hohete," he replied as Ibrahim Hafez's daughter finished unbraiding her hair. She stopped for a moment to gaze at him. "But someday she will end this dream and creation will collapse upon itself, until the One-Who-Has-Many-Names, whom you call Jah, decides to dream once again. Then her creation will be born, anew." They sit together in silence for a while as Narada senses the nature of her thoughts without invading her privacy.

"The Oromo boy who into the compound before sunrise he comes, why does he?" she finally asks.

"Yes, that is Ma'Mun."

"And why here does he come?"

"I am his teacher."

"And what to him are you teaching?"

"How to sit quietly and deepen his union with the Great Mystery...Please come if you wish and sit with us, Hohete."

Her smile lit up the room.

Morning prayer with Ma'Mun was over when Arsalaan knocked on the door and was allowed into the Hafez compound. He looked as wild and disheveled as ever. But the shards of animal bone in his hair and dry blood on his ragged clothes were replaced by brown mud stains everywhere. Ibrahim Hafez looked aghast at the madness that stood in front of him and wondered if Arsalaan, even with a bath and new clothes, would ever be presentable under any condition to anyone, much less to his family and his clan.

The previous night Hohete and her father had dragged a large wooden tub used for washing across the courtyard to a corner of the compound and erected a makeshift curtain made from one of Ayaat's old, tattered shawls. They placed three wooden buckets full of water next to the tub and covered them with straw baskets to keep out the tiny creatures that fly. And the two women rose early to boil water in a large, covered pot resting on burning charcoal. The water hissed and sizzled, voicing its complaint that it would not be enough to wash away Arsalaan's dirt and smell of accumulated years of madness, self-loathing, and neglect.

Arsalaan stood near the palm trees in the middle of the courtyard like a child not knowing what to do. Hohete stepped outside and, like her father, saw a man that who was not only scruffy; she saw something else: his fear.

"Amantahu," she said as she approached him.

"Amantashe," Arsalaan replied and slightly bowed his head as he stood in front of her.

Hohete reached out and handed him a piece of dark soap. "The water and tub for you, over there they are waiting," she said, pointing her finger in the direction of the drawn curtain in the corner. "My father, your new clothes after you wash and for them ready are, hand them to you he will. A comb for you to pick at your hair, I also bought. Your head in years has not been touched, I bet," she said with a smile.

Arsalaan stood, expressionless, with his hands folded in front of him, looking at her as Ibrahim Hafez watched. An awkward moment passed between the three of them, as no one knew exactly what to do next until Hohete finally said to Arsalaan, "Pour two pails of water into the tub, I suggest, and with that wash. The third pale over you my father will pour, when the soap to rinse off you are ready."

"I will?" inquired Ibrahim Hafez, with a bit of surprise as he never was asked.

"Yes Abbah." She ran back inside her father's house, and quickly returned with a large piece of cloth for Arsalaan to use as a towel. But he was already behind the curtain, pouring water and taking off his rags, so Hohete hastily gave the cloth to her father.

"Abbah! Auntie and I inside will stay until for us safe it is, and to come out us you tell."

And with that, Hohete crossed the courtyard, disappeared into Ayaat's house, and closed the large, ornate wooden door, but not quite quickly enough to miss seeing Arsalaan's dark-brown backside as he bent over in the large tub. She closed her eyes to his nakedness and slowly finished closing the door.

Twenty minutes passed when Ayaat and Hohete heard sounds coming from outside and recognized it was not the voice of Ibrahim but that of Arsalaan, singing loudly as if he did not have a care in the world. And for some inexplicable reason that eluded Hohete, his voice irritated her. Her agitation seemed to lessen when hearing Narada and Ma'Mun talking outside with her father. Another twenty minutes passed before she heard a soft knock on the door. As she opened it, there stood Arsalaan in the new clothes Hohete had purchased for him. He looked clean and radiant, with water still dripping from his thick, curly hair. Ibrahim Hafez stood off to one side, looking exhausted, with the front of his white shirt and lungi soaking wet, as if he had wrestled with a one-hump camel over water and lost.

A broad smile graced Arsalaan's face as he looked at Hohete for her approval, and she, too, smiled and nodded her head. He held up his hand with the wooden comb and asked, "Would you please with my hair, help me?"

Hohete's smile immediately disappeared. "To cut it off and over again start, you might want to. Your hair, as bushy as a bird's nest it is, and hours to do it time might take."

"If time you have, yours I am."

Hohete walked past him, got a wooden stool, and placed it in a sunny corner of the courtyard. Hohete then went back inside her aunt's house and soon returned with a small bowl with coconut oil and a large piece of cloth. She set the bowl down near the seat and spread the cloth in front of the three-legged stool. Then, snatching the comb from Arsalaan's hand, she commanded, "Come and sit," pointing to the material on the ground, "so messing up your clothes you will not, and what I can do let me see." Ibrahim Hafez and Ayaat watched as if they were the guests in another family's house.

Like a domesticated dog, Arsalaan followed Hohete to the three-legged stool and sat down as he was told. And as if one of Narada's characters in the story was speaking directly in her ear, a thought suddenly occurred to Hohete: Valerie and me, men with many problems dealing with them we are.

CHAPTER 32

THE LION'S TAIL

It was well after sunrise when Hohete walked through the Fajaruddin gate and stopped to watch a boisterous crowd of Oromo men and women disputing in Oromo regarding where women in the ensuing chaos were supposed to sit. People's heads gathered in several small clusters, talking to each other while arms gestured and pointed to various places on the ground. A man pulled on a woman's arm as she struggled to keep a sack of potatoes balanced on her head while two other women held onto the other arm and tugged.

A young boy, bent over and with his arms outstretched, chased a hen through the pandemonium as it darted about, cackling and scurrying around and under people's legs each time the youth went to grab it. In spite of the bedlam, people joked and laughed with one another as women found places to sit on their heels or with their legs outstretched on the ground. Amid the commotion, women claimed spaces and spread pieces of bright-colored cloth down before stacking rows of small mounds of tomatoes or onions or potatoes or peanuts. Other women arranged bundles of oranges and lemons in rows or organized fresh herbs and tiny mounds of spices on pieces of palm leaf, bringing a semblance of order to the disarray.

Women hawking the same produce sat together and chatted and laughed with one another as muddled turmoil gradually gave way to the emergence of a magala. Behind the squatting women, a young boy stood next to a beige-colored donkey weighed down by all its years and two full satchels of water—one down each side. Using a tiny cup, the boy knocked rhythmically, against the wooden frame that held the bags, chanting "water for sale," as the persistent flies hovering around the donkey's eyes were jarred by each knock and unable to settle.

A familiar face, unexpectedly, appeared in the crowd, and ran up to Hohete, smiling broadly and a little out of breath. "Amanta-hu," cried Ma'Mun.

"Hiya Aman…Amanta-he, Ma'Mun."

"Hiya Aman…so, sister Hohete, my name you know."

"Yes, in our compound each morning, Ma'Mun, I see you, so of course your name I know."

"But you never do I see."

"But women, everything we see."

And they laughed together as he smiled and looked up at her.

"Something from our new magala would you like to buy?"

"Oh no…not now, Ma'Mun. On my way to the Oromo well I am, but maybe on my way back I will," she said and turned away to resume her walk along the path.

"With you may I walk, sister Hohete?"

"If you wish…"

"Ato [Mr.] Narada in your house to stay, what is it like?" he asked with a boy's curiosity and look of innocence that endears a woman's heart.

"Like any of my father's guests he is…very gracious and giving."

"A jinn is he? Because a jinn if he is, a powerful one he must be."

Hohete stopped and turned to the young boy. "Why to say that do you, Ma'Mun?"

"Well, the other night after his story, my grandfather and me, with him in the field we sat. The storyteller, my grandfather's eyesight back he gave it. True it is, because it I saw."

"To anyone this have you told, Ma'Mun?"

"Not to tell, he said to us."

"Then why me you are telling?"

Ma'Mun became quiet and lowered his head to stare at the ground without answering her. Hohete gently lifted his chin. "Ma'Mun, if to anyone this you repeat, Narada in danger you may put. Understand do you?"

"Yes, sister Hohete."

"Harm to him come do you wish, Ma'Mun?"

"Certainly not, sister Hohete...my grandfather, Daanish Nour, the same thing he told me, but you knew, I thought."

Hohete looked up and down the path before recommencing her walk, and Ma'Mun still tagged along. "Sister Hohete, why all the way out to the Oromo well for water do you go when wells in Ja'Usu some there are?"

"Because the water from the Oromo well, for drinking the best it is, so out there I go."

"Oh, my grandfather, something to ask you me he told," said Ma'Mun. Hohete stopped, again, to look at the boy and waited for him to continue.

"Arsalaan, my grandfather him to see he wishes. Please, Arsalaan can you tell?"

"Why not you or your grandfather yourself tell him? Why me ask?" And she quickened her pace, feeling a little annoyed.

"'Cause a little frightening he is, and him you know," said Ma'Mun, trying to catch up.

"Him to know I do not," Hohete countered.

"Well, him a bath you gave."

"Listen, Ma'Mun," she replied, taken aback by the implications of the boy's remark. "A bath for Arsalaan I prepared. Him a bath I did not give. If with me to walk you want and the water back help me to carry, then come. But drop the subject of Arsalaan, and about anything else we can talk." She stopped again and faced Ma'Mun. "OK?"

"OK."

"Good," she said before starting off again with Ma'Mun now walking beside her.

"Him you like, huh?" he asked.

Hohete ignored this comment, refusing to engage in any more conversation with the boy, and Ma'Mun began singing in Oromo.

Patriarchs Aschenaki, the one who distresses, and Safdar, the one who breaks the enemy's ranks, were resting on luxurious, sky-blue pillows from Persia and drinking tea on the uppermost platform in Aschenaki's main room when Nabeel, one of his sister's sons, appeared in the entrance, announcing that someone was banging on the compound door. Folding his short leg at the knee so he could sit upright, Aschenaki asked his nephew to find out who was knocking on the door.

Nabeel was back in an instant and said, "Uncle Arsalaan's at the door."

It took a minute or two for Aschenaki to grasp the weight of what was said as he put down his small glass of tea and looked at his companion, Safdar, who also seemed confused by the news.

"Well, Nabeel, please..." and before he could finish his instructions, Arsalaan stood in his brother's entrance, smiling up at him.

"Amantahe, my brother," said Arsalaan.

"Hiya Aman...Amantahu, my older brother," Aschenaki replied with uneasiness. He would have gotten up if his right leg could support his weight, but as it could not without forcing him to move awkwardly, he held out his hand for his older brother to come and join them. Aschenaki was in shock at seeing his brother no longer in filth and rags but standing before him in clean, new clothes. Patriarch Safdar quickly rose to his feet and offered to give Arsalaan his place next to his brother, but Arsalaan refused as he made his way onto the platforms and walked over to greet his brother. He knelt down and embraced Aschenaki tenderly before standing up again to first, bow before reaching out for Patriarch Safdar's hand. Aschenaki yelled for his young wife, Pariza, who came quickly from a side room and stopped in amazement when she recognized her favorite in-law.

"Arsalaan...oh, Arsalaan," she cried, running into his arms, weeping and crying for joy.

The commotion must have disturbed their mother, Rona, who now hurried into the room and, when she saw her eldest son, wailed for all to hear, calling Arsalaan's name over and over again as she, too, ran to embrace him. Now Aschenaki's entire compound was in an uproar as family members rushed to the entrance to witness the miracle that stood before them. The men clapped as the women began a lilting shrill for the entire neighborhood to hear. They celebrated Arsalaan's return when they had given him up for dead. Most of them, including Aschenaki, had seen him in the city dressed in rags, dragging dry bones and animal guts up and down the street. Upon seeing him, they'd turn their heads or hastily walked away to spare themselves the hurt they felt and the embarrassment of seeing one another. They had accepted long ago that Arsalaan was lost to them forever when he became Ja'Usu's noble tragedy and turned into the hyena man.

Aschenaki looked upon this reunion and all the fuss with mixed emotions, although anyone watching would have thought he was as happy as everyone else and overjoyed to see his older brother. But what was on his mind was whether Arsalaan had returned to claim his rightful place as patriarch of the family, as he was the older of his father's two sons. If he had, Aschenaki had no intentions of giving up so easily his long-standing position as family head, given his brother's abdication of the role such a long time ago.

By late afternoon the word had spread like a sandstorm throughout the 426 members of the clan that Arsalaan had returned and was at his father's—and now his brother's—home. So it was only fitting for Aschenaki to show due respect and invite his older brother to stay for dinner and have conversation with him. But secretly, he wanted Arsalaan to leave and go back to feeding his filthy hyenas.

The household was in a festive mood as relatives arrived, unannounced, to welcome Arsalaan's return to the family as though he had just returned from a very long journey. Everyone knew he had actually gone mad after his father's untimely death, but they were curious to see for themselves whether he really had recovered and changed.

Mother Rona busied herself with ordering more food and organizing the family's women to prepare food for the relatives walking through their compound door. Her older sister, Ad'ifaah, took over the mud-brick kitchen next to the main room and directed Aschenaki's two wives, Fadwah and Pariza, on what to fix and how to cook the meal, as if they did not know from making food every day. Pariza, the youngest at eighteen, jumped about like someone chased by an angry whip. Vardah, Mother Rona's oldest child and only daughter, went with her own two sons, Nabeel and Duha, to Ghazi's shop, where the hyena man used to scoop up guts and haul away animal bones, to buy more goat meat.

As Aschenaki sat with Safdar in what used to be his father's house, watching his long-lost brother now come home, he smiled amiably and talked and laughed as his young daughter by his first wife, Tazkia, served them tea and sweet breads. Underneath this pretense, the patriarch's feelings of inadequacy and self-loathing returned like retribution, exposing the darkness that lay whimpering like a frightened hag wedged in his heart.

The festive day was coming to an end, and Patriarch Safdar, the one who breaks the enemy's ranks, had left long ago. The women, eating apart from the men, were sitting in the courtyard, talking and laughing about some details of Narada's story as children played and danced around them. The desert sun, turning a deep orange, advanced over Ja'Usu's western wall, crossing Somali land and Djibouti as light and dark shadows crept across the compound's grounds from west to east and slowly made their way up the whitewashed wall of the main house.

Duha rarely spoke. When he did, it was in a language that only he and his younger brother, Nabeel, could understand, and so Nabeel always spoke to others for the two of them. They sat between their two uncles and were quietly speaking in their private language when Nabeel suddenly asked, "Uncle Arsalaan, feeding hyenas, what is it like?"

"Holding a lion by its tail it is like, until you they get to know. But when comfortable with your smell they are, and feed them you do, as gentle as house cats they become."

"And people paid you them to feed as they watched?" asked Nabeel, age nineteen.

"Yes...sometimes."

"And you are living now, my brother, where are you?" Aschenaki asked.

"In the compound when Father was alive I bought. The three buildings repairing I am and there plan to live."

"So with us to stay you do not wish?"

"Oh no, my brother; the patriarch of this family you are, and by rights your house this is. No, here I will not stay."

The women could be heard in the courtyard now, giggling and laughing as they talked about Arthur making love to Valerie in a place they called hotel. Their laughter distracted Aschenaki from speaking to his brother as he tried to hear exactly what was being said. Fadwah was overheard imitating Valerie's passion when she came to a climax with Arthur. The women erupted in laughter as Aschenaki's face turned blood red. He struggled to listen more intently to what else was being discussed, but the women's voices were reduced to a whisper, with short wisps of giggling and more laughter. Aschenaki was sure they were talking about him, and his face showed traces of his growing anger.

"The governing council, me and Jumah to arrest, why do they want us?" Arsalaan finally asked, breaking the silence between them.

"What?" asked Aschenaki.

"The patriarchs us to arrest, why are they trying?"

"My dear brother, nothing about any arrest do I know."

"After Narada's storytelling last night, right after the fire went out, henchmen from the council the two of us to arrest they tried...Jumah and me, but in the crowd returning to the city, them we lost."

"You and this Jumah fellow, the storyteller's fire last night you built?"

"Yes, my brother."

"Why? Why Narada helping you are?"

"A long story it is, but helping us let me say he is."

"Helping you, how?"

"Here in clean clothes before you now sitting I would not be, if for Narada it were not."

Aschenaki was very much alarmed at this revelation but said with as much sympathy and composure as he could muster, masking his real distress, "My dear brother, Narada in our midst to have, such a blessing he is. In addition to his talent as a story-teller, the minds of many people in Ja'Usu opened he has done. Everyone…about him they talk, and his tale about Arthur and the health conductors in wonder the people are. May I ask, your relationship with him, what is it?"

Arsalaan wanted to confide in Aschenaki and share with him what Narada had revealed, that their father was murdered and did not die of natural causes. But if he disclosed this information, he knew his brother's temperament would stop at nothing to bypass Ja'Usu's legal system and take revenge against whomever he thought may have committed this monstrous crime. Even innocent people could lose their lives and the real murderers remain at large. No, better to hold off for now, he thought; and instead he said, "To look at life in a different way, Narada helping me he is, and for that grateful I am. So with his fire him I helped."

"And this Jumah person, who to you he is?"

"Jumah…one of those unfortunate street boys he is."

"The ruffians from people they steal and homes they rob?"

"Yes, but helping them, too, turn their lives around the story-teller is doing."

"I bet he is," Aschenaki sarcastically said, immediately realizing he was exposed. "I mean, I hope successful he will be."

"So, my brother, the council to back off Jumah and me and not after us come, please tell."

"I will see what I can do."

CHAPTER 33

A MONSTROUS THOUGHT

Morning prayer had ended; yet a small group of merchants gathered outside the holy edifice while a few lingered at the entrance. They engaged in a spirited conversation and sporadically looked into the hall at the nine patriarchs already sipping their coffee and eating biscuits. Several patriarchs casually watched the men when one of them walked away from the rest, kicked off his sandals at the door, and strode across the hall's Persian carpet to stand before the governing council sitting on the rug.

Ghayoor folded his hands in front of him and, with his head lowered to show respect, waited for the council to recognize him. He was a small, thin, middle-aged man with a white cap on his head and a dyed carrot-orange beard. Patriarch Liyaqat, one who is worthy and deserving, nudged Chief Patriarch Murabbi sitting next to him, who munched with abandon on his biscuit. Some crumbled in his lap.

"Amantahe, Ghayoor, to help you how may we?" asked the chief patriarch, finally looking up.

"Hiya Aman, Chief Patriarch Murabbi...council members. Amantahu. Your family, sir, how are they?"

"Well they are, Ghayoor," said Murabbi.

"And your wife, Chief Patriarch?"

"Fine she is, Ghayoor."

"And your children, Chief Patriarch, well also are they doing?"

"Yes, Ghayoor, my whole household, well it is. To help you, how may we?"

"Sir, something very odd has happened and I…I mean, we… the shopkeepers, to your attention we want to bring it."

"What oddness has taken place that about we need to know, Ghayoor?"

"Well, sir, all the Oromo women on Ja'Usu's streets, disappeared they have. Outside our shops sitting they are not, and food and other wares selling they are not; even your own shops' Oromo women have gone, my patriarchs."

"So…"

"Well, sir, it means the number of people shopping on our streets we do not have. Less Ja'Usu citizens to our shops are coming, because the Oromo women in front of our shops sitting they are not, and food selling they are not. When Oromo on the street in front of our shops there are, the people not only their daily foods buy but also inside our shops come in. They look around, and whatever else they need to buy, they do. But now, the Oromo gone they are, so Ja'Usu women inside our shops to come, no reason they have. Our main streets—Fajaruddin, Masresha, and Mustakim—empty they are, and the shopkeepers in an uproar they are. Sir, the Oromo women right away to come back, them we need."

Ghayoor now stood quietly, looking over his shoulder every now and again to see his fellow shopkeepers standing in the holy edifice's entrance, watching him. He smiled and nodded his head at them, reassuring everyone that he was doing fine as they, like him, waited for the governing council's immediate response.

"So our women shopping, where going are they?" asked Taqiyy, the pious, the righteous, who already knew, like everyone else, the answer to his question.

"Patriarch Taqiyy, Ja'Usu women outside the Fajaruddin gate at the Oromo's new magala, now shopping they are."

"But our decree all around the city we posted, warning Ja'Usu inhabitants not to step outside the gate at that market to buy," said Abdul Muntaqim, slave of him who punishes wrongdoings and seizes retribution. "These women, to arrest them we should and an example of them make. Then away from the Oromo magala they will stay."

"All our edict did," countered Patriarch Taqiyy, "is let everyone know where vegetables to buy they could go. So food for their families, to the Oromo magala our women forced to go they are. Them to arrest! The Oromo, food for us they grow, and it we buy; how are we going to them arrest?"

"Now the council this matter will take up, Ghayoor, and let shopkeepers quickly know what about the situation to do we are prepared," said Chief Patriarch Murabbi.

"Thank you, sir...council members, to bring the Oromo women back to Ja'Usu streets, anything you can do, grateful we will be." Ghayoor made a stiff bow before quickly walking away to tell the merchants outside eagerly awaiting his news.

"On our hands a real problem we have, and a solution now we need," said Murabbi.

"The Oromo, them we should arrest," replied Patriarch Safdar, one who breaks the enemy's rank.

"And if food for selling our women we detain them, from whom to buy do we? And if this action we take, Ja'Usu inhabitants, how will they react, do you think?" countered Patriarch Taqiyy.

"And besides, if the Oromo we arrest, our shopkeepers' situation we will not solve," continued Patriarch Aschenaki, the distressed.

"A solution I have, but the council afraid I am it you will not like," Patriarch Taqiyy said, "although in my clan, the situation already discussed has been, and forward to move prepared we are." Everyone's eyes turned to him.

"Oh, what might that be, Taqiyy?" asked the chief patriarch.

"My family, up and down Beza gate, land we own," Patriarch Taqiyy began, "including the plot where the road right across from this holy edifice begins. This land to the Oromo to rent, we are prepared for..."

Before Patriarch Taqiyy, the pious, the righteous, could get the rest of his proposal out of his mouth, the council was in an uproar. Patriarchs shook their heads in loud disapproval while Chief Patriarch Murabbi dropped his half-empty coffee cup in his lap, spilling the dregs all over his expensive cotton tunic.

"No! Absolutely not," exclaimed Patriarch Tahawwur, the rash, who, in addition to his head shaking, squeezed his eyes shut as if to block out the monstrous thought and pounded his fists against the ornate Persian rug.

Aschenaki sat quietly weighing the practicality of Taqiyy's offer. "Our righteous patriarch, Taqiyy, a proposal on our carpet he has put; no matter how detestable it may sound, we should study it, I think. That is...unless anyone here a more acceptable proposition for us to consider has."

There was momentary silence as council members struggled to adjust their minds to grasp the reasonableness of Aschenaki's request. Tahawwur, the rash, moved his head from side to side and then up and down, eyeballs twitching, as he resisted the urge to say "no." The chief patriarch, who had already instructed Beena to bring him a small bowl of cold water and a cloth to wipe away the large coffee stain in his lap, was busy studying his crotch.

"About to say I was," continued Taqiyy calmly, "my family the land across from this holy edifice to the Oromo to rent willing we are, so their magala in the city they can have. This arrangement, to all shopkeepers in the city fair it would be, because all Ja'Usu streets to this building lead and to their magala would also lead. So if any of the city's nine main roads you take, from their gate to here, all shops on the way here you will pass. A magala in the heart of Ja'Usu, our merchants…all of them and the Oromo as well…everyone will be satisfied."

"Most Oromo women, their vegetables on Fajaruddin, Mustakim, and Masresha they sell," said Patriarch Ihtesham, the respectable and honorable one. "So if our women down any street to this magala…to here on Beza come, shopkeepers on Fajaruddin, Mustakim, and Masresha, fewer people walking down their streets they are going to have."

"Yes, true that may be, Ihtesham," replied Patriarch Liyaqat, the worthy and deserving, "but the few shops on Harisah, Beza, Khawar, Fozeia, Ehan, and Dabbah, more passersby they will have, which means more business for them they are going to get. Right now, those merchants to the people in their immediate neighborhoods only they sell, not to the rest of Ja'Usu, who seldom these streets walk down."

And for the first time in a long while, the light peeked through cobwebs in the minds of Patriarchs Abdul Muntaqim, Liyaqat, Izzat, Safdar, and Tahawwur, who suddenly realized that their clans would benefit from an Oromo magala opening across from the holy edifice. It was their families that lived on and around these six streets with fewer shops, and, because there was less commerce on these roads, their clans remained poorer than Murabbi's family on Fajaruddin, Istesham's clan on Masresha, and Aschenaki's family on Mustakim. These three clans controlled the shops on these major streets and, together, amassed more silver and gold than the remaining six families all together.

Now these five patriarchs realized what was behind Taqiyy's rent-to-the-Oromo proposal, and they smiled at him—that old sly and clever dog, they thought—as they envisioned the money and wealth that would be theirs if they went along with his proposition. They looked at their three fellow patriarchs, Murabbi, Istesham, and Aschenaki—who also understood the shift in bargaining power that had just occurred—as now their rivals. Taqiyy had not only found a way to appease the Oromo but also to create a new revenue base for the majority of the council members and their families.

Patriarch Safdar, the one who breaks the enemy's ranks, was elated and the first to speak. "In reconsidering, my dear Taqiyy's proposal, solve our Oromo problem it does, and the best for all concerned it would be. So I encourage that his generous offer of land to rent to our brethren the Oromo for their market we support."

"Oh, yes…much more to agree to I could not," said Tahawwur. "Patriarch Taqiyy's scheme…I mean proposal…I, too, support."

"To you to say I want, my esteemed Patriarch Taqiyy," chimed Patriarch Liyaqat, the most worthy and deserving, "in light of our long history with the Oromo, very courageous of you and your family it is, renting land at the beginning of Beza to those poor, hardworking Oromo women to propose so their own magala they can have. Very righteous and kind you are, and your generous proposal I, too, now support."

"The best solution to our Oromo problem, I must confess, and good for Ja'Usu to have them back in the city it will be," said Patriarch Izzat, with high rank and honor. "For Taqiyy's plan I also vote to support."

"Narrow-minded I have been," confessed Patriarch Abdul Muntaqim, slave of him who punishes wrongdoings and seizes retribution, "and to my dear Taqiyy, whom my eyes he has opened, and a better way let me see, to you I apologize. My mind I have changed, and my fine friend's proposal I now accept."

The three remaining council members, Chief Patriarch Murabbi and Patriarchs Ihtesham and Aschenaki, were silent and looked at one another, waiting for someone to speak.

"While the governing council's rule that a majority vote wins it is," began the chief patriarch, sounding very sweet and diplomatic, "we always...always approve items with a unanimous vote. And for the three of us I think I speak—for Patriarchs Aschenaki, Ihtesham, and myself, that is—to patriarch Taqiyy's generous proposition we have not yet spoken. In favor of this proposal we are not, although, it is a bighearted one. So unless an objection there is, this proposal to the Oromo this land to rent does not pass."

"An objection there is," Patriarch Tahawwur quickly countered. "Six of us the majority vote have, and since you acknowledge, Chief Patriarch Murabbi, the council's rule that with a majority vote a measure will pass, on this particular issue, Taqiyy's proposal passes. And we, the majority, request that our fellow patriarch as quickly as possible the land across from this holy edifice to the Oromo for their market rent."

There was an awkward silence between the nine patriarchs as each one considered what this standoff meant when Patriarch Aschenaki, the distressed, spoke up. "My brother patriarch, correct you are. The three of us in the minority, your majority vote we must accept. But before Taqiyy's proposal we accept, each patriarch supporting this majority ruling and not sticking with our traditional unanimous vote must so say, I would like."

One by one, each patriarch voiced whether or not he was in support of the majority rule, which ended in the same final count—six for Taqiyy's proposal and three against. His proposal was forcibly approved.

The chief patriarch was visibly disturbed. "In Ja'Usu a real problem we have, and to deal with it now we must. Trouble with the Oromo it is not; them to manage we can. This Narada fellow and his damn story it is. A troublemaker and rabble-rouser he is, and influencing the Oromo he is doing…the peace and tranquility of this council he disturbs, and us as families up against one another pitting he is. Out of Ja'Usu, today, let us throw him, I move, before this night's story he begins."

"Narada, alone him we should leave, I think," replied Taqiyy. "Every time his activities to undermine we try, backfired on us it has. Maybe the truth when first we met us he told—a powerful jinn he is. His story let him finish. Three more nights only he has, and then gone he will be."

"His story in Ja'Usu after finishing he will leave, you say; that how do you know? What if he does not?" asked Abdul Muntaqim, slave of him who punishes wrongdoings and seizes retribution.

"This storyteller or jinn or whatever him you call, the spotlight then he will not have," replied Patriarch Izzat. "Then to leave, him we can ask—and by force if he does not."

"To Ibrahim Hafez's house still food we are sending?" asked Patriarch Liyaqat. "Maybe, we should stop."

"In this matter, with my brother Taqiyy, I agree," said Aschenaki to everyone's surprise. "Since Narada in Ja'Usu has been, everything we have tried to do, wrong it has gone. His story let him finish; and if on his own he does not leave, him to a donkey we can tie and back to the desert without water send him. So our agreement with him let us fulfill and his food send, his fire on storytelling night alone leave, and the arrest of his fire builders stop."

The chief patriarch was more than shocked at Aschenaki's change of attitude toward Narada and was about to speak up when he began to weigh the possibility of being on the wrong side of another council vote and face more embarrassment and defeat. So he kept quiet. There was no other response to Taqiyy's and Aschenaki's advice, so the motion to leave Narada alone passed without putting it to a formal vote. Then the patriarchs adjourned for the day.

The Storyteller's Fifth Night

It was twilight and the coming of story time when Patriarch Aschenaki recognized his brother walking alongside Ibrahim Hafez's daughter with a young boy, whom he assumed was Jumah, and the rest of the Hafez family. They followed closely behind Narada as he made his way from the rear of the gathering down to the first ring of the circle. And like on previous story nights, the crowd spread across the flatlands outside Ja'Usu's main gate, but this night the gathering was larger, with more than 1,500 people waiting for the storyteller. Starting with the inner circle, they rose to their feet in waves when they saw him.

This night, however, something unusual added to their greeting. Men gently beat their chests with an open palm, and women sang a lilting high drone, perhaps honoring Narada for enlivening their spirits and awakening in them their creative potential to shape their own destinies. It was not that the people gathered could identify or articulate this innate gift the storyteller set free in them, but their hearts intuitively felt the blessing bestowed each night when he, the storyteller, commanded they be still.

But the patriarchs, with the exception of Taqiyy, the pious, the righteous, marred by the weight of their own self-interests and vain conceits and their tenacious belief in the supremacy and permanence of themselves, reined in yet emboldened by the pretensions and false pride of a religion stilted by the imperfections of being human, were not pleased. They slipped in and out of experiencing Narada's story. Except for one, they viewed a scene here, witnessed a passage there, without grasping the full thread of the narrative. But too proud to disclose their inability to follow the story, eight patriarchs concealed their difficulty from one another while sitting on the platform built exclusively for them. Each of them pretended to be immersed in the narrative, but in reality eight patriarchs were oblivious to the experience Patriarch Taqiyy and the other gatherers were having.

Hohete and Arsalaan stood together on one side of Narada while Ma'Mun and his grandfather, Daanish Nour, and Ibrahim Hafez and Ayaat stood on his other side. Narada smiled and waved to the crowd. They cheered even louder before he gestured for everyone to sit while he remained standing. He then bowed to the Earth: first to the north, and then to the east, and then south, and lastly to the west before sitting down on his mat and folding his legs.

Looking out over the gathering, Narada was delighted to see something different about the seating this night, which the patriarchs noticed as well and were not too pleased about. The Oromo were no longer a ragtag group of nomads seated on the periphery of the gathering. Tonight they wore their finest clothes and wraps and were scattered in small groupings throughout the crowd, waiting like everyone for the story to resume. Only Jumah and his gang of thieves sat uneasily at the rear of the gathering and remained in the shadows, looking about for anyone who might want to arrest them.

Imitiyaz and Tabsassum, the fire builders, were back and stood in the center of the ring with their torches lit. They waited for Narada's signal to light the fire the people now considered sacred, except for the newcomers and the patriarchs. And as the dry wood caught fire, a hush came over the crowd, and some held their breath in anticipation of the story they knew was about to begin.

But then something unexpected happened. Narada stood with a clay water jug in his hand and walked toward the fire while, from the opposite end of the inner circle, a short Oromo man dressed in white stood up with a large drum that hung by a strap over his shoulder. He, too, made his way toward the center. When he drew near the storyteller, he began beating out the rhythm of a human heart with a constant tha-thump...tha-thump...tha-thump. Then the rhythm and tempo burst into an explosion of sharp, rapid strokes that heated up the animal skin stretched tightly across the wooden drum.

When the drummer's petition ended, the cadence slowed and softened as the voice of the storyteller filled the air. "It is fitting that we give thanks to Jah, the Most High, and for all those who have come before us. We ask that they appeal on our behalf to the Great Mystery to uplift our hearts and minds so that we are constant in our knowing that we are children of One Mother... Jah, the Most High. From One Mother we came, and into the arms of the Divine Mother we shall once again return."

Raising the jug of water above his head for all to see, the storyteller recited for all to hear, "So on this evening, I pour this libation on this sacred earth to show our gratitude to Jah and to honor our ancestors for our healing."

When the people in the inner rings of the great circle stood and placed a hand on the person's shoulder next to or in front of them, the rest of the gathering—except for the ones too young or too old or too crippled to stand—rose to their feet, and they, too, put a hand on the shoulder of a man or woman near them, until the people were entwined from hand to shoulder and shoulder to hand. And those who could not rise reached to touch the leg nearest to them as Narada intoned: "To the Great Mystery who sometimes is called Jah or Igziyabher, or is sometimes known as Olodumare or Olorun, or sometimes called Allah or Brahma or Divine Mother or often called Yaweh or God or Lord, we pour this water on your earth in remembrance of you...for these sacred elements are you...Amin."

And the slow, rhythmic pulse of the drum quickly rose and fell as the gathering intuitively knew what was being asked of them, and the people said, "Amin." Narada poured a few drops of water on the ground.

"And to our ancestors, the river people who emerged along the ancient Nile, the Niger, and the Congo rivers, say Amin." And the inhabitants of Ja'Usu and the Oromo together said "Amin" as Narada poured drops of water on the land, and the drum raised its voice before quickly fading away again.

"To our ancestors from the Empire of Isonghee, now known as Zaire, which introduced the mathematical abacus, say Amin." And the gathering said "Amin" before the drum picked up the call and then rapidly softened once again.

"To the ancient Egyptian kingdom once known as Kumet and before that as Punt, say Amin." And all who heard the storyteller's voice said "Amin" before the rhythm of the drum rose and fell. And the storyteller poured more libation.

"To the our ancestors from the ancient African civilizations that settled in the Nile Valley and to our ancestors, the Bantu peoples who spread across the sub-Sahara for over two thousand years before the birth of Christ, say Amin." And those gathered said "Amin" as the drum sang their praises. Narada poured drops of water on the earth.

"To our ancestors from Kush or Nubia who ruled Egypt from its capital Meroe and invented metal technology, and to our ancestors of the ancient Nok culture who thrived in the forests of Central Nigeria and who the Yoruba claim as their ancestors and were known for their arts; and to the rise of the great empires of Ghana, Mali, and Songhai, say Amin." And the people said "Amin" when the drum raised its voice again before returning to a whisper. And a few more precious drops of water were poured once again.

"And we mourn for the lives of our brothers and sisters who, caught up in the slave trade's net, are maimed and killed, who died in dungeons or in holes of slave ships during the middle passage; say Amin." And the people said "Amin" as the drum screamed in agony for Africa's dead before quickly fading into nothingness. And drops of water fell like blood on the ground in remembrance of them.

"And to our brothers and sisters who, though enslaved, yet survive in spite of their suffering to bring forth seed of African descent. We appeal to the Great Mystery to heal their children of the wounds inflicted on their fathers and mothers so they may return in spirit to Mother Africa, who patiently waits for her children at the water's edge. Let the people say Amin." And the gathering said "Amin" as the drum cried out for Africa's sons and daughters, and sacred drops of water were poured again on the earth.

"And to our Oromo and Ja'Usu brethren who fought with one another and died, together, to erect this city in the desert, may they find peace, love, and understanding in one another as they continue to commune with the living, and let the gathering say Amin." And the crowd said "Amin" as the drum raised its voice before reverting, once again, to a whisper.

"And finally, for the Oromo and Ja'Usu children waiting to be born, we welcome you here and pray the actions of city patriarchs and Oromo elders, together, prepare the way for your arrival and affirm your right to be born. In the name of our ancestors, let this gathering say Amin," said the storyteller, and the people echoed "Amin," which was repeated again and again as the pulsating drum leaped and pranced over the crest of the people's spoken words, proclaiming a future of hope and promise and new beginnings. "Amin…Amin…Amin…"

Narada signaled for the people to sit; then he walked several times around the flames of the fire before returning to his place in the circle. After sitting down, he closed his eyes and said what no one else could hear, "May all the crawling creatures and the flying little ones in the air, may you go underground or to your nests or hives and sleep until I choose to wake you." And the multitude of snakes and lizards and toads and scorpions and sand crabs and fleas and anything that crawled or flew in the air did as they were told.

The sky was now dark as sparks of red-hot embers rose into the night sky, and a silent celestial gathering of stars took their places in the heavens. And spirit that was fire and the luminous multitude of stars above were of one accord, as African Spirit always is and ever will be in the consciousness of the people. And the all-knowing, all-seeing life force gathered up the people so the community of gatherers were of one accord as Narada intoned in an unspoken, unknown tongue for the Akasha Records of Celestial Light to open.

And from a mysterious wellspring, deeper than any vibration or sound they had ever felt or heard, the first word, the almighty Aum or Amen or Amin, the Holy Ghost was audible within and among them. And for the first time since Narada's reading began, the people were not afraid. The deep rumbling softened and became gentle like the sweet kiss of a mother's lips. It stilled the people's minds so they thought no thoughts, and from a peaceful wellspring as vast as the cosmos itself, the storyteller's voice was heard.

CHAPTER 34

A GENTLE WARRIOR

Arthur arrives at Luther's one-bedroom cottage on Oakdale Drive with a list of questions he's eager to have answered and starts asking them as soon as Luther opens his door. "Good evening, Luther. I've been thinking about how we first met and wonder how you happened to be in Ensarro on that particular day. Do you have lunch there often, waiting for someone like me?"

"Come in, Arthur; I'm glad you're on time. Please take your shoes off and leave them here," he says, pointing to a wooden rack close to the floor. Luther, dressed in white cotton pants and a loose-fitting white shirt, ushers Arthur into his living room as the flickering glow of a white candle dances joyously on a table near the window. The sweet scent of jasmine emanates throughout the room as if the very walls are in full bloom, but no floral incense is in sight. There's a most delicate arrangement of cut flowers on a second small table on the other side of the room, but the entire space is sparse, with only a forest-green rug on a hardwood floor and two antique wooden chairs placed next to a wall. Gold-colored fabric is draped over the top of a stand, concealing something resting between the chairs. Judging from the room, Arthur presumes Luther lives alone and probably doesn't entertain much.

"You know, Luther, even though I admitted to you at Ensarro that I called out to God when I was at the Hilton, I'm really not into the God thing. I'm really not."

Luther is amused by Arthur's comment and laughs easily. "The God thing, I haven't heard that phrase before…the God thing. Would you mind if I use it sometimes?"

"Please, be my guest."

"Arthur, how did you arrive at the conclusion that you're not into the God thing, as you put it?" asks Luther.

"What do you mean?" replies Arthur.

"I trust you've thought many times about the existence of God. Isn't that so?"

"Yes, I have…over the years."

"So, what brought you to this position that you don't believe in God?"

"Sometimes, Luther, I used to wake up in the morning and feel I was an agnostic, because I had doubts. And then other times, well…there were days when I'd say to myself there is no God, especially when thinking about all the evil in the world…and the natural and man-made disasters that occur, and the people hurt and killed as a result; and I say to myself, there can't be a God if he lets these things happen. And if there is a God…like the one portrayed in the Old Testament…I don't like him much. He's always angry, and a vengeful god who allows people to suffer."

Luther walks over to the other side of the living room, drags one of the chairs into the middle of the space, and gestures for Arthur to sit down.

"You don't believe in a lot of furniture, do you, Mr. McKinnie?"

"Call me Luther, son. I generally sit on the carpet when I'm, here, alone. It's better for my health. You know, the getting up and sitting down. It forces me to keep my back straight; and at my age, it helps me keep my spinal cord flexible."

"How old are you, anyway?" asks Arthur.

Luther either doesn't seem to hear Arthur's question or ignores answering it as he pulls over the other chair and places it on the rug facing Arthur. "The existence of God can be scientifically proven, you know. Did you know that?" he says.

"That's hard to believe, Mr. McKinnie...Luther, because if it were so, scientists or somebody would have already discovered the fellow and published their findings. So, I very much doubt it."

Luther apparently finds Arthur's remark delightfully funny, and he laughs. "That's a good point. I'm glad you won't take on face value what I say to you. That's a good attitude to have when conducting experiments...like scientists do. Question everything and anything. I want you to take the mind tools I'm going to give you and learn to use them like one would discover how to handle a microscope or a hammer or a screwdriver. Learn to use them properly, and you'll realize for yourself, through your own direct experience, what's real and not real—even whether there is a God or not. And if you do encounter God, perhaps you'll also discover her true nature. But instead of calling your efforts science, let's call your process of inquiry self-realization, all right?"

"I've never heard anyone talk about searching for God as a scientific experiment."

"What I've described to you is the essence of the scientific method. Is it not?"

"Well..." Arthur hedges.

"Think about it. A scientist comes up with a hypothesis—an idea or proposed principle that hasn't been substantiated—and takes it to her laboratory to design and then to conduct an experiment to prove or disprove that hypothesis. And in conducting her experiment, she proves or disproves her hypothesis, and she gets the same results every time the experiment is performed… and other scientists can replicate her work…well then, her hypothesis must be correct. Do you agree?"

"Yes, that sounds right," says Arthur with hesitation in his voice, as he's never given the scientific method much thought.

"Well, that's how I want you to approach your meditations," says Luther. "You're going to take all your questions and doubts to your own inner laboratory and discover for yourself what's real and not real…what's true and not true. Are you open to that?"

"Yes, I actually welcome…I'm comfortable with that approach."

Luther draws his chair in a little closer to Arthur and leans over to say, "Good…because I also must tell you, you'll have to become a gentle warrior as well."

"A gentle warrior…what does that mean?" asks Arthur.

"Your laboratory is the quality of your internal life…your inner experience," says Luther. "And sometimes you will run into obstacles along the way…deep-rooted attitudes and beliefs…your desires…forces at work within your family passed down from one generation to the next…your habits…the way you prefer to see yourself and the world, you may have to let go. These hindrances and more will challenge you at times, but they'll surface in your consciousness only when you're ready to overcome them. So you see, you must become a gentle warrior, ready to do battle with your demons and face them whenever they arise. Do you understand?"

"Yes, I think so."

Luther smiles easily. "Good, but I'll always be there to help you, so let's get started." Arthur watches Luther as he immediately closes his eyes and wonders if he's supposed to do the same. Luther recites a silent prayer, as his companion isn't into the God thing, before opening his eyes to find Arthur sitting in front of him with a quizzical expression.

"Now, Arthur, keep your feet squarely on the floor in front of you and sit up straight, without your spine touching the back of the chair. Come on, sit up. Rest the palms of your hands facing upward, like so, on the juncture between your thighs and lower abdomen. Good. Are you comfortable?"

"Yeah, I feel fine."

Luther studies Arthur's posture; then he stands and makes a slight adjustment to the position of his back and hands before returning to his chair. "Remember this posture, what it feels like, and resume this position whenever you meditate. Relax into it. Never allow your body to become stiff or rigid.

"OK, close your eyes and bring your full attention to that point right above the bridge of your nose...between your eyebrows." Luther reaches over and, with his index finger, gently touches that point on Arthur's forehead. Sitting back in his chair again, he watches Arthur for a moment. "With your eyes closed, gently raise your gaze to that point between your eyebrows...but don't strain in any way...OK, cool."

"OK, cool" seems so out of place for Luther to say that Arthur loses his composure and doubles over laughing. Luther waits patiently for him to regain his self-control and, once this is accomplished, they sit in silence.

Arthur feels relaxed and listens to the distant voices of children playing on the street and the horn of a car beep twice as it travels up the block. But his mind, like a monkey swinging from branch to branch, keeps jumping from one thought to another, making it impossible for him to focus on any one thing for too long. Luther watches Arthur intently, especially the slight rise and fall of his chest as his companion inhales and exhales.

"Still gazing at that point between your eyes, Arthur, I want you to bring your full attention to your breath...watch your breath...your breathing in and breathing out without controlling it in any way...as if you're taking in air and breathing out has a life of its own. And when you find your mind wandering, gently bring it back to watching your breath."

Luther sits with Arthur in silence for some time with his own eyes closed, calmly listening to the young man's breath, and prays for his protection from the mischievous spirit that dwells in the young man's building. May it depart and find peace.

"You can open your eyes when you are ready," Luther says softly, knowing his charge is now keenly sensitive to the sounds around him.

He watches Arthur as he gradually opens his eyes as if stirring from a deep sleep. In fact, the immediate surroundings had been so still that Arthur did momentarily sleep. He rubs his eyes, waking up, and gazes around the room before settling on Luther smiling at him.

"Yes, you did fall asleep for a while, and that may happen in the beginning, especially when you're tired and don't get enough sleep. When you find yourself sleeping, gently bring your attention back to your breath without getting frustrated with yourself, because you can only focus on your breathing for short periods of time. It sometimes happens that way. What can I tell ya?" Luther throws up his hands like one using the expression c'est la vie, that's life. The gesture reminds Arthur of a fat Chinese Buddha statue he once saw and is greatly amused. Luther enjoys the moment as well, almost as if he planned to end their quiet sitting in this way.

"These are your mind tools for now, Arthur," says Luther after regaining Arthur's attention. "Sit completely still in the posture I showed you and practice watching your breath without controlling it in any way...and try to stay awake, Arthur. Sit twice each day at the time of yoga or union, when night transitions into day and again when day changes into night."

"Since I live alone, I have no set time for eating in the evening, and I eat dinner in restaurants a lot. So I may not always be home to sit at this union time."

"I'm sure you'll figure it out, but try to set a consistent time for when you sit in the morning and evening, even if it's just before going to bed," says Luther. "However, at that time, you may be more prone to sleep."

"I'll try."

"Arthur, quiet sitting is a discipline that many people who just try are unable or unwilling to master because their will power is not developed enough to sustain their practice. But you received a blessing when that malicious spirit possessed you. Do you know that?"

"Why do you say that?" asks Arthur.

"Because when you felt that spirit rise out of you...for your own survival, you knew you had to learn how to protect yourself. Otherwise, you'd remain susceptible and run the risk of other possessions. It was then you cried out to a God you don't know for help, and the response is you sitting here in front of me today. So this training, here and now, is a way to strengthen and nurture your inner life, even if you doubt the existence of God, so you don't have to fear a reoccurrence of spirit possession."

Luther's explanation is a revelation to Arthur, a sudden leap in understanding of a truth he now grasps at the core of his being. Direct and so simply put by this intriguing black man he doesn't even know. Arthur wonders why he hadn't arrived at this same conclusion and made the connection.

"So, tell me, Arthur...will you commit, today, and prepare a place in your busy life for meditation? It will require patience and your tenacious persistence to cultivate this discipline in your life; at least, until it becomes a habit you choose to surrender to."

Arthur has an uneasy feeling he's revisiting a crossroads he's been at before, where life-altering decisions have to be made. And if he's arrived at this juncture in the past, why has he returned to the same place again? Did he take the wrong turn the last time around and now has the opportunity to choose once again? These were curious and odd thoughts. Like, at birth, does a baby choose to take or not to take its first breath, or is that choice demanded of the child by a higher power? Or is the position he finds himself in as significant as a choice to live in darkness rather than walking in the light, or has that choice already been made by his past actions? Arthur sees Luther patiently waiting for his response, while his own insight into his dilemma sets him back in his chair as if a powerful wind has him up against a wall.

"Do you really want to be a gentle warrior, Arthur, and remove the inner obstacles to let the power and voice of Spirit to work within and through you?" asks Luther in a quiet voice. His dark eyes pierce Arthur's soul.

"What did you say?" asks Arthur, startled by Luther's comment while hanging on to the man's every word. Luther says nothing more as he awaits Arthur's reply.

"I commit to your meditation practice, Luther, if it leads me to knowing for myself that there is something I can call Divine," says Arthur.

"So your practice is conditional. And how long do you think you will stick with it, Arthur?"

"Until I know for myself one way or the other."

"I'm here, Arthur, to help you regain your footing on a path you've walked before," says Luther with an unfathomable grin. He abruptly stands and extends his hand. "I would like to see you again around this time next week. Can you fit this day and time into your schedule?"

"Yes, I'll make it work."

"Cool."

Together, they laugh again and embrace one another before Arthur walks to the door and puts on his shoes. It's not until he steps outside that Arthur looks at his watch and realizes he's been with Luther for almost two hours. Looking up at the fading blue sky, he notices a lone bright star near the fullness of the moon and is reminded of his promise to sit as best he can at the time of yoga when day vanishes into night and night makes way for the coming of day.

Walking down Oakdale to his car, Arthur wonders why Luther said he'd walked this path before. And how did his mentor know about Critical Mass Health Conductors' fourth principle about removing inner obstacles? Arthur promises himself to keep the commitment made to Luther and vows to practice daily, at least for now.

CHAPTER 35

FIFTY-SEVEN TEASPOONS OF SUGAR

"If you've read anything about our patron, Harriet Tubman, you know she wasn't afraid to take risks; and she was courageous, even with the huge bounty on her head. They wanted her dead or alive," says Arthur, standing behind the podium and talking to leadership at the health conductors' second training session. "We're told, for example, that Harriet was one of the pioneers in using the railway as part of her underground railroad. She reasoned that it was often safer to use public transportation because no one would suspect a runaway slave to board a public train. More than once, she'd held a paper or magazine in her hands to make like she was reading because white folks knew slaves were supposed to be illiterate. Harriet was illiterate, too, but she had faith that she'd be holding the paper the right way, instead of upside down, so she could appear as though she was actually reading.

"Another instance of her risk-taking and bravery was the time she walked down the main street of a small town in Maryland, in broad daylight, and recognized one of her former masters walking toward her. She wore a large sunbonnet that day and pulled it down over her head, holding on to two live chickens by their feet tied with a rope. When the master approached, she looked down and pulled on the rope, so the chickens got agitated and started cackling. Harriet used this opportunity to look away and avoid the eyes of the master, who she thought would surely recognize her.

"So we look to Harriet to build up our own courage and determination as we struggle to change, perhaps, long-held habits and beliefs that we know are destroying our health, like cigarette smoking or feeling so tired and stressed out after work that we give up on exercise or binge on comfort food late at night while watching television.

"Thinking about our own efforts to make better lifestyle choices, we need to sometimes ask ourselves, what would Harriet do? That's why, tonight, we're giving you this blue wrist band." Arthur holds up the rubber bracelet for them to see. "It says, in large gold letters, 'What would Harriet do?' If you wear it, it will not only promote Critical Mass Health Conductors but also remind you and me of Harriet's courage and ingenuity in times when we have doubts or need support to live up to our own commitment to making better health decisions. Thank you."

The gathering gives him a round of applause as he leaves the podium, and Aisha Middleton takes his place. It's time for testimonies from those in triads who have something to share with the rest of the group. "So now we'd like to hear from you about what your triad experience has been like for you and your group over the past month. Would anyone like to start?"

Aaron from the public health department is the first to raise his hand and stand. "Most of my immediate staff know that I'm participating in Health Conductors, so they ask me what are we doing and whether my experience walking the lake with Arthur and John has been beneficial. Sometimes they'll stop by my office just to ask. Well, today I had three employees, who don't report directly to me, stop by and ask if they could join conductors now because they are a triad and want some assistance in getting started. My immediate thought was to invite them to this training, tonight; but if I did that, I know others in the department would want to join as well, and we're halfway through our three-month training." Aaron sits down.

Several affirmative nods signal that others, too, had employees approach them about Health Conductors. Herbert Curry, the evaluator, pulls out his pen and notepad as these anecdotal stories from conductors-in-training demonstrate genuine interest in the program from external sources. He wants to document them.

Reggie Johnson, from United Youth Leadership, then stands and says, "You know, my triad has all men—Samuel over there, and Greg, here with me. We go bike riding every other weekend and do at least twenty to thirty miles in and around the Bay. We've been out twice so far. I know there's interest in Health Conductors because we picked up two other brothas, one from my job and a friend of Greg's, who rode with us the last time because they liked riding with a group. And I'm sure they'll come back for our ride next Saturday. So we're starting a movement, oh yeah, oh yeah!" He raises his fist in the air and hoots several times before returning to his chair. This generates sidebar conversations and laughter.

"Well, I want to tell you," continues Carol Anderson from Black Youth Radio, "I was sick and tired of my triad ladies after the first week, 'cause they call me every night around nine o'clock, both of them asking me if I'm ready for bed. Hell no, I'm not ready! I got so many calls that at about a quarter to nine, I've started rushing whatever I am doing 'cause I know they're gonna be ringin', asking me what I'm doing. Do you hear me? I mean, I almost have anxiety attacks." And there's more laughter and applause heard from around the room. "So, finally, I decided to have my pajamas on by eight thirty, no matter what I am doing, so I can tell them when they call that I'm ready for bed. And do you know what? Since then, I've been getting into bed…though I don't always put the lights out, but I'm in bed by nine thirty. Yes I am." And Carol sits down.

Testimony from other conductors-in-training continues for another thirty-five minutes under the momentum of new vitality and energy, as one person after another delights in telling his or her story. Any stress leadership may have felt or been under, dealing with the day-to-day politics and human interaction in their offices, dissipates by the time testimony is over.

Arthur leaves the room to answer a phone call as Hachi introduces Pat Cleveland, a young, petite African American woman from the public health department who is there to conduct the fats and sugars seminar. The call's from Valerie. Arthur immediately realizes from the tremor in her voice that something is wrong when she says, "Hello, Arthur?"

"Hi, Valerie, how are you?" he asks.

"Her voice trembles. "I'm fine, but Ralph's sick, and I just needed someone to talk to."

"I'm glad you thought to call me. What's wrong with him?"

"He has ALS, Lou Gehrig's disease," Valerie struggles to say.

"I've heard of ALS, but what exactly is it?"

"It's a disease affecting the nervous system and brain and spinal cord. His nerve cells are degenerating, causing muscle weakness in his arms and legs, even his ability to swallow and eat food or talk…even his breathing will eventually be affected. They say Ralph has no more than a year or two to live."

"My God, Valerie, how long has Ralph had this?"

"It's been about three years now."

"And in all this time, you've never mentioned it when we've talked on the phone or gotten together. Even when we were in

San Francisco when I asked about Ralph, you told me he just worked all the time. Why?"

"I don't know, Arthur. I really don't know," she replies, sounding physically exhausted and breathing heavily from the years and months she carried this secret and held it back from him.

He's shocked at this revelation and wants to probe, to find out why she's never mentioned it, but he realizes it's not about him tonight. "And have you been Ralph's caretaker all this time?"

"Well, when he was first diagnosed, he was still functioning. I mean, he'd lose his footing sometimes, especially when stepping off the curb, but neither of us suspected anything was wrong. Then, on occasion, he started dropping things he held in his hands. That's when I insisted he see a doctor. They gave him a battery of tests before they diagnosed him with ALS. But he could pretty much function on his own then. But now..."Her voice trails off, as if she has taken too many sleeping pills or is about to pass out from too many drinks.

"Valerie...Valerie! Are you still there?"

"Yes, I'm here...I'm just tired, that's all. Ralph's in a wheelchair now, when he's able to get out of bed. I have to massage his limbs every day...they get stiff. Now the disease is beginning to affect his ability to swallow, and they're saying eventually he'll have to be hooked-up to intravenous feeding."

"Valerie, do you have help taking care of Ralph?

"Yes, I have help now. Luckily, he has good health insurance that includes home assistance. A nurse visits twice a week, and a home aide comes in every morning...except the weekends... and helps out. That's when I run to the store and do errands and things. All other times, I'm alone, and I'm fine with that. I really am. It's just that, like tonight, I was feeling overwhelmed by the responsibility."

"And how are you able to work?" asks Arthur.

"Arthur, I've been working in curriculum development for so many years that I can take assignments and work at home, what with the Internet and all."

"Valerie, I am amazed at what you're telling me. In all these years, you've never said a word about any of this."

"Arthur, please don't be mad," she says.

"Valerie, I'm not mad. Maybe, a little disappointed that you didn't have enough faith in me to know that I'm here for you and that I would understand."

"Maybe someday we can talk about it again, but not now."

"Do you want me to come to New York and see you?"

"No…not now, baby. I just wanted to hear your voice and talk for a while. I feel a burden has been lifted in telling you, even if my confession is a little late. Good night, Arthur. I need to get to bed and sleep. Don't worry, I'm all right."

"Can I call you in a few days to see how you're doing?" asks Arthur.

"Arthur, you can call me anytime. I'm here."

"Good night, Valerie."

"Good night, Arthur. I love you," is transmitted through the line as an intimate breath softly resonates in his ear and heart, and he knows what she said is true.

Health conductors-in-training are standing in the back rows, watching Pat as she counts out loud the fifty-seven teaspoons of sugar she's putting into an empty two-liter bottle of Coca-Cola as Arthur walks into the room. Many in the group appear genuinely shocked, judging from their gaping mouths, that all this sugar is added to one bottle of flavored soda water. If one didn't know it, you'd think they're watching a scary horror movie or a gruesome murder mystery on television. It all seems rather trivial and meaningless as Arthur thinks about his conversation with Valerie and Ralph's disease, which will eventually transform him into living stone.

"How much added sweeteners, including sugar, do you think the average American eats in one year?" Pat asks the group.

"Fifteen pounds...twenty-five pounds...fifty-pounds," several people shout from their seats.

"Any other answers?" she replies with a voice that contradicts her small size. "Almost one hundred pounds a year, which is almost a quarter pound of sugar and other calorie-rich sweeteners, like high fructose corn syrup, in one day. It's no wonder that two out of three Americans are overweight or obese. And you know far too many of us are walking around with too much extra padding, which can lead to serious health problems like heart disease, type two diabetes, and certain kinds of cancers."

"So last month," says Sonia Cespedes, "we talked about the metabolic syndrome and were told that being overweight was one of the traits of having this syndrome. Is that correct?"

"Yes, that's right," Pat replies.

"Well, some of us believe...because I've been in groups of black women who have talked about it...that we're just a big-boned people, that we're big by nature, and that this is the way we're built...big...or do you think that's a myth and our weight gain is really because of a sugar-laden diet?"

Several women in the room look uncomfortable with the question, perhaps because they support this point of view giving credence to their being so grossly overweight. One of the women, Martha Grimes, from Alameda County Social Services, starts pulling on her loose-fitting blouse that hangs like an open parachute over her rotund waistline as if she can conceal what surely she can't hide.

"I've heard that explanation as well, Sonia," says Pat, scanning the room so her eyes don't rest on any particular person. "There can be many reasons for weight gain and being overweight, including certain glandular diseases; and that would have to be diagnosed by a doctor. But the fact remains that there's too much sugar and carbohydrates, which turns into sugar, in our diets…the so-called soul food diet. Look what we're eating at church socials, and what's our traditional meal at Christmas, Thanksgiving, and at family reunions? Besides the meat on our plates, we're eating candied yams and rice and macaroni and cheese with, maybe, a little room for some salad or overcooked greens; and we're washing it down with large glasses of sugary soda. Now, ain't that right? Can I get a witness?"

Uneasy laughter explodes around the room as participants come to grips with the truth in her remarks. "And don't think we ain't got…excuse my English, 'cause y'all got me riled up now… don't think we ain't got our eyes peeled on that dessert table, watching to see if the sweets ain't laid out already. And we're asking ourselves, when dey gonna start serving dessert? And then we gorge ourselves on the butter pound cake, the coconut cake, the red velvet cake, the sweet potato and pumpkin pies, the German chocolate cake, and, if we're lucky, we might grab ourselves a little of Grandma's peach cobbler…and if we're real, real lucky, we're gonna add some vanilla ice cream on top of dat. Now, ain't dat right? See, I know…I know, 'cause as little as I am, I've been there, too…uh-huh…uh-huh."

There's now raucous laughter feverishly prancing around the room as several women—including Martha Grimes—cover their mouths, embarrassed, because Patricia has peeped their whole card. Some of the men raise a hand in praise of the Lord and whoop or slap high fives with one another as there's commotion all around.

"So, you see, our diets have too much sugar and other sweeteners," continues Pat when the room calms down. "We need to be more conscious about what we're putting in our mouths and our children's stomachs. Sugar is addictive. It's like being strung out on cocaine or heroin…really. And it's hard to break this addiction because sugar's in everything...everything, 'cause it's what makes us go back to buy some more.

"We should also try to stay away from eating processed food and eat more fresh foods...foods with lots of color like greens and tomatoes and carrots and fruits—although if you're diabetic, you'll have to be careful about not eating too much fruit, because fruits contain lots of sugars. But stay away from sugary drinks and sodas altogether, and as an alternative, drink lots of water. Ain't nothin' wrong with water. OK, everyone, let's get back to business. Are there any more questions about the consumption of sugar before we turn our attention to good and bad fats?"

CHAPTER 36

A HOP AND A LEAP

One Week Later

Arthur turns onto Oakdale Drive and immediately finds a parking spot not far from Luther's house. Walking up the block and looking at his watch, he realizes it's about a half-hour or so before the time of yoga. He is pleasantly surprised, and actually looking forward to sitting with Luther. Up ahead, children are playing a game on the sidewalk; and even from this far away, it's apparent they're enjoying their play. Their frolicking bubbles over into peals of laughter as four children jump up and down while watching a fifth child hop up and down.

As Arthur draws closer, he's stunned to recognize that the figure in the middle is not a child at all but Luther McKinnie playing a game of hopscotch with them. Nine square boxes drawn with colored chalk are on the pavement in a long column with several pairs of boxes drawn side by side. Luther's keys are eight squares away, and he hops on one foot, advancing through two of the boxes before he's able to put both feet down with one foot in each box. Arthur's mentor stops on the two squares and fakes losing his balance. The children scream with excitement, waiting to see if his feet will leave a box or if he will fall over, which will mean he loses his turn.

Luther makes believe he's regained his balance before taking a white handkerchief out of his pants pocket and wiping his forehead. Then, for the children's merriment, he acts like he's afraid to move on and pantomimes that he needs help, and the children are ecstatic. Finally, Luther finds the courage to hop and jump to the seventh box where, standing only on one foot, he gracefully bends over and picks up his keys lying in the next box on the pavement. After retrieving his keys, he makes a perfect 180-degree leap in the air and lands facing the opposite direction—with one foot in each box—like a graceful but overweight ballet dancer. He then hops and jumps without a mistake to where he started. The children and Arthur cheer and roar with laughter as an elderly white man walking on the other side of the street, startled by the commotion, raises his shriveled-up fist at the kids before noticing Arthur and Luther staring back at him. Abruptly aborting the gesture, he hastens his pace as if he hadn't seen or done a thing.

The kids cheer and grab hold of Luther's arm as he walks over to greet Arthur. They don't want him to leave and plead for him to stay, enjoying the attention of an old man who plays like a child. Luther promises he'll return another day and says his goodbyes while tapping each child lightly on the top of the head. Then he takes Arthur's arm, and together they walk up the street.

"Do you often play with these kids?" asks Arthur.

"Not often, but I enjoy being with them. They're starved for adult attention, you know. And they rarely talk to or see an old man like me. So I play with the children every now and again, and they always leave me with a good workout. Jumping rope is the most challenging for me, but I manage; and for them it's good fun."

"And their parents don't mind?"

"Why should they mind?" replies Luther. "They know me. I don't go to their homes, but they see me in the yard or out front. They know where I live, and I watch out for the children until their parents come home."

Arthur follows Luther up the stairs and into his house. After they remove their shoes, Luther moves one of the living-room chairs to the middle of the floor and then rolls over the covered object that sits on a stand between the two chairs. Arthur retrieves the other chair and places it, like on the first occasion, in front of his mentor, who sits patiently smiling at him.

"I know this sounds a little weird, but you enjoy smiling at people, don't you Luther?" asks Arthur.

"Is there something wrong with smiling, Arthur?" asks Luther.

"No, but your smile is special...mysterious in some way. When I see you, I, too, want to smile...and it's calming, like everything is all right, and it seems always different...reflecting a change in mood, perhaps?"

Luther is delighted and smiles even more. "And what do you think my smile is saying now?"

Arthur studies Luther's face for a moment. "Well...I think you have something to tell me or ask, and you are waiting for me to get settled and sit. Am I correct?" Arthur takes his seat and smiles, waiting for his mentor to respond.

"So you're comfortable with me, now?"

"Why do you say that?"

"'Cause you're trying to humor me," says Luther.

"Is it working?" says Arthur, laughing easily. "Luther, I still don't really know you, but I'm comfortable in your presence."

"Good...well then, tell me, Arthur, in the past when you've thought about the God thing, what images of the Divine came to your mind? How did you picture God?"

"Luther, is this the question you wanted to ask me?"

"Yes..."

Arthur has to adjust to the question, as it wasn't anticipated. "Well, I don't know," he replies, searching his mentor's face for a clue as to where the conversation is going. "I know this may sound infantile," he finally continues, "and maybe it's because how I was raised, but as a child, I pictured God as an old white man with a beard...a long white beard like Charleton Heston in the film "The Ten Commandments." And in Sunday school, I learned that God sat on his throne in heaven with Jesus Christ sitting, I think, on God's right side. Saint Peter stood at the pearly gates...I don't recall why they were called pearly...but he decided who was fit to enter and who had to go on down to hell."

Luther listened carefully, nodding his head occasionally to assure Arthur he was listening. "Our consciousness," he finally says. "Think of what a blessing and a gift it is, Arthur, that you and I exist and are aware of our existence. And that awareness... that we exist...is not only within us but in all humankind. And that consciousness is more than the sum total of the consciousness in all human beings. It is more than that...it's aware of itself. You and I, Arthur, are little waves of that consciousness that have risen from this infinite ocean of consciousness, and we will return to that ocean when we pass away. Why not acknowledge and honor that wave of consciousness within us...that *is* us...that is beyond us...that vast ocean of consciousness that surrounds us?

"Now's the time for yoga, so let us sit for a while and see if we can expand our little wave of consciousness into that endless ocean of consciousness—the mother of us all. So relax into your meditation posture and close your eyes, Arthur. Gently raise your gaze to that point between your eyes...and when you're ready, focus on your breathing."

They sit in silence for half an hour before Luther reaches over and touches the tip of his index finger to that spot on Arthur's forehead and silently invokes a prayer. Arthur then begins to hear the first, faint sound of the harmonium's voice, a small reed organ uncovered now and delivering one long sustained note. Luther's hand is on the keyboard while the other hand pumps the bellows filling it with air. That one note expands in tone and then blends with added notes into a harmonious cord as Luther softly begins to hum a haunting melody. The hum gradually turns into repetitive phrases as he chants to the Divine Mother until his incantation settles into a rhythm and upbeat cadence, hinting at his Southern roots. The repetitive chant now rises and falls in intensity as Luther sings with longing and passion, tapping his right foot on the floor.

Arthur, however, is self-conscious and increasingly uncomfortable for reasons unknown to him. And the more he strives to be receptive to Luther's singing, the more his uneasiness grows. Suddenly overwhelmed by his discomfort, Arthur retreats and fights against the music by trying to ignore Luther by focusing on his breath, to the exclusion of everything around him. Thoughts now flood his mind, undermining his attempt to sit quietly. He questions why he's allowed himself to be lured into this predicament by Luther's words and can't recall his own rationale for agreeing to meditate each day. Arthur considers whether he should have taken Hector's advice and returned for his protective beads. That option would have been far easier, he realizes, and a quicker fix than sitting still with eyes closed next to a man who remains a mystery to him. Another five or so minutes pass before tears well up in Arthur's eyes and stream down his face. With the tears is a flashback of the overpowering fear and hopelessness he felt in Valerie's hotel room that day when he called out to God to save him.

Arthur's body shudders from the raw emotion of the memory, when he was out of control and utterly defenseless against the spirit that possessed him. He feebly starts to mouth barely audible words to Luther's chant, as if it's a life raft too far out of reach. The words stick in his throat like the madness of a defiant ego under siege. He's almost in a panic as Luther's chant floods his mind, along with a rising tide of sadness and false pride, as tears continue to roll down his cheeks.

Then something in him gives way as he recollects Luther's council that he must be a gentle warrior. Hearing this inner voice, Arthur is suddenly released from the incessant chatter inundating his mind and surrenders to the moment. Rebelling against his self-judgment, he raises his voice and joins Luther in praise of the Mother he does not know...Luther's Divine Mother.

And in the silence, the stillness that follows after the chant, Arthur begins to discern the faint sound of a deep vibration that his knowing self has never heard, but his soul knows right well—the commanding monotonic hum that undergirds the entire universe. The rumbling absorbs the total sum of what he is, drawing him deeper and deeper within until, peering into this inner darkness behind closed eyes, he finds himself standing on the edge of his own consciousness, looking into a black abyss. Arthur's frightened by the darkness. His fear screams him away from the edge, and he opens his eyes to find Luther calmly smiling at him.

Arthur looks around the room, reassuring himself that the world is still in place and just as he left it. He listens to the street sounds outside; a car passes by. "Luther," he says with an unsteady voice, "I felt I was standing on the edge of my own consciousness looking out into a vast and dark emptiness, so I had to back away."

"And why did you back away?" asks Luther.

"Why? If I went any farther, maybe I wouldn't come back."

"And would that matter?"

"Yes, it matters. I have responsibilities and work to do." Arthur realizes immediately that his impulsive response covers up the real reason for his retreat—that he was consumed by fear. A chill goes up his spine, and he's now more curious than ever about who this man really is who calls himself Luther McKinnie. "Who are you, Luther? I mean, where do you come from?"

"I'm spirit in human form just like you, Arthur. We're little waves rising from the ocean of Spirit. As you continue your practice, the fear you may feel now will dissipate and will steadily be replaced by a feeling of peace and ever-new joy. I promise you—that is, as you gradually prove it to yourself." Again, Luther smiles. "Do you have a Bible?"

"My grandmother's Bible, but I haven't looked at it in years."

"Well, open your grandma's Bible and read Psalm 139, the Mystic's Prayer, before starting your meditation at night. It speaks to this vast ocean of Spirit and our relationship with it."

"Read it every night?" asks Arthur.

"Yes...until your own experience echoes this truth, especially, the verses in the psalm that read:

> If I ascend up into heaven, you are there; if I make my bed in hell, behold, you are there.
>
> If I take the wings of the morning, and dwell in the uttermost parts of the sea;
>
> even there shall your hand lead me, and your right hand shall hold me.
>
> If I say, surely the darkness shall cover me; even the night shall be light about me.
>
> Yes, the darkness cannot hide you; but the night shines as the day; the darkness and the light are both alike to you.

"For now, I want you to end your practice in the mornings and evenings with the last verse in the psalm, 'Search me, O God, and know my heart; try me and know my thoughts. And see if there be any wicked way in me, and lead me in the way everlasting.'

A famous preacher of African descent by the name of Howard Thurman always began his sermons with this verse. Will you do that, Arthur?"

"But why, Luther—remember you told me to question everything and everyone? And doesn't that mean you?"

Luther laughs. "I was waiting for that pronouncement. I would like to be able to say what I said and leave it at that...to say, 'Just trust me on this one'; but I know that answer won't satisfy your desire to know, so let me say this, and don't ask me now how I know.

"Remember when you were in the hotel room and were possessed? When you called out to God for help? Well, if you were vulnerable then to this spirit, you still are now. It will no doubt try again to possess you. Your regular practice and the verses from this psalm will enrich your inner life...strengthen it and protect you from spirit possession. That's why I'm giving you these verses from the Mystic's Prayer to say along with your practice."

Arthur has an odd thought but immediately dismisses it. "Yes, Luther, right now I accept your reasoning. I'll memorize these verses from the prayer."

"But you must not say them by rote memory. These verses must become your very own. Do you understand?"

"Yes, Luther, I understand."

"Good."

Luther then questions Arthur in detail about where he meditates in his apartment and suggests he find a space where he can place a chair only to be used for that purpose. He tells him to buy a piece of raw silk long enough to drape over the back of the chair and onto the seat and down to the floor, so that when he sits, his feet will be on the cloth. Luther explains how the life force or energy drawn into the body during meditation comes into the medulla oblongata, and that the silk insulates the body so the energy generated will not be dispelled into the floor.

"Do you have an altar in your home, Arthur?" Luther asks.

"No. What would I do with an altar?" Arthur is amused by this inquiry.

"You may have one and don't think of it as an altar. Do you keep photographs of family who have passed over?"

"Yes...photos of my grandmother, my father and brother, Mark, and a younger sister who died before her seventeen birthday, Azizah."

"And where do you keep their photos—in an album, or are they in picture frames hanging on the wall or sitting on a tabletop somewhere?"

"They're in picture frames. I keep them on a table in my living room."

"Then it's an altar, isn't it?" asks Luther. "You placed their photos together on a table so you can see them...remember them. They're your family, and perhaps, sometimes, you even dream and talk to them. So why not set your chair in front of their table? Invite your ancestors to join you when you sit to meditate."

"Will they come?" asks Arthur.

"Perhaps, if your prayers and meditations go deep enough... are long enough."

"And how will I know they're there?"

"Now, that you'll have to discover for yourself, my friend."

Arthur is silent, lost in thought as he thinks about the implications of Luther's suggestion. He wonders if he should introduce this idea, quiet sitting with ancestors, to the Health Conductors—or would they believe such a proposition too fanciful, too way out and beyond the scope and interest of the project's mission or against most of their Christian beliefs?

"Remember, Arthur," continues Luther, "you're not worshiping your ancestors...you're acknowledging and honoring them by inviting them to sit with you...let them serve as intermediaries to the Divine when you are in need of advice."

"Luther, I am not convinced I believe in all that right now."

"I know, Arthur. The important thing is to continue your daily sitting. Let where you place your chair and table and photos in your apartment grow on you. In time, you will know where to place them. Everything doesn't have to be done in a day. But it is an essential part of our African heritage—you know, the honoring of ancestors. Family members considered ancestors are ones who had good character when they were among the living, when they were role models for other members in your family and in the community."

"Yes, I understand."

Arthur is high on Luther's teachings and advice when leaving his mentor's East Oakland home. It's a clear evening. A sliver of the moon and a bright evening star are already visible in the east. His mobile phone rings, and it's Natalie. Arthur swears she only pops up when he's feeling good to break his happiness. "How are you, Natalie?"

"Hi, Arthur. I just want you to know that my attorney has mailed the divorce papers, and you should get them by FedEx tomorrow. I hope you'll sign them and return them to his office as soon as possible."

"What's the rush?" asks Arthur.

"There's really no rush, Arthur. I just want to get this over with so we can both move on with our lives."

"You know, Natalie, for what it's worth, I never slept around, as you put it. It is true, I did cheat on you…once…maybe twice, and for that I do apologize. I hope you don't give up on men because of your experience with me, and…"

"What do you mean, Arthur? I'm not gay! Why do you think I'm gay?" she cries with annoyance in her voice. She is about to say more when Arthur interrupts.

"Natalie, I didn't mean to suggest that you're gay. I meant no offense, really. I used the wrong choice of words. I'm sorry. I just want you to know that I wish you well. I'll sign the papers and return them to your attorney as soon as possible. Good night, and have a happy life." And he hangs up without waiting for her reply.

By the time he parks his car, climbs the stairs, and turns the key in the doorknob, Arthur's no longer thinking about Natalie but rather about the photographs on the living-room table. He walks over and looks at the pictures, now seeing the family photos in a new way, in a new light.

The malicious spirit in the apartment underneath, sensing Arthur's arrival, rises through the floorboards and settles in his kitchen. It's fascinated by Arthur, now that it's invaded the young man's vessel and successfully possessed him. It's confident that if it can enter his human form once, it's only a matter of time before it will enter again. Arthur is now its obsession; if it had a material mouth, it would salivate like a dog seeing a bone. Hypnotized by the allure of Arthur's physical frame, it fantasizes about using his body again, like when it made him ride BART back and forth all day from morning to night. If only it could possess him again and ride him to a bar for a drink. It knows it has to be devious and more skillful at sliding in and out of Arthur's physical element without him noticing. If it is to master possession of him, it realizes it must be patient and learn how to wear him like old familiar clothes—a well-worn leather glove.

Its surging obsession with Arthur is tangled up with wanton passions, a frenzied collection of dark, lower memories of a lascivious nature when it was also human. Watching Arthur is so exciting that if it had a body right now, it would surely be orgasmic. It needs a dick to masturbate and to feel the heat rise into its disembodied loins. Seeing only blood red now, it retreats down into the darkness.

CHAPTER 37
OCEAN WAVES

Dr. Phil Morgan sits outside the Berkeley clinic on a bench, reading a magazine, when Arthur arrives to take him to the health conductors' training. He's grown a short beard since their first meeting, and is casually dressed in a comfortable pair of jeans and brown leather belt with a big silver buckle. He also sports a light-blue work shirt and a pair of brown leather boots. Phil greets Arthur through the open window and gets into the car.

"Doc, what do you think of us referring to meditation as a spiritual tool in your stress-reduction seminar?" asks Arthur.

"Are you kidding? That's politically unwise. You'll stir up a hornet's nest in your audience. I've encountered that problem before, and I don't want to go there again, especially when dealing with black folk who are Christians. I suggest we stay away from anything that smacks of religion or spirituality when talking about stress management. I prefer not even using the word 'meditation' at all; I will simply call what's introduced as quiet sitting or just plain sitting, quietly."

"Why is referring to meditation as a spiritual tool a problem?"

Stopping at the corner of University Avenue and Sixth Street, they wait for the light to make a left onto the overpass heading for the freeway going south. Then Phil responds, "Look, mainstream religious types, including black churchgoers…they have a real problem with meditation because pastors tell them it's bad…it's navel gazing. It comes out of Eastern religions that are polytheistic and people who don't accept Jesus Christ as their only Lord and Savior.

"And besides, some pastors fear that if their congregations start meditating, churchgoers will eventually cut them out as their middleman to God, so to speak, and they'll be out of a job. Besides, most preachers know little or nothing about quiet sitting, 'cause they don't practice it themselves, and think meditation is the same thing as prayer. And it makes them nervous when you ask people to sit quietly with their eyes closed and virtually tune them out. Oh no…no…no, let's stick with quiet sitting as a stress-reduction tool, that's all."

Health conductors are presenting testimonials when Phil and Arthur walk through the door. Doris Whitehead is standing and describing how one of her triad members tried to back out of a commitment to walk Lake Merritt last Sunday morning with the group.

"She told us she forgot Sunday was coming up, and she couldn't miss church. We told that hussy…" Doris turns to her companion immediately and lightly touches her on the shoulder. "Sorry, Carol, I didn't mean to call you a hussy," she says, interrupting her own testimonial before turning back to the room. "Anyway, we listened to Carol on the call and then told her she'd made a commitment, and church that morning was gonna be walking with us around the lake."

"Did she keep her promise?" asks Aisha from the podium.

"Yes, girl; we all walked the lake last Sunday and then stopped for breakfast, where she ate two orders of bacon. That girl can eat!"

Carol jumps up and tries to put her hand over Doris's mouth, and the room breaks out in laughter. "Girl, you don't need to say all that. I think you said enough, so it's time to take your seat."

Arthur introduces Phil to Hachi Lightfoot, who is standing on one side of the room, watching Aisha lead the testimonials. After greeting one another, they recall meeting at a black physicians' social affair and discover they know several mutual colleagues. Arthur hears Aisha closing the testimonial segment of the program and acknowledging that their guest speaker for the evening is ready for his presentation. Conductors-in-training turn their attention to Phil, and he waves to everyone. Hachi offers to present Dr. Morgan to the group and takes the lead as Phil follows her to the podium. After a brief introduction, citing Phil's credentials and his service as director of the city of Berkeley's substance-abuse program, Hachi leaves him to begin his seminar.

"Good evening, everyone. OK, let's begin," he says. "First, let's talk about what causes stress. When your blood sugar is up, nine times outta ten, people are under stress. Practicing simple relaxation techniques makes your blood sugar go down, and then your stress level goes down. These techniques help some people get off medication.

"Stress exacerbates or causes ninety percent of all diseases. It affects the brain. The brain controls most of the body functions. Proper nourishment or diet, exercise, and stress reduction means a longer, healthier life. Together, these three action steps are a curative lifestyle.

"How many of you have heard of the fight-or-flight response?" Phil surveys the room to find that most of the leadership has a hand raised. "I'm glad to know most of you know about the fight-or-flight response, but for those of you who don't, let's review it together. So here's the scene: A hungry tiger is at one end of a large field, and you're at the other end. The tiger sees you and begins to run toward you. What are you going to do...stand your ground and fight or run away? Regardless of what you decide to do, your body has its own reaction and gets ready to deal with the situation.

"So what actually happens, biologically speaking, when you have a fight-or-flight response? You have an adrenalin rush. Adrenalin is a hormone or chemical produced in the body that carries messages from glands to cells to maintain chemical levels in the bloodstream to control the condition of the body. Adrenalin release is toxic in high doses, because it causes the blood vessels in the body to start to deteriorate.

"So, what happens to the body in a stress or fight-or-flight response, like being attacked by a tiger? Your brain waves speed up like a stormy ocean. Your heart starts pounding faster, and your blood pressure and blood sugar go up. Blood rushes to major muscle groups in the body to prepare for flight. And blood is cut off from flowing to the skin, so you won't bleed much. It's cut off from your stomach, because you don't need to digest food at that moment. Your immune system shuts down because, if you have a pimple on your nose, you don't need to ward off infection at this moment.

"Another stress hormone is cortisol, which is also released by the same gland that produces adrenalin. This hormone breaks down the tissue to convert it into energy. So, together, the hormones adrenalin and cortisol are called the stress hormones.

"Now, what happens if you're under constant stress? Stressed-out people start looking for things to calm them down, like smoking, habitual eating, drugs, alcohol, etc. Stress knocks out the immune system; and if you already have cancer, it will cause your cancer to spread. Stress also produces anxiety, which affects the brain. Chronic stress is like a simmering fight-or-flight response that just stays below the boiling point. It's damaging to the body. Any questions so far?"

No one responds, although everyone is attentive to what Phil has to say. "OK. How do we learn to counter this fight-or-flight response? We can offset this response by engaging in deep relaxation. So how do you relax? Anyone care to tell us how you personally relax?"

Herb Curry, the project's evaluator, raises his hand and says, "I try to play at least one game of golf on the weekends. That's how I relax."

"I like to read," says Regina Bradley, a registered nurse.

"Well, it turns out," continues Phil, "that if you ask most people living here in the West, they'll pretty much say the same thing. They like to play golf, read...take time to sew, and perform other kinds of leisure activities, but deep relaxation is not the same as leisure activities. Is sleeping relaxing?" Phil waits for an answer that doesn't come; then finally he says, "Sleep is not deep relaxation. Why? There are two kinds of sleep, dream sleep and deep sleep. In dream sleep, the brain waves remain active; in deep sleep or delta sleep, you are no longer aware that you are relaxed, and your metabolism, food digestion, is down by eight percent.

"In order to relax, you have to be awake and relaxed; and when this occurs, your metabolism is down sixty to eighty percent, and your brain waves slow down. Remember, when you're under stress, you have rapid beta waves."

Phil reaches for the half-full bottle of water a trainee has in their hands and shakes it. Everyone watches as the shaken water becomes turbulent in the plastic container, and when he stops shaking it, the liquid settles down. "Thank you," he says, handing the bottle back to its owner.

"For deep relaxation, you must remain awake—and yet relaxed. It's a kind of restful alertness. When you're relaxed, your blood pressure goes down, your blood sugar level goes down, adrenalin and cortisol levels go down, and your immune system is strengthened, not shut off.

"So now that we understand what chronic stress is and how it affects the body, how can we activate the deep-relaxation response to counteract our stress? Let's take a ten-minute break and I'll show you several deep-relaxation exercises you can do at any time to help reduce stress."

Martha Grimes from Social Services rushes over to Phil as he leaves the front of the room to say, "Dr. Morgan, would you be willing to conduct this workshop at my church here in West Oakland? Because we got a whole lot of people who suffer from hypertension, and they need to hear what you have to say."

"Sure, I'm open to the idea, but let me present the exercises; and if you're still interested when I'm finished, I'll give you my phone number at the clinic, and you can reach me there."

Before resuming after the break, Phil is introduced to Aisha, and he hands her a CD he wants her to play later in his presentation. Conductors-in-training take their seats, and Phil returns to the front of the room.

"My question to you before we stopped was, how can we activate the relaxation response? Well, it turns out that there are many kinds of deep-relaxation techniques, but they all start with quiet sitting, or sitting quietly, where you engage in little or nothing at all. So I'm going to teach you two simple quiet-sitting exercises that, once learned, you can do any time on your own. So, everyone…let's sit up in your chairs…put all your pencils or pens, notepads, and papers down. Of course, if your cell phone is on, please turn it off."

Several people check their phones, and a number of people put their notepads and writing instruments in their bags or on the floor.

"In a minute or so, I'm gonna ask you to close your eyes and sit quietly and do nothing. And when I do, I want you to just watch your thoughts without chasing them. Don't block your thoughts in any way. Just let them come and go as they please. Don't grab onto a thought and let it carry you away.

"OK, close your eyes now, and we're going to sit quietly, watching our thoughts for five minutes...starting now." And Phil looks at his watch to gauge the time.

When a little more than five minutes passes, Phil asks the group to open their eyes and waits until everyone is back with him. "How many of you felt yourselves slowing down? Please raise your hands."

All arms are raised except for Doris Whitehead's and John Sutton's; they'd fallen asleep. "If you find yourself sleeping while doing this exercise," says Phil, "when you realize you've nodded off, just wake up and resume your sitting."

"The discipline of watching your thoughts without letting them carry you away; that ain't easy," exclaims Reggie Johnson.

"Yes, you're right. Training the monkey mind does take time and practice, but after a while, you'll get the hang of it. OK, that exercise may not work for everyone, so the next relaxation exercise is visualization. The fact is that we, as human beings, are seventy percent water. Things that remind us of water tend to calm us down, like the sounds of the ocean or of moving water. So, we can use water as a quiet-sitting device, but you don't have to concentrate on water to achieve a benefit. Keep it simple. Don't try to count the waves rolling up on the beach or anything like that.

"You can even get yourself a CD of ocean sounds or say to yourself, 'Ocean waves.' That will work, too. So, in this next exercise, we're going to use the sound of ocean waves," and Phil signals to Aisha to play his CD. As the music's volume is gradually raised, Phil asks the group again to close their eyes and listen to the sound of rushing water washing up on the shoreline for five minutes. He looks at his watch every now and then, and quietly paces the floor. But several people open their eyes to check where Phil's at in the room, before quickly closing them, again. When the time is up, he asks everyone to open their eyes and inquires as to whether they can feel the sense of peace and tranquility that fills the room. Leaders affirm they can, with the exception of four participants who fell asleep during the exercise.

Dr. Joe Braxton even started snoring after the first four minutes, forcing the exercise to be aborted as his snores generated giggles and then a steady stream of laughter from the group. It took a couple of shakes to wake him up and a minute or so for the good doctor to regain his composure.

"Man, those ocean waves will do you in," he says, rubbing his eyes. Then he looks at the people next to him and notices several of his colleagues staring at him.

As soon as Phil's workshop ends, several women walk over to speak to him. Although each of them has a question to ask or perhaps just something to say, what they really want to know is whether Phil's married, as he doesn't wear a wedding ring. They may not want to know for themselves but rather for a niece or cousin or a girlfriend who is casually or seriously looking for a righteous man. And here's a young doctor without a ring. Why? So as they stand around Phil, waiting to be heard, the women watch him closely for any telltale subtle sign on the way he holds his arm or bends his wrist or moves his eyes, praying to God that he ain't gay.

"Dr. Morgan," a woman named Elizabeth says, "have you read the research on the impact of chronic stress on pregnant African American women?"

"Yes, there's been several studies done on black woman and chronic stress, showing that high cortisol levels among pregnant woman of African descent, regardless of their socio-economic status, not only adversely affects the mother but the fetus as well. It causes over thirty thousand infants each year to be born prematurely."

"So, do you think if black women practice these deep-relaxation exercises regularly during their pregnancies, it would reduce their stress and help them bring their babies to term?" she continues, unaware she's batting her eyes at him.

"Absolutely...absolutely."

"Thanks, Phillip—and by the way, why aren't you wearing a wedding ring?" asks Elizabeth with a broad smile. The rest of the ladies suspend their side chatter to hear his response.

"Please tell me your name?" asks Phil.

"Elizabeth."

"Elizabeth, I'm not wearing one because I haven't found the right woman yet."

"And where did you say you worked at?" she inquires, still smiling, now speaking with an affected Southern drawl.

"I'm at the Berkeley Substance Abuse Clinic."

"Thank you, Phillip," she says, walking away like a woman who's mastered how to draw a man's attention. The other sistahs close ranks around the unmarried doctor and immediately engage him in conversation.

CHAPTER 38
TWENTY PIECES OF SILVER

Morning prayer was over at the holy edifice, and Beena, the young virgin, was already serving the patriarchs their morning coffee and biscuits when the commotion broke out. Munqad, one of the longtime guards at the Fajaruddin gate, rushed as quickly as his spindly old legs could carry him into the edifice to speak to the governing council.

"When breakfast we are having, interrupted we always are; why is it?" asked Chief Patriarch Murabbi, patron and guardian of the people, with irritation.

"Sorry, Chief Patriarch, but a bunch of Oromo young men outside there are. Their prayers in our holy edifice they want to say. Of course, they cannot, them we told, but to the same God we all pray, they say. To do what shall we?"

"Next what is it? First, a market outside our doors they want, and now the Oromo our holy of holies to take over they want," Patriarch Ihtesham, the respectable and honorable one, retorted as he crushed the dry biscuit held in his hand.

"Outside, how many they are, Munqad?" asked the chief patriarch.

"Only four or five, but now if in we let them, maybe more tomorrow will come."

"Absolutely right you are," said Patriarch Aschenaki, the distressed one. "Go away, tell them."

"Patriarch, they will not."

"And again tell me, what say they?" Aschenaki inquired.

"Our brothers they say they are, and the same God we all worship. So, my patriarch, allowed in here they should be."

"Such information, where getting this they are?" Murabbi asked his fellow patriarchs.

"Obvious, is it not?" Ihtesham responded. "At the gathering last night, everyone brothers they are. This the storyteller said."

"Look," said Taqiyy, the pious, the righteous, "a point they have. To the same God all of us we bow down. So their heads, their hands, and their feet in the correct ritual way if they wash, enter to pray as they wish, them we should let."

"What! Your mind, have you lost it, Patriarch Taqiyy?" replied the chief patriarch. "And in if we let them, tomorrow or the next day, with all the men in their nomadic existence they will return. That do you want?"

"So, if they do," exclaimed Patriarch Liyaqat, one who is worthy and most deserving, "this holy edifice for the first time in more than a decade morning prayer with believers will be full."

"Liyaqat, right he is," Patriarch Izzat, one with high rank and honor, calmly replied. "The only ones regularly here are this governing council and a few of Ja'Usu's merchants come. That is all."

Patriarch Aschenaki listened to the exchange and wondered if the six patriarchs who voted in favor of the Oromo magala across from the edifice had struck some kind of bargain with the Oromo elders. "My dear Taqiyy," he began, "when your land to the Oromo for their market you leased, with them their use of our holy edifice did you also discuss?"

"This holy edifice we did discuss, Aschenaki, but permission here to enter I never gave them. The Oromo elders, I told them such an approval up to Ja'Usu's governing council it is."

"And..."

"Their request with the council to raise I only promised, which on this morning to do I had planned. These young men here, today they should not be."

"Patriarch Taqiyy, completely mad have you gone?" asked Murabbi, now visibly shaken. "And how many of you this promise to the Oromo knew?" Five patriarchs—Izzat, Liyaqat, Abdul Muntaqim, Tahawwur, and Safdar—reluctantly raised their hands.

"I see," said Aschenaki, who remained unruffled. "So, Patriarch Taqiyy, outside please will you go, and to the Oromo men who gather speak. Their elder's request for the council to consider presented it is being. And to their elders, shortly, we will respond. Please...that for the council, would you do?"

"Yes, Aschenaki, to them I will talk. To this council I sincerely apologize. For this situation this way to happen, I never intended. To them, immediately, I will speak." Patriarch Taqiyy hastily got up and started for the door.

The chief patriarch, confused and disheartened, looked at his fellow council members sitting with him and asked, "Presenting such a request, Ja'Usu's history with the Oromo knowing, why would all of you agree—or seduced by the storyteller have all of you been? Tell me, please, a bad dream tell me this is."

Although Aschenaki also waited for their response, he already suspected what had happened when Taqiyy and the rest of them went to rent Beza to the Oromo for their market. The Oromo elders must have pushed for more concessions, and the patriarchs agreed to bring this matter before the governing council. He also was certain that if this issue of the Oromo worshiping in their edifice was put to a vote, the six patriarchs would approve the request, and Murabbi, Istesham, and he would be the losers once again.

Patriarch Taqiyy returned and informed the council that the Oromo men had left and apologized once again for the way their appeal was handled. The chief patriarch, however, remained unnerved and glared at Taqiyy like he was a traitor.

After Taqiyy resumed his place on the carpet, and Murabbi stopped scowling, Aschenaki asked, "Please tell us, Taqiyy, what incentive the Oromo did they offer that prompted you to this council for consideration their request to present?"

"By their straightforwardness and their sincerity, I was moved," replied Taqiyy, directing his remarks to all the patriarchs. "The Oromo with us to fight they do not wish or against our traditions go. The elders, Oromo culture trying to change they are. Away from being nomads on the desert to change they want…according to the season moving here, moving there…and their own community outside Ja'Usu's gates to build they wish. In harmony with Ja'Usu inhabitants without feeling by us subjugated, truly they want."

"So, Taqiyy, offer you what did they?" repeated Aschenaki.

"After renting the Beza land, to increase their rent by paying an additional twenty pieces of silver more each month for one full year, they offered. And in return the Oromo here allowed to worship, they want, and their own meeting one morning or evening each month inside this edifice to hold."

"This desire of theirs, why do they want it?"

"No permanent buildings of their own for their elders to meet in do they have, because nomadic living and meeting under tents of cloth and animal skins always they have been. The Oromo from their nomad life to move away they want, and farmers on the land to cultivate they want. Outside Ja'Usu's walls, a community of their own to build they would like. A proud people they are, but our help they are asking for. Meeting in this holy place once a month where their young men can speak about what it means to live in community, the Oromo elders wish to have."

"And after the year is up, what happens?" asked Patriarch Ihtesham. "Then what will they do?"

"Their own holy place outside the Fajaruddin gate by the end of the year to build they expect."

"So if the Oromo request we all approve," said the chief patriarch, mockingly, "this silver you will pocket and get rich, huh, Taqiyy? Or the twenty pieces of silver each month with the five other patriarchs on the council to split you were going to?"

Taqiyy was thoughtful for a moment as the five other council members, who voted for renting his family's land for the Oromo magala, looked his way. "My dear Chief Patriarch Murabbi," replied Taqiyy, the pious, the righteous, "this additional silver to the governing council should be given, I thought, so a fund for our city to support public works we can start. To think what do you, Murabbi?"

The chief patriarch was thrown off guard by Taqiyy's proposal and did not quite know what to say. He stumbled over his words, surprised that anyone in his right mind would give away silver for the council to direct how it would be used.

"Serious are you, Taqiyy? This silver to the council you would give? And these funds, Taqiyy, them who would control?" Murabbi asked with a sly grin, thinking that he had caught Taqiyy by the balls.

"As chief patriarch of Ja'Usu's governing council, the silver on behalf of all of us you would hold. But to this body you are accountable...all nine of us, what these funds support, together we would determine. Would such an arrangement for you work, Chief Patriarch?"

"Well...well, it would, I guess," Murabbi replied, stammering over his words, "but mighty strange it all sounds. A city fund we have never had."

"Well, times changing they are," retorted Taqiyy. "On whether the Oromo to worship with us and meet on their own once a month in this holy place to allow, now can we vote?"

Patriarch Aschenaki, the distressed, was troubled at the prospect of sitting next to a smelly Oromo dirt farmer, even though they worshiped the same God, Jah, and in the same way. Even though during morning prayer he sat in the back, propped up against a wall to stretch out his feeble leg, the thought of sharing their worship space with the Oromo was repulsive to him. His face, however, was a mask that concealed his distaste, although he did plan to vote in favor of the Oromo proposal. Better to appear on the side of the majority, he reasoned, than once again face an obvious defeat.

But it was clear to him that something had to be done about the storyteller's growing influence in Ja'Usu, and it had to be done soon. Otherwise, he reckoned the council would become more and more divisive, and its control and power over the city would continue to be diminished. He resolved to ask the chief patriarch and Ihtesham, the respectable and noble, to stay after the meeting to discuss what should be done.

The chief patriarch did not know what to think and looked down at the maroon carpet to hide his confusion. Murabbi liked the notion of a city fund that he controlled but was uneasy about the trade-off: allowing the Oromo to sit among them.

"To a vote, the Oromo proposal now can we put it?" Taqiyy asked again.

"All in favor of the Oromos' request with us to worship and meet here once each month, please your hand raise," said Aschenaki. All arms were lifted, except for Murabbi's hand, which moved just a little, but not enough to tell whether he was for or against the appeal.

"Chief Patriarch," inquired Aschenaki, "what say do you? For or against it are you?"

"I…I am…" Murabbi replied in a barely audible whisper, "for it, I think I am." Without his mind's consent, his hand, on its own accord, slowly rose above his head.

The patriarchs' usual morning convening finally concluded when Aschenaki signaled Murabbi and Ihtesham to remain seated. Taqiyy and the other five family heads stood and remained preoccupied with their own agendas, unaware of their fellow patriarchs who stayed behind. Aschenaki waited for the other patriarchs to leave the hall before turning to his two companions. "About Narada's growing influence in our city, something now has to be done, I believe. Behind this Oromo upsurge he is, I know; and causing division within our governing council, he has succeeded. This storyteller, crafty he is; and maybe in Ja'Usu planning to stay and taking over he is."

"Right I think you are, Patriarch Aschenaki. In last night's story, this Arthur fellow quietly to sit he is learning as this Oromo-looking elder stuffs his head with all kinds of nonsense, did you see?" asked Ihtesham, the respectable and honorable. "Well, Narada to us the same he is doing? And our people out there on the land look…this storyteller, watch how at him they look and on his every word hang. They, too, sitting quietly they are as their heads with his sinful story he stuffs. To puke it makes me want."

"This storytelling devil, perverting our religion he is," continued Murabbi. "What with the Oromo in prayer joining us they want. Him we must get rid of, and quickly, before Ja'Usu apart he tears."

"But the problem is, how?" asked Ihtesham. "Delicately this we have to handle, because the people, him they like; and a powerful and evil jinn now convinced I am he is."

"Narada, powerful he might be; right you are, Ihtesham…a jinn truly he is. But a human body now he inhabits, and a flesh-and-blood body, destroyed it can be," said Aschenaki.

"Saying what are you, Aschenaki?" asked Murabbi, speaking once more in a whisper as he sensed the formulation of a conspiracy brewing.

Aschenaki had a plan but decided not to share it with either of them. Murabbi, old and often bewildered in council conversations, might say anything to anyone under pressure. And Ihtesham, the respectable and honorable one, he knew he would trade off his own mother for a price. So he thought it best to keep his scheme to himself, at least for now, so as not to become vulnerable to what they might do or say if his plot went awry. "Nothing now I am saying. To know I do not, but a way to get rid of Narada without directing blame on any of us there must be. As soon as a scheme I figure out, only the two of you to know I will let," said Aschenaki. "Ihtesham, up please help me. Here too long I have been sitting." Limping away, Aschenaki knew what he had to do and already started planning his next move.

CHAPTER 39

VENERATION OF ANCESTORS

The morning sun had crested over the eastern horizon when Narada finished his meditation with Ma'Mun and Hohete, and someone banged loudly on the compound door. Ibrahim Hafez ran into the courtyard and yelled over the cow dung, rock, and earthen wall to find out who was so rudely knocking at this early hour, only to discover it was Arsalaan who had been running and was out of breath. Hohete's father was visibly annoyed when he opened the door, and Arsalaan profusely gave his apologizes before begging to see Narada.

Ibrahim Hafez led the former hyena man turned house builder into his home to find Narada and Ma'Mun already seated on the mat in the main room as Hohete went to get their tea.

"Amantahu," greeted Arsalaan.

"Hiya Aman," said Narada and Ma'Mun.

"May I sit down?" asked Arsalaan, turning first to the storyteller and then to Ibrahim Hafez. Hohete's father nodded before returning to the courtyard, and Arsalaan quickly joined Narada and Ma'Mun on the dais. "Narada, what you requested of me I tried doing. To Jumah and the street boys I gave jobs, but their labor, good it is not. Work they really do not want, only the pieces of silver to them I give. For silver to work they do not understand."

"What happened, Arsalaan?" Narada inquired, even though he already knew as Hohete returned with tea.

Arsalaan suddenly became distracted when Ibrahim Hafez's daughter entered the room with tiny bells tinkling around her ankles. He could not respond to the storyteller's question, and a grin as wide as a half-moon appeared on Ma'Mun's young face. Hohete noticed Ma'Mun's expression right away before turning to Arsalaan, whose eyes were locked on her, and an odd sensation passed through her spine. She was at once self-conscious, with Arsalaan staring at her with his wild and penetrating eyes, but at the same time, she felt a curious sense of power that she could take his breath away.

This certainly was unusual, as it most often was the other way around, at least in Ja'Usu culture. When an unmarried man entered a room and greeted a Ja'Usu woman for the first time, if she was interested in him, she would immediately leave the area. This spontaneous but customary act by an unmarried woman conveyed to the man and everyone around that "this man who enters the room takes my breath away, and in order to regain my breath…my composure, I must leave the room."

Narada noticed as well and knew that Arsalaan could see and hear no one else but Hohete. Ma'Mun tapped Arsalaan on the knee, and when he finally drew his attention, Arsalaan looked up and smiled at him. "Our teacher's question, did you hear?" asked Ma'Mun.

"No," replied Arsalaan, whose mind was once again enthralled by Hohete's presence. He stared at her ankle bells and then watched her serve tea before she turned to him and asked with the innocence of a child, "Tea would you like?"

"Yes, of course…I mean…yes, tea I would very much like," he said as Hohete struggled to keep from laughing. "Please,

Narada," Arsalaan continued, almost sounding like he was begging, "a question for me do you have, Master?"

"Arsalaan, why did you say you could not work with Jumah and the boys?"

Hohete returned with another cup and served Arsalaan's tea before sitting down to join them, which was also unusual for a woman to do as they were discussing the business of men. Arsalaan became distracted by her presence again and only came to his senses when Ma'Mun touched him lightly on his knee.

"Narada," he resumed, "those ruffians, one day for me last week they labored, and this morning to return they were supposed to, but to show up they did not. At the end of that one day, every boy a silver coin I paid, and to come back in the morning them I told. On the second day, late in the afternoon they showed up. And at the end of the day, another coin for each boy Jumah demanded. I refused; a full day of labor them they did not give, Jumah I told. So angry he became, and this morning not one boy showed up. Wild and unreliable they all are. With them I cannot work. Sorry...that is it."

"Hohete," said Narada, "do you not have something to say?" Ma'Mun was attentive and quiet and knew that something curious was about to happen.

Ibrahim Hafez's daughter looked at Narada and wondered if he had resumed reading her mind without telling her. "How did you know I had something to say?"

"Hohete, the signs are written on your face."

"Well...something to say I do have," now glancing over at Arsalaan, "only if Arsalaan comfortable with what I want to say he is."

"Yes, please...your mind speak, Hohete. Grateful I would be...really."

She looked at the two men and Ma'Mun, and, after clearing her throat and adjusting her position on the straw mat, as if she needed to give herself permission and room to speak, she said, "Last night about you, Arsalaan, a dream I had, and here this morning I knew you would be. In the dream to the street boys talking I saw you, and with them angry you were."

Hohete stopped talking and glanced at them to see if she still had their attention. But she was also reluctant to continue, thinking perhaps she was speaking out of turn for a woman to talk to men in this way or, even worse, being openly discourteous. Then she thought of the women in Narada's story and was encouraged by their example to speak her mind.

"Go on, Hohete, we are all eager to hear what you have to say," said Narada.

"Well," she began slowly, trying to choose her words carefully. She turned to Arsalaan and, suddenly, like pouring water out of a pail too fast, she exclaimed, "With the boys in the wrong way you are working, I think. I mean…like you said, wild they are… living on the streets they have been…as they please coming and going. Labor they are not used to, and training they need, but some of them to be trained they do not want."

"So, what do I do, Hohete?" asked Arsalaan.

"In my dream, this is what I saw. A stairstep way to train them you must make, and each boy for the things he really accomplishes you pay."

Arsalaan and Ma'Mun looked confused. It was evident they did not follow her logic, and clearly they did not understand.

"OK," continued Hohete, "right now every boy a silver coin at the end of the day for their labor you pay…yes?"

"Yes."

"What did each boy do? What did they do?"

"To know I do not. Work as a group I gave them."

"Not good that is…each of them the same amount of work, they did not do. Each boy a small thing to do give them, and for that small thing done correctly only pay them."

Arsalaan and Ma'Mun were still bewildered as they looked back and forth at one another and then at Narada, who remained silent.

"OK, for instance…a boy for your courtyard to sweep you want, and the garbage in a certain place to put it you also want. For his labor before he starts, how much will you pay tell him, and only after he finishes you see and say how good it is, yes? Then him you pay. OK…your courtyard he sweeps, and the garbage he puts away, but after he labors, still many things on the ground there are. What then say you? Arsalaan, what say you?

"Good enough it is not?"

"Yes, so him you do not pay. Then him you show, again…and to get angry you do not, Arsalaan. What remains to do, him you show. After he finishes, you pay him what you promised. That is all. Now, understand do you?"

"Yes, but suppose no labor at all the boy does, and away he walks?" asks Arsalaan.

"In the beginning before his labor, him you told…yes? Only when he finishes and you like it, you pay. If good labor he does not, him you do not pay."

"That arrangement he may not accept, and work for me at all he may not."

"If a little thing to do he cannot accept, and something much more difficult to do you give him, how could you? Small labor for every boy to do you must create before something harder to do you give them. And when something well they do, tell them… praise them. Then, a harder labor give them…something that more time to complete, it will take them, so every boy at their own pace learns to labor.

"The boys who do not like labor, find out you will; the boys who like labor, the little things them you give, gladly they will do. And Oromo boys, many there are. All I have to say, I have said." Hohete quickly stood and walked away.

"What do you think about Hohete's suggestion?" asked Narada after a moment.

Arsalaan was still looking her way long after Hohete left the room, before turning to Narada and saying, "My wedding Hohete, would Ibrahim Hafez consent? What do you think? That is, if me she will have."

As if responding to his name, Ibrahim Hafez appeared in the doorway with Nabeel, Arsalaan's young nephew, beside him. He came with a handwritten note from his other uncle, the Patriarch Aschenaki. The boy walked into the room and greeted his uncle and the others before turning to Narada with his message.

"Amantahu," he politely said to the storyteller.

"Hiya Aman, Nabeel."

"Sir, for your reply to wait, my uncle asked me."

"Nabeel, please tell your uncle that I would be delighted to accept his invitation to share a meal with him, but not today. It would have to be tomorrow, after storytelling this evening."

Nabeel looked at the message still in his hand and then at Narada. "Sir, please…opened my uncle's note you have not, so without reading it him how can you answer?"

"I already know what the note says, Nabeel, so please tell your uncle that I will come to his home in the early afternoon, tomorrow. Hiya Aman, Nabeel."

And without waiting for anything more to be said, Nabeel made a courteous bow and took three steps back before turning around and leaving the compound.

"Why, my brother, you to see he wants? What does he want?" asked Arsalaan. Ma'Mun, curious about everything, also looked to the teacher for an answer.

"Your brother, speaking for Ja'Usu's governing council, wants to know how long I will remain in Ja'Usu since I am nearing the end of my story."

"Teacher, to leave us planning you are?" asked Ma'Mun.

"After the seventh and final night of story, I will leave you, my friend."

"Why so soon?" Arsalaan inquired.

"It is my fate that I can never settle in one place too long. I become restless and must move on."

"Teacher, with you may I go?" asked Ma'Mun.

Narada placed his arm over the young boy's shoulder and drew him near. For he knew Ma'Mun was sincere and would follow him to the ends of the Earth, if he was asked. "Ma'Mun, your grandfather needs you, and your life's purpose is here."

"My life's purpose...What is it, teacher?"

"You will know when the time comes. I promise you."

The Sixth Evening's Story

Patriarch Aschenaki was not happy when he walked through the Fajaruddin gate and saw the throng of people waiting to hear and see the sixth night of Narada's story. He was certain he could have prevented this calamity had the storyteller accepted his invitation to share a meal that afternoon, but Narada was obstinate and insisted on tomorrow. So, limping along, he made his way with his wife, Pariza, to the patriarchs' platform while nursing his frustration and waited for Narada's hideous narrative to begin once again.

Patriarchs Murabbi and Ihtesham soon joined him on the dais with their families in tow and hurried over to see if Aschenaki had figured out a way to rid the city of the storyteller. They huddled together and spoke in whispers, as if someone might realize they were up to no good and plotting something.

By now these storytelling events had become festive occasions. As soon as Ja'Usu families walked through the gate, their children ran ahead to buy sweet biscuits and dried fruit from the vendors. But the Oromo remained a mystery and disappointment to the sellers. They neither bought food nor brought any.

Their elders approached Narada's evening and the resumption of his chronicle as a sacred experience, as the source of their inspiration on many fronts came from his narrative. And their sentiments were communicated to Oromo families, so food and children's play had no place at these gatherings.

When those seated in the inner circle saw Narada and stood, the Oromo were the first to notice and immediately rose to their feet, while most Ja'Usu families were slow to act and still talking. As soon as they noticed the Oromo standing, not wanting to be left out, they also rose and now looked to the Oromo to let them know what was proper to do.

The storyteller walked over to the burning fire in the center of the ring and looked out over the gathering as twilight tiptoed into night. Narada was pleased that, with their earnest desire to hear and see the story night after night, the people had grown accustomed to sitting in silence and calming their incessant thoughts to focus on the narrative unfolding before them. Many of those gathered were already sitting quietly with closed eyes as if their natural yearning for the joy and peace experienced in quiet sitting had already touched their hearts and minds.

He also sensed a nascent impulse in the people, restoring the splendor and mystery of community between the living and the dead; a renewed communion or reconciliation to be brought about through the veneration of ancestors. For Narada's invocation to the many peoples of Mother Africa and the libation poured on the earth during the previous night of storytelling had surely taken root. The tremor his incantation channeled rattled Ja'Usu's rigidity and stagnation that stunted the city's development and growth; it strengthened the people's courage to confront their fears while facing the future and the unknown, and it revived the collective memory of the people to assert what the African Spirit had taught them over the centuries about what it means to be spirit in human form.

But remnants of melancholy and longing to affirm permanence and place also lingered, especially with older men, like the patriarchs and merchants who banked their wealth on everything staying much the same, who wrapped themselves in status and power and hoarded silver and gold, and who took great pride in exercising control over the Oromo and Ja'Usu's people. Their sense of self was defined with and by these things. And any change in Ja'Usu that they had not initiated or did not control was viewed with foreboding and suspicion.

In some misguided way, social change for them betrayed their cultural heritage, disrupted their way of life in the desert, corrupted their ancient traditions and beliefs, and, especially, threatened their faith healers' reciting a stilted religion that had ossified with time. They held fast to an age-old way of life given to them by their prophets, and they looked into the face of change and spit in it.

The veneration of ancestors was seen by them as heretical, a blasphemous and subversive act that could never be condoned, even if it meant turning their backs on acknowledging and honoring the descendants of their own families. These men, especially Patriarch Aschenaki, saw Narada as a destructive, deadly influence in their city. He was a growing menace that had to be dealt with.

But this night, Narada would not dwell on them. He was exultant in the gathering's awakening, for these were his children whose hearts and minds were budding for Spirit to make a way.

"It is good that we give thanks to Jah and our ancestors for the blessing of life and our renewed awareness that we exist by the grace of the Most High," he proclaimed to the crowd. "And we ask our ancestors who came before us to appeal to the Great Mystery on our behalf to open our hearts and strengthen our minds, so we do not forget that we are children of one Mother. And from that Mother we are born, and into the arms of the Divine Mother we shall return once again."

Raising a bowl of water above his head for all to see, the storyteller continued, "So on this sixth night of story, we pour libation on the earth to show our love and devotion to Jah, and we honor our ancestors throughout the ages who ushered us into the living. We invite them to join us."

And when the people in the second ring of the great circle placed their hands on the shoulders in front of them, the people behind them placed their hands on the shoulders of the men or women in front of them until all the people were linked one to another. And the people in the first ring touched the hem of the Master. And those who were crippled and could not stand reached for the leg nearest them as Narada poured libation for the spirits waiting to be born.

"And with the birth of each Oromo and Ja'Usu child, may this ancient city in the desert discern your unique purpose in returning to this world and help you recollect and live up to that purpose for the benefit of this community. In the name of our ancestors let this gathering say, Amin," concluded the storyteller. And the people said, "Amin...Amin...Amin."

Narada returned to his place in the inner circle and directed the people to sit before silently commanding the little creatures that crawled on the ground and flew in the air to go to their places of shelter and sleep. Then, once again, he summoned the Akasha Records of Celestial Light when the ground shook, but this time the people were unafraid. And then he began to read from the Akasha on the sixth night of the story.

CHAPTER 40
TABLE AND CHAIR

Arthur arrives at Ensarro with a copy of W. E. B. DuBois's book, The Souls of Black Folk, to meet John Sutton, who is already seated at a table. It's lunchtime, and the cozy restaurant is bustling with regular customers who, like Arthur and John, eat there at least once or twice a week. Ethiopian art adorns the walls: a portrait of a young girl with braided hair and a traditional white dress and a painting of two Orthodox Christian priests holding sacred tablets and dressed all in white. On another wall hangs an igelgil, a deep-dish basket with a tight-fitting lid covered with tanned cow hide, used to carry prepared food on long journeys. And next to it is a rectangular hand painting on tree bark of Ethiopian warriors on horseback with spears, fighting a hostile tribe on foot.

"I've been rereading W. E. B. DuBois's book and have come to the conclusion that the two opposing or antithetical forces that DuBois describes in his premise may be able to be resolved," says Arthur, sitting down at the table. A waiter, whose large eyes resemble those of the priests in the painting, approaches with two glasses of water and menus bound in maroon leather jackets.

"What are you talking about?" asks John.

Arthur opens his well-worn paperback edition and searches through the pages for the paragraphs he wants to share with John. "OK…here," says Arthur. "DuBois is talking about the inner life of African Americans when he writes:

> One ever feels his twoness—an American, a Negro; two souls, two thoughts, two unreconciled strivings; two warring ideals in one dark body, whose dogged strength alone keeps it from being torn asunder. The history of the American Negro is the history of this strife—this longing to attain self-conscious manhood, to merge his double self into a better and truer self.

Solomon approaches the table with a small pad of paper and short pencil in hand. "TenayisTalliñ, indemin allew [how are you], Ato Arthur and Ato John?" He smiles and waits with great pleasure for the response in Amharic that he taught them during their last visit.

"TenayisTalliñ, Ato Solomon, indemin adderu?" says Arthur as John simply looks at the proprietor.

"Ine dehna, igziyabher yimmesgen" [Me I'm very well, thank you].

"OK, Solomon, that's all my tongue can say right now," replies Arthur with a light chuckle.

"No, you're doin' good, Ato Arthur…very good. Are you two having your usual?"

"Yes, that would be fine," says John, not wanting to be left out of the conversation. The proprietor nods and leaves to place their order.

"Is that the end of the reading you want to talk about?" asks John.

"No, there's a little more," Arthur replies, looking down at the page to find his place. He continues:

> This waste of double aims, this seeking to satisfy two unreconciled ideals [one American, one Negro] has wrought sad havoc with the courage and faith and deeds of ten thousand...people—has sent them often wooing false gods and invoking false means of salvation, and at times has even seemed about to make them ashamed of themselves.

"So in the past when I've read these passages, I totally agreed with DuBois. They are two warring factions—one American and one of African descent—and they are antithetical, but I'm not sure any more about being irreconcilable. They're warring in us, because inherent in the American striving is this white-supremacist worldview...and it wants to be in control of everything that is and everything that will be, at any cost.

"How did you arrive at that?"

"Come on, John...You know what I'm talking about. The epitome of this striving is the Frankenstein myth that's portrayed in movies over and over again. The Western mind will not be satisfied until it can play God and create a human being, whether it's through artificial intelligence or an actual living, breathing body—or both. Look, scientists can already replicate human organs like the heart, hands, legs, and arms, and they can manipulate genes. You think they're gonna stop there? It's in Western culture's DNA, and we breathe in this mindset—including a white-supremacist worldview—when black babies are born and take their first breath. And yet we're also born of African ancestry.

"Africa is also in our DNA, and while it may not be reflected in the geopolitical reality of Africa today, the Afrocentric worldview is entirely different than the Western mind. It seeks to be in harmony with all that is and ever will be. So now do you see why these two strivings, as DuBois calls them, are at war within us?

And these two psychic forces, dating back to slavery, we still pass down and struggle with from one generation to the next. Don't you see?"

"And you don't have to tell me which of these two factions is winning the war, 'cause I already know," says John. "But where do you go from there, when you say it's possible to reconcile the irreconcilable? I'd like to know."

"John, the grip of these two energies in us is so deep that we're not going to be able to reason or think our way out of this internal conflict. If that were possible, black folk would have done it already. But maybe they can be reconciled experientially through meditation."

"Oh, now I get it…that's why you wanted to have lunch with me today. Since you know I'm a devote Christian and a pastor, what you really want to know, Arthur, is what I think about meditation. Am I right? Am I right?" John is amused by this revelation and laughs loud enough for others in the restaurant to look their way.

"Well, now that you've said it, yes, I want to know what you think about meditation. Because I think DuBois's insight describes very well the spiritual disease plaguing African Americans…and the stress this internal war produces might be at the heart of our community's health crisis. So I'm suggesting meditation may be the appropriate medicine for the cure."

"OK, but you're paying for this lunch, 'cause my time and this consultation ain't free. And the answer to your question is, it ain't gonna happen…it ain't gonna happen…huh…huh! African Americans have Christian roots, and even if they're not active churchgoers, they're not gonna turn en masse to meditation to cure what you or DuBois call our spiritual disease."

"Why not?" asks Arthur.

"First of all, as conservative as black folk are…especially Christian black folk…they're not gonna embrace any practice that comes out of the East."

"Why not?"

"Why not? Because they see these practices...meditation, or whatever you want to label it, as disciplines that come from Buddhism or Hinduism, which are about attaining enlightenment or union with God."

"And there's something wrong with that?"

"There's no focus on looking to Jesus Christ for salvation or acknowledging the primacy of the Holy Bible. It's all about looking into the self for peace and the experience of cosmic consciousness. Many black people, especially if they're devoted churchgoers, look upon meditation as spiritual navel gazing—or worse, as satanic and blasphemous. I know...I've talked to pastors about this very subject."

Noticing the two men in heated conversation, the waiter places a large tray of doro wat, cooked yellow lentils, a mixture of boiled potatoes and cooked cabbage, and mixed greens with tomato salad on their table, along with a plate with pieces of injera, and leaves without comment. John quickly blesses the food.

"I do value your comments, John, but where do you personally stand on the issue of Christianity and meditation?"

"How long have your been seeing this guy for meditation lessons, Arthur?"

"OK, so now you're gonna deflect my question by asking one of your own."

"No, I'm gonna answer your question, but I just wanna know," says John.

"Almost two months—" begins Arthur.

"Almost two months, and you've come to the conclusion that meditation is the answer to saving the black man from himself?"

"I'm still in the process of discovery, John, so I'm raising these issues with you because you're my friend, and I know we can have this discussion."

"Well, I appreciate your confidence in me, Arthur, and yes, we can have this conversation."

They eat together in silence as Arthur waits for his companion's response.

"Arthur," John finally says, after wiping his mouth and hands on his table napkin, "there's a fella named James Finley who at one time was a Trappist monk. He talks about contemplation as a Christian term for meditation. He also reminds us that at the heart of the gospel, Jesus says, 'I and my Father are one.' Finley writes that the early Christians understood Jesus's words as a call to enter into Christ's divine oneness with the Father. They felt they could respond to this call by entering into that oneness experientially, and they sought to experience this through meditation and prayer. They wanted to attain this oneness in Christ and the Father that, as he puts it, is beyond thought, beyond memory, beyond the will, beyond feeling."

"Is that your desire, too, John?" Arthur stopped eating and looked at him.

"What you talkin' 'bout? I'm a black preacher. You wanna get me thrown outta my church?" And they both laughed together before resuming their shared meal.

"Arthur, what do you believe in, since you don't profess to be Christian?"

"I don't know what I believe in, John. You could say that I'm still in the process of discovery, and that's what appeals to me about meditation…aside from feeling a deep sense of peace and tranquility after sitting. What I like about the practice is that it doesn't demand that I accept anyone's dogma or belief system. It simply asks that I be present in the moment, which I'm finding is not that easy, but I feel that I'm spiritually growing…perhaps even healing in some way through the practice."

John's question—"What do you believe in?"—remains with Arthur after leaving Ensarro and driving back to his office. He didn't share with John the first thought that came to his mind—that he believed in the love of a woman. How strange that sounds, now that he's divorced and thoughts about Natalie are less and less frequent. The only other woman in his life…

While waiting for the traffic light to change, Arthur taps the speaker phone over his driver's seat and directs the automated system to dial Valerie's number. After several rings, she answers. "Hello, Arthur. It's funny, just before the phone rang I knew it was you calling. And you did."

"How's Ralph doing?" asks Arthur.

"He's about the same. Although he's talking less, because I think the disease is now affecting his speech."

"And you…how are you?"

"I'm OK. I'm doing OK. I just got another consultant contract I can do at home, so I have my work, which I enjoy, and I'm still free to take care of Ralph. So I'm fine."

"I was having lunch with a friend and colleague, and he asked me, 'What do you believe in?' So, since you knew it was me calling, perhaps you also know what my answer was to his question. Can you guess?"

"Arthur, I have no idea," she says, laughing with a quality of intimacy and warmth.

"My first thought—and I didn't share this with John—was that I believed in the love of a woman."

"OK? Now did you mean the love of a woman in a general sense, or did you have a particular woman in mind?"

"That's why my response seemed odd at first. Natalie divorced me, and I'm not longing for her to return. I'm actually relieved that our relationship is over, and I'm surely not seeing anyone else, so my unspoken response was strange—that is, until I realized I was thinking of you. Valerie, every time we meet or talk on the phone, you say that you love me, and I know you do, and I want you to know I take comfort in that. And I also love you."

"Arthur, that's sweet. It's good to feel loved, don't you think? Aside from Ralph, you're the only man I've ever loved, and it pleases me to hear you say you know that I love you and that you love me. So now that we have confessed our affection for one another, it's time for you to tell me your secret."

"What secret?"

"Arthur, what happened that afternoon in my hotel room? I opened the door, and you were sitting in the middle of the room, looking quite exhausted. What was going on with you?"

Arthur drives into a parking space and turns off the ignition key as his mind weighs the consequences of telling Valerie the truth. "Valerie, I'm reluctant to tell you something that I don't really understand myself and have only spoken about with two other people. One was a therapist, who thought I needed to be medicated, and the other was a Santeria priest I saw for a consultation."

He tells her about the inclination of his spirit to leave his body when he's depressed or under stress and his disembodied experiences flying in the air. He describes his encounter with Sonia and Hector, who said his ability to leave his body at will is a gift, and Hector's insistence that he wear protective beads to ward off evil spirits, especially the one that resides in his building. He shares with Valerie the one experience of trying to leave his physical form and the sudden appearance of a skull and crossbones warning him of danger.

And, finally, Arthur describes his experience riding the BART back and forth all day between her hotel room and his apartment and about ending up at the end of the day in her room, feeling totally exhausted and out of control. He describes how he felt, knowing he didn't want to move or take another step, yet feeling compelled to return to the BART and make another trip across the Bay. He explains how he forced himself to sit in her room and prayed to God for help when, suddenly, he felt this unclean shadow like hazy gray smoke leave him.

"Then, I looked up and saw you standing at the door." There's dead silence at the other end of the line, and Arthur fears Valerie has already hung up because she's overwhelmed and doesn't know what to say in response to his confession. He's desperate to hear her voice...for her to say something, anything...and is about to hang up when he hears her sigh.

"Arthur, why didn't you trust me enough to tell me this, earlier?" she asks.

"I guess for the same reason you weren't able to talk to me about Ralph."

"Touché, well said. Arthur, when I walked in the room that day I, too, saw something, but it wasn't gray smoke. There was a bright light around you, and in that light a man was standing behind you. He wore brown-colored beads around his neck, and his hands were resting on your shoulder."

"Was he a short black man and a little chubby with dark skin?"

"No, this man was tall and thin with a beard—had a medium-brown complexion. I could have sworn he looked at me before he faded away in the light."

"Why didn't you say something?" asks Arthur.

"Arthur, it was so strange...so otherworldly, I didn't know what to say. I've never seen a ghost or something like that before. I thought, at first, you'd tell me what was going on, but then I realized you didn't even know. So I decided not to say anything when maybe I should have. But whatever I saw, it wasn't there to harm you.

"Did you go back to Hector's and get your protective beads? Arthur, that scares me, you being possessed. Were you possessed the night you made love to me?"

"No, Valerie, it took place the day after we slept together."

"Are you sure?"

"Yes, I'm sure, and no, I didn't go back for the beads. I decided instead to learn to meditate."

"And that's going to protect you?" she asks. "Arthur, please go back to Hector's for the beads."

"I'll think about it."

"Arthur, I know what that means when you say you'll think about something. And have you started meditating?"

"Yes, a man named Luther has been teaching me for the past two months."

"And is it preventing you from being possessed?"

"I haven't felt a reoccurrence since I started."

"How do you know?"

"Valerie, I can't tell you how I know, but I know...So, you believe what I've told you?"

"Yes, Arthur; when I was a child, my grandma talked about these things happening to people. And after my grandfather died, she'd tell me when she felt his spirit was around. He smoked a pipe, and after his death, Granny often said she smelled the aroma of his tobacco; and when that happened, she'd say he was around. And when she dreamed about Grandpa, she'd tell me about their conversations in the dream world. So yes, Arthur, I do believe you."

There's silence on each end of the phone for a moment until Valerie confides, "I had a dream about you. You were climbing a very high mountain, like in the Rocky Mountains or the Himalayas, and they were covered with snow. The wind was blowing, and you were crouching on a ledge in the crevice of a rock. Your arms were folded around your knees. It was peculiar, though, because you weren't trying to stay warm. You weren't even cold. Then I woke up. Arthur, I hear Ralph, and he needs me, so I have to go. Ciao." She hangs up.

⁂

Arthur stops at the International Fabric store on upper Broadway on his way home and buys the raw silk Luther recommended he use. He also finds a Mexican bodega on San Pablo Avenue and purchases half a dozen white candles in tall, plain glass jars.

It is Mrs. Alvarez's cleaning day, and she has already left his apartment by the time Arthur parks his car and walks in the door. He changes into house clothes before removing his family photos from the table in the living room. Picking up the table, he places it next to the far-end wall in his empty dining area, where it can't immediately be seen. He then searches in his hallway closet and finds a red, gold, and forest-green silk scarf he sometimes wears. After spreading it over the tabletop, Arthur rearranges his family photos on the table, leaving space for the white candle in a jar, which he sets just in front of the pictures. Stepping back and looking at what he has done, Arthur detects there's still something missing. And after sitting down to consider it, he realizes he must find a small vase for the setting to put fresh flowers in.

And it occurs to him that, although Luther suggested he create this space, he senses he's created such a space before, as if all the items on the table and the arrangement itself are thought pieces from another time and place. Arthur gets up and returns to the altar, as if waiting for a sign or recollection of a distant memory that remains elusive, like grasping for frantic leaves in a gusty wind or grabbing at fleeting shadows on a wall.

The malevolent spirit from the lower unit senses that his obsession is home, and he rises up through the ceiling and floorboards into Arthur's kitchen to observe the human body it claims as its own. It's been around Arthur long enough to be conscious of his thoughts and scoffs at the idea that any practice or altar can keep him from taking what it now considers to be rightly its. It stares at Arthur looking at the table and chair, now draped with raw silk, and struggles to not let its emotions override its reason—to wait patiently for the right time to mount this human donkey and ride him straight to a neighborhood bar. And so, like Pavlov's dog salivating over the promise of food, it studies every twist, turn, and gesture Arthur makes and waits…waits for that moment to repossess this human form.

Arthur showers and dresses for bed before returning to the dining room and altar, where he lights the candle on the table in front of him and sits down on the chair with the raw silk draping under his feet. He gradually settles into the stillness, undisturbed by the sporadic clatter from the street outside or the soft groans and creeks of the old building he sits in or the quiet undulation of his own breath. After a time in the profound peace and serenity that embraces him, surrounds him, he discerns in the silence the faint resonant hum that undergirds the universe and surrenders to it—to the extent his mortal fear will allow. And after a time, in the darkness behind closed eyes he whispers, "Search me, O God, and know my heart; try me and know my thoughts; and see if there be any wicked way in me, and lead me in the way everlasting. Aum…Amen…Amin…and So It Is." Meanwhile, the restless spirit from downstairs looks on.

CHAPTER 41
HARRIET'S CHILDREN

The ceremony is about to begin when Martha Grimes, from Alameda County Social Services, rushes over to Arthur and anxiously says she's not ready to become a health conductor, yet. "Why?" he asks.

"I'm just not ready to be anybody's role model. I need more time to work on myself and would like to repeat the training the next time it's given. Is that OK?"

"It's your choice, Martha. There are others here who also have expressed concern about being a role model, but they recognize the struggle to make better health decisions is an ongoing struggle, so we should never expect to reach a final destination. But you can repeat the training anytime it's offered, even if you are a health conductor. So are you sure you'd prefer not to graduate with the group tonight?"

"Yes, I'm sure, but I'd like to stay, if y'all don't mind."

"Of course; it's totally up to you."

Mary Roebuck, the project manager, takes the stage and calls the group to order, letting those standing in the back know the graduation is about to begin. Leaders have brought their families, including their children, to the affair. Some of the women are dressed in African prints and head wraps, while many of the men wear dashikis and colorful kufi caps.

Tonight Harriet Tubman's portrait is in an ornate dark wood frame resting on a wooden easel and front and center on the stage. A piece of maroon-colored cloth lies underneath her photograph, and next to the easel is a large vase filled with cream-colored roses with blood-red borders mixed with fern. Two straw baskets are placed far apart on the maroon cloth, and a lit white candle resting in a gold-plated candelabra is next to each basket.

Mary, standing behind the podium, welcomes the seventy or so people in attendance, including graduating leaders and their families; program trainers; Pat Cleveland, the sugars and fats instructor; Dr. Phil Morgan; several of the Trust's board of directors; as well as public officials from the City of Oakland and Alameda County. In all, twenty-one members who participated in Hachi's social experiment are about to take their oaths as the first graduating class of Critical Mass Health Conductors.

After introducing Aisha Middleton, mistress of ceremonies for the evening, Mary leaves the stage and checks in with the caterer, whose name is Africa, about the meal. Aisha's evident exuberance bubbles over in excitement as the leaders clap and cheer, and she proudly acknowledges what they have accomplished together. She gives voice to what they collectively feel but have not yet expressed—that in completing Hachi's experiment, they have recovered, to their surprise, the latent, transformative power of coming together in support of one another. And as a result of their communal efforts, they have enhanced the health and well-being of everyone engaged in the project and are now prepared to serve by example as culturally rooted agents for social change.

"And as we do in all of our events," continues Aisha, "let us honor our ancestors and draw on their strength and their courage as we aspire to improve the health and well-being of our community. Ronald, will you come forward and offer the libation, please?"

Ron Upchurch stands and signals to a young man in the front row, who then picks up the green plant next to him and places it on the floor near the stage. He returns to his chair, retrieves a pitcher of water, brings it to the front, and stands alongside Ron. Ronald steps forward with his African drum and starts his petition on behalf of the gathering, striking the drum like the sound of a man wearing shoes tripping over his own feet. This rhythm is soon replaced by a brisk tap…tap…tap, exploding like a hundred woodpeckers beating all together on hardwood. This rapid cadence then slows and settles into a sustained life-giving pulse of a human heartbeat, thump…thump…thump.

As on the day the development committee met at Silvestre's, Ron calls on the Most High, who is sometimes called Olodumare or Olorun or Exi-ab-hare, or sometimes called Allah or Brahma or Yaweh, or sometimes called Lord or God, to bless the gathering. He petitions the ancestors who led rebellions against slavery and channeled runaway slaves north through the Underground Railroad to join their gathering and then acknowledges those of African descent yet waiting to be born.

After each appeal, the young man standing next to him pours a few drops of water on the plant in the flowerpot. And before ending his invocation, Ron asks the ancestors to watch over them and keep safe those who are about to become health conductors, to support them as change agents, promoting health and wellness. "And let us say, Ashe…Ashe…Ashe…"

Then Aisha returns to the podium. "Some of you…family members and friends may wonder why we have a portrait of Harriet Tubman displayed, here, surrounded by flowers and baskets laid out on a piece of cloth with white candles. We do not worship her, but we chose Harriet as our patron…our role model in establishing what we've come to call our Overground

Railroad, which is to improve the health and well-being of our community. And as our role model, Harriet Tubman is health-conductor number one…our first health conductor. She presides over all that we do.

"All those graduating this evening will receive a permanent health-conductor number. Later, we will explain why. But for now, please understand that no one will be able to choose the number one, because that number has already been awarded to Harriet Tubman. We selected her as our patron because throughout her life, she demonstrated courage and strength and bravery against what many would consider insurmountable odds. In spite of suffering from an uncontrollable sleeping sickness, Harriet returned to the plantations in the South, again and again, to free her brothas and sistahs. And she never lost a charge while leading runaways north. She also held the rank of general in the Union army, where she served as a spy behind enemy lines and a doctor treating the wounded. In her later years, she established a house in Auburn, New York, for poor and aged colored folk, where she died on March 10, 1913, at the age of ninety-three.

"So during health-conductor trainings when, perhaps, we felt a little discouraged about what we were doing…or we didn't know how to proceed with a task or deal with a problem, we asked ourselves, 'What would Harriet do?' And to remind ourselves to ask, we were able to look at these blue bands around our wrists that say, 'What would Harriet do?' to help us with our difficulty, to resolve whatever seemed like a problem. Harriet's photo is with us this evening, as it will be for all our future functions, to give us courage and strength and remind us of our commitments to ourselves…to one another, and to our community. Health conductors are Harriet's children."

Aisha introduces Arthur before stepping away from the podium. For the benefit of the families and invited guests, he presents evidence of the health crisis facing the black community and speaks to why and how African American leadership came together to find a culturally rooted response to the crisis. Arthur introduces the health conductors' guiding principles and goes over the commitments conductors are prepared to make in support of building a healthy black community.

Aisha then returns, following an enthusiastic round of applause for the Trust's director, as Arthur leaves the stage. She introduces Hachi, who, after briefly describing the conductor program, says, "I was going to ask our soon-to-be graduates to stand and share with you, our guests, what they personally gained from their training experience. But over the past three months, we've heard their testimonies, so I'm not going to ask them to stand and give it now. Instead, I would like the family members or friends of these community leaders to share if you've noticed any changes in the health behavior of our soon-to-be graduates. Have you seen any positive changes in them and, if so, have these changes influenced you or members of your family to also look at your or their own health-related behavior...anyone?"

The room is quiet except for the rattling of a few papers, and someone coughs; after a minute or so, a middle-aged woman in a black dress timidly raises her hand in the back and, when acknowledged, stands. "Good evening, everyone; my name is Eunice Braxton, and I'm married to Joe sitting over there," pointing to Dr. Braxton, who turns to look at his wife of thirty-one years. "He's been on blood-pressure pills for the past three years and has always complained about taking them...wanting, instead, to manage his blood pressure through a low-salt diet and getting more exercise to reduce his stress. He does exercise...well, not enough, if you ask me. But as a result of this program, he regularly sits and meditates mornings and evenings, and that seems to be helping. So now, he tells me, it might be possible for him to get off the pills...we'll see.

"And now I've started to sit with him in the mornings and can feel the benefit of listening to ocean waves. So I thank you, Dr. Morgan, and this program for sharing this meditation stuff with him. Thank you, and that's all I have to say." She sits down.

A hand is raised on the other side of the room, and a young, slightly overweight man, James Wycliffe, sporting a close-cropped beard and wearing a hand-dyed batik shirt from Ghana, stands and says that his wife, Lauren, was invited by Carol Anderson to join her trio. "I was concerned when she came home and said that her group decided to work on preparing vegetarian meals."

Lauren and Carol, sitting with the other graduating conductors, exchange comments in a whisper and look over at James.

"I'm sure they're over there talking about me now," he continues as he looks over at the two women. "You see, I like my meat, and I wasn't prepared to give up eating it for even a day. Now, don't get me wrong, I like vegetables and all that, but they're foods to go along with your meat. Can you feel me? So I wasn't gonna give up eating meat because Lauren joined this here group. Well, after her trio met, Lauren comes home and tells me and Sophie that one night a week, we're gonna have a vegetarian meal. I was so mad, I couldn't even pronounce the word 'vegetarian.'"

The room erupts in laughter.

"I said to myself that I'd eat out the night Lauren was gonna prepare that you-know-what-kinda-meal, but I forgot to ask what day that was gonna be. So I came home one Thursday night, sat down to dinner and had this wonderful spaghetti dish with a tasty red sauce, French bread, and salad. And when I finished, I got up to get some more spaghetti and sauce because it was good, and they...Lauren and Sophie, they start laughing. Sophie says to me, 'How did you like the vegetarian meal, Dad?'"

His daughter, sitting next to him, holds her face in her hands and giggles as the rest of the audience breaks out laughing. After people settle down, James continues, "Now, I still like my meat, but I'm open now to having a veggie-meal at least once in a while." The room cheers him on as he sits down, and Sophie pats her father on the back.

"Again, to our families and friends," says Hachi, "by a show of hands, how many of you think you've been positively influenced or helped in some way by one of our leaders, here, this evening? How many of you are now more conscientious about your health because of their efforts? Please raise your hands."

Twenty-nine people raise them.

"That's a pretty good number," continues Hachi. "So you see, everyone, health conductors have already had an impact on many of us. And after each future training, we will assess the program's strengths and weaknesses so we can continue to improve and refine health conductors as we expand its reach in the community.

"Our goal is to train 4,650 health conductors, ten percent of the African American population in the Bay Area, over the next five years. And in reaching this goal, we expect to achieve that mysterious tipping point when a project like this one will no longer be necessary. Why? Because there will be so many African Americans living in the Bay Area who will know about the health-conductor movement...or, better still, know a health conductor... that they, too, will become more conscientious about improving their own health and well-being.

"And when we reach this tipping point, the chronic health crisis we now face as a community will come to an end. So we ask for your help in growing this movement now by signing up, yourself, for the next health-conductor training that will begin next month. And invite another family member or a friend to join you. You can sign up online on the Trust's website or fill out one of the registration forms on the back table before leaving here tonight. Thank you."

Aisha returns to the podium with a copy of the health conductor's Certificate of Membership and Affirmation and explains how each graduate's number indicates when he or she completed the training. In addition, she describes the ritual: after reading the declaration, each graduate will come to the podium, place a flower on the maroon cloth to honor Harriet, and place an envelope with a monetary donation in the straw basket. Donations will go into a special fund held by the Trust to cover costs associated with hosting the next health-conductor graduation. Each graduate then picks at random one of the small stones with a tiny number hidden on the other side of the stone. They also pick up their affirmation, share their number by saying it out loud to everyone present, and sign the affirmation.

Almost a full hour passes before all the leaders are done. Aisha is the last person; after selecting a stone, she proclaims her health-conductor number: seven. As she heads for the table, John Sutton quickly walks to the front of the hall and closes the ceremony with a prayer that concludes with a blessing for the food they're about to eat. "And let the community say, Amen."

"Amen."

CHAPTER 42
THE MASTER BUILDER

It was early morning when Arsalaan walked through the Fajaruddin gate with Ma'Mun and headed toward the Oromo wellspring in the oasis—the source where Hohete first met Narada and gave him water. Ma'Mun led the way as they walked along the dirt path from Ja'Usu to where the Oromo elders waited to meet them. A procession of camels rambled across the footpath ahead of them to reach the thorny brush on the other side of the path, while Oromo boys herded their goats with a switch to keep them moving. White egrets circled overhead, following the camels and goats that moved across the land. They waited for them to drop their dung so they could descend and pick through the warm mass for undigested seeds and berries and sometimes worms to eat. Theirs was a quiet harmony between boys and camels and goats and birds, crisscrossing the arid land foraging for food—the younger boys tagged along behind the older ones and played. As if the children's energy was contagious, the baby goats and calves sporadically leaped in the air, fitfully ran about, or suckled on their mother's teats.

Once they reached the oasis, Arsalaan drank from the well and noticed a small black-and-yellow bird flit over the tops of the palms before settling on the highest frond. In spite of the slight weight of its tiny body, the long stem bent down until the bird spread its wings and flew west across the verdant green and over a large tent covered with tattered rugs and old straw mats.

A wiry old man with a bare chest and a faded piece of orange cloth wrapped tightly around his waist appeared out of nowhere and greeted Arsalaan. He led him and Ma'Mun across the oasis to the tent where the elders and several younger Oromo men were waiting. The old man and Ma'Mun stepped aside to let Arsalaan be the first to enter. And when the twelve or so men in the tent saw him, they immediately rose to their feet and bowed to greet him. Daanish Nour stood in the middle of the group, and Ma'Mun moved to his grandfather's side as they all sat down on a well-worn Arab rug laid out for this occasion.

One of the younger men moved forward and placed a white porcelain cup in front of Arsalaan and suggested he sit across from Daanish Nour. Then he poured from an old pot the hot, sweet tea all the men were drinking. Another man stood and placed a few dry biscuits wrapped in a piece of palm leaf on the rug in front of Arsalaan before returning to his place in the tent. The men, including Daanish Nour, resumed quietly drinking their tea while their eyes remained on their guest.

"Arsalaan," said Daanish Nour, "our invitation you accepted; we are pleased. That Ja'Usu people to the bush are willing to come and us Oromo to meet, it is not often."

"As probably you know, the hyenas to feed I used to, and outside the Masresha gate I lived, so many Ja'Usu with me they will not meet either, but in time this will change," said Arsalaan.

"Of the storyteller's narrative, what do you think?" asked Daanish Nour.

"Back from the dead, me he has brought. Sitting here I would not be, if not for Narada."

Arsalaan took another sip of his tea. Daanish Nour seemed to wrestle with a thought before he leaned forward to say, "About the storyteller, something with you of my encounter with him to share I also have, but until another time I will wait. Arsalaan… Narada has prompted Oromo living as nomads to stop, and our own community outside Ja'Usu walls build. The Nubian master builder of the holy edifice you helped, we know about. And your house in Ja'Usu between Mustakim and Khawar at this time building you are…Ma'Mun tells us. Correct this is?"

"Yes, correct it is."

"Well, homes for us, too, you build we would like, and our young men houses to construct as well teach. Something like this, you can do? Of course, for your labor, you we are able to pay."

Arsalaan was certain Narada was behind Daanish Nour's request but decided to wait and ask later about this when they were alone. It was surely a blessing, as their desire to build community came also with the need to assemble communal structures and erect Oromo homes. And although he would never have anticipated this opening, Arsalaan understood that fulfilling the Oromos' wish offered him a way to make a living for Hohete and her family, if they would have him.

"Homes for you my honor to build it would be, Daanish Nour, and Oromo men as well to train I will. But Ja'Usu's street boys as well I want to teach; this you I must tell. For many of them it may not work out, but some of them, good builders they might become. A problem for you would this be?"

"No, not at all…with me, Arsalaan, please come and walk." Ma'Mun and another youth rushed over to help their elder up. "Over me, do not fuss. Why your help do you think I need? Old and blind you must think I am. Ma'Mun, walk with us please come."

Arsalaan and Ma'Mun now stood beside the Oromo elder in the open air directly outside the makeshift shelter. Daanish Nour, shielding his eyes from the morning sun, looked off into the distance. "My staff, Ma'Mun, please fetch me."

As soon as his grandson returned from inside the tent and handed the old man his shepherd's crook, Daanish Nour strode off toward the ancient city. Arsalaan walked beside his new benefactor, and Ma'Mun followed. They walked together in silence across the land, passing dry brush and desert mice that were out of their burrows and standing on their hind legs to watch them coming.

"Since you said, Arsalaan, that back from the dead Narada brought you, I, too, in you wanted to confide that our storyteller brought me back from darkness. But in front of the others I did not want to say, because the secret we would keep, Ma'Mun and me promised, at least until Narada's story he finishes."

"Elder, what mean do you?"

"Your word do I have, Arsalaan, that my secret you will keep until to my brethren I reveal it?"

"Yes, Daanish Nour. Whatever you say, no one from me will hear it."

The three now left the centuries-old path to the Fajaruddin gate and veered to the right toward the area where the gathering sat and Narada told his story.

"One night after story, Ma'Mun and me, behind we remained the storyteller to meet. We Oromo to his narrative had been listening, but at the edge of the gathering we stayed and to one side sat. Then, our place we knew.

"After the gathering left, Narada we approached. We were coming, he seemed to know, and waiting for us he was. On the ground near him we sat, but the storyteller rose, and on the straw mat he was sitting on he had me sit. About many things we talked, but two miracles that night occurred. And as a result of these wonders, more than what he appears to be he has convinced me he is."

"Ibrahim Hafez himself, me he told that Narada, a powerful jinn he is," said Arsalaan.

"What he is I do not know, but Narada, more than a jinn he is. The Oromo, a name for him we do not have. The first miracle: totally blind since birth I have been, but that night while next to him sitting, for the first time to see I suddenly started. With sight Narada blessed me."

"Abbabba, Grandfather, may I tell him?" Ma'Mun shouted from behind. The old man and Arsalaan stopped and turned to face the boy.

"What tell him?"

"After my grandfather's sight he was given, a flute to play started, but the teacher it was not, and no one in the darkness we could see. The music played, and teacher and Abbabba and me, until morning we all danced."

"The second miracle was that?" asked Arsalaan.

"No," Daanish Nour responded as they resumed their walk. "This staff to guide my way I always carry, and at my age to walk it aids me, but since that night this stick I really do not need. Now out of habit, I carry it. Youthful and strong now my body feels, and on my own I stand and walk. The second miracle this is, but one more there may also well be."

The old man abruptly stopped again and rested his staff on the ground. "Arsalaan, where we are, do you know?" Arsalaan and Ma'Mun looked around to get their bearings.

"Well, Narada's fire over there they build," replied Arsalaan, "so about where the storyteller sits this is, and next to him we sit—Ma'Mun and you, the Hafez family, and me."

"And here, what else is?"

Arsalaan looked uncertainly at Ma'Mun and then at his grandfather. He did not see anything, but then he turned to search the ground around them and still came up with nothing. "Nothing else here there is," he said. "To understand I do not."

Daanish Nour and Ma'Mun were now smiling at him, and he knew his confusion was amusing them. "Arsalaan," said Daanish Nour, "your eyes close and a few steps forward walk. Something that you can see, it is not."

Arsalaan did as he was directed, and after slowly advancing three steps, he experienced something peculiar and stopped. He then took a few steps back, and the sensation suddenly went away. Once more, Arsalaan cautiously moved forward before stopping after two steps, and the odd sensation returned. It felt like a mass of needles were gently piercing his skin from the top of his head to the bottoms of his feet.

He opened his eyes and examined his body; then he touched his legs and chest and arms with his hands. Arsalaan looked at Daanish Nour with surprise and awe. The sensation was still there—this feeling that his skin was being kissed or softly pricked by spiny needles from a cactus plant. He moved out of the area, and the sensation went away. Then he walked back to the space, and the awareness returned before Arsalaan stepped away, once again. "This I feel what is, Abbabba?"

"To know I do not. But a few days ago, when here to where Narada and I sat that night we met, this amazing thing I discovered. Then Ma'Mun, here, I brought without why telling him, and he, too, the same thing as you describe felt…thousands and thousands of needles touching his skin…and now you. What it is I do not know, but something with the storyteller to do I think it has. Do the two of you this prickling feel when next to the storyteller the nights of his story you sit?"

Arsalaan and Ma'Mun searched each other's faces for an answer before Arsalaan abruptly threw his hands up to the sky. "To know I do not. Maybe this wonder here always has been, but experienced it before I never have."

"Abbabba, to know also I do not. Maybe another miracle it is," said Ma'Mun.

Daanish Nour picked up his staff and placed it over the area without it touching the ground. "To this spot on the land every day I now return, and cactus needles always here they are. What this is I feel. Maybe something with Narada's spirit to do with this is."

"But Grandfather, how can that be?" asked Ma'Mun.

"An old man I am, and many things I know, grandchild, but this…to know I do not. Narada about this mystery I will ask. But what I do know, Arsalaan, the first building for the Oromo a holy edifice like the one in the center of Ja'Usu you will erect. And this area, with prickly cactus needles, the heart of our edifice it will be."

"If this mystery here at this spot remains, Daanish Nour, so it will be."

"Abbabba," cried Ma'Mun, "a house for you and the other families first before Arsalaan an edifice builds, do you not want?"

"Oh no, Ma'Mun, a place for worship and for our families together to come, first we must build. Then, homes for our clan we will construct."

"Mud brick to make, we will need a place, Daanish Nour," said Arsalaan.

"Up to you to decide it is, my brother and master builder." And the old man turned with his staff pointing in a new direction and walked away, with Ma'Mun running to catch up.

CHAPTER 43

A CUP OF COFFEE

After Ibrahim Hafez greeted and welcomed the two sons of Aschenaki's married sister, Vardah, they asked to speak to the storyteller. Their uncle, the family's patriarch, had sent them to escort Narada through the city's streets and to his compound for their scheduled meal together.

The two brothers approached Narada, who was sitting on the lower platform in Ibrahim Hafez's main room, and bowed to show respect. Then Nabeel, the older one, spoke for both of them. "Amantahu, Ato Narada."

"Hiya Aman, Nabeel and Duha. Are your father and mother well?"

"Yes, thank you, Ato Narada, our father and mother, well they are," Nabeel replied, and again the two brothers bowed their heads.

"And your uncle and his mother and other family members, are they also well?"

"Yes, Ato Narada, our uncle and our grandmother and the rest of our family, also well they are." And again the two brothers bowed.

"And how about your cat and the two birds your mother keeps in a cage, are they also in good health?"

Ibrahim Hafez, who had ushered the boys into the compound and was standing behind them, smiling, knew that Narada, following Ja'Usu's tradition of asking about the family's health, was playing with them.

"Oh yes, our cat and my mother's birds, well they are doing," Nabeel said, bowing his head as Duha covered his mouth to conceal his amusement. Nabeel jabbed his brother with his elbow in the side.

"And so, are we ready to go?" asked Narada.

"Yes, Ato Narada, my brother and I, to go we are ready."

Narada was the first to walk out the compound door and onto the narrow lane as Nabeel and Duha rushed to keep up. But the path was too constricted for them to walk side by side, so Nabeel, wanting to be a good escort, tried his best to pass his guest so that he could lead the way. Duha was content, however, to follow along and watch as his brother jockey with the storyteller for front position. When they reached Fajaruddin and turned left toward the heart of the city, Narada slowed down and let Nabeel take the lead. The young man surged ahead, not realizing that the storyteller had slowed down to walk beside his younger brother.

"Duha, do you ever speak for yourself?"

Duha heard Narada speaking but chose to ignore what was said, like he did with most people when they addressed him directly. His reaction usually discouraged them from attempting to communicate with him again.

It was not that he did not want to speak. In Duha's early childhood, he had grown tired of talking to people only to be made fun of when they realized he spoke a language they could not comprehend, a dialect all his own. They would say to him, "How are you?" or "Your name, little boy, what is it?" And his response would be gibberish in their ears. So over the years, he learned to keep his thoughts to himself; and if he had to communicate with others, he would do so through whispering to his brother, Nabeel, who for some inexplicable reason always understood him.

"Do not be afraid, Duha. I, too, speak a language that is all my own and no one else but Jah truly understands. It is a language of the heart conveyed through thought." Duha turned and looked at Narada as he struggled to form words that would not be born.

"After thirteen years of not giving voice to what you think or feel, you must be full and long to release what is in your heart and mind. Is this not so, Duha?"

Tears now streaked down the young boy's cheeks and dropped on the cobblestone as they walked together down Ja'Usu's main street.

"We can remove this barrier, my son, so you may speak and be understood by all. But first, you must face the root cause of why your voice went silent and hid behind a language only your brother understands. If you summon the courage that is truly within you, together we can push this barrier out of the way and release your breath that carries speech so you may freely converse with anyone."

Duha and the storyteller reached the end of Fajaruddin and were entering the heart of the city across from the holy edifice when Nabeel, who had walked on ahead, now returned. "I apologize, Ato Narada. Sorry ahead I went, and you and Duha behind I left…to realize I did not. Please, my uncle do not tell."

"Nabeel, your absence gave your brother and me the chance to talk, so no apology is necessary. Your confession is safe with me." Nabeel looked at Duha with an unspoken question as he joined them walking down Mustakim road toward Aschenaki's compound.

Ordinarily, Patriarch Aschenaki left all household matters to his mother, Rona, who then, as head of the household, dictated her wishes like a command to his two wives, Fadwah and Pariza. But today was no usual day, as Narada was coming to lunch, and he wanted his plan to work and for everything to go off right.

To the consternation of the women, Aschenaki had given directions that he and Narada should not be interrupted or disturbed, and he also instructed when the coffee should be served at the end of the meal. His older sister, Vardah, got annoyed with him when he announced that he did not trust Pariza to wait on him and the storyteller properly, and that he wanted Vardah to serve the food. Pariza was merely to bring the coffee, and only when he called her. Under no circumstances after the coffee was served should he and Narada be disturbed.

During the course of the morning, Aschenaki had limped along behind each of the four women more than once to discuss the details of his anticipated meeting with Narada—that is, until his mother pleaded with her son to rest his leg and sit down. The young patriarch finally conceded to her wishes and painstakingly climbed to the highest-level platform in his house and, once seated, closed his eyes to review in his mind how everything should unfold. He was both annoyed and surprised when Nabeel interrupted his reverie and announced that the storyteller had arrived.

As planned, Aschenaki waited for Narada to present himself at the entrance to the main room before exaggerating his effort to stand with the aid of his wooden crutch. He thought such a gesture would display humility on his part and play upon the storyteller's sympathy for his obvious infirmity.

"Amantahu," said Narada, standing in the doorway of the large room.

"Hiya Aman, my dear storyteller," the patriarch replied as he struggled to his feet. "My humble abode that you are able to visit I am so happy. Step up and sit by me, come."

Narada climbed the two levels and joined his host on the highest dais, where Aschenaki now made an effort to sit back down. This was staged as he had learned in childhood how to manipulate his malformed body efficiently to minimize any unnecessary move or action.

"So Narada, tell me, our city in the desert, so far enjoyed it have you? Our people friendly and hospitable do you find?" Aschenaki leaned back on the two fluffy pillows he had arranged for himself and looked kindly on his guest.

"Ja'Usu is like a desert flower with its nine ancient gates, and it is unique because it keeps you somewhat isolated from your brothers and sisters living elsewhere on the Earth. If it were not for the caravans traveling from the east, you would be cut off from the rest of the world. Yet, in spite of the city's remoteness, Ja'Usu is a beautiful oasis with much potential, if it can embrace change and address the needs of its poor. Have you enjoyed listening to my story?"

Aschenaki suddenly began to cough and covered his mouth as a way of stealing a moment to determine how best to answer the storyteller's question. Clearly, he wished he had never prompted the governing council to accept Narada's proposition to tell a story, but he had. And this obscene storyteller's repulsive narrative personally brought up for him issues about his family's past and concerns about its future, what with Arsalaan's return. Narada's story, going on and on, challenged his standing on the council and even pitted council members against one another, which caused him great anguish and much concern. But he said nothing about these things. Instead the patriarch, summoning as must empathy as he could muster, simply smiled and replied, "To me, a story about a future world and a future people taking seven nights to tell, to me astounding it is. What an imagination you have, Narada. Our people are enjoying it, I think, immensely." This finally said, Aschenaki looked away and clapped his hands, and his sister Vardah walked into the room, carrying a bowl of warm lemon water and two cloth towels so they could wash and dry their hands.

"Amantahu, Ato Narada," she said. "That you are here with us, I am so excited."

"Haya Aman…Amantashe, sister Vardah."

"Oh, so my name you know." In keeping with the status of a married woman, Vardah politely smiled and looked away to avoid making eye contact with her brother's guest.

Then Aschenaki asked, "Narada, if meat or not you eat we did not know, so two stews we have cooked. A very nice vegetable stew my mother likes to make…potatoes and carrots and some kind of greens, to know I do not. Also my wives, Fadwah and Pariza, a goat stew for you they have made. What would you prefer?"

"The vegetable stew would be fine. Thank you."

"Vardah, our guest the vegetable stew for him please bring, and for me, meat I like…and some fresh water…please." Aschenaki's sister collected the wet towels and bowl and left the room.

"Narada, why so important is accepting change?" Aschenaki asked.

"Change is the nature of our existence, Aschenaki. Change creates an opening for the Spirit you call Jah to express itself in new ways. It allows for the evolution of the human spirit. Would you not agree?"

"Oh yes, Narada, but always a good thing change is not if to instability and greater suffering it leads."

Aschenaki's sister returned with two dish-shaped baskets—one with goat stew on flatbread she set before her brother, and the other with curried vegetables she gave to Narada. Vardah then left, only to return with two glasses of water and small hand towels, which she placed on the mat between them before bowing to Narada and leaving the room.

Aschenaki spread one of the towels across his lap and, in keeping with Ja'Usu custom, used only the fingers of his right hand to tear off a piece of bread and wrap it around a bit of meat before placing it in his mouth. Narada thought it curious how the young patriarch, now totally absorbed with the food on his plate, ate like a ravenous dog eating quickly for fear that a stronger beast might snatch it away. So although they sat together in the same space, Narada understood Aschenaki usually ate alone, emotionally reclusive, placing his own needs and desires before everything else and everyone. And for this reason, he felt sorry for the little man who remained unaware that he had dug himself into a deep, dark hole.

Aschenaki soaked up the last drops of his stew with his remaining piece of bread and began licking each finger on his right hand before remembering his guest was also there. Looking up with some embarrassment, he was relieved to see that Narada was still eating and mulling over his own plate.

"Well, Narada, a delicious stew mine I must say was. I trust your meal agreeable to you it is?"

"Your mother is a fine cook. I would like to thank her for the meal."

"Oh, necessary that is not…for you, her I will thank," said Aschenaki. Then he added, "My mother a good cook she is, why do you say?"

"I can taste her unique seasoning, the years of experience, and the love for her family she mixes in the curry."

"You know, Narada, absolutely right you are. Cooking as a labor of love I never thought of, but I, too, my mother's love in her cooking can taste. Such a wise man you are."

And for an instant, Aschenaki forgot the storyteller's treachery and almost felt remorse for what he planned to do. He clapped his hands and called for Vardah, who came immediately to collect the empty eating baskets and the soiled towels as they drank the water.

Then Pariza stepped into the doorway, carrying a tray, and asked in a childlike voice, "Asche, do you wish me to serve the coffee now?"

Aschenaki was furious, and it took all his willpower and strength to mask his obvious disdain for the mistake he had married. How could a woman be so stupid when he had distinctly instructed her, three times, to only serve the coffee when he called her?

"Pariza…Pariza, an odd little bird you are. Why not…yes, the coffee now why not serve?" Then turning to Narada, speaking in the calmest voice he could rally, he asked, "Our Ja'Usu coffee, do you drink?"

"Yes, your coffee is some of the best in the world."

"Good. Pariza, coffee let us have." And he dismissed her with his eyes.

Exasperation and anger flooded his brain while his wife's bare feet pitter-pattered across the red clay floor. The little woman smiled at the man who ruled her life as she stepped onto the lower platform and set the metal tray down on the mat between them.

"Asche, the coffee too shall I pour?"

Aschenaki would have lost it if it were not for Narada, who raised his cup from the tray and held it out for Pariza to serve the brew. The storyteller caught the fear in her eyes, not of him but of Aschenaki. The latter, seeing the little diversion, reached behind his pillow and grabbed the tiny vial he had hidden there. As Pariza poured the coffee, Aschenaki quickly emptied the few drops of a clear liquid into the cup on the tray and then slid the empty bottle under his tunic.

He waited nervously now, gambling on Narada's sense of courtesy to pass him the coffee Pariza had poured, which the storyteller did. Aschenaki observed intently as Narada reached for the other cup on the tray and held it out for his not-too-bright wife to fill. Once done, masking his sigh of relief, he watched his guest put the coffee cup to his mouth. Aschenaki sipped from his cup and waited, but not before Pariza said, "Asche, some tea biscuits with honey shall I bring you?" She knew this delicacy was his favorite and wanted so much to please him.

The young patriarch almost choked, but with as much composure as he could rally placed his coffee cup back on the tray, looked at his wife, and said with a strained smile, "Pariza, my sweet, Narada and I conversation now we must have; so perhaps, for biscuits later I will call you. OK?"

"OK, Asche." She left the room and closed the wooden doors to the kitchen area behind her.

Aschenaki picked up his coffee and rested his back against his pillow as Narada again held his cup to drink. Like a house cat that had caught a mouse and knew its prey's life was near its end, the patriarch was serene and still as he watched the storyteller consume the last dregs of coffee in his cup.

"Do you not like your coffee, Aschenaki?"

"Oh yes, Ja'Usu coffee in our traditional way Pariza makes it. First, the dry beans over charcoal until dark-roasted they become." He took a sip from his coffee and licked his lips before resuming. "Then the beans the women grind and place them in a pot to cook...and a trick, here, there is," he stopped to take another sip before having to suppress his laughter. "Over the beans just the right amount of boiling water they must pour, so the coffee, too strong or too weak it will not be. And they let the brew continue to boil for the right effect to have. I mean taste...the right taste to have." Aschenaki could no longer contain his glee, and his laughter bubbled over in loud hysteria.

"And how long do you think the poison will take before I die, Aschenaki?"

"Saying what are you, Narada?" he replied, pretending to be shocked.

Seeing through Aschenaki's pretense, the storyteller stared at his host until it was clear to the patriarch that Narada knew precisely what he had done.

"Not long, Narada," he said calmly with a sneer. "Very long it will not take, and all the time in the world for your demise to wait I have. You know, a pain in my leg ever since you arrived you have been, spreading mystery and magic…making everyone believe some kind of jinn you are when nothing more than an overblown beggar who tells stories you are. In Ja'Usu, your welcome you have worn out." Aschenaki now no longer concealed his contempt.

"And how do you plan to explain my death to your family and the council and the city?"

"A problem that will not be, Narada. Arsenic is a colorless liquid, you see, and no taste or odor does it have. And enough in your coffee, I put it. Maybe a little white foam from your mouth as you die will appear, but after away it I wipe, no evidence there will be…none."

Aschenaki relaxed back on his pillow and placed his hands behind his head while he warmed up to his subject, as if he had rehearsed these lines from a play once read and was onstage now for his first and only performance.

"To my family that you simply keeled over after drinking the coffee I will say, and if anyone to blame there is…well, Pariza it will be, but all right eventually she will be…I promise. And to the council…several patriarchs and I simply a story make up like you we will, and that will be that. Maybe one or two patriarchs the timeliness of your demise will question, but them I can handle. And for the rest of Ja'Usu, well…unsavory rumors about you with Ibrahim Hafez's disgraced daughter, whom a liking to you she has taken, and all your indiscretions revealed they shall be. By the time with you we have finished, your name, Narada, and your ludicrous story that so much trouble has caused will be tarnished and forgotten eventually will be."

"Poor Aschenaki, I am sorry to tell you there is a wrinkle in your plan."

"Storyteller, no wrinkles there are. To get up now you can and, perhaps, in the streets die, which for me, better it might be. Or gracefully right here sit and eventually no more be. About thirty to forty minutes, my experience tells me left you have."

"Someone is going to die here today, but it will not be me, Aschenaki."

"Mean what do you?" exclaimed Aschenaki.

"I switched our cups when you were speaking to Pariza. So it is you who drank the poison, not me."

"Serious you cannot be!" Aschenaki said with shock. He suddenly turned pale and felt around his throat, as if his body would certainly convey the truth. Then he began to laugh again. "Storyteller, there you almost got me. But me you cannot fool. From the poisoned well you drank, not me."

"Then why am I sitting calmly while you are beginning to sweat and your head is starting to ache?"

Aschenaki was now alarmed, because he felt these symptoms just as Narada described, and he screamed out in distress. Fear took hold of him as his eyes bulged out of his head, and he tried to scream for help. Words did not come; only hot, dry, air escaped from his throat as he found it difficult to both breathe and speak at the same time.

"Did you know, Aschenaki, arsenic has been used as a medicine by the Chinese for over twenty-four hundred years and will be used in future medications to treat a variety of diseases? During the reign of Queen Elizabeth the First in England, for example, well-to-do women mixed arsenic with vinegar and chalk to whiten their skin and, they thought, prevent it from aging."

Aschenaki's eyes rolled back in his head, his muscles cramped, and his stomach was on fire as he gasped with pain. "Please… please, something you must do," he pleaded.

"Perhaps I can take your mind off of your dilemma by telling you more about the history of your favorite poison, Aschenaki. Did you know in the Middle Ages and in Europe's Renaissance period…from the fifth to the fifteenth century, arsenic was the most favored method for murder committed by royalty? So, today, it is often called the inheritance powder, because impatient heirs were known—or suspected, I should say—to use it to ensure or accelerate their inheritance. Is that why you killed your father, Aschenaki, to speed up your inheritance and ensure that you became your family's next patriarch?"

"What! Such a thing, why would you say?" Aschenaki looked confused, and his clothes were dripping wet from perspiration. A red stain appeared on the mat between his legs as blood seeped into his urine.

"If you tell me the truth—and I will know if you are lying—I will save your life."

Finding the sudden strength to lean forward, the patriarch reached for Narada's foot and pleaded, "Please save me, and anything you want to know I will tell you."

"Did you murder your father, Aschenaki?"

A feeling of pain and agony welled up in the young patriarch's eyes and spilled over onto his face. "Yes, my father with small doses of arsenic over several weeks, I killed him."

"Why would you do such a terrible thing?" asked Narada.

The young patriarch struggled to take a breath and speak. "Dying he was anyway, and Arsalaan to become patriarch he wanted. But my brother, the responsibility he did not want. Me he should have chosen…but no, Arsalaan to wait for he would have. Me he did not even see. All my life for Arsalaan I have been passed over, and enough I just had, so with the same poison that me is killing, my father I killed."

"And what do you think Arsalaan would do if he found out that his own brother had murdered his father?"

Aschenaki coughed and gasped for air as his heart pounded in his chest. Yet, he felt a great release in unburdening his secret to someone and lay back on his pillow to wait for the spirit of death he knew would eventually come.

"Aschenaki, you are not dying," Narada told him.

"Narada, nothing for me now you can do there is, so alone leave me."

"Aschenaki, I could have given you the poisoned coffee you intended for me, but instead, I chose to drink it myself; so you are not dying, at least not today."

The patriarch heard, but it took a moment for him to comprehend what was said. He slowly sat up, looking dazed and confused. "Mean what do you? If dying I am not, why do I feel like I am?"

"I made you feel like you were dying, but I assure you, you are not. It is true I could take your life, but it would not go well for your family or for your brother, Arsalaan, who has chosen a different path. And revenge is not a course he should take, so you are not going to die today."

Aschenaki shook his head as if trying to wake up from a bad dream and stared at Narada like he was seeing him for the first time. "Well, dying are you?"

"On your watch, no...but I need to tell you that in my Father's house, there are many mansions; and unfortunately, you have chosen a hall that holds many like-minded and misguided souls like yours. There are repercussions for what you have done; and in time, in order for you to grow as spirit in human form, you must come to grips with everything you have done. But for now, there is only one thing I ask of you."

"What is it?" asked Aschenaki. "Anything I will do."

"That 'doing anything' is what has gotten you into trouble, Aschenaki."

"OK, what you ask of me I will do."

"When Arsalaan comes to you and asks for your approval as family patriarch to wed Ibrahim Hafez's daughter Hohete, you will give your blessing, gladly. And you and your family will treat them with kindness and respect all the remaining days of your life. Do you understand?"

"Yes…yes, I understand," he replied, like a man who has just been risen from the dead.

"I know all things, Aschenaki, and do not have to return here through the desert to check up on you. I can reappear in Ja'Usu in the twinkling of a moment, so do not go back on your promise. Do you understand?"

"Yes…yes, I understand…I understand," he said as he hung on Narada's every word.

Narada stood and dusted off his clothes before turning to step down off the two platforms and walk out the door.

"So powerful jinn you really are," Aschenaki called after him.

Narada looked back at him but said nothing before passing the four women in the courtyard and walking out the compound's door.

Duha was leaning against the wall outside his uncle's place when the storyteller stepped across the entrance and onto the street, and he rushed over to greet him with a bow of humility and respect. When he opened his mouth and gibberish came out, Narada knew that Duha had made up his mind; he wanted to speak.

He lightly touched the boy on his forehead with the palm of his hand, and Duha's eyes closed as his spirit was instantly transported to another place in another time. Surveying his surroundings, Duha's spirit noticed a male youth yelling at an older man he knew was the boy's father.

"You have done nothing to help me!" the boy screamed. "And what you have done, you were supposed to do. So what! You are still poor and dumb, and I hope my children are nothing like you!"

The old man felt deeply hurt and was offended, not only by his son's words but more by the bitterness and anger he saw in his son's eyes. Still, the father's own flesh and blood was desperately crying out for something more; something he did not have or know enough to give. The old man raced through memories to uncover where he went wrong but found nothing that justified the depth of his son's torment. With sadness he gazed at his boy and wondered whether his child felt the love he had for him, and this unknowing hurt even more.

"You speak nothing but gibberish," the father finally said to his son, and the boy turned his back and walked away, never to see his father ever again.

Duha's eyes opened, and once again, he faced Narada, who looked at him kindly. "Was anyone familiar to you in your vision?" he asked.

"Yes, myself…" replied Duha.

"Who were you?"

"At his beloved father, the boy screaming I was."

"And why were you shouting at him?" Narada prodded.

"A boy I met, trash he called me, because my father poor he was and me in rags dressed. At the boy I got angry, but on my father I took it out."

"And what happened after that?"

"My father again I never saw."

"Why?"

"Wrong I knew I was, even when those things to him I said. All back I wanted to take it, but off I kept putting it…too proud to say I was sorry."

"And what happened, Duha?"

"My father died, and him I never saw." Duha lowered his head as tears fell upon the cobblestone street.

"And in honor of your father, whom you wrongly shamed, your spirit chose to speak only gibberish in this life." Narada looked up and down the empty street before his eyes rested on Duha, and in an instant, the storyteller transformed himself into the human form of the angry boy's father in Duha's vision.

"I knew you were angry, son, but did not know how, because of my own ignorance, to chase away your anger. Instead, I was consumed by your words and could not help you. Please forgive my ignorance. I did not mean to wish away your ability to speak. I am sorry."

Duha grabbed his father from a previous life around his waist and hugged him tightly. "Father, it is I who should beg for your forgiveness. I did not mean what I said. You gave me what you could, and most of all you gave me your love, and I am forever grateful. Please forgive me, Father...please...please, Father."

"I love you, son, and I forgive you." And with these words, Narada returned to his own human form.

"Your situation reminds me of a story of a young man I will meet in the future," exclaimed the storyteller. "He will have a fist-fight with his older brother and, to pay his brother back for his wrong, will climb onto a rooftop as high as a mountain to jump. You harmed yourself when you walked away from your father."

Duha, still thinking he was clinging to his father from a previous life, was startled by Narada's voice and let go, only to see he was holding on to the storyteller.

"The boy, does he jump?" asked Duha.

"No, he is talked out of leaping to his death. So you see, words have power; so use them wisely. Please do something for me, Duha. Go into your uncle's house and say to him these exact words: 'Narada says he will always be watching you.' Will you do this for me?"

"As you ask, how can I do, when gibberish you know I speak?"

"Not anymore, Duha. Your father from a past life has forgiven you. You are free now to speak to anyone, and they will understand you. So please do as I ask, and say to your uncle Aschenaki, 'Narada says he will always be watching you.' Your uncle will surely understand."

With that said, the storyteller strolled down the street as Duha looked his way and repeated softly what he had been asked to say to his family's patriarch—and listened, for the first time, to the sound of his own voice.

"Storyteller, thank you…Ato Narada, thank you, I mean! Thank you!"

CHAPTER 44

THE SEVENTH NIGHT

It was midmorning, on the day of the conclusion of Narada's story, when Hohete and Ayaat walked into Arsalaan's compound, still without a door. The master builder, anxiously awaiting their arrival, kept one eye on the entrance while he stacked mud brick in one corner of the yard. When the women appeared, Arsalaan was so eager to greet them that he stumbled over bricks on the ground and would have landed in the dirt had it not been for a stack of blocks that broke his fall.

Hohete laughed, and he rushed over to meet them.

"Amantahu, sister Hohete and mother Ayaat."

"Hiya Aman," they replied as Hohete placed her pastel blue scarf over her face, leaving her eyes uncovered.

Arsalaan led them into the largest of three buildings, where he had met with Narada and Jumah, and invited the two women to sit down, but not before scurrying around the room and fluffing up his few pillows and wiping away the dust that had settled on the straw mat. He sensed their amusement and could feel their eyes on him as they sat on the first-level dais. Although Arsalaan had rehearsed what he would do and say, now that

Hohete and her aunt were there, he seemed at a loss as to what he should do next.

Then, remembering he had prepared hot mint tea for them, he rushed into a small adjoining room and returned with a tray with three teacups and the sweet biscuits he had purchased from a vendor the previous day. Hohete smiled with amusement behind her scarf as he poured their sweet tea, careful to not spill a drop, and then ripped open the package of tea biscuits that fell out onto the tray. Arsalaan stepped onto the dais and sat down to drink his tea and reached for a biscuit, but he felt awkward in the silence, which was suddenly broken by Hohete's laughter as she looked at her aunt. Ayaat just stared at their host with a broad smile, revealing several of her missing front teeth. This look from the old woman thoroughly confused and unnerved Arsalaan, who thought perhaps he had insects still crawling on his beard or had spilt tea in his lap. This amused Hohete even more. Without saying a word, Ayaat picked up her tea and walked to the doorway, where she squatted within hearing range of her niece and the man she was sure was a strange fellow.

"Hohete," Arsalaan said in hushed tones while looking at her aunt, who appeared not to be listening. The old woman's face was placid as she looked out into the distance beyond the compound but listened to Arsalaan's every word. "For quite some time, what to you to say I have been thinking. Ja'Usu custom tells me with my brother, Aschenaki, first I should meet, and to your father to speak ask him. But close to Aschenaki I am not as with other members of my family I am.

"Then to your father myself to speak, I thought. But after how I should deal with the street boys you instructed me, directly to you to talk I decided. And then, if you wish, advise me how to proceed."

"With what to proceed?"

"Hohete, good business partners we would make, I think, and your man I want to be...if you would have me. I mean together to live I want us, and through the marriage ceremony one family to become, so my woman you are and your man I am."

"Oh my Jah...Oh my Jah!" shouted Ayaat, still squatting in the entrance but raising her arms to the sky.

"Please, auntie!" Hohete exclaimed before turning back to him. "No, Arsalaan, your woman I cannot be and with you a family start."

"Hohete, why not? You liked me I thought," he said with great disappointment.

"You I do like, Arsalaan, but like Arthur loves Valerie in Narada's story, loved I want to be, not like someone's business partner be. With your work I can and will help you, but you in my bed I cannot accept."

"But Hohete, why not?"

She reached out and gently held his hand. "Arsalaan, cursed surely you have heard I am. At least, Ja'Usu believes I am...your family believes it. My fault that Waheed at an early age passed away, people say this, and without an heir. And when the streets alone I walk, at me people curse and stare. So if as my man I took you, you Ja'Usu would make fun of and perhaps pity. And after a while, that curse you also would believe; and because of it, me you would begin to hate and even me leave. Only if me it is you truly loved, like Arthur loves Valerie, a family on our own terms raise we could and strong enough be. So you see Arsalaan, being your woman I cannot accept."

Hohete rose from the mat and stepped onto the floor, which made her scarf drop from her shoulders. She looked at him with kindness before raising her hand and lightly touching Arsalaan's face. He gazed into her eyes, their allure accentuated by the charcoal on her eyelids and the fragrance of rosewater and coconut oil in her long dark hair.

"As your business partner, if you still want me that we can be. And with your boys, you I will help." Hohete turned and walked away, and Ayaat joined her.

The Last Night of the Story

It was a large gathering with as many Oromo families present as there were Ja'Usu inhabitants to witness Narada's last night of storytelling. The ritual and prelude to each evening's narrative was so familiar to the assembly that many people arrived early to sit close to the storyteller and share in the communal prayer. They waited patiently for Narada, whom some now considered a prophet, and passed along a rumor they heard that soon he would leave.

The patriarchs, including Aschenaki and his immediate family, were already seated when the storyteller arrived with his arm around Ma'Mun Ibn Nour's shoulder and Arsalaan and Ibrahim Hafez walking on his other side. Hohete and Ayaat followed behind them. The sacred fire in the center of the ring was ready as Imtiyaz and Tabassum stood with their burning torches raised, waiting for Narada's command to light.

As on previous evenings, the people in the inner circles were the first to see the storyteller. They rose to their feet, which signaled to the rest of the gathering—except for the patriarchs and their immediate relatives—to stand. This evening was different for most of the patriarchs, who had grown accustomed to acting in unison when it came to not acknowledging Narada. None of them could have anticipated or foreseen Patriarch Aschenaki struggling to his feet with the rest of the assembly when the storyteller first appeared. Certainly it was not out of deference, but he did so because he was now sure that Narada was a formidable being that was all-knowing and all-seeing, a powerful spirit that could be everywhere and anywhere all at the same time. How else could it be, he wondered, if his young nephew, Duha, who had never spoken an intelligible word in his entire life, could stand before him and say as clearly as a donkey's bray, "Narada says he will always be watching you"? This miraculous event was fixed in Aschenaki's mind as a chilling promise and fearful warning that, hereafter, would compel him to straighten his back or suffer to stand anytime he heard the name Narada.

The sight of Aschenaki standing for the storyteller was perplexing and too much to bear for members of the city's governing council, except for Patriarch Taqiyy, the pious, the righteous, who had come to appreciate Narada's effect on Ja'Usu. Beginning with the third night of the story, Taqiyy had stood with the rest of the gathering when the storyteller appeared. The other patriarchs sat and looked at one another on the platform and shook their heads at Aschenaki in utter disbelief.

"Aschenaki!" Chief Patriarch Murabbi finally shouted. "Mad have you gone!"

But Aschenaki, more afraid of Narada and the risk of being exposed with the gruesome secret he buried deep and chained inside, ignored Murabbi and said nothing. He tucked away his crime in an inner fortress, sustained by fear and the rationalization that what he had done—murdering his father—was for the good of his clan. He would keep his promise to Narada for his own safety and well-being, if you could call his bizarre behavior an expression of wellness.

Once the libation to ancestors ended and future generations blessed, Narada asked Imtiyaz and Tabassum to light the fire as the gathering sat down, including Jumah and his ragtag boys, who remained in the shadows on the edge of the crowd. Narada, sitting between Hohete and Arsalaan, sensed the internal struggle the two were engaged in. The master builder grappled with his feelings for Ibrahim Hafez's daughter, and Hohete worried that Narada might leave Ja'Usu without fulfilling his promise to secure her future with a loving man. After folding his legs underneath him and closing his eyes, he commanded the multitude of crawling creatures to return to their nests and flying wings to find rest. Then he conveyed a thought-seed that would be received as intuition by Hohete and Arsalaan: This night at the end of story, my spirit leaves as my body passes away; and when you prop up my physical form between your arms, you will find each other there. And know that what sustains your breath and fills your heart is Divine Mother's love revealed in one another.

Hohete grabbed Narada's hand as if the world were coming to an end and looked at him with fear and anguish already in grief upon her face. Arsalaan also gazed at the storyteller and then noticed the tears in Hohete's eyes. And as they happened to glance at one another, they immediately felt that something in them was being born as Narada's narrative was coming to an end. Arsalaan wanted to reach out to Hohete and tell her how much he loved her, like Arthur loved Valerie, but knew this was not the place or the time.

The storyteller took Arsalaan's hand and held it on his folded knee while he looked into the fire and watched the crackling flames rebel against the darkness. The people's eyes were already closed as they waited, patiently, in their quiet space for the story to once again unfold. And from a wellspring, deeper than any vibration or sound they had ever felt or heard, arose a sound that made their bodies tremble and the ground shake, but the people were oddly not afraid. And as the rumbling diminished and the earth came to rest, the storyteller intoned for the Akasha Records of Celestial Light to open. Then the moving images behind closed eyes reemerged as Narada read for the seventh and final night from the book of stories.

CHAPTER 45
THE SNOW LEOPARD

The night air is cool, clear, and crisp. Looking up at the heavens, past the glare of fleeting city lights, Arthur imagines an escape, even for an instant, from the insular limits of his daily routine moving between work, and home and community. A twinkling star not far from the planet Venus catches his attention while he waits for the traffic light. When it turns green, the driver behind him honks his horn and wakes Arthur from his musings.

Driving back to his apartment, Arthur wonders why he's exhausted when he should feel upbeat and energized from the health-conductor graduation. He mulls over the day's events in his mind: time spent in the office responding to e-mails; explaining to Gracie, at least three times, why the cost of the graduation was over budget; and reviewing the Trust's financial report from the previous month. He considers whether to join the other project leaders—Hachi, Mary, Aisha, and Herb the evaluator—at Pecan restaurant for a celebratory glass of wine but decides, instead, to go home and rest.

He drives north on San Pablo Avenue, which is nearly deserted except for several homeless people pushing their possessions in rickety carts or searching for a doorway to huddle or hide in out of the chill and harm's way. The light turns red at the corner of MacArthur Boulevard and San Pablo, and Arthur slows to a stop. A sudden, sharp knock on the side window startles Arthur, and he looks up to stare down the steel barrel of a gun.

"Open up, mothafucka, and get the fuck outta the car…now!"

It takes a moment for Arthur to comprehend what's happening as his mind is jerked away from heady musings about the nature of community empowerment, social change, and personal transformation. His immediate impulse makes him immobile, as he's suspended between thoughts of securing the door or stepping on the gas in hope that either action might protect him against the young man with a gun. It takes another moment for Arthur to come to the sobering reality that locking the car door or speeding away can't stop a bullet.

"Did you hear me, mothafucka? Get outta the damn car!"

Perhaps it's an unintended mistake; or that Arthur doesn't move fast enough; or that his attacker can no longer contain his anger, his rage; or possibly he just needs to hurt somebody. The gun fires, and the assailant screams, cursing the air he breathes, Arthur, and everyone else he wants to feel his pain. Blood gushes from the stub of what used to be the assailant's right thumb, pieces of glass splatter into Arthur's face, and then Arthur's body is yanked from the car and dumped onto the cold concrete.

In an instant, Arthur's spirit is jolted out of its body and is staring down at a lifeless form. It notices, more out of curiosity than from any emotion, blood oozing from the body's head; the figure on the pavement is strangely still. His spirit draws closer to examine the physical form when it's distracted by the sound of a Honda crashing into a parked car up the block. The automobile then backs up before belching white smoke and peeling rubber as it screeches madness like a gigantic rat on steroids while racing up the street.

Arthur's spirit stands next to the body lying on the concrete and wonders what's to happen next. It then reaches for its smartphone to dial 911. It's this repetitive attempt to lift the black leather cover to the phone that first alarms his spirit when it realizes that something is terribly wrong. His essence looks down and watches his right hand reach for the phone as his fingers pass right through the leather casing on his belt like it isn't really there. In vain, it tries several more times to pick up the cell phone before turning its attention to the body on the ground. His spirit then bends down and looks into his own bloody face.

The light turns red as two cars, one behind the other, stop at the intersection heading east on MacArthur. Arthur yells and waves to get their attention. The driver's door in the first car opens, and a middle-aged man with a potbelly stands with effort, leaving one leg in the automobile and a hand on his steering wheel as he cautiously looks in Arthur's direction. The driver in the second car quickly opens his door, and a young Asian man rushes toward Arthur's unseen spirit, talking loudly and pointing to the body on the pavement. The driver with the large belly, assured now he's not alone, gets out of his vehicle and looks around again before waddling over to the Asian guy now bending over Arthur's lifeless form. Arthur's spirit tries, unsuccessfully, to communicate with the young Asian who already has his mobile phone out and dialing when the other man steps up to look at the body while putting his hands on his hips.

"He must have gotten hit by a car or something," the Asian man says. "We shouldn't move him, but let's see if he has a pulse."

The middle-aged motorist, still standing over the other man, looks up and down the street before saying, "I think he's dead."

Sirens are screaming in the distance as the young man touches Arthur on the neck. Unable to find a pulse, he gets up, looking straight through the spirit standing directly in front of him and says, "It might be a hit and run, which would make this a crime scene."

"You think?"

Cars are now approaching on both San Pablo and MacArthur when the potbellied motorist realizes he'd be more comfortable directing traffic than standing over a dead man. As the young Asian runs back to his car and grabs a blanket out of his trunk, the other man waddles over to the solid yellow line in the middle of the street and starts directing traffic.

The younger driver is carefully covering Arthur with a blanket when an emergency fire truck arrives, followed by the first of two ambulances. Two firemen hurry over, and as one bends down to examine Arthur, the other asks the Asian man what happened. The older motorist then hurries over to join their conversation. Paramedics from the first ambulance unit joins the fireman attending to Arthur's body as three police cars arrive with their sirens blaring. Officers cordon off the area and begin to divert traffic while their emergency lights remain flashing bright red, white, and blue. Two officers take statements from both drivers before letting them go.

Arthur's spirit observes all the activity around it before following an emergency worker holding his wallet over to the apparent officer-in-charge. "Hey John…this guy's name is Arthur Renfro, and he wasn't run over by a car. At least, we don't think so. It looks like he's been shot and is bleeding from the head. His vital signs are weak. The poor guy may not even make it to the hospital."

"Where are you taking him?"

"To Summit Medical."

"Are you sure he was shot?"

"One of your officers over there with the flashlight," he says pointing in the direction of the cop, "found bullet fragments, and judging from the hole on the side of the guy's head, he was shot. There's also a severed thumb over there on the ground."

"Does Renfro have both his thumbs?"

"Yea, we checked. It's not his thumb. This is definitely a crime scene."

The firemen watch as two paramedics place Arthur's comatose body onto a stretcher and secure him in the ambulance. A tall, thin medic with dark circles under his eyes hops into the back of the vehicle and, unbeknown to him, is followed by Arthur's spirit. They sit side by side as the medic adjusts Arthur's IV, and his spirit stares at the body that is his own. The driver quickly shuts the doors, heads for the driver's seat, and turns on the ignition key and emergency siren before racing into the night.

Arthur is rushed into the emergency room, where he's quickly moved from the paramedic's gurney to the triage table. After the emergency physician checks his pulse and eyes for signs of life, they give him a tracheotomy to secure his airway, and a nurse checks his blood pressure. The doctor removes the bloody bandages around his head and neck. Seeing the swelling of his brain and the formation of blood clots, he orders a nurse to call the neurosurgeon. While IV fluids are added to Arthur's intravenous tube, two nurses strip away his clothes and cover him with blankets before wheeling him to another room for a CT scan.

Thirteen minutes elapse before he's rushed into surgery. Arthur's spirit hovers over the operating table, looking down on someone tinkering with a machine and getting ready to put a mask over his face. Other people rush into the room, along with two men dressed in blue scrubs, who appear to be the surgeons. A nurse is helping one man adjust a mask over his nose and mouth when, suddenly, Arthur's spirit is distracted by a sliver of blue light hovering in the air on the other side of the room.

Returning his attention to the figures in the room, Arthur's spirit observes the man placing the mask over his body's face as the hovering blue light widens and expands into the opening of a passageway. Although Arthur's spirit wants to stay with its body to witness what's going on, it involuntarily starts to effortlessly float toward the light until it drifts toward the entrance to what appears to be a long, spiraling tunnel as dark as the night. In the distance shines what resembles a radiant white star. His spirit drifts into the spiraling channel and gradually accelerates in speed. A profound sense of peace and calm assurance now embraces Arthur's spirit as it glides in silence with increasing speed on a path toward the bright light at the other end of the tunnel.

As his spirit advances, the star draws nearer until its brilliance is as large as the circumference of the channel, and the sensation of movement slows until his essence involuntarily stops and hovers in place. But what he sees as far as his spirit eyes can see is a shock. No deceased friends or relatives waiting with open arms to greet him. No astral plane with celestial earth and green meadows. No powder-blue sky or deep-blue rivers and lakes. No ethereal plants or flora. No multicolored birds or butterflies to flutter happily around his head. Nothing close at hand or even in the distance, save the resumption of slowly moving forward while engulfed in bone-white brightness as far as his spirit can see. Arthur's spirit is confident there's purpose to his journey and floats forward without fear to whatever destination awaits him. He recollects being ten years old and asking his father about death and what's in the afterlife as they sat together watching television one Saturday afternoon.

"Dad, what happens after you die? Where do people go?"

"Nowhere, son; that's it. There's nothing after death. You just go blank," his father replied as the comedy show continued with ludicrous eruptions of canned laughter every fifteen or so seconds. Arthur's spirit remembers looking up at his father in disbelief, wondering why he and his brother, Roland, had to sit through boring church services if there wasn't a heaven after all.

The opaque whiteness suddenly starts to clear, and his spirit notices up ahead the steep side of a mountain with patches of white snow. Not long after, his spirit slows and comes to rest, high up, on a narrow, rocky precipice. As it turns around from what feels like landing on hard, gray stone, as far as his spirit can see are snow-capped mountain ridges and peaks rising above low-lying valleys covered with sparse evergreen trees; at least, they look like trees. Looking up, his spirit sees only a cheerless, grayish-white canopy and suspects that if the mountains and trees are real, then what's above him must be real sky…a celestial sky. Peering into the distance, his essence searches for any movement at all but sees only a desolate range of jagged rocks and empty whiteness all around.

His spirit crouches on the mountain ledge and wraps its spirit-arms around its knees and is suddenly reminded of Arthur's telephone conversation with Valerie when she told him of her dream. You were on a crevice in a rock, and your arms were folded around your knees. But you weren't trying to stay warm…you weren't cold. You were looking up.

And for the first time since his murder on San Pablo Avenue, Arthur's spirit is overwhelmed with grief for having been forced out of the living and leaving loved ones unexpectedly behind, without warning, and with so many things left undone. He thinks about Valerie and how she will take his death. And then about his mother, who he knows couldn't imagine him dying before her; and about his brother, Roland, who at thirty-two never thinks about death. And how will the Trust and the Board and Gracie and Ramona and Critical Mass Health Conductors feel about his passing? And who is going to arrange his memorial service, and how many people are going to attend? Will Natalie be there, and will she cry? But most of all, his thoughts return to Valerie, and he realizes, while staring into the void, how much he loves her and is distressed at not having the chance to say goodbye.

Arthur's spirit notices the brightness on the horizon getting darker as shades of gray gather like storm clouds and move toward him. Confusion engulfs his essence, and it feels very much alone as he squats on the ledge, staring off into a vast unknown. Is this his purgatory or a personal hell he must endure for a transgression he can't recall? An increasing panic seeps into his being as the darkening clouds come closer.

Looking down, his spirit realizes climbing down from this rocky outcropping is out of the question. Even if it successfully made it off the mountain, where would his spirit go? His essence examines the hard, gray stone underneath its spirit feet and the concave walls bordering the shallow ledge. There's no sign that anyone has been there. And then his essence recollects it is no longer among the living. His spirit carefully reexamines the walls—the cracks and crevices—before turning its attention upward, only to be startled by what stares back at him. If his spirit still possessed a material heart, it would register fear and beat faster. If it had lungs and air to breathe, the creature above him would have taken his spirit's breath away.

The snow leopard sits on an outcropping and looks down at him. Its penetratingly large, green eyes are ablaze under a thick mass of gray and white fur highlighting dollar-sized black spots and small gray circles within black rings. Rather than showing aggression by baring its teeth or slinking away, it lies down on its haunches and continues watching him. Although the large animal makes Arthur's spirit uncomfortable, his essence takes comfort in knowing it's not alone. Yet, his spirit ponders, if the leopard chooses to attack, there's no place for the two of them to go but off the side of the mountain. And then it occurs to his spirit that the big cat may be considering the same thing. This revelation arrives with increasing apprehension.

Arthur's spirit isn't aware when its initial panic is absorbed by the leopard's stare; when its fright is replaced with a sense of peace and calmness. When it finally recognizes the soothing effect the cat has on his essence, the leopard rises off its haunches, looks up, and gracefully leaps almost twenty feet to higher ground.

The dark storm clouds that were once moving toward him are now receding in the distance, and his spirit wonders whether the appearance of the rolling clouds had anything to do with his sudden shift in mood and changing emotions. Did the leopard show up to transform his fear into calmness? Now, no longer alone, his essence perceives the snow leopard as a good omen. And with this new thought, it decides to climb off the precipice and follow the leopard up the mountain wall.

Examining gaps in the rocks near and above him, Arthur's essence carefully wedges its spirit toes and fingers into a vertical crack and begins to climb. Lifting itself up and off the ledge renews his spirit and strengthens its conviction to continue in its ascent. Reaching for a tiny outcrop to pull itself up and then inserting a spirit foot in a crack in the rock, his spirit slowly makes its way up the mountainside, climbing higher and higher.

Growing in self-confidence its ascent is now easier, not from the agility of physical limbs that aren't there or the strength of muscles it no longer possesses but from a sixth sense that it has made this climb before. This suspicion quickens but is mixed with a sense of urgency and dread. These emotions zap his spirit's energy and demands that it rest. During these pauses in the climb, Arthur's essence fights the urge to look down and, instead, glances up to always find the snow leopard twenty or thirty feet away, looking at him...watching until his spirit resumes the climb.

Suddenly, floating on a sporadic breeze, Arthur's spirit thinks it faintly hears a stringed instrument playing, not a familiar melody, but ancient half tones and modulations that bring to his consciousness flashes of images, like the taste of fragrant spices once savored but long forgotten. These remembrances become intense, making Arthur's spirit a bit dizzy and forcing his spirit again to stop. At these moments, it clings to the mountain for fear of losing its grip and falling back into the abyss. The sounds swell and wane in definition and clarity as his spirit nears the mountaintop.

This time, when blindly reaching upward for something to grab hold of, his spirit hand discovers what feels like the trunk of a small shrub or tree. Holding on to the shaft, Arthur's spirit lifts itself up onto the crest of the mountain, only to be startled by the snow leopard sitting on its haunches two feet in front of him. The animal calmly licks its fur on a massive gray-and-white paw when, to his spirit's astonishment, a dazzling white light surrounds the cat's body, and it morphs into a human form. The once snow leopard emerges as a tall man with dark-brown ringlets falling down onto his shoulders. His walnut-colored chest is bare, except for sandalwood beads that grace his neck and the immaculate white lungi or wrap that's around his waist. He looks at Arthur's spirit with dark, almond-shaped eyes and a youthful smile that belies his age. He's amused at Arthur's astonished face, whose spirit eyes open wide in wonder.

Unlike the barren rock and chasms below, this mountain plateau is a tropical sanctuary with wildlife and flora. Tall, green palms and trees bear ripe, hanging fruit of mango, banana, and papaya. And not far beyond, a babbling waterfall gushes warm spring water into an aqua-blue pond with bouquets of pink and white lotus blossoms floating on the surface of the water. Arthur's spirit is enchanted with the fragrance and the bright red, green, and canary-yellow parrots flying overhead in this ethereal paradise. With a sudden surge of emotion coupled with long-forgotten memories his spirit knows well, Arthur's spirit remembers and lies facedown on the astral earth and embraces the feet of the snow leopard, now a man.

"Please forgive me, Master. Until this moment, I had no idea it was you."

"Did you recognize me when you tried leaving your body while lying on your bed, and I appeared as skull and crossbones, warning you to stop? Or did you feel my presence in Valerie's hotel room when you were desperate and not yourself? I've watched you for over two thousand years, Arthur, when your spirit was born. Like a butterfly pursuing nectar from the most exotic flowers, you've darted from one life to the next, and I've watched and protected you."

Arthur's essence lay prone before this being, not knowing what to say or do, while silently thinking about why it called this being before him "Master."

"More than a few incarnations ago, Arthur, when knowing your divine nature became important to you, you asked of me to become your spiritual guide, and I said no—I would not. That's when you started calling me 'Master.' Do you now remember?"

"No, sir, I do not...and you said 'no'?"

Another memory surfaces that causes Arthur's spirit to rise to its feet and look at the Master. While asking with his eyes for an answer to his question, a flood of memories and emotions surge through him, carrying the agony and heartbreak from past encounters with this being near him, remembrances that drown out the initial joy of their reunion. Arthur's spirit steps back to put distance between himself and the Master who, understanding all things great and small, is already aware of his thoughts even before they reach Arthur's awareness.

The Master looks at his young spirit with compassion. "Twice before you have struggled up this mountainside after leaving a life, and each time you have asked the same question. Do you feel compelled to ask it again?"

Arthur's spirit recalls its earlier experiences in scaling the mountain and greeting the Master on his final ascent. Memories inundate his consciousness like a river overflowing its banks and brings with these recollections how he felt when the Master turned his spirit away. Apprehension and frustration now surface, once again, and settle on his spirit's tongue as he looks longingly into the Master's incomprehensible eyes and says with a trembling voice, "Master, I beg you, allow me to stay this time and accept me as your disciple."

"No," is the Master's stern and only reply.

"After two…now my third attempt to seek your permission, again, you turn me down. Why?"

The Master's face, once compassionate and gentle, is now as inscrutable as stone. His eyes are unyielding and impenetrable while remaining unmoved by Arthur's plea.

"Why transform into a snow leopard to guide me up the mountain if you know your answer to my repeated plea will always be no?" The Master's face softens into a slight smile, but he remains silent while looking calmly at Arthur's spirit.

"If you don't accept me as your disciple here and now," says Arthur's spirit, "I'll jump off this mountain and shall never return."

"Then jump," the Master says with an enigmatic grin.

Arthur's essence, without giving his threat a second thought, steps to the edge of the mount, leans back with open arms, and plunges into the vast unknown. Verses from the Mystic's Prayer swiftly surface like fragments of ticker tape in his consciousness as his spirit surrenders to the fall. If I ascend up into heaven… you're there…if I make my bed in hell…you say you're there…If I take the wings of the morning…and dwell in the uttermost parts of the sea…even there your hands…hold me. Arthur surrenders his spirit-heart to the Divine as it wonders if this sensation of falling is similar to what it might be like leaping to one's death off

Golden Gate Bridge. Events in his relatively short life pass before his eyes like a dramatic Technicolor film in slow motion before his spirit hits jagged rocks and loses consciousness before plummeting to the hard astral ground.

The two neuro-surgeons, Drs. Ravinda Singh and Paul Schultz, the anesthesiologist, and three operating-room nurses work on Arthur's body to save his life. They're distracted by the disquieting beep of the vital signs monitor. Arthur is flatlining and going into cardiac arrest. Dr. Singh demands a dose of Vasopressin to be injected into Arthur's left arm while Dr. Schultz performs CPR on his patient's chest. After thirty long minutes and no success in reviving him, Dr. Singh announces Arthur's death at 2:43 a.m. and then peels off his latex gloves and storms out of the operating room.

The Master's celestial form is now aglow, like August's full moon on a clear, starlit night. And his radiance transmutes into a wave of joy as he commands two of his initiates to fetch Arthur's broken spirit at the bottom of the mount. Returning in an instant, they lay Arthur's limp spirit on the astral earth in front of the Master. He kneels down and slowly passes his outstretched hand over the length of the young man's spirit before lightly tapping his astral forehead. With his essence now cradled in the great being's arms, Arthur's spirit opens its eyes and looks up into the beaming face of the Master.

"There is one thing that our Divine Mother does not possess," the Master says, "and you must give it of your own free will...that's your love. She knows the tenor of your heart and the course of your thoughts and only reveals herself to the ones who freely surrender their love to her…that you have done, Arthur Renfro; that you have done, my beloved disciple."

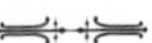

A nurse carries a white shroud over to where Arthur lays on the operating table and, beginning at his feet, unfolds and pulls the cloth over the full length of his body, only leaving his head exposed. Dr. Schultz, resigned to his patient's death, looks at Arthur's face and checks the pupils of his eyes one more time before saying, "Let's quickly see if we can locate his next of kin."

He pulls the mask from his face and walks to the door when he suddenly hears the unexpected beep of a monitor. Thinking the nurse has forgotten to turn off the machine and detach the sensors from Arthur's corpse, he walks to the monitor and, to his astonishment, the cardiac flatline is now undulating in normal waves across the screen. Stunned, he quickly locates his stethoscope, places the rubber tips in his ears, and positions the metal chest piece over Arthur's heart, which is now beating strongly. Calling out to the only nurse in the room, he orders her to bring Dr. Singh back to surgery.

The other neurosurgeon casually enters the operating room and, following Dr. Schultz's request, examines Arthur's body. "Even though this man's heart is now beating strongly," says Dr. Singh, "and I grant you, that in itself is quite miraculous…but since you already pronounced him dead, this fella is no doubt brain-dead from lack of oxygen."

Dr. Schultz rolls over the EEG, attaches the sensors to Arthur's body, and switches on the monitor. Within three seconds the machine registers strong brain-wave activity as Drs. Singh and Schultz look on in disbelief. Shamus Kiltey, the anesthesiologist, immediately steps forward as a nurse begins to reattach an IV to Arthur's inner arm. She then looks up and waits for further instructions while the two surgeons continue to stare in disbelief at the screen.

"Well, let's move on," Shamus impatiently demands, startling both surgeons before they regain their composure and quickly resume operating on Arthur's broken, bloody head.

Arthur's spirit sits on astral turf near the Master. "You've met Luther. He has encouraged you to turn your attention inward, ever deepening your relationship with Spirit. Be steadfast in your practice, Arthur, and deepen your devotion as our Divine Mother draws ever near. And in her stillness, listen to her eternal heartbeat as Luther has instructed you to do. It is that vibratory cosmic energy proclaimed as Aum in the Vedas, Amin in the Quran, Amen in the Biblical narratives, and bearing witness as the Holy Ghost in the New Testament. Listen to the heartbeat as it manifests in you. It will instruct you in all things."

Spellbound by the tenor of his teacher's voice, Arthur's spirit closes its eyes and listens to the vibrant energy the Master describes until the deep, rumbling tremor absorbs his entire being while his spirit remains fully aware of itself. The Master's physical form also melts away, only to return in an astral day to resume his conversation with his new initiate. Arthur's spirit opens its eyes to find the Teacher blissfully smiling at him.

"Master, are you returning me to the living?" Arthur's spirit asks.

"Yes, Arthur, you have much work to do among the living."

"But how can that be? I was shot in the head and face with a gun and died, so how can I go back now?"

The Master laughs as a spark of light flashes in his eyes, like a bolt of lightning before a thunderclap. "You're still in surgery,

Arthur. I'm helping the three doctors working on you as we sit here together. You'll walk away from their operation just fine."

"Master, how are you helping them?"

"I'm sharpening their focus and concentration as they move your surgery along with their trained hands. You'll have a slight scar no bigger than an inch next to your left eye when healed, but your vision will be perfect, and your mind will be fine."

"I thought your disciples remain with you," says Arthur's spirit.

"Arthur, you don't have to see my body for me to be with you. I will always be close—forever and a day, as you say. And soon, as your devotion deepens and your willpower grows strong, I will show you how to visit me in your nightly dreams."

"Will my face be disfigured?"

The Master laughs again, enjoying this exchange as a red-, yellow-, and green-feathered parrot comes to rest on his shoulder. And in an instant, Master and bird and mountain paradise fade into nothingness as Arthur's spirit also disappears.

CHAPTER 46

MUCH MORE WORK TO DO

The rapid eye movement under Arthur's closed lids ceases as his right eye opens, and he looks out onto an unfamiliar place. His throat hurts as his one eye notices a plastic bag filled with a clear liquid hanging from a hook on a metal stand beside the bed. He watches the drip, drip, drops of the fluid trickling into plastic tubing attached to the back of his left hand. It's then that Arthur realizes he's in a hospital room and seeing only with one eye. Cautiously he raises an arm and lightly touches the bandages over his left eye and ear and up over the left side of his head. He sees someone slumped in a chair not far from his bed asleep with a blanket over their chest. In response to a sudden impulse, Arthur jerks the tubes in his nose out before falling back to sleep.

Its 6:32 a.m. when Arthur opens his right eye again and sees a woman standing by the bed, holding his hand. "I'm so glad to see you've joined the living, again," she says to him. "Do you know who I am?"

Arthur looks away and studies the room for a second time, knowing he's been spoken to but a little fuzzy on what was said. Turning his head to look again, he stares at the woman for almost a minute before moving his head up and down to confirm that he recognizes her.

Valerie calls for the nurse without letting go of Arthur's hand. A woman appears in the doorway and walks over to the patient's bed. Arthur tries to speak, but while he knows his lips are moving, he finds he cannot talk. He raises a hand to his throat to discover something stuck on his neck.

"Sir, there's a tube down your throat to help you breathe, so you can't talk right now. Wait…let me call the doctor," the nurse says and leaves the room. She returns minutes later followed by the intern on duty. The physician pulls from his lab coat a pen-flashlight and shines it across Arthur's one eye and looks at the monitor beside the bed before turning to the nurse and then to Valerie.

"Who took the feeding tube out of his nose?"

The two women glance at one another without responding and then at the intern, who feels a tap on the back of his hand. Looking down, he sees Arthur pointing to himself.

"He wants that thing you got down his throat removed," says Valerie.

"We can't make that decision right now, although I would like to. One of his surgeons, Dr. Singh, will stop by this afternoon to check on him. You can ask about removing it then." Turning his attention back to Arthur, the intern asks, "So how are you feeling, Mr. Renfro? Move your head up and down if you're feeling OK and from side to side if you're not feeling well."

Arthur looks quizzically at the women before slowly nodding his head up and down. "Good," says the intern. "And do you have a headache?" He stares at the doctor for a moment before slowly shaking his head no. But then he points to the tube down his windpipe, and Valerie conveys to the physician that his throat hurts.

"Yes, I know," says the doctor. "Trachs are never comfortable, and hopefully your surgeon will order it removed, but you'll have to wait for Dr. Singh. Until then, he can write notes if he wants. Nurse, please bring Mr. Renfro something to write on and a pen."

"Those supplies are already in the drawer next to his bed, doctor," the nurse replies.

"I'll stop by and see you when I make my rounds again, Mr. Renfro," says the intern when his cell phone rings, and he hurries out the room, presumably to take the call. The nurse leaves right after the doctor without adding anything more.

Valerie opens the drawer next to Arthur's bed and searches for the writing pad and pen. Finding the pad and a half-used pencil, she places them in Arthur's hands and quickly demands, "Now, tell me how you feel, Arthur Renfro."

He looks up at her and then at the pad. Valerie questions if he actually does understand, but then Arthur scribbles something slowly on the paper. "I feel like I've fallen off a cliff, Valerie," he writes, and then looks at her.

"You might've gone off a cliff, my dear, but you've fallen back into life where you belong. At least, while I'm still here," Valerie replies with a smile and sigh of relief in her voice. "I'm glad you know my name, Arthur. I was worried you wouldn't...Well, now I know you're going to be all right."

Arthur makes an effort to sit up in the bed, with Valerie's help, and is about to explore the bandages over his left eye and head when she catches his arm and stops him. "Don't, Arthur. Let's wait for your doctor who's coming soon. Do you remember what happened to you?"

Valerie can tell by looking at his one eye that he's searching for an answer before a wobbly hand scribbles on the page. "I don't know," he writes. And then, "What happened to me?"

Tears well up in her eyes as she reluctantly tells Arthur that he was shot and found lying in the street. He stares at her as if she speaks a foreign language he doesn't quite understand. Valerie grabs his hand and holds it tight.

"I met your mother and brother. They were here yesterday and are staying at your apartment. I got your keys from Gracie. Your mother called this morning, and they'll be back this afternoon. I ought to call her, though, and let her know you're awake and all right."

Observing Arthur as she speaks and judging from the bewildered look on his face, Valerie wonders if he comprehends what's being said. She tries to mask her concern.

"You've had people here every day, Arthur," she continues. "You're a popular man. They wait in the lobby for news, since the hospital only let's immediate family members into intensive care. Every now and then, Roland or I go downstairs and let everyone know your status. They think I'm your wife, you know," she whispers with a smile. "Your staff and board members were also here last night, and several health conductors, too. Some of them have been here every night since you arrived, Arthur."

Arthur remains attentive, looking at Valerie without scribbling on his pad. She decides to change the subject. "See all the flowers your friends brought you?" she says, stepping back a bit to let him see.

He looks around the room again. "You'd think I was dying with all these flowers in the room," he writes. Valerie's relieved that he understands.

"You're not dying, so don't say that. Arthur, an older man came to visit you the other day, and it was odd because they let him into intensive care. When he came in the room, he called me by my name, which surprised me, since I don't know anyone here. His name was Luther, and I asked him how he knew my name. He said you must have mentioned me to him. Did you?"

Arthur listens, but doesn't begin to write. "Anyway," she continues, "he told me not to worry...that you would heal and be all right."

A young African American physician named Dr. Roundtree walks into the room and examines Arthur's medical chart. Without comment, he leaves and goes over to the nurse's station before returning to the room.

"I'm glad to see you're awake, Mr. Renfro," says the doctor, "and surprised you're sitting up in bed. I see the nurse gave you some paper and a pen; that's good. You know, you've been in a coma for the past five days. How does it feel to be awake?"

Arthur writes something down as Dr. Roundtree approaches the bed and reads his note. "My throat hurts, and I'd like some water."

"You can't drink water until we remove the tube from your windpipe, but judging from your progress, I know it will be soon." He places the rubber tips of his stethoscope in his ears and leans over to listen to Arthur's heart. "I've looked at your chart, and your vitals are good. Your blood pressure's normal, the swelling in your brain has subsided...Actually, Mr. Renfro, you're making a remarkable recovery for someone just shot in the head."

Dr. Roundtree then holds up his hands in front of Arthur's face and asks, "How many fingers do you see?"

"Seven," Arthur writes.

"And how many people are currently in the room?"

"Three, including me," he scribbles and shows it to the doctor.

"Good. What's your wife's name?"

Valerie looks away, wondering what Arthur is prepared to say. He gazes at her for a moment before scribbling on his pad, "Valerie Harper."

"Excellent, Mr. Renfro. You know, you're a very lucky man to be alive, judging from your injuries. Are you in any pain?"

"No, just a sore throat," he jots down on a page.

"I can give you more morphine for the pain, if you like." Arthur thinks for a moment and shakes his head no.

"One more question, Mr. Renfro: how does your head feel?"

"It hurts a little. Why do you ask?" he writes.

Dr. Roundtree laughs. "Mr. Renfro, you were shot in the head. Fragments of the bullet were lodged in your brain and caused some swelling. And by the time you reached this hospital, you lost a lot of blood. So I am surprised to see you so well. What's the last thing you remember about the incident, Mr. Renfro?"

Arthur turns to Valerie as if she knows the answer before turning back to the doctor with confusion on his face. "Just stopping for a light, that's it," he writes.

Dr. Roundtree picks up Arthur's chart at the end of the bed and writes something on it. "One of your surgeons will drop by to talk with you, and I'm sure the police…well, they'll be back… I'm sure."

"What about his other eye, doctor?" says Valerie. "When will you know if he'll be able to see with it again?"

"I think it best you speak to the surgeon who performed the operation about the bandages and his eye, Mrs. Renfro. I'll check in with you tomorrow. OK?" And without waiting for a response, Dr. Roundtree leaves the room.

Arthurs begins writing on his pad and holds it up for Valerie to see. "How did you know I was here?"

"Gracie called me. Now do you really think you could be in the hospital without my knowing it? And by the way it all sounded, I thought you might pass away before I got here. Don't ever scare me like that again, Arthur Renfro."

And he writes her a note: "It's not my time to die yet, Valerie. I have much more work to do."

CHAPTER 47

THE FUNERAL PYRE

Those who gathered opened their eyes and stretched as if waking from a dream. Some women wept in silence while others shrieked out loud. But only Narada knew if the women's raw emotion was because his story had come to its natural end or was due to Arthur almost getting himself killed.

Many of the men sat quietly and simply looked around to see what others were feeling or doing. Other men pondered odd and random thoughts about the story: What would it feel like to get shot with a hand machine and be forced out of your body? How does a jinn make himself a leopard and then change into a man? Do people actually live in the cold on mountaintops with all that stuff called snow? Is it really possible to open up a body and keep on living? If you don't have a body, how can you fall off a cliff? And if you are already dead, is it possible for a jinn to bring you back to life? And more was thought and said.

There were men and women who, after hearing and witnessing all seven nights or most of Narada's story, believed his narrative was genuine and true. But there were also those who questioned whether the storyteller made it all up and who believed that such a future world could not possibly be real. But all the people that were there, even if they only heard one or two nights of the tale, were convinced that Narada was the greatest teller of stories they had ever heard or would ever hear, and they all began to cheer for him.

Suddenly, a chorus of alarm went up from the women sitting closest to Narada as the news spread by word of mouth to the outer edges of the assembly that their beloved storyteller was dead.

Women began to sob and wail in disbelief as men stood motionless, in shock. Others in the crowd pushed their way toward the center of the circle to see for themselves if Narada was really gone. Though his head leaned back and his mouth was wide open, his physical frame was propped up in a sitting position and embraced by the two people next to him, Ibrahim Hafez's daughter and Arsalaan, both weeping uncontrollably. Daanish Nour directed Oromo men to form a wide circle around Narada's body, Hohete, and Arsalaan so they would not be overrun or crushed by those in the throng who not only wanted to see the storyteller but also touch his dead corpse.

The nine patriarchs and their families remained on their platform, gawking at the crowd when they heard the unexpected news. Several members of the governing council wondered if there was some mysterious link between Aschenaki standing for Narada earlier that evening and the storyteller's sudden demise. But knowing Aschenaki, how would they ever learn the truth? Chief Patriarch Murabbi, patron and guardian of the people, and Patriarch Ihtesham, the respectable and honorable one, had no plans to find out.

While there were those who lingered, sobbing and wailing, after viewing Narada, most of the gatherers joined a long, slow procession home in shock that someone who had brought so much life and promise and joy into their day-to-day lives was suddenly no more.

While Arsalaan released his hold on Narada to gently lower his body to the ground, Hohete was inconsolable and rocked back and forth, still weeping as she held the storyteller's lifeless form. Ibrahim Hafez and Ayaat eventually had to pry her loose so they could lay Narada down. Hohete's father tried to comfort his daughter. He told her they would carry Narada back to their compound, where she could watch over him and help prepare him for burial. Arsalaan, Daanish Nour, Imtiyaz, Tabassum, and several Oromo men listened and looked on.

But out of the darkness, Ma'Mun stepped forward and said in a clear voice for all to hear, "My teacher into Ja'Usu bring he does not want to be, because in the morning for his body the governing council will come, and away to take it they will want."

"This to know, how do you, Ma'Mun?" Arsalaan asked.

"Because my teacher me he told."

"This, my son, you when did he tell?" asked Daanish Nour.

"Yesterday morning after our quiet sitting, Grandfather," Ma'Mun replied, knowing his teacher's passing was surely foretold.

"So tonight Narada knew he was going to die?" asked Arsalaan.

"Oh yes; as much as he loved us, his destiny as an eternal wanderer demanded he move on, he told me. The words he used those were." Ma'Mun searched the faces closest to him to judge whether they believed him or not.

"So, with Narada's body, what shall we do?" Ibrahim Hafez asked, looking at the men before his eyes settled on Ma'Mun.

"The Oromo, him we will take, and our women for burial Narada they will prepare," said Daanish Nour.

"My teacher, buried he does not want to be," continued Ma'Mun. "A funeral pyre placed where he sat he wants, and at sunrise his body until nothing remains but ash burn."

"So be it," replied his grandfather before directing four Oromo men to lift up the storyteller's remains and take them to his tent. But they stopped when they approached the corpse and saw Hohete staring up at them.

"Daanish Nour, with you I would like to go, and with your women Narada's body I shall prepare. No one more than I, him I loved, and near him to stay I want."

Daanish Nour looked at her father, Ibrahim Hafez, and then at Arsalaan for approval, as it was unheard of for a Ja'Usu woman to assist the Oromo in preparing for the dead. Ibrahim Hafez nodded his consent as Arsalaan looked on.

"Well, let us proceed," commanded Ma'Mun's grandfather. "Much time before sunrise we do not have."

Hohete allowed the four Oromo men to place his body on their shoulders as Ma'Mun quickly lit the camphor lamp he was carrying and led the small procession across the flatlands toward the desert. The tiny flame he carried through the darkness left a pale halo on the earth as they moved farther and farther away from where the rest of the group remained.

"Arsalaan, Imtiyaz, and Tabassum," said Daanish Nour, "dry wood by sunrise, the three of you can you find? The fire for five to eight hours will have to last and hot enough for his bones into ash to turn."

"Dry wood we can find, but not enough wood on the land for those many hours to burn there is," replied Arsalaan, gazing at his companions, who also agreed.

"Well, the best we can, we must do." Ma'Mun's grandfather studied the faces of the men for any response and walked away when there was none.

Chief Patriarch Murabbi, the patron and guardian of the people, did not want to wait until morning before convening a session of the council to discuss the storyteller's sudden and unexpected death. So before leaving their platform at the gathering, he requested his council to meet at the holy edifice within the hour. The eight patriarchs were already seated on the carpet in the rear of the hall when Murabbi arrived. He was out of breath and struggled to speak while approaching them.

"Patriarchs," he gasped as he lumbered toward them, "a dilemma on our hands we have. Fortunately, or maybe unfortunately, I should say, our most famous storyteller is no more and with a small problem left us."

"A problem…what is it? Dead he is…dead," replied Patriarch Ihtesham, the respectable and honorable one.

"Tonight, his story, how many people to hear came?" asked Murabbi.

"Probably over two thousand," Patriarch Liyaqat, the worthy and deserving, guessed.

"Do you not see? That storyteller, by the people of Ja'Usu and the Oromo now revered he is. With his death, a new prophet now him they could crown—or worse, a god. Then where would we be?" Murabbi examined their faces, begging for an answer. "Come on…where would we be?"

The city's leaders were baffled and sat staring at one another, except for Patriarch Aschenaki, who stared at the carpet. He wondered if the poison he put in the coffee was what killed Narada and pondered whether the storyteller would come and take revenge on him.

Murabbi was still standing and waiting for an answer. "Do you not see?" he continued, clearly upset. "This storyteller, all along with our minds he has been playing, and in Ja'Usu behind all the weird events that have taken place he is. Aschenaki's brother, the hyena man he was. Now normal clothes to wear he goes back to…Sorry Aschenaki, what I mean you know…The street thugs, holding up people they stop, which a good thing I guess is…the Oromo their own magala they demand, and to worship here in our holy edifice they want. Enday! Discord here in our own governing council there is…and now our dear brother, Aschenaki, for some inexplicable reason, for Narada before his last night of story he stands up. This man, dangerous dead or alive I tell you he is, so take charge now we must and his corpse quickly get rid of."

"Chief Patriarch Murabbi," said Patriarch Safdar, the one who breaks the enemy's ranks, "gone already he is. Dead…dead…dead he is."

"Do not fooled be, Safdar. The people the storyteller's body will entomb and a shrine make it to be. And in time, a holy edifice near or around the tomb they will build and our religion corrupt into something never meant it was to be. And if that happens, our hold on the city, threatened it is, and doomed we are. This do you not see?"

"Brother Aschenaki, think what do you?" asked Patriarch Izzat, holding high rank and honor, who watched him brooding. "Lunch with the storyteller yesterday afternoon you had, we are told. What to you did he say that Murabbi's concerns we might understand?"

Aschenaki first looked at Izzat and then at the other patriarchs as if seeing them for the first time, and fear crept into his consciousness. In responding he might unwittingly expose his secret of killing his father, and he began to sweat. "My sister's youngest son, Duha, thirteen years old he is, and gibberish ever since birth has only spoken—a language only his brother comprehends. As soon as the storyteller my home left, Duha to my door came and in a clear voice that for the first time to me in a way I could understand said, 'Narada will always be watching you.'" The patriarch looked far off to a distant place and added, "Bewitched me Narada has."

"Well," said Murabbi, pointing to Aschenaki. "See! How our dear brother this storyteller has affected, do you see? Around are we all going to sit and wait until for another one of us he comes?" Then, "Hey, Aschenaki…snap out of it!" he shouted. "Narada like any other man ate and shit, so to your senses come. His body we need to find and it get rid of, quick, so the people from the dead he rose they can't say or him a martyr make. Now, do you all understand? My Jah!"

The chief patriarch paced back and forth in front of the other council members before he turned to them and commanded, "Abdul Muntaqim, slave of him who punishes wrongdoers and seizes retribution, please some men at dawn take and to Ibrahim Hafez's house go, where surely Narada's body they have taken. Pick him up and here bring it while we decide, now, how of it to dispose."

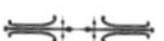

Hohete and an older woman, who prepared Oromo for the grave, bathed Narada's body in fresh water from the well where Ibrahim Hafez's daughter first met the stranger from the desert. Together, they rubbed his corpse with wood ash and wrapped his body in white cloth Daanish Nour got from three Oromo families. After the storyteller's remains were ready, Ma'Mun's grandfather chose four men to lay his body on camel skin and carry it back to where the people were already gathering. This time, Hohete led the small procession to the funeral pyre, wrapped in the white Oromo cloth that remained.

More than three hundred people were at the funeral mound as they waited for the faint glimmer of sunlight to appear over the eastern horizon. There was a chill in the air, and they huddled together in small groups and wrapped themselves in white shawls that hung almost to the ground. Oromo and inhabitants from Ja'Usu were present, as Ibrahim Hafez had quickly spread the word among his clan that Narada's corpse was to burn at sunrise.

Ma'Mun Ibn Nour astonished everyone when he commanded with authority Arsalaan, Imtiyaz, and Tabassum to build the funeral pyre on a bed of cow dung and wood and sprinkle it with ghee. He instructed them to place his teacher's body with his feet pointing south, in the direction of the Lord of Death, and his head pointed north toward the Lord of Wealth. They covered Narada's corpse with dry wood, so when finished, the funeral pyre resembled a large, rectangular bed.

When Daanish Nour quietly took his grandson aside and asked how he knew such things, Ma'Mun disclosed that Narada was in his thoughts and showing him the proper way. "Oh, and Grandfather," Ma'Mun confided, "about the wood, do not worry, Narada says. Enough there will be."

As the faint glow of sunlight slowly bled into the fleeting night sky, first turning gray and then a pale pink, Daanish Nour and Ibrahim Hafez walked together toward the funeral pyre and turned to the gathering that was now silent. Daanish Nour was the first to speak, reciting an Oromo burial prayer; followed by Ibrahim Hafez, who shared with the assembly a traditional Ja'Usu prayer for the dead. When they were done and walked away, Imitiyaz and Tabassum stepped forward and lit Narada's funeral fire. As soon as their torches touched the ghee and dried cow dung, it went ablaze. As the fire burned, Ja'Usu inhabitants continued to straggle through Fajaruddin gate, some out of curiosity to see what was burning at such an early hour. White and gray smoke swirled high in the sky. Arsalaan sat among the others in the inner circle that had formed around the fire, next to the Hafez family, Daanish Nour, Ma'Mun Ibn Nour, and Jumah and the street boys. Hohete sat next to Arsalaan with her face covered, weeping inconsolably. And as people joined the gathering they, too, like on Narada's story nights, formed rings around the inner circle and squatted on the ground. Hours passed as men and women with children kept coming and watched Narada's corpse, now ablaze. It continued to burn without the fire needing to be fed more wood, ghee, or cow dung; and the people were amazed.

A thought had taken shape and was brewing in Arsalaan's mind as he looked at Hohete with her head buried in Narada's remaining white cloth. He got up, walked over to Daanish Nour and Ma'Mun, and picked up the oil lamp on the ground between them. Walking over to Narada's pyre, he seized a burning stick from the blaze and lit the lamp, and then he placed it on the ground not far from the funeral mound. And without knowing a reason why, he felt compelled to walk clockwise around Narada's fire three times while thinking about what he wanted to say. Then he stopped to face the crowd. The people watched and waited, knowing Arsalaan, once the hyena man, was about to speak:

"The sound of my voice is not like music to your ears, I know, since many of you me have known...Ja'Usu streets walking, you have seen me...dead and rotten meat to the hyenas outside Masresha gate giving, where the hyena man used to sleep. Well, the hyena man, gone he is. Gone for good he is."

Arsalaan stopped and looked at the ground as he moved his toe in the sand. But he was not finished with what he had to say, and the gathering knew it, so they waited patiently for him to speak again when he lifted his head.

"An educated man I am not, but a Ja'Usu and Oromo custom or tradition I know it is, no sign of affection between a man and a woman in the open is allowed. Well, that tradition in front of Narada's funeral fire right now I am breaking, because a new way us he has shown. Hohete Hafez, you it is I love...more than Arthur loves Valerie, and all of you to know it I want. And if you and your father, Ibrahim Hafez, me as your man will have, you I will love and cherish, Hohete, always."

Arsalaan looked over at Ibrahim Hafez, who raised a hand in approval as Ayaat smiled. Then he turned to Hohete, who had replaced Narada's white funeral cloth around her head and face with the blue scarf she wore around her neck and held her head up to look at him. Arsalaan was about to sit down but realized he had something more to say.

"That Hohete Hafez and myself cursed, many of you truly believe we are; and because cursed you have a duty and a right to call us names when on the street you see us, you think. What to yourself you think a right you have, but in public if in any way you dare disrespect us, you personally search out I will, and..."

"Arsalaan!" Hohete cried, and he looked over at her as she placed a quiet finger over her closed lips. She stood and walked over to him and reached for his hand as Ja'Usu's inhabitants gasped. Then, as they turned to face the funeral fire, Hohete leaned over and whispered in his ear, "You I love it is, Arsalaan, and Narada's love embraces us and our families also it is."

Together they watched the fire burn, and for an instant thought they saw Narada dressed in white, smiling at them from the other side of the flames. A wisp of radiant light suddenly flashed above the funeral pyre and swiftly rose into the heavens before bursting into a multitude of tiny glowing pieces; then vanished like they were never there.

CHAPTER 48
MYTHS CREATE WORLDS

Luther McKinnie tipped his gray fedora to the old man from Jamaica sitting in front of Arthur's apartment in a wheelchair with a small blanket across his legs. He walked into the building and turned the doorknob to apartment number one on the first floor, entered the empty, musty unit, and closed the door. The apartment was dimly lit, with bands of light streaming through the thin spaces in the window blinds, alternating light and dark shadows onto the dusty hardwood floor. Luther strolled through the flat from one room to the next until he stood in the doorway of the back room where the window shades were pulled down, leaving the space devoid of light. Yet he could see as if the darkness was the day.

He sat down in a worn, straight-backed chair that was in the middle of the room and took off his hat and rested it on his lap before looking in the direction of the spirit sitting on the floor in the corner of the room. Its spirit legs were outstretched in front of its disembodied fat torso, and its back leaned against where the two walls met. The room was still and quiet as the spirit and Luther looked at one another without alarm or dread.

"Francis, I wanted to personally come and thank you for helping to bring Arthur, the young man living in the apartment above you, back on to his spiritual path. If it wasn't for your possessing him, he might have waited until another life before returning to the path he committed to so very long ago. Thank you."

"Who are you, and how do you know my name?"

"I have many names, each for the physical form I wish to assume. You may call me Luther, but many have called me Narada, Orumali, or the Master. I've watched you, Francis, from afar for some time now."

"I am nothing, so why have you been watchin' me?" asked the spirit.

"I have great sympathy for those who have been cursed because I, too, was cursed. And you were cursed, Francis. When you were a child, your father and mother, who didn't know any better, told you, like a recurring chorus from a diseased song, that you were a nigga and wouldn't amount to nothing in this life."

"Now, wait a minute..."

"They slapped you around because they hated themselves and hated you, because when they looked at you, they saw themselves, like the generations before them who learned from slave masters to despise themselves. And when that self-loathing was turned into flesh, it spread like a cancer from one generation to the next. And now here you are, Francis, carrying that legacy of rage and self-loathing forward, wreaking havoc on the living."

Francis scrutinized the figure sitting before him, a body he could barely see in his self-imposed darkness. "My, my, now ain't you the one with beautiful words," he said with a sneer. "Luther... Narada...Orumali, whatever you want to call yourself, you ain't nothing but a black man yourself. Shit! I think you wanna outfox me for the body upstairs. And why you want to do that? Seems like you already got a body for yourself. Huh! Why you wanna gang up on me?"

Narada didn't respond and sat quietly, waiting for Francis's aggressive energy, fueled by heated emotions, to subside. "Francis, I once knew an old rabbi who was called Ari Ha'Kadosh, or the Holy Lion, and he lived in the sixteenth century. The Jews had been expelled from Spain about that time and were wandering east and west for a safe place to live and call their own. Well, this old Rabbi, Ari Ha'Kadosh, wanted to understand the spiritual meaning of his people's homelessness and wanderings. He discovered—symbolically, mind you—that the Jewish people's predicament was the mirror image of what had happened to the Divine."

Francis laughed uproariously at Luther's remarks, which helped his spirit calm down. "Oh, I know this has got to be good. And...?"

"You see, before the universe was created, the rabbi thought, the One-Who-Has-Many-Names, who is Infinite, had to make room for all things that were finite or had limited form. So the Divine created a space, a void, and placed in this emptiness a seed filled with a great light, just like a woman who conceives a child and has to make space in her body for the baby to grow. And from this seed, which was the Infinite's great light, emerged a colossal flame. And in the center of this flame were a host of concealed shells, and each vessel contained a piece of the Infinite—a little piece of the light inside it that was to set sail everywhere, creating the finite world.

"But you see, Francis, it was impossible for anything with a fixed, limited, finite form like these shells to hold the Infinite, which has no boundaries and must be free. So most of the frail casings broke open, letting out the Infinite that couldn't be contained. Like when the baby in the mother's womb needs more room to grow and develop, it separates from the mother and is born. And these shattered fragments of the Infinite, these fragmented pieces of great light scattered everywhere, above and below.

"According to the rabbi's creation myth, which he believed mirrored the spiritual condition of the homeless and wandering Jews, these scattered sparks of infinite light are also in you and me. They're in every form of life and matter—the stars, the planets, in the beings that inhabit the many astral realms. These fragments of infinite light are everywhere throughout the Divine's mystery. The sole purpose of our existence is to search for these sparks of light, no matter where they may be found, within and without, and to set them free to merge with the Infinite."

"But it was a myth," said Francis with scorn.

"Myths create worlds, Francis."

The foul spirit in the corner was moved almost to tears by Narada's story, but it didn't want its unwelcome feelings to be known to this intruder for fear he would see it as weak and take advantage of it in some unforeseen way. "So what does all this have to do with me?"

Narada, knowing of all things great and small, was already aware of the thoughts and interior life of his companion. "Francis, although you have indomitable will, which is a commendable quality, you can only hold up in this gloomy place for just so long before the infinite light that is you will no longer be contained. Everything that is finite is constantly changing and evolving to fulfill the ultimate purpose of the Infinite, which is awesomely mysterious and unknown. The question is, Francis, will you be dragged along, kicking and screaming all the way, or will you work in harmony with the Infinite to fulfill your unique purpose in her creation?"

"Well, am I not fulfilling that purpose now if, as you say, you've come to thank me for bringing that young man upstairs back to his so-called path?"

"Yes, you're right, Francis, because we all play our parts in the Infinite's motion-picture show of light and shadows in a world of dualities—good and evil, happiness and sadness, love and hate, harmony and chaos, light and darkness, kindness and cruelty. Which do you choose, Francis?"

"You said you were cursed. Why was that, Luther? What did you do wrong?"

"My brother, Daksha, had two sons who, soon after the world was created, wanted to be the first to create a race of men. I played a cruel prank on his sons in asking them how they could create a race of men if they hadn't first seen the ends of the universe. They agreed with me and happily went searching for that end. Of course, I knew they would never find it, because this universe is infinite. When my brother found out what I had done, he put a curse on me."

"And what is that curse?" asked the spirit.

"That I remain a wanderer, restless and homeless, forever, for sending his two sons on an endless quest to find the borders of the universe."

Francis's raucous laughter was unbounded at Luther's misfortune—until he understood the profound significance of what his intruder had said. "Do you mean that you were born when the world was created?"

"Before the world was created, Francis, from a pure thought of the Infinite."

If the spirit in the corner could have melted into the mildewed wallpaper and run away, it would have been gone. It was unable to move, feeling frozen in the dark place it called home. Its mind trembled in fear while its soul opened like a flower blossoming in the warmth of the sun.

"You can no longer stay here, Francis, to trouble Arthur anymore. Now you have a decision to make, and your choice will impact the willful intention of your many lives to come. It is your blessing to be at this crossroad, Francis. Will you choose, driven by your own fear and agony, to remain in darkness, or will you make the harder choice—to become a gentle warrior and revive your labor to walk in the light?"

Francis, however, still under the yoke of fear and self-loathing, had grown accustomed to the gloom and, acting upon its own anger and rage, had grown comfortable with living vicariously through the lives of others. It was confident that in time, it would learn to satisfy its lust and other cravings by manipulating and possessing human hosts, like putting on a pair of well-heeled shoes, to fulfill its desires and they do its bidding. How could it give up what it knew to be true for Luther's promise of goodness and light?

Francis's spirit was suddenly surprised to hear and feel a heartbeat that couldn't be its own, the pulsating of blood in arteries and veins that it no longer possessed, the mysterious thumping of a human organ that had the capacity to experience joy and sorrow and pain. Placing its spirit hand over its spirit chest, Francis listened with awe to its beating breast and the rhythmic thump…thump…thump whose cadence took it back to the small dresser drawer and pillow it lay on as an infant, crying for its mama's milk.

And the sun and moon floated silently in a daily pageant across the southern sky, promising the world a spectacle of wonder and joy and smiling faces and mystery. But the miracle that was life dried up like a wrinkled prune or a drop of spilled milk on hot concrete the first time his daddy called Francis a little nigga and his mama slapped him silly. Then the joy and promise of the world turned mean as he grew into boyhood and learned to chew and swallow his own anger. That is, until he saw himself as nothin'…wasn't nothin'…felt nothin' except when he tormented the lives of others so they could feel his pain.

But Francis's spirit was also tired of this dreary, dead place and, in moments of clarity like this one, yearned to move out of the darkness and daydreamed about living in the light. Struggling to overcome its own fear and false pride, it looked up and said to Luther, "If I become this gentle warrior you speak about, and learn to walk with infinite light, will you help me?"

"I will be your eternal guide, Francis, and keep you safe. Even when you lose your way, moving from one life to the next, I will be with you, Francis, forever and a day."

Francis, with tears in his spirit eyes that overflowed onto his dark, pudgy spirit face, rose to his feet and exclaimed, "Yes, Luther, show me the way." Luther stood up and embraced him, and Francis' spirit was absorbed into a great light.

Placing his gray fedora on his head, Luther walked out of the building and down the front steps to find the Jamaican man still stoically sitting in his wheelchair. Luther walked over to the old man and said, "Has the world changed very much since you were a little boy?"

"Sonny, I don't even know what planet I'm on," the man replied with a wry smile.

"Get up, old man."

"Can't you see, man, I'm in a wheelchair?" he replied, dismissing the command in Luther's voice.

"I said get up and walk with me."

The old man looked up for a moment as his mind teetered between rebellion and faith. Seeing the confidence and strength in Luther's eyes gave him hope. And without giving it another thought, the old man struggled to his feet and took Luther's outstretched arm; and they walked down the street, and the two of them disappeared into the ether.

ACKNOWLEDGMENTS

This is a work of fiction, and all the characters are imaginary; however, the contemporary story on the development and initiation of Critical Mass Health Conductors is based on true events that began in Oakland, California, in 2003. The characters in this thread of the narrative are loosely based on real people whose names have been changed to protect their privacy and shield them from any embarrassment I may have caused in how they are portrayed in this fictional story. I am indebted to the Health Conductors' leadership and the more than one thousand community volunteers who completed the training and became cultural revolutionaries to improve the health and well-being of people of African descent in the Bay Area in those early years.

The nonprofit organization that initiated this project, and continues to manage and support the development and growth of Health Conductors, is also real—the Bay Area Black United Fund (BABUF). I especially thank the agency's President and Chief Executive Officer, Duane Poe, for permitting me to use the rightful name of this initiative in this fictional work. There are other organizations and businesses depicted in the narrative that are also real, including the Alameda County Public Health Department; Summit Medical Hospital; and two of Oakland's most popular restaurants, Ms. Ollie's and Ensarro.

I would also like to thank my mother's old friend, and now mine, Mrs. Dottie Smith, in Teaneck New Jersey; and my good friends, Anthony Gittens and his wife, Jennifer Lawson, in Washington, DC; and Stanley Sneed and Mary Roebuck in Saint Croix, USVI. Each of them gave me a quiet place to stay and write during many months of travel. I am also grateful to Alscess Lewis-Brown, a writer and director of The Caribbean Writer program in Saint Croix, whose technical advice on story development and creative writing was immeasurably helpful. And I would not have had the psychic space to write if it were not for my true friends, Arnold X. Perkins and Robert Wilkins, who, perhaps unbeknown to them, have been immeasurably supportive during the development of this novel. Thoughts of gratitude also go out to my brother and his wife, Michael and Saphronia Carter, for their genuine goodness and support in addressing pressing family matters that would have taken me away from completing this work, were it not for them.

I am also forever grateful to Astrid Berg, for her astute judgment and hands-on technical assistance as my consultant editor, and to Liz Weldon, whose talent and artistry produced the ancient city of Ja'Usu's map.

And most of all, I am humbled and eternally grateful to the One-Who-Is-Called-by-Many-Names; to my beloved Guru; my ancestors; and the community of souls, here on Earth and in the beyond, who have contributed to the writing of *Narada's Children*. As so it is…

Woody Carter
Richmond, California, September 2015